THE DEVIL'S WATERS

Also by David L. Robbins:

Souls To Keep
War of the Rats
The End of War
Scorched Earth
Last Citadel
Liberation Road
The Assassins Gallery
The Betrayal Game
Broken Jewel

For the stage:
Scorched Earth (an adaptation)

THE
DEVIL'S
WATERS

DAVID L. ROBBINS

THOMAS & MERCER

Published by Thomas & Mercer
P.O. Box 400818
Las Vegas, NV 89140

ISBN-13: 9781612186061
ISBN-10: 1612186068

To the selfless men of CSAR, combat search and rescue.

To Sherrie Najarian, for whom I have searched, and by whom I have been rescued.

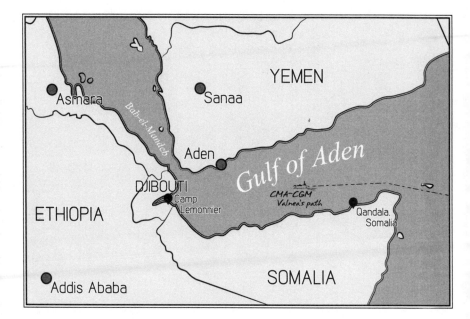

"That Others May Live"

motto of the USAF pararescue Guardian Angels,
known as the PJs

Chapter 1

2010

On board HH-60 Pedro 1
Hindu Kush
Afghanistan

The earphones in LB's helmet buzzed.

"Where'd he go?"

LB lay still. He'd stretched out on the Pave Hawk's vibrating floor and wasn't going to give up his spot just because the pilot sounded a little edgy. These helo jocks were good, and what little they didn't know about the valleys and mountains of Afghanistan, multiple arrays of electronics could tell them. GPS, FLIR, Inertial Nav—the cockpit up front shimmered with green gauges, digits, and shifty electronic lines. LB lay in the back of *Pedro 1*, comfortable. He had his own job to do once they reached the village. He lolled his head to the side to glance out the window, into the canopy of high blue over the serrated edges of the Hindu Kush.

Beside him, Wally couldn't help himself; he had to look. He rose to his knees, pivoting to get a peek out the windshield. The moment he did this, Doc's boots filled in the vacated space.

Wally's voice sizzled over the intercom. "Whoa."

In that moment, the squall socked away the sky and mountains. The floor under LB's rump and rucksack shook as their copter disappeared into the fat, blowing mist.

Around LB, everyone—the flight engineer, back-end gunner, even old hands Doc and Quincy—peered out the windows. This wasn't a fascination with weather, how thick a whiteout nature could whip up at nine thousand feet in the Afghan mountains. The men were on the lookout for *Pedro 2*, the other Pave Hawk on the mission, with its own giant rotating blade somewhere, invisibly, close by.

LB couldn't enjoy having the floor all to himself if no one was competing with him for it. The others had noses pressed to the windows like pooches, paying him no mind. The pilots and engineer continued their radio chatter. Even in their clipped speech over the intercom, LB deciphered some nerves. He slid back against the door, shoving himself to a sitting position, and shouldered beside young Jamie to get a gander at the storm.

"Whoa is right."

The HH-60 blasted through the squall at 120 miles per hour. Snow and sheets of fog streaked by in hurrying, purling ghosts of opaque white. Visibility ramped down to zero.

The air frame rattled, suspended beneath the spinning rotor. The HH-60 was built for rugged, not smooth, flying. She was neither sleek nor pretty. The aircraft was designed to be hard to bring down, not much else. Left and right, mountain peaks and sheer walls zoomed by, completely obscured. Somewhere in this same blank morass flew *Pedro 2*, another HH-60.

"*Ringo 53, Pedro 1*," the pilot called to their HC-130 fuel plane cruising two thousand feet overhead, above the storm. "You got eyes on?" "Negative, *Pedro 1*. Blind on your position."

LB muttered, "Shit." The intercom picked this up.

Wally shot him a cool rebuke from behind his Oakley shades.

LB ignored him. Wally was a captain and a CRO, but that didn't have much juice up here, where all their tails were equally on the line. On his knees, LB squirmed between Doc and Quincy. He stuck his head into the narrow alley between the engineer and back-end gunner for a clear view of the cockpit.

LB didn't look out the windshield or at the gauges and flowing emerald lines on the heads-down display. He was interested not in computers or satellites right now, but in the pilots, the hands on the controls.

He'd been in this situation before, a year ago in southern Afghanistan, Paktika Province. Same drill: high altitude, sudden whiteout, PR mission. The air force after-report said the copter pilots lost spatial orientation only minutes after being swallowed whole in clam chowder clouds. They stopped trusting their instruments, got hesitant, and decided to abort. They banked the Pave Hawk out of the mission flight path. In the thin air at ten thousand feet, the rotor couldn't generate enough lift. The HH-60 sank into the unseen side of a mountain. The blades sheared into catapulting pieces in every direction; the fuselage slid backward, then somersaulted into five barrel rolls down the slope. Many miracles occurred in those tumbling moments. When the dented hulk of the HH-60 finally came to rest against a stone hut, in the dust, smoke, and adrenaline, no one had a single broken bone or even a gash, just a lot of bruises and some puking. Wally was there, too; he held up his breakfast burrito and emptied coffee mug. He earned himself a new call sign that morning: Juggler.

Today's storm raged in northeast Afghanistan; the conditions were lousy all over this country. LB studied the men in the cockpit for situational awareness. Were the pilots keeping it together? The squall tossed them around, but *Pedro 1* was built to take enemy fire; it could stand a good buffeting. In his twelve years as a pararescueman, LB had seen men and machines outperform any reasonable expectation, go far past what could be decently asked of flesh or metal. He'd been present, too, when machines failed and men broke. It was always a coin toss what was going to happen.

Wally sidled next to him. He made an okay sign with fingers and thumb, asking how LB was holding up. LB made a sour face.

Wally bent his helmet's mike close to his lips so the pilots could hear him clearly.

"How we doin' up front?"

"The terrain's taking us up another thousand. Not happy having to climb in this soup."

"Stay with it, guys. We'll make it."

The helicopter lurched in a stomach-churning jump over a wind burst. *Pedro 1* was giving her all. Young Jamie blew out his cheeks, no fan of roller coasters. Wally turned on the four PJs, sticking out an upturned thumb. Doc and Quincy looked to each other. Both were experienced soldiers—Doc a former marine, Quincy come over from the SEALs. Neither had been in a crash. Jamie was the newest PJ. This was just his second PR mission. He waited for the others.

Wally waggled the thumb, asking for a vote. As much as LB enjoyed frustrating Wally's attempts at leadership—they agreed they'd been together too long—he was the first to stick up his own thumb. This time, Wally was right on the money. The safest thing to do in these conditions was to press forward, fly the flight plan loaded into the instruments, prepped for in the briefings. As long as *Pedro 1* stayed airborne and performing along this route, and *Pedro 2* did the same, they should rely on their avionics. Flying white blind was not as big a risk as losing confidence and faith.

The blowing ropes of fog and snow drew Doc and Quincy to one last, agonized glance out the windows before they voted thumbs-up. Red-cheeked Jamie made it unanimous.

Wally turned forward, toward the cockpit.

"We got a vote back here, Major. We want to push through. There's a kid up ahead. He needs to meet us."

The pilot pivoted enough to eye Wally, with LB beside him. Jamie, Doc, and Quincy came to their knees so the pilot could see the entire team.

The pilot's lips parted to speak. He closed them, nodded, and returned to his instruments and the storm.

Smartly, Wally slid to sit on the shivering floor before the others could grab all the legroom. The PJs settled in with lowered chins and folded arms to await the consequences of their vote. LB kept on his knees. Wally lifted his chin to him, in thanks for the support. LB hit him on the shoulder, too hard.

The weather broke like a fever, after enough shaking and sweats to exhaust everyone in *Pedro 1*. The perfect sky and troublingly close cliffs reappeared with only a dozen miles left to the village. LB stayed on his knees, watching the pilots until the clouds parted and *Pedro 2* corkscrewed out of the mist fifty yards ahead, right where they'd been thirty minutes ago when the storm stole them.

Wally thanked the pilots. He cast another thumbs-up around to the PJs, but no one came out of their own hunker to respond. LB sometimes felt bad for Wally and his sunny demeanor, his cheerful brand of leadership that often fell flat. Not this time. LB was sore and tasting the bile in his throat from the thrashing of the squall. He wanted to be on solid earth, even Afghanistan's stony ground.

The pair of choppers barreled through a long, deep valley, carved between sheer slopes along the northern ridge of the Hindu Kush. *Pedro 1* and *Pedro 2* poured on the speed, beating at the flimsy air to put some distance between them and the squall rolling up behind them.

The pilot crackled over the intercom. "Figure fifteen minutes on the ground, boys. That system's funneling right down the valley. I don't want to be here when it hits."

"Roger that." Wally tapped his wristwatch at the PJs to keep an eye on the time.

The back-end gunner shoved aside his window. He lowered his visor and put both hands on the .50 caliber. On the left, *Pedro 2* slowed and stood off, hovering high above a rocky creek carving through the valley. *Pedro 1* surged forward.

LB secured his gear and med ruck, his M4 carbine. He unplugged his helmet from the HH-60's intercom and jacked into the team's radio comm on his Rhodesian vest.

He pointed at Wally. "Juggler, radio check."

Wally responded. "Lima Charlie. How me?"

"Loud and clear."

One at a time, LB made contact with the others until all had transmitted and received. Each team member checked his own radio the same way.

Pedro 1 slowed, hovering several hundred meters shy of the LZ. Out of the copter's rear, a liquid gush blew from the tank release valve as the pilots dumped two hundred pounds of weight to accommodate the passengers they'd come to retrieve. At eleven thousand feet, every extra pound had to be accounted for and balanced so the chopper, after setting down, could fight its way back into the air.

LB rose to his kneepads. The others did the same in a circle. The chopper descended quickly, squeezing another pinched look from Jamie. Out the window, a stream coursed, swollen with winter runoff from snowy peaks on all sides. The HH-60 zoomed in low over the creek, then halted in midair while the pilots final-checked the landing. With an ease missing from the rest of the flight, the chopper touched wheels down.

The PJs unclipped their cow's tails from the floor, and Quincy slid back the door. The back-end gunner swept the barrel of his .50 cal across the waiting village elders. Wally hit the cold ground first. LB and the rest formed up behind him, crouching beneath the spinning blades. Dust and small stones whipped at their boots. The elders' dark *chapan* coats and beards wavered on the rotor wash.

LB lengthened his strides to pass the much taller Wally, raising a hand to the locals. A younger one, in a blue *pakul* hat to match his long frock, stepped forward. This one's beard was the shortest, the hand he extended the least thick. Wally and Doc arrived beside LB. Jamie and Quincy spread out, attention on the first huts of the village a hundred yards off, the steep terrain rising behind it, and the sere shrubs along the stream.

"Welcome to Rubati Yar," the young man shouted in English. "I am teacher."

LB pulled off his glove to clasp the offered hand. Wally did not remove his sunglasses.

LB asked, "Where's the boy?"

"Come."

Wally nodded, stepping back. He rested a hand on the M4 carbine slung at his chest, near the trigger. LB motioned Doc to follow.

The teacher led them away from the stream, up a pebbled trail into the village. Rubati Yar was made up of a few dozen stacked-stone shacks, corrugated tin roofs, stave sheds, and goat pens clinging to a flat patch on the side of a mountain. One cinder trail ran beside the water ten kilometers downhill, leading west to the poppy fields of the Khumbi Khulkhan highlands. Twenty miles east sprawled Pakistan, twenty to the north lay Tajikistan.

In this sparse, far corner of Afghanistan, a boy had stepped on a land mine.

Yesterday a marine LRP team, walking this high-altitude stream, had been flagged down by the villagers of Rubati Yar. They showed the marine captain a boy in rough shape. Half his foot was blown off; black flesh framed the wound. The marines put in a call to Bagram Air Base for an air evac. The PJs spun up at first light.

LB labored for breath climbing the hundred-yard path into the village. Behind him, the river valley thrummed with the beating rotors of *Pedro 2* hovering a mile off, the slowing blades of *Pedro 1* near the stream, and high above, the circling HC-130 that would refuel both copters on the return to Bagram. Pausing to catch his wind, LB gazed south, where the squall crawled after them over white and russet peaks.

Doc passed him on the path. Four years younger than LB at thirty-six, Doc was the second-oldest PJ in the unit. Doc smacked him in the back on a Kevlar plate. Both men hauled almost a hundred pounds of medical supplies, weapons, communications, and armament up into the village. A breath at this height was a lot less nourishing than one at sea level.

"S'matter, old man?"

Doc ran marathons. LB lifted weights.

The Afghan teacher held out an arm, signaling that the walk was almost over. The boy's hut lay just ahead.

Chickens scattered from their pecking at the corners of the village. A black-clad woman faded into the darkness of her hut, eyeing the passing PJs. Boys stood in doorways, dressed like little beardless men in the same woven coats and hats as their elders. Their hands, too, had begun to take on the roughness of this land, their eyes the mistrust, inheritances of such isolation. LB made no gestures, nothing to be misinterpreted. He closed in behind the teacher and Doc through the ancient alleyways of the village to a waiting open door.

The teacher entered first, bowing in greeting. Doc followed, LB behind him.

Inside, a dirt floor lay under threadbare prayer carpets. The window frames held no glass, only shutters. LB imagined the cold this household endured most of the year on the side of a mountain, night broken by homely candles, meals, and heat from a mud oven.

The boy lay in a cot on goatskins. The teacher moved to stand beside the father, who did not come forward to greet the Americans. Deeper in the shadows of the hovel, peering around the father, hid two women, drawing veils across their faces below the eyes. One, the younger, crooked an arm over her distended belly, pregnant. The teacher explained that these were the man's wife and widowed daughter.

Doc advanced first. The mangling of the boy's left foot didn't seem so bad until LB flicked on his flashlight. He caught his breath.

The outer half of the boy's small foot had been sheared off. From toes to heel, the wound ran jagged as if bitten by teeth, not a forgotten land mine. The part of the foot the kid had left was bloated and purpled. The swelling carried into his calf. In places, the dying flesh had ruptured. A pasty pale green ooze let off a cloying, putrid stench, the signature of wet gangrene.

LB aimed the flashlight where Doc put hands on the boy. He slid his med ruck to the ground and, not pulling the light from Doc, dug in for antibiotics and morphine.

Doc laid a bare palm to the boy's forehead to feel the elevated temperature of sepsis, then to the quickened pulse in his neck. Doc folded back the hem of the boy's long robe, exposing the whole leg. Swelling and necrosis stopped below the knee, but were headed that way. Gingerly, Doc wrapped his fingers around the calf and squeezed. The boy moaned on the goatskins. He brought young hands over his face to cover his pain. The calf creaked, filled with gas by the bacteria devouring the foot. In the corner of the hut, the father cringed. Behind him, both women quietly cried.

Doc fired up his own flashlight to illuminate LB kneeling beside the cot, inserting an IV into the boy's hot arm. He injected one milliliter of morphine to ease pain and anxiety. Because the kid was septic and the morphine could lower his blood pressure even more, he plugged in a bag of lactated Ringer's to maintain fluids. Last, he piggybacked both antibiotics, penicillin and clindamycin, to slow the march of gangrene up the boy's leg. LB rested the plastic bags on the boy's chest. Doc held up the boy's leg under the knee so LB could fast-wrap the ankle and calf in gauze. The boy whimpered, breaths fast and shallow, then clamped his jaw bravely.

LB walked outside, gesturing for Doc, the teacher, and the boy's father to join him. In sunlight, the father behind the beard appeared much younger than he did in the hovel. His eyes glowed, raw with tears and worry.

"Tell him," LB said to the teacher, "his son is going to lose that foot and some of the leg. We won't know how much till we get him back to the hospital. The doctors will do the best they can."

The teacher did not look into the father's face while he said this.

"Tell him his son's going to live. But we have to go right now. Make sure he knows he's coming, too."

With urgency, the teacher repeated this.

Doc said to LB, "Let's just lift him on that cot and carry him down."

"Good."

When the teacher finished translating, the boy's father whirled in his long coat for the open hut door. Inside, he told the family what was happening. The women wailed until he shouted them silent.

Doc rested a hand on the teacher's shoulder. "What do you teach?"

The man smiled shyly at the attention. "Reading and writing."

"Can girls come to your school?"

"No. They have a separate school."

"Is it any good?"

"I don't understand the question."

Back home in Vegas, Doc had four daughters, a wife, and a female dog.

LB turned the teacher by the arm. "Come on."

Inside the hut, the father stood ready at the head of the cot, the women pressed into a dim recess. The teacher moved to the father's shoulder. LB and Doc bent to hoist the foot of the bed. Doc lent only one hand to the cot; the other supported the IV bags.

"Up."

The four maneuvered the cot out the door. The boy, like his father, shed years outside. He was no more than eight, smooth skinned with long black lashes fluttering under the morphine. The women filled the doorway, sniffling. The daughter's veil had gone crooked from her crying; her mother reached to straighten it over the girl's puffy face.

"Hang on," LB said. "Set him down."

The men lowered the cot to the rocky path. LB walked back to the hut, curling a finger for the teacher to follow. The father trailed.

The women retreated in the doorway. The mother hurried to obscure her daughter's face.

"Wait," LB said, holding up a palm. "Wait. Teacher, tell them to stand still."

The man spoke for LB. The women did not disappear into the house.

From behind, Doc called, "What's up?"

The father rushed forward, in front of his wife and daughter. He bellowed, waving LB and the teacher back from them. LB held his ground.

"Tell his daughter to take down the veil. I need to see her face again."

The teacher rattled his head. "This is not possible."

"Make it possible. Tell Pops here she might be sick. We need to check her out."

The women watched the discussion from the doorway, with the father blocking the way. While the teacher spoke, the father waved his arms more, raising his voice in ire and pointing at LB.

11

The teacher faced LB with shoulders down. "He will not allow it."

"Then tell him to look. Look at her hands. Her feet and ankles. Face and neck. He's gonna see they're swollen."

The father rejected this before the teacher had finished translating.

"He says she is with child. This is natural."

Doc piped up. "Ask him if she ever has seizures. Ask if she shakes, do her eyeballs roll up in her head."

The father shouted over the question. He aimed a leathery finger at the boy moaning on the cot.

"C'mere." LB pinched the teacher's coat to draw him close. "Ask Mom."

"I cannot speak to her."

LB let the teacher go. He stuck his tongue in his cheek, considering what to do. He shrugged at Doc, who shrugged back.

Doc set down the bags to put his M4 into his hands. He moved between the father, the teacher, and the women. Doc spread his legs and set himself. The two Afghan men raised their voices and hands, but neither advanced on the stolid Doc, who held both at bay.

LB stepped around them to the mother. She positioned herself in front of her pregnant daughter, both with veiled faces and frightened eyes. They did not retreat, though the father hollered and pointed for them to do so. Doc kept the man back not with his weapon but with a raised, warning finger. Neighbors came out of their own stone hovels to investigate.

Quickly, LB pantomimed what he wanted the mother to do, lift her daughter's long frock to show her ankles.

The wrinkles beside the mother's eyes deepened as she looked at LB. After more loud objections from her red-faced husband, she nodded and spoke.

LB called to the interpreter, "What'd she say?"

"Her daughter sometimes shakes. Her hands and face are swollen, and her feet. She does not need to show you."

LB returned the mother's nod.

"It's called eclampsia. It'll kill the baby, and maybe your girl here. Her blood pressure's too high; we've got to treat it. We can fix it in Bagram."

LB held out an arm, inviting. The mother waited for the teacher's translation, then took her daughter's hand from atop the girl's belly. She left the doorway, towing her daughter. Leaving the hut, she shouted behind her into the dark.

Inside, deep in the shadows, what LB thought had been a pile of clothes shifted, rose, and ambled forward. An old man, grooved and pitted by decades of mountain wind, scuffed into the light past LB without a glance or a word. He passed the cot, patting the boy's head.

The angry father finally closed his mouth when his wife and daughter strode past him without deference, heading down the hill. Doc slipped his M4 back over his shoulder. The teacher, father, LB, and Doc hoisted the cot. Carrying his corner, the father sulked, conflicted, until his eyes fell again on his boy, soon to lose a foot. This was not a bad man.

LB freed a hand to press the push-to-talk on his unit radio. "Juggler, Juggler. Lima Bravo."

"Go, LB."

"Leaving the village now. Came for two. Bringing back five."

A pause, then, "Typical. Roger."

The cot slowed them on the path. LB grew breathless headed down from the village, just as he'd been going up. The old man and two women arrived first at the copter. They waited outside the reach of the idling HH-60's slowly turning blades.

The four men carried the cot close to the copter's open door, easing the boy down. Quincy and Jamie hurried to tend to the women and the old man, who looked to have taken his longest walk in years. The father and teacher intercepted the two PJs.

Wally stepped to LB, lips pursed and skeptical, eyes masked by his reflecting shades.

"Where we gonna put 'em?"

Wally was right to ask. There wasn't room in the HH-60's bay for the five-man PJ team plus this whole Afghan family. *Pedro 1* had dumped only enough fuel to evacuate the father and son. The two women and the old man were unexpected, another four hundred pounds of load at eleven thousand feet. The chopper couldn't spill fuel while on the ground. The purge valve was located right below the jet engines. If the exhaust didn't ignite the fuel puddled in the dirt, static electricity from the whirling propellers probably would. A fuel dump had to be done in the air. The alternative was a fireball.

Wally cocked his head. "You ever think things through before you do them?"

Wally motioned for the chopper's engineer to hand down the Stokes litter. Reaching to his vest, Wally flicked the comm switch to *Pedro 2*'s frequency. The copter flew a bone pattern, a slow oval above the valley miles off. Framed between peaks, the storm line crept closer.

"*Pedro 2, Pedro 2*, Hallmark."

When the copter answered, Wally informed the pilot to come in for a pickup. Dump five hundred pounds first.

He turned to LB. "All right. Let's load your folks up. Me and Quincy'll wait for *Pedro 2*. These are your patients, LB. You go with them."

LB loosed a sigh. That had been his exact plan, to wait with Quincy for *Pedro 2*. Wally had leaped to it before he could say anything.

This was vintage Wally. The man had a nose for credit, what would get him noticed and promoted from captain to major fastest. Staying on the ground in unfriendly territory to assist the evac of a local family would make a nice little act of selfless courage, good reading in the paperwork afterward. LB was a first sergeant, not bucking for more. PJs weren't officers; CROs were. LB was going to stay a pararescueman. He wanted to wait for

Pedro 2 so he could stretch out for the ride back, that was all. But now that Wally had laid claim to the second chopper, LB made a plan. He considered it a game, like chess, to thwart Wally. Not because the man wouldn't make a respectable major. Wally was a stickler and too good-natured by half, but a fine officer. Wally had guts and skills. LB just liked opponents, and Wally so often made himself one.

Jamie and Quincy herded the family under *Pedro 1*'s accelerating prop. The pilots intended to take off the instant everyone was on board. Turbulence from the squall was already cascading down the mountains towering above Rubati Yar. The teacher stayed back with the village elders and others who'd gathered by the stream. They grabbed their hats as the winds from the storm and copter built.

The valley grew noisy as *Pedro 2* neared. High above, *Ringo 53* droned, circling. Both copters were going to need refueling soon. *Pedro 2* closed to a hundred yards from the stream and slowed, showing its belly, waiting for *Pedro 1* to clear.

Because the boy would be taken off the chopper first at Bagram, he needed to be loaded in last. LB pointed for the father to climb on. Jamie and Doc followed, to help the mother and pregnant daughter climb on. Concern for his two sick kids and the approaching storm had convinced the father to make an exception for these American soldiers touching his females. Last, Jamie lifted the old man into the bay by himself.

LB shouted, "Start strapping 'em in," and Jamie and Doc began strapping gunner's belts around the Afghans to anchor them to the floor.

"Quincy, get on the other side of the basket. Wally, we'll hand him up to you. Start tying the kid down."

Wally jumped into the copter.

On the count of three, LB and Quincy lifted the boy. Wally grabbed the head of the Stokes litter to guide it onto the HH-60's floor.

LB indicated the IV bags for fluid and antibiotics lying in the skins beside the boy. "Hang those up."

"Got it."

The copter's engineer found a fruit roll-up to lay on the kid's chest. LB tossed it back, explaining that the kid was headed for surgery and couldn't eat.

The rotor spun faster, ready to go. The engine whined to a higher pitch, and the copter bounced, eager to be airborne.

With Wally focused on the IV bags, LB pointed to Doc, then at the kid. Doc nodded.

LB slammed shut the HH-60's door. Grabbing big Quincy's sleeve, he ran past the cockpit, knocked knuckles on the cowling, hauled Quincy out of the prop wash.

With no hesitation, the blades whirled harder, the chopper's wheels growing light on the bare earth. Inside, Wally framed himself in the large window of the shut door, leaning across the Stokes litter and the kid in it.

Wally's gloved palms flattened on the impact glass. He eyed LB from the rising copter.

Wally didn't order the HH-60 to set back down and let him off. He knew the gangrenous boy had to get to Bagram fast. Both choppers hung on the edge of the chasing squall. Like the good officer he was, Wally assessed the situation. He took the appropriate action and did nothing.

LB waved up from the fading ground. Wally mouthed the words that had given LB his call sign years ago.

You little bastard.

Chapter 2

Today

Gulf of Aden
3 miles off the coast of Qandala
Somalia

Yusuf Raage lifted his arms as if he might catch the falling treasure.

He stood alone atop the superstructure beside the radar arrays and quiet smokestack. Below him and all around the freighter, on top of containers, dozens of his men watched his gesture of triumph. They raised their own fists, weapons, voices, at the parachute drifting millions of dollars down to them, and at their clansman and captain, who'd made it so.

Beneath Yusuf's boots, from the wheelhouse, came cheers also from the *MV Bannon's* crew, seventeen Malay ratings and five Indian officers celebrating the white cask splashing down. When the chute collapsed into the blue water, the crew stamped their feet, pounded the steel walls, to ring in their freedom.

In the brilliant afternoon, a single-engine plane flown by white men in sunglasses banked low, keeping an eye on the transaction. Yusuf lowered his arms to his hips to stand like a king on a hill, a warrior king who had taken this hill, not one born to it. For six months this steel behemoth had been his prize. He'd captured it on the open sea, brought it here, dropped anchor three miles offshore from his home village. He'd made the ship a fortress, then priced it and sold it. The lives and possessions on board had been under his hand. At times he'd threatened the captives, claimed at key points in the negotiations that he would sink the *Bannon* with all hands if his ransom demands were not met. In the end, he'd hurt no one, as was his intention. The price paid after half a year was the amount he'd asked for after three days. The barrel of money bobbing on the ocean freed Yusuf, too. He did not need to stand here any longer.

A long skiff raced to the cask a hundred meters off the starboard beam. Yusuf's cousin Suleiman dragged the barrel out of the water. He cut away the chute. In the slow-circling plane, one of the insurance company's Frenchmen snapped photographs. Yusuf was not concerned that his picture was being taken. It served his purposes to be known.

———•———

Barefoot, Yusuf stood before the cask. The barrel rested on the long chart table in the *Bannon*'s sun-bright bridge. He wore a ceremonial *ma'awis* sarong, a loose silk *khameez* blouse, and an embroidered *taqiyah* cap. Acting like a priest, he laid hands on the cask.

Beside him, Suleiman held a handgun on Ashwin, the *Bannon*'s captain. Another younger cousin, Guleed, pointed a rifle at Chugh, the first mate. The Indian and Malay crew were lined up in front of the long wheelhouse windshield. The remainder of Yusuf's team, two dozen from his Harti subclan of the Darood, waited around the ship; still too soon to put down their guns and grenade launchers. Five live goats had been ferried on board for the final feast. Somewhere on deck, cutthroat knives were being sharpened, fires readied. The Frenchmen in their plane circled and photographed all this.

Yusuf raised his head as if from a depth to open his eyes on the *Bannon*'s captain, Ashwin.

Yusuf held out an onyx-handled blade. In English, he said, "Come, Captain. You do the honors."

The Indian, smaller than Yusuf by a head and a hundred pounds, stepped forward. The man had handled himself and his crew well during the ordeal of the ship's hijacking and long negotiations. They'd surrendered the ship quickly; only a few had been fired upon by Yusuf's pirates. In captivity, the discipline of Ashwin's men's had rarely wavered; they'd offered no resistance nor chicanery and had kept their ill opinions of their Somali captors largely to themselves. No one jumped overboard. Why would they, three miles from a lawless coast into shark- and seasnake–infested waters?

For twenty-seven weeks, Yusuf saw to it that the hostages were well fed, though the captain seemed too distressed to eat. Every Sunday the crewmen were allowed to contact their families by satellite phone. The trouble was made not by the seamen, who had no interest in anything beyond their liberation, but by the ship's European owners, who poor-mouthed their ability to pay. After this, his sixth hijacking, Yusuf knew well all the ship owners' ploys. The longer they allowed the pirates to hold their ships, the better their payouts from their insurance. The owners always waited until the economics shifted in their favor before settling up.

In front of the audience of his captive crew, the little captain held out a brown hand for the knife. Privately, Yusuf was sorry to see the weight Ashwin had lost.

Yusuf bent to the man's ear. "Understand. You will open this barrel. If there is a bomb or anything unpleasant inside, it will surprise you first."

The captain smiled wanly, beaten down by his imprisonment. Ashwin snipped the plastic straps. Yusuf retreated, motioning for the captain to crack the lid. Nothing emerged from the white barrel but the reflected glow of green.

Ashwin folded back the cask's top. He did not step away but stayed rooted in front of the money. Yusuf, done with the captain now, retrieved the knife and shunted him aside. Suleiman walked the short man away on the end of his pistol, as Yusuf planted his broad palms on 3.7 million American dollars. A rush charged up his arms, expanding his chest. He exhaled slowly through his nose, for everyone on the bridge to hear. The Indians and Malays watched him over Guleed's leveled Kalashnikov. Funny. Of all the things Yusuf had held hostage—this weathered ship, three thousand cargo containers, the owners' schedules and profits—these little brown lives were what the money had bought back. His gaze fell into the cask to the banded stacks of bills, sheaves of dollars. How wonderful to be worth this.

Yusuf considered his own two cousins and his clansmen, waiting. He knew their poverty because he'd shared it, and he'd ended it. Today, they had this value too.

Plucking one bundle of the cash, Yusuf held it with both hands over his head like the heart of a beast.

"Kill the goats."

His cousins lowered their weapons. Suleiman came to Yusuf's side. Guleed clapped and jogged out of the wheelhouse to issue the order that would begin the butchering and cooking of their last meal aboard the *Bannon*. The Indians and Malays, for the first time in months, were left unguarded. They moved unsurely, like men wearing shoes that were too big.

Yusuf spoke to the captain: "Take your men outside. Let the French snap your pictures from their plane to show your families you're all right. We'll eat, then we'll be gone at sundown. The ship will be yours again."

The little Indian asked, "Will your men return what else they have stolen? Our computers, cell phones, cameras, clothes?"

Yusuf waved a bundle of dollars beneath his nose to sniff it like a bouquet. He laughed down to his bare feet on the cool floor. He said only, "Suleiman."

Yusuf's lieutenant, narrow-faced and gold-toothed, raised his handgun. "Get some sun, man."

The captain nodded in the manner of an educated fellow, completing his judgment of Yusuf and likely all Somalis as thieves and worthless. He stepped away with an incline of his head, still the pirate king's prisoner.

Alone on the bridge, Yusuf and Suleiman counted the ransom. The cousins combed through banded bills to be certain of the denominations, all thousands and hundreds. When they were assured of the amount, Suleiman unzipped several satchels. Yusuf tossed him bricks of dollars.

The merchants were paid first. For the three months the *Bannon* rode at anchor offshore, the villagers of Qandala had kept Yusuf's twenty-man guard teams supplied. In daily motorboats, they ferried out fresh food, drink, Kenyan *qaat* leaf to chew, laundered clothes, time cards for the guards' cell phones. Yusuf pitched to Suleiman enough packets for $300,000, a 200 percent profit. The chief of the suppliers was Suleiman's brother-in-law. His sister had married outside the Darood clan, a Rahanweyn, the farmer caste, *ashraf.* This generosity should help keep the peace.

Second came the large share for the financiers, faceless money that flowed from offices in Dubai and Mombasa. These funds were made available to only the best crews, all arrangements done in secret. They paid for Yusuf's equipment, and in return took a one-third interest. The moneymen had provided skiffs and motors, weapons and ammunition, radios, food, and the fuel used at sea while Yusuf and his boarding crew searched for a suitable target.

The financiers' portion required a large duffel. One million, one hundred thousand dollars. A massive profit. A car and unnamed armed men would arrive at Yusuf's compound tonight.

Next came the local elders, *odayal*. The Darood chiefs granted anchoring rights off Qandala; from the south, the Hawiye of Hobyo in the Mudug allowed Yusuf to hunt in their waters. Suleiman stuffed two bags each with $184,000, 5 percent.

Now, the class A and class B members of the crew. One B share was worth the prearranged amount of $10,000. Yusuf's company of men had hired forty-five of these as militiamen to guard the hostages and the ship during the negotiations, as interpreters, cooks, janitors. Most of these were teenagers, poor boys who flocked to join the pirate companies, many of them younger relatives of class A shareholders. They were unproven, often illiterate, but they were given tasks and weapons. Most of their guns were left without bullets in case the hostages revolted, tempers flared, or someone grew angry or dulled by too much *qaat*. They pilfered from the captives in petty ways that Yusuf allowed, and earned a pittance from the pirate trade that would change their lives for the better. Suleiman snagged $450,000 out of the air from Yusuf.

That left $1.5 million for the A shares.

These men had risked their lives with Yusuf on *bad-weyn*, the deep water, to capture this ship. For a week in April, well before the monsoon season, Yusuf, Suleiman, and a dozen others had floated in the Gulf of Aden on their dhow mother ship. Hundreds of freighters passed them, all bound north to Suez or south from it. The commercial ships formed convoys passing Somali waters, escorted by coalition warships from forty countries that shadowed the convoys and spoiled for a fight with pirates. Other Somali crews trolled these waters, but Yusuf's dhow was familiar to them, and they kept a distance. For a week in the gulf, Yusuf, Suleiman, and ten others bobbed and plotted, navigated, caught and cleaned fish, did their shifts in the deep of the night and the stink of diesel. They found no ships they felt sufficiently vulnerable; all were either too fast, too tall, or too close to the warships. Yusuf turned his dhow east into the Indian Ocean, away from the nuisance of the coalition's guardians. For ten days more they scanned the blue swells for passing freighters and tankers, looking for a sluggard, loaded to the hilt, low freeboard. They found the *Bannon* five hundred miles west of the Seychelles doing only sixteen knots, stacked with containers, unwary of pirates. Yusuf and his crew sped alongside in wooden skiffs. They raked the steel sides with bullets, held high their rocket grenade launchers to threaten the behemoth into slowing more. They boarded her easily with grappling hooks and ladders. They fired no more shots, cowed the ships' mates into hostages, and turned her for the Somali coast, home to Qandala.

Counting out the money for this team, Yusuf grinned that they were not worthless men, though they were brigands. They were hard men of the sea, fishermen before, pirates now.

He had twenty-five class A shares to distribute, each valued at $68,000. The assault team of fourteen had voted Suleiman an extra half-share for being the first to board the *Bannon*. One half-share was to be given to the widow of a clansman who'd drowned months ago on an earlier, unsuccessful trip; three shares would be split between the families of six men captured last spring by a Chinese warship, jailed now in Kenya.

These shares went into another duffel, to be handed to the men at a celebration at Yusuf's compound in Qandala tomorrow. The remaining shares were split between first mate Suleiman, who stuffed two into his own sack, and Yusuf, six as captain.

The two shook hands. Yusuf's larger mitt swallowed his older cousin's slim fingers.

"*Mahad sanid.*"

"*Mahad sanid, saaxiib.*"

Yusuf turned a circle in the wheelhouse, granting his memory a last panorama. The captain's leather chair, the bank of radar monitors, compasses, controls, the wheel and throttle, high above a mountain of containers. These had all been his. Stolen, yes, but answerable to him. That was sufficient power to envision himself this ship's true captain, not its captor. The money in his sack did not release him so quickly from this image as he'd like.

"Yusuf."

"Yes."

"Time to go."

Yusuf shouldered his leather bag, $400,000. The weight impressed him, helped him shrug off the lure of the *Bannon*.

"Hold the door open, cousin."

Suleiman pulled back the starboard door. Yusuf lifted the hard plastic cask. He hefted the barrel outside, onto the starboard wing. With one great shove, he heaved it over the rail, to fall to the ocean a hundred feet below.

The chest opened its white and emptied innards, a clamshell with the pearl gone. The current dragged it down the length of the ship and away. Shots rang in salute. The French photographers' plane, believing the bullets were aimed at it, skittered off to a safer distance.

—•—

Sharks thrashed at the heads and hooves, the scraps of the goats tossed overboard. The Somalis, raised to believe in animal omens, cheered. Fires burned in fifty-gallon drums cut in half, filled with charcoal, fitted with grills. Hoses washed away blood from the slaughter, drawing more sharks.

The *Bannon*'s cooks pitched in to prepare the meal. When the meat was done and carved, the Malays ate with their guards, glad to be rid of them soon but glad, too, for a hearty meal. Ashwin and his officers stayed apart, clucking tongues at the mess, finally free to express their disdain. Suleiman circulated, keeping order. Yusuf watched from four decks above in the smoke of the braziers.

Below, his men concocted stories to spread once back on shore. Perhaps the blood they'd washed overboard had belonged to a Malay crewman they'd butchered. The sharks ate the pieces of his body. They spoke of the many seamen they'd had to kill to capture this ship, then beaten the rest to keep it. The cruelties of Yusuf, the cleverness of Suleiman. How the captain, owners, and insurers of the great freighter *Bannon* bowed to them. The terrible things done at the command of Yusuf Raage, the bloodiest of Somali pirate chiefs.

Yusuf did not come down for the meal but stood in full view throughout. He let the tales about him whip up with the rising shore breeze.

After an hour, with the sun low over the rocky coast, the meal was abandoned, the fire pits left to smolder. Five fast skiffs sped out to the *Bannon* from shore. Yusuf climbed down from his perch. His cadre of young guards, filled with goat and curd, some glassy-eyed from chewing *qaat* leaves, lined up on the starboard rail. Weapons hung lazily over their shoulders and in their hands, the job done, money and sleep on their minds.

Guleed, younger and even thinner than Suleiman, lowered the long gangway. The metal stairs dipped to the waterline. Yusuf beckoned for the Indian captain, Ashwin.

"You did not eat, Captain."

"Nor did you. Captain."

"I'll eat tonight." Yusuf shook the bag in his grip. "I'll eat well. Right now, I need you and your officers for one more chore."

"We are finished. You have your money."

"I don't have it in my vault. Nor do I have myself behind my walls." Yusuf pushed a finger at the purpling dusk. "It would be a very easy matter for a warship helicopter to visit us while we're headed for shore. We'll be very exposed. Wonderful targets. You see? Everyone wants to hold up a Somali pirate's head."

Ashwin seemed disappointed. "You are a clever man."

Yusuf chortled. "Who starts these rumors? Yes, perhaps. Now, to the point. You will ride in the skiff with me. Each of your officers will go in one of the remaining boats. After the sharks have not eaten us and we're on shore, the skiffs will bring you back here. You may weigh anchor and go wherever you like."

Ashwin did not wait for Yusuf's dismissal. He turned to inform his officers.

The first of the skiffs puttered alongside the dropped gangway. Suleiman, waiting on the platform, climbed in. He carried his own bag and the dollar-stuffed duffel for the financiers. Five militiamen clambered aboard with him, then Chugh, the *Bannon*'s first mate. This was repeated until all the Somalis and Indian officers were on their way toward shore, each skiff bearing one of the money satchels. Yusuf stepped off the gangway into the last boat. He reached up to Ashwin, allowing him to be the final man off the ship. In the fading afternoon a shark's shadow rippled under the surface.

The skiff skipped over the even seas, running flat out. Yusuf did not know the boy at the tiller, but the lad beamed, seeming honored. On the sandy shore, a reception party waited for Yusuf and the money. The *Bannon* grew small in the skiff's wake.

The two miles to shore went fast. Yusuf stood in the bow, a figurehead for the skiff. Nearing the beach, the boy did not glide in to have Yusuf step out in knee-deep water like the other skiffs but powered onto the shore, wedging the hull into the sand for a dramatic arrival. Yusuf braced himself at the bow, then hopped over the gunwale. He did not turn to Ashwin to bid farewell.

One hundred meters inland, the beach became a hardscrabble desert. Scrub brush grew in the sand, wind-tossed plastic bags hung snagged in the scraggy branches. Huts of rock, driftwood, and mud had been raised at the rim of the beach by Qandala fishermen who had no boats. The town itself stood two miles away at the end of a dusty track.

The late-day sky remained quiet, without helicopters or photographers' planes. A lone buzzard wheeled. Yusuf looked up to the bird and marveled that it knew.

Yusuf's twenty militiamen formed up behind him, Suleiman in the lead. Even the boy in the dried-out skiff jumped down with a rattling old AK-47 to stand with Yusuf. The boy must have been Darood.

To Yusuf's right, out of the way, a handful of old men in long robes were gathered. Each gray beard quivered while they spoke among themselves. They were not the law. No one was.

Across thirty meters of sand, with gun stocks pressed to their hips and barrels level, stood a firing line of Rahanweyn, as many as fifty. Yusuf did not bother to count; he was well outnumbered. Their weapons were a mix of vintage carbines and beat-up submachine guns, enough for fools to feel brave. At their head slouched Suleiman's brother-in-law, Madoowbe. This was his proper *naanay*; privately he was called Wiil Waal, "Bold Boy." He was too fond of chewing *qaat*.

Yusuf motioned forward young Guleed.

"Take the money bag to the *odayal*. Stay over there."

"No, cousin."

Yusuf patted the teenager's narrow shoulder. "Who would you have me send? Who else can I trust?"

Guleed spit in the sand. He stared after it a moment, committing himself to the duty of murdering Wiil Waal later. He jogged off with the bag. Yusuf called after him, "Good boy."

When the elders had received their cash, Suleiman gestured for the satchel with $300,000 that was to be given to the Rahanweyn. He dropped the bag at Yusuf's bare feet.

In the beached skiff, Captain Ashwin ducked, to peer over the gunwale.

Yusuf spoke to Suleiman at his side. "Do not raise guns. There's no need."

"You and I define need very differently."

"He's your family. I'm sorry."

"He's a *footo delo*." An asshole.

Yusuf chuckled. He let the laughter stay in his voice when he called across the beach to Madoowbe.

The man shouted in reply, "*Salaamu alaykum.*"

"I have your money. A very good amount."

"How much?"

"Three hundred thousand dollars."

Wiil Waal's men whistled and stirred around him. Though he would surely cheat them, this was enough to go around. The tall man took several strides ahead of his clansmen. When he did, he revealed the woman behind him. Suleiman's sister, Aziza.

Bold Boy would put his wife in this sort of danger. He would use a Darood woman as a shield against Darood men. Yusuf spit in the sand where Guleed had.

He propped a hand against Suleiman's advance.

"You do not lead while I'm alive."

Suleiman did not retreat, but did not press forward.

Madoowbe called across the darkening beach, "How much do you have in your own bag, Yusuf?"

"*We'el,*" someone behind Yusuf muttered. Bastard.

Yusuf held it up for Bold Boy to see.

"Four hundred thousand."

The Rahanweyn leader strode farther away from his clotted guns. He stood alone and fearless halfway to Yusuf like a gladiator on the sand. Bold Boy waved his arms as he spoke, agitated and high.

"I have fifty men here who worked for you for three months. Hauling everything you needed back and forth to that fucking ship." This lash at the *Bannon* struck hard in Yusuf's ear. Bold Boy spoke like a farmer, with no love of the ocean.

"Your men did a fine job."

"We did. And now you tell us that you, one man, are worth more than my fifty. We had expenses!"

He yelled this as if it were some final argument that could not be overcome.

"You keep our bag, Yusuf. We want yours. We earned it."

Ten steps behind Bold Boy, his wife, Aziza, pressed hands to her mouth. Yusuf knew her, and she him. He would never hand over the satchel on his shoulder, for it was not money he would surrender.

Yusuf heaved his duffel to the sand.

"Come get it," he said. "*Ha cabsan.*" Don't be afraid.

Madoowbe turned to his fifty clansmen for a short, manic laugh. He asked them, "Why would I be afraid?"

He pivoted back to Yusuf, pointing with the barrel of his gun. "Bring it to me."

Yusuf bit his lip. Bold Boy had forgotten his place.

Madoowbe waited halfway between the two armed clans. This looked like courage. Yusuf hefted his satchel. To Suleiman, he whispered, "Do nothing."

Yusuf took the fifteen strides slowly, kicking his sarong with his steps. Madoowbe covered him with the rifle.

"Will you shoot me?" Yusuf closed the distance until he pushed his chest against the black ring of the rifle's barrel. "In front of the elders? My clan?" Madoowbe's eyes were wide and wild, *qaat*-stained and seeing more than he ought, that he might kill Yusuf the pirate and take all the money.

Yusuf dropped the satchel. He had no desire to die today. To live, and to save his clansmen, he gave himself over to wickedness.

"Wiil Waal."

Madoowbe slatted his eyes. Yusuf dared him to his name. Be bold. Boy.

Yusuf surged forward and pushed his chest into the barrel, moving the gun backward, for an instant raising Madoowbe's finger off the trigger. In the split second that gained him, Yusuf shoved the gun barrel down, aiming it into the sand. Madoowbe squeezed, firing near his own feet. Yusuf flashed his free hand to the small of his own back, snatching the onyx-handled knife from his waistband under the *khameez*. In a blinding backhand sweep, the well-whetted blade hacked deep below Madoowbe's left ear, slicing the neck vein. Swiftly, with a crossing flick, Yusuf slashed again at the Rahanweyn's throat. The two gashes cut a sudden V below Madoowbe's chin, both burbling. Bold Boy jerked back a step, coughing. He spit blood from his lips and new gills onto Yusuf's blouse, spraying red over the bag of money. Yusuf caught him before he could spin away, snatching Madoowbe by the tunic. He took away Madoowbe's rifle, barely held. Bold Boy wriggled, painting more blood on Yusuf.

Madoowbe's mouth rounded, gasping for air that would not reach his lungs. His eyes batted in shock and at what frightful thoughts he might have. His long legs bowed. Before he could collapse, Yusuf gripped Bold Boy's hair. He let the Rahanweyn's knees bend but held the torso erect. Madoowbe knelt to Yusuf, dying. He continued to spew blood from his heartbeat and wasted gasps.

With tacky hands, Yusuf twisted Madoowbe around to face the fifty Rahanweyn. Madoowbe spilled out the smell of copper, of earth. Yusuf raised his own nostrils above the ruby draining out of Bold Boy, soaking in the sand. He reached for the salt air of the ocean at his back. Let me bleed that, he wished, should I die in the next seconds, not this farmer's smell. I am *rer manjo*, of the sea people.

Yusuf threw Madoowbe's rifle down beside the money satchel. He tilted the man's head left and right, working him like a marionette, to shame him and make him look like a puppet in front of the fifty rifles. The noggin was loose and quiet in Yusuf's grasp; Bold Boy was dead. Yusuf tossed him on his face into the wine-dark sand.

He bellowed, "Rahanweyn!" He flung a blood-bathed hand at the clan. To a man, they pointed back with their weapons.

"You know me! I am Yusuf Raage of the Darood Harti! I have never cheated a man among you. I have never hidden behind a woman!"

Yusuf took steps closer to the guns, near enough to tower over all the Rahanweyn and Aziza. She covered her mouth, glaring. If alive, Yusuf would ask later if this was hatred he saw, or relief.

Yusuf pointed the onyx-handled knife back to the corpse. His wet and warm blouse clung to him.

"That piece of dung was not worthy to lead you. He's not worth losing your life for. Listen to me now."

Across the beach, Suleiman kept the Darood reined in. No guns were raised among them. The threat was in Yusuf's hands and thundering voice. He whirled on the farmers.

"If you pull one trigger, my men will kill you all. They will hunt down your families and kill them too, no survivors. We will throw your children and your women into the fires of your villages. You know we will do this. And if not the men behind me, other Darood men will come and they will do it."

Yusuf set his jaw. The buzzard above cawed oddly, sweetly. Was he calling out his brothers? Was he tasting the odor of Bold Boy? Yusuf took his eyes off the Rahanweyn. If he could not die at sea, let it happen with his eyes upward.

He saw only the lone bird, no others anywhere. That was the omen. One buzzard, one death. Madoowbe had fulfilled this.

Yusuf tucked the knife away at his back. He walked off from the Rahanweyn past the body of Bold Boy to retrieve his money sack. He lifted the bag with effort; the weight made him slouch. Wickedness left Yusuf feeling tired.

Suleiman led Yusuf's men forward. Guleed bowed to the elders and ran to join them.

The Darood formed up in front of Yusuf, still with their guns lowered. Suleiman bore the Rahanweyn's sack of money, $300,000.

The boy who'd piloted Yusuf's skiff stayed behind. In the beached boat, the Indian captain Ashwin stood in the bow, and though he could not have understood the Somali shouts back and forth, he clapped slowly for clever Yusuf.

Suleiman dumped the merchants' money in front of the fifty. They made way for the twenty Darood. Suleiman jabbed a finger at his sister but walked on. Her eyes glistened without telling why. Many Rahanweyn kept their guns up and ready, the path through them staying barbed and tense. The buzzard soared in tighter, lower circles. Yusuf shuffled behind Guleed.

Aziza put out her hand to stop Yusuf. She turned over her brown palm.

Yusuf unclasped his own bag. He dug out two banded packets, $20,000. With his waning energy, he slapped them in her hand.

"Next time," he growled to Suleiman, "find her a Darood."

The buzzard lighted in the sand near Madoowbe. It did not approach the corpse but folded and watched.

Chapter 3

On board HC-130 Kingsman 46
Above the Gulf of Aden
Off the coast of Djibouti

The wind made LB's cheeks rubbery. He brought his goggled face in from the 130-mile-an-hour gust.

With a slicing motion, he signaled the loadmaster to cut the net holding back the pallet. Immediately the four-foot-square package rolled down the lowered ramp, off the edge, and into the air at 3,500 feet.

The wind snatched the package and sped it far behind the chopper. The static line played out, then snapped taut. Two cargo chutes blossomed before the RAMZ plummeted out of sight.

Instantly the loadmaster reeled in the flapping static line. When he turned with a thumbs-up, LB waddled as fast as he could in swim fins down *Kingsman 46*'s open gate. Reaching the edge, he catapulted spread-eagled into the sunny morning.

Below, the white cargo chutes had opened perfectly, and the RAMZ drifted in fine shape to the turquoise water. LB counted to five in freefall, admiring as always the world from a great height, the wide Gulf of Aden, the tan shore of Djibouti. He pulled his main cord, felt the shudder of silk unfurling from his container, and as always when it filled, lost his breath in sudden and marvelous deceleration. He loved jumping in scuba gear, much lighter than combat tack and armor. Just fins, shorty wetsuit, low-profile mask, small tank, regulator, and fanny pack with signaling devices and survival gear.

Big Quincy, second in the stack, opened his chute above. Next, Doc popped. On top, the new lieutenant, Robey.

Djibouti was the LT's first deployment, today his first training jump with the PJs. LB didn't know the kid well. They'd had just ten days together during spin-up training at Nellis, much of that dedicated to mundane tasks, nothing to test or reveal the young combat rescue officer's makeup. They'd been in Djibouti four days. Robey seemed okay. Black kid, probably had a good life story so far. Confident, fit, standard CRO material, straight out of the Air Force Academy and the Pipeline.

The folded Zodiac package under its twin chutes neared the LZ. The gulf ran choppy today; whitecaps and swells cruised by, whipped by a warm *khamsin* breeze blowing south off the Sudan. The RAMZ neared the rippling surface. Just as it touched down, one of the larger waves rose up to meet it.

LB muttered, "Uh-oh."

The package splashed down without much spray. The wave had reached up at exactly the wrong moment, softening the impact. The RAMZ hit the water slower than the twenty-five miles per hour needed to spring the release mechanisms and disconnect the big chutes. The package rolled over in the water as it was supposed to, exposing the wooden pallet and big painted orange triangle to the surface. But the chutes remained attached. Instead of collapsing into the water, they stayed round and full in the wind. Like something not wanting to share, the silks dragged the package through the waves, towing it away from the fast-dropping PJ team.

LB tugged on both toggles to brake his own descent. He needed to land downwind to make sure the package floated past him. This was standard procedure for RAMZ drops, any waterborne cargo ops, in the event this very thing happened. If the team landed upwind, the package would just sail away and leave them behind. Aboard *Kingsman 46*, the loadmaster had another RAMZ to drop just in case. But that was a backup for a fuckup. Using it would be humiliating.

LB peeked at the other chutes following him down, to be sure they all knew what had happened. Quincy and Doc were well lined up on his lead to land ahead of the moving package. At the top of the stack, Robey glided in too high. The kid had banked into the wind with the rest of them on a final turn but needed to dump air now to get down. LB couldn't watch Robey long; he had to line up his own descent.

Swooping in low over the seas, LB kept pressure on his toggles to milk the last of the chute's airfoil lift. He lined up on the RAMZ straight downwind. He picked his spot, estimating the crate's path through the water, adding fifty yards. Quincy would land another ten yards behind him, then Doc and hopefully Robey, so someone in the line would snare the RAMZ sailing past.

With seconds left above the gulf, LB quick-released his chest strap and belly band; he was attached to the container and chute now only by the pair of crotch straps. Hauling both toggles down to his waist, he braced for the water. As he took one last look at the RAMZ package to make sure he fell in line with it, his fins hit. LB arched his back and flipped the ejectors on his leg straps, freeing himself from the chute.

He kicked to propel himself away from the tumbling canopy and lines. Just in time, he surfaced to reach up and smack Quincy on his fins floating past. Behind and above Quincy, Doc drifted down right where he ought.

LB groped for the mini-bottle strapped at his side. He spun the valve to turn on his air and popped the regulator in his mouth. Breathing easy, he trod water directly in the way of the oncoming package and rogue chutes. One last time, he looked for Robey and found him coming in too high.

"Get down, get down," LB growled around the regulator's mouthpiece.

The young lieutenant made a clumsy turn in an effort to spill altitude. Instead of landing behind Doc in the water, Robey soared past all three PJs and the RAMZ bearing down on them.

LB grumbled a curse. There was nothing he could do for Robey right now. He focused his attention on intercepting the package.

The RAMZ crate came right at him. LB kicked to the side to let the open chutes, struggling gamely, glide by. The pallet was being dragged at four or five knots. LB didn't want to try to snare it from a standstill in the water; he couldn't be sure his grip would hold. He broke into a crawl and a robust kick in the same direction. The package sped alongside, LB swimming fast and close enough to heave a gloved hand on top. He snagged a board and held on until he could get his other hand attached. With a two-legged kick of the fins and a hard pull, he hauled himself on top just as the pallet cruised by Quincy.

LB dropped a hand, snaring the PJ's thick forearm. With a heave, both men knelt on board.

Quincy made short work of the parachutes. He didn't bother searching for the release mechanisms but snatched his dive knife out of his leg sheath to slash through the left-hand lines. The chute crumpled. Quincy snipped the right-hand lines, and the second chute fainted into the water, done. The momentum of the RAMZ bled away just as the package bobbed up to Doc.

LB yanked out his regulator. "Where the hell is Robey?"

Doc pointed upwind. "That way."

The gulf's chop was high enough to block LB's vision beyond thirty yards, even sitting on top of the pallet. No sign of Robey. LB didn't bother with profanity. "We'll deal with that. Let's unfold this thing."

The three PJs knew their tasks. Quincy dove back into the water, regulator in his mouth. In seconds, he released the canvas diaper wrapping the RAMZ package. This floated away, a shadow under the surface. The coiled Zodiac began to separate from the pallet. Doc ducked under to find the bow of the inflatable, then swam it outward while Quincy did the same at the stern. LB remained on top of the pallet, popping open all the bands needed to pack a raft and outboard engine tightly enough to drop them from a plane.

Once the boat was free of all restraints, LB slipped into the water. He found the scuba tank attached to the boat's air intake, opened the tank's valve a half turn. Compressed air bled into the Zodiac; LB made sure he inflated the craft slowly to avoid crimps as it expanded.

The Zodiac uncurled and swelled enough for Quincy to climb aboard, then grab the bucket the riggers had secured inside and start bailing. LB increased the flow of compressed air, and the Zodiac took shape faster. Doc hoisted himself over the side, taking charge of setting up the outboard engine. LB waited until the air tank had tightened the Zodiac's skin, then kicked himself over the side. He scanned the rising and falling waters for the young LT, but there was no sign of him. Quincy bailed, while Doc set about dewatering the outboard.

LB despised this part of RAMZ ops—rocking in a raft over choppy seas on a hot day, waiting to get the seawater out of the engine's carburetor. Add to that the smells of sun-warmed rubber and gasoline, rising heat, and the neoprene wetsuits they all wore. The motor dewatering could take one minute or fifteen. Motion sickness never struck LB first, but if someone puked, he was next.

Doc yanked the starter cord on the outboard motor, keeping the purge valve open to force out the water. He pulled several times, spitting dribbles from the valve.

LB pleaded, "C'mon, Doc." The raft bobbed over a series of rollers. Quincy looked green.

LB turned his attention back to the shifting horizon of water. If they couldn't see Robey, he couldn't see them. The young CRO floated somewhere nearby, surely wondering on this first training day in the Horn of Africa what the hell he'd gotten himself into.

After minutes of swaying on the seas and churning stomachs, Quincy lost patience. He replaced Doc at the motor, took over pulling the cord. The big man put his back into the job, and on the fourth pull closed the dewatering drain. With his next yank, the engine sprang to life. LB spit out the taste of rising gall while the motor coughed its start-up smoke. Quincy worked the choke, revving the rpms, and the Zodiac lurched forward.

LB took up the raft's painter to stand in the bow. Quincy drove in widening spirals. Ten minutes passed before they found the new lieutenant, waving for them at the crest of a swell. The current had swept him several hundred yards north from the RAMZ's LZ.

Quincy zoomed to Robey, then cut the engine to drift beside him.

Robey puffed his cheeks. "Really glad to see you guys."

The morning heat climbed, the gulf water simmering at a tropical temperature. The straw from the freshwater bladder in Robey's backpack hovered near his lips. In the open ocean, he wouldn't die of dehydration for another few days, if the sharks let him live that long. Robey could have made the swim to shore, only four miles off. But that wasn't the point.

Changing the way a man thought could be done by teaching him. Altering the way he reacted without thought meant tampering with his instincts.

LB didn't know much about the kid floating beside the Zodiac because Robey himself couldn't know. The most important item had yet to be determined. Limits. The comfort zone. That's why they were out here training. To find the boundaries in each man and in the team, then shove them back.

Robey looked relieved and expectant. None of the PJs offered him a hand into the raft. Robey lapped a brown arm over the inflated side. With his foot, LB pushed the young lieutenant's arm back into the water.

Robey gazed up from the bobbing sea. "LB?"

"You're not here right now."

Quincy and Doc said nothing.

"Let me into the raft."

"No. You flew over the RAMZ. You landed upwind, and it left you behind. What if it was nighttime? What if it's pitch-black and we can't find you? Now you're not one of the rescuers, not a CRO or a PJ. You can't help the team because you've become a liability. We can't do our mission because we're looking for you. Somebody else, some survivor we were supposed to rescue, might die in the meantime. Rule number one for a PJ: Never become the one who needs rescuing. Ever. So you stay in the water till we locate you. Sir."

Robey tightened his lips. He floated another yard from the raft.

LB looked away from Robey. "I can't see you. Blow your whistle."

The lieutenant glared up. He took a sip from his straw to moisten his mouth, then put the plastic whistle tied to his buoyancy vest to his lips. He blew a shrill tweet.

"Didn't hear it. Too much wind and waves out here at night. Keep it up."

The three PJs waited, rolling over the rippling seas while Robey blew on the whistle.

"Hey"—LB addressed Quincy and Doc, behind him—"did you hear something?" They looked away. Both had gotten this business from LB early in their PJ lives.

"Hit your strobe. Maybe we can see you."

Bobbing, glistening from seawater and sweat, Robey turned on the flashing light attached to his vest. The emitter pulsed meekly in the African sun. His face took on a pinched, determined mien, a laser focus that LB knew well, a young man's defiance.

LB looked far out to sea beneath a shielding hand. "I think I caught a glimpse of something. Dunno. Pull out your buzz saw."

Digging below the water to his fanny pack, Robey unraveled a long string attached to a Cyalume glow stick. He bent the stick to activate the chemicals inside, then twirled the vivid green light around his head on the string.

"Guys," LB finally said, pointing at Robey, bobbing five yards away, "there he is."

Blank-faced, the LT dropped the ChemLight into the water. He cut off his flashing strobe to kick closer to the Zodiac. LB reached down, and Robey grabbed his hand.

LB lowered the lieutenant's grip to a rubber handhold on the raft's side.

"Hang on tight, sir. Quincy?"

The big PJ cranked the engine. He gunned it, spinning the Zodiac around.

For fifteen minutes the PJs coursed back and forth across the waves, collecting their spilled chutes and containers. They hauled them in like fishing nets while Robey clung to the handhold, ignored.

When they'd recovered the chutes, Quincy pointed the Zodiac west to the beach, where the riggers waited with Land Rovers and a trailer for the raft.

The Zodiac couldn't reach top speed because of Robey's drag. The PJs all sat in hot wetsuits and itchy sweat. LB saw little sense in making himself, Doc, and Quincy pay any longer for Robey's mistake.

LB let the kid hang on for two more bouncing, tough minutes, then gave Quincy the kill signal. The Zodiac slowed to a few knots. Robey couldn't heave himself over the side. Doc reeled him in.

Chapter 4

—·—

Camp Lemonnier
Djibouti

At the Barn, all the team's equipment was cleaned first. Doc, Quincy, LB, and Robey sprayed down the Zodiac, flushed and re-oiled the engine. Robey handled his end of the chores in silence. After the raft and chutes were squared away, they went their separate ways to deal with personal gear, then lunch. LB rinsed his wetsuit and scuba stuff, then hung them to dry in his locker. The team was in a surly mood, anticipating the debriefing set for 2:00 p.m., in ninety minutes, after lunch. Everyone, including the PJs and support crew who weren't on today's training mission, was required to attend.

With the great hut emptied, LB climbed the ladder to duck into his tent beside Doc's. The two preferred the roominess of the Barn, having the Ping-Pong table to themselves, and quiet after hours, so they made their racks in tents on the top of a high, broad shelf below the steel rafters and ductwork. The rest of the team was quartered in CLUs, contained living units, modular trailers stacked on top of each other throughout the camp.

The Barn served as the PJs' nerve center at Camp Lemonnier. A long, narrow table was the domain of the chute riggers. In the Ready Room, the unit's comm and intel computers fanned themselves. The briefing room also showed movies. On the broad concrete floor, rows of hardware and vehicles waited for action, folded and strapped to skids, each able to be dropped onto land or water. The fridge held cases of bottled water to offset the constant African heat.

Doc and LB agreed that Djibouti was a dusty, hot skillet where litter and grit rode on a bug-filled wind and no bush lacked a thorn or poison leaf. The locals were treacherous or high, and when they weren't, they were pitifully poor and heartbreakingly earnest. The national beer was a weak joke. For the two of them, the Barn was the best place in the whole country.

LB stretched out on his sleeping bag for a quick nap. He grew drowsy fast. Before he could drop off to sleep, boot steps below opened his eyes. A cheery voice called up.

"Hey!"

LB muttered. This was his own fault; he'd left the tent flap open and his bare feet hanging out where Wally could see them.

Wally hadn't been scheduled on today's training drop. Too bad. More than once, LB had seen him actually land on the pallet.

LB had known him for fifteen years. Back then, Wally Bloom was a lanky cadet at the Air Force Academy, the best jumper at the school, captain of the competition team. LB had been a young Ranger lieutenant, passing through the academy for a month of high-altitude jump training. Wally was the instructor who gave it. They'd crossed paths that long-ago summer and never got untangled. Now Wally was an even better jumper, the unit's top CRO, and LB's captain. PJs weren't easy men to command, though Wally tried to make it look like they were.

"Hey," LB answered without sitting up on his sleeping bag.

"You going to lunch?"

"No. Bring me a sandwich."

"How'd the RAMZ jump go this morning?"

LB folded hands across his chest. He'd learned to sleep like a soldier, accustomed to the ground.

"Depends on your perspective."

The unit gathered around the big table and on bar stools. Missing were Wally and Robey.

At 1405, LB stepped outside to look for them. He found both CROs just inside the chain-link gate. Wally leaned on an ATV, listening while Robey spoke animatedly.

LB approached into the sun. "Meeting's started."

Robey stilled his gestures. At LB's arrival, his face bore the same simmering mix of anger and restraint he'd had in the water.

Wally answered. "Robey tells me you lit him up pretty good this morning."

"Did he? If the lieutenant will come inside, I'll gladly give him an afternoon session. He can tell me which one he liked better."

Wally shook his head. LB didn't like dealing with Wally's disapproval through sunglasses. He preferred to see a man's eyes, the giveaway. Underwater, calm or panic showed there before it did in the body. Same thing in combat or a storm, or poker. The dying always died first in the eyes.

"Wasn't his fault," Wally said. "The right-side toggle tore when his canopy opened. He only had half control of the chute. Sounds like he did a helluva job landing anywhere near the RAMZ."

"That so, LT?"

Robey nodded, holding something in.

"Why didn't you tell me?"

The rear door of the Barn opened. Doc shouted for them to come on, then retreated into the cool.

LB turned to Robey. "Sir?"

The young CRO licked his lips. "Look. This is my first deployment. That makes me the new guy. I figured it was best to keep my mouth shut."

"You had no problem talking to the captain here."

Wally raised a hand. "I ran into Quincy at lunch. He told me what happened. I approached Robey."

LB asked again, "So why'd you stay quiet and take it? I was wrong."

"Didn't see the need."

"For what?"

"To show you up."

"Really? You're worried about making me look bad?"

"Yeah. You're LB. You're the man. It's called respect."

LB set a hand on Robey's shoulder. The kid was almost as tall as Wally.

"LT, I was an officer in the Rangers for eight years. I served in South America and the Middle East. I've done two PJ tours in Iraq, three in Afghanistan, all of them with the captain here. This is my third time in Djibouti. I'm not worried about looking bad, or being shown up. At this point, I care about one thing, and that's the mission. If I'm wrong and you don't tell me, if you let me make a mistake, that's what makes me look bad."

Robey hesitated before nodding. This clearly wasn't the direction he had figured LB would take.

"Now, let me be real clear about this, so we don't run into it again. You're an officer. I'm not. You chose to be an officer. You've got to show the same commitment to leading men as me and the other guys show at being PJs. Your job is to lead. Period. You never sacrifice that responsibility for your own comfort or need to avoid conflict. Never. You're in the fucking military. Conflict is what you do. What if I'm wrong on a real mission? You gonna worry about my feelings then?"

Robey opened his mouth to speak. LB cut him off.

"Sir, please don't answer me. You haven't thought this through enough to answer."

Wally said, "They're waiting on us."

LB nodded. "One last thing. See this?"

He tapped the patch on Robey's sleeve, the same one they all wore.

"That others may live, Robey. That might be the toughest motto in the military. The PJs you lead from this point on are going to trust you with their lives. They need to know you'll lay it all down for them. They've got to count on you being right and saying so. You lead, Robey. Whatever shape that takes. However bad it hurts."

LB rammed a thumb at Wally.

"I've known this one since he was twenty. I trained him. I argue with him as often as not. He's too good-natured by half, but I'll say this. I have never seen him refuse to step out in front. You stop worrying about me and start watching him."

Before Wally could say anything about the compliment, or Robey could mutter a young officer's thanks for the tough lesson, LB took a step backward.

He put his hands on his hips, a teakettle of a man when he stood like this, short and stout. "One last thing."

Robey said, "Okay."

"The men and women who turn to you will be in bad trouble. They will be in the shit. You'll be their lifeline. They may be frightened, even panicked. They may be bigger and stronger than you. Under no circumstances can you lose your composure or your control of the situation. A PJ is trained to do his job past the breaking point of any other soldier. More than anything else, that's what makes you a PJ. You got that? Sir?"

Robey squared his jaw before he answered. "Got it."

Wally signaled LB that the tongue-lashing was done for now. Robey slipped on his sunglasses, too.

Backpedaling, LB watched the pair of CROs follow. In the meeting, he'd rip LT again in front of the team. Let the kid have some practice getting on his feet as an officer, defend himself. Give him a free shot, even things up.

Chapter 5

---·---

Qandala
Puntland
Somalia

Yusuf waited until all the children were seated before he would come down.

In the courtyard below, women arranged the children so the littlest ones had seats in the front. Next came the girls, and behind them, the boys were made to kneel. They, being boys, wanted to stand.

On his adobe parapet, a sundown breeze furled his robe. Yusuf turned away from the bustling below to gaze east at the blue water beyond two miles of meager land. Tonight's sky would stay starry; the monsoons were over. One great ship rode at harbor, a Saudi vessel. The freighter was not his, but had been taken two weeks ago by another crew. Yusuf did not know how the negotiations were proceeding. From his catwalk along his walls he'd watched the supply skiffs parade back and forth. Yusuf had not ventured onto *bad-weyn* in seven months.

For a lark that he'd planned, he reached for a bag of coins. He tossed them in the air, scattering them over the courtyard at the feet of the children. This ruined the women's careful seating and made them glower at Yusuf. Suleiman's sister, Aziza, for whom the wedding celebration was being held—Suleiman had found her a Darood, though she'd had to settle for being third wife—was not amused. One long-faced woman, Hoodo, smiled up at Yusuf out of her *hijab* scarf. He had no wife, and lived only with servants in his compound. His position in the clan, his militia and wealth, would let him have any woman he fancied; he could even pay a husband and take the man's wife for his own. Since his return to Somalia, Yusuf had satisfied himself with prostitutes in Mogadishu and Bosaso. He told himself he lacked both the need and the time. This argument no longer held, because he had already begun to make the time, and the need nudged him, looking at Hoodo. She was known as an excellent cook and dutiful. At gatherings Hoodo always teased him, then asked for Yusuf's stories. She looked beautiful tonight, draped in an indigo *coantino*, almond eyes surrounded by henna dots, diagrams on her slender feet and hands. He'd long considered buying her. He might speak to her grandfather before the year was out.

While the women rearranged the children, Yusuf gazed over his compound. Chinese candle lanterns hung on lines above smoking pits where camel and goat meat fried. A diesel generator powered his machine to make ice; tubs of it cooled Western colas and beers. Small bundles of *qaat* were available inside the house for those who preferred the leaf to drink. Two Japanese SUVs, black and white, had been polished by his servants to be admired. *Odayal*, pirate captains, a hundred crew and clansmen, and a dozen of Yusuf's private gunmen had come for the party. An emissary from the jihadists had arrived as well, without invitation but graciously requesting at Yusuf's door an audience at a convenient moment. Yusuf welcomed the al-Shabaab sheikh. The man wore an old revolver in a holster across his chest. This was no cause for concern; every man at a Somali wedding wore a dagger, sidearm, or rifle. After the vows were taken, before the feast, they would fire in the air in salute, to spur the groom for his wedding night, even if it was to the number-three wife.

Yusuf descended the wooden stairs. They creaked under his bare feet. He was the biggest man at the party and in the village. He lacked the thinness of Suleiman, the narrow head and yellowness of eye. His cousin had returned home to Somalia from London first, after fifteen years. Yusuf had stayed in England's plenty five years longer, enough to let his face grow round and well fed, his hands and feet great.

The children sat like a garden of stones when he stood before them, the pirate king and warlord of Qandala. He raised a wide palm for silence from the women and children and attention from the men of the gathering.

"*Nin aan dhul marin dhaayo maleh.*" A man who has not traveled does not have eyes.

This was the way a story began.

For the children, Yusuf pointed beyond the walls of his compound, to a land far away where tales were lived. To the Darood, the captains, elders, and the sheikh, he spoke of a closer nature.

"A lion walked the land that was his home. He walked far, across plains and rivers. His domain was as broad as his legs could carry, for nowhere the lion stood was he not king.

"On one day, he moved in the shadows of a forest. He followed a sound and a scent. He was hunting."

Yusuf bent low for the children. He worked his hands like the paws of a stalking beast. He cocked an ear and sniffed the wind.

"The lion found his prey sitting against a tree. He crept closer, silently. Before he could leap and strike, the prey jumped to his feet. The lion halted, amazed. What stood before him was a tall and beautiful *jinn*."

Yusuf rose erect, playing the genie. He spread his arms in greeting.

"'Welcome, lion. I have expected you.'"

Yusuf crouched again, the wary lion.

"'How could that be, spirit? You were asleep. And I was silent.'

"'I am greater than you. That is how.'

49

"'I am king. This is my land. You are not greater than I.'

"At this, the lion roared his mightiest. Leaves shook off the trees, the ground broke beneath the lion's feet."

Yusuf raised both arms high to depict the size of the lion's roar. The children dropped their own jaws.

"The *jinn* wiped a fallen leaf from his shoulder. He opened his mouth and bellowed with the sound of thunder. No! Of a mountain rising out of the earth. The lion was staggered by the genie's voice."

Yusuf played the lion, puffing his chest, defiant.

"'I am king of this land. You are not greater.'

"The lion swiped a powerful paw against a tree, slicing out a chunk that made the tree crack and topple. The *jinn* stepped away from the tumbling tree. With one finger, he pushed over another, bigger tree. The lion bared his long teeth so the *jinn* could see.

"'I see. I grant that you are more powerful.'"

Yusuf stepped one leg back to bow deeply, as the lion accepting the truth of the genie.

"Then the lion clapped one paw against the earth, making a deep rumble in the forest floor. He did this again and again. Each time he struck the ground, an animal appeared in the clearing around him. First another lion, almost as big as him. Then a camel, then two. Then cheetahs and more lions, apes and elephants, crocodiles, rose out of the river. Hawks, seagulls, and buzzards lighted on the branches. All creatures of the forest, plains, rivers, and skies came to stand with the lion."

Yusuf turned in a circle to invoke all the growling, flapping, crouching animals.

"And the lion said to the *jinn*, 'But as you see, spirit, I am king of this land.'

"The *jinn* nodded to the lion, and all the animals of the kingdom who were joined against him."

Slowly Yusuf rotated once more, fingers under his chin to play the spirit considering all the beasts at the lion's command.

Yusuf gathered the hem of his robe. He sped the genie's spinning, faster on his toes for the children and adults, until the genie leaped, clicked his heels, and ran away.

The children laughed and hooted after the defeated *jinn*. The boys in the back threw their coins, then scrambled to reclaim them. Hoodo came forward clapping loudest, then joined the women taking the children off to bed. Men lingered in the courtyard, pleased with Yusuf's storytelling, before filtering away to resume smoking, talking, and grooming their hungers for the coming feast. Yusuf watched from behind a corner. The sheikh stayed alone and quiet, the way the *jinn* had waited for the lion.

Yusuf came out of hiding to approach the sheikh. The Islamist inclined his covered head.

"That was a wonderful story."

Yusuf returned the small bow, his head not covered. "It was one of my mother's. She was a great storyteller. A poet also."

The sheikh flattened a palm across the chest strap of his holster. A pious gesture.

"Allah has given you the same gift, Yusuf Raage. I am Sheikh Birhan Idi Robow."

Yusuf smiled. "I did not know. I apologize. But I see I chose my story better than I knew."

"Perhaps. May we leave your elegant party for a few minutes? So we may talk in private."

Yusuf raised a hand to catch Suleiman's attention. He told his cousin he would be back quickly. His intent, which Suleiman caught, was to have Suleiman climb the parapet and keep watch over this conversation.

Yusuf led the sheikh out a back door, through the adobe compound walls. His home lay on the eastern outskirts of Qandala, surrounded by open ground and sparse scrub. Sheikh Robow plucked a brittle stick from a bush.

"Do you recall how many trees Somalia once had? When I was a boy, I played under acacia, mahogany, yagar. We had forests like the one in your story. I pretended to be just such a lion. Now, look at this." Robow dropped the stick on the pebbles. "We are so poor from civil war that we sell each other charcoal. And we have no trees left."

Yusuf, still barefoot, aimed a hand east to the ocean.

"We had fish. Tuna, mackerel, swordfish, shark, shrimp, and lobster. We fed ourselves and made a living. The fish are gone now. Poachers from a dozen countries took them with gillnets, and no one to stop them. They paid no taxes, nothing. They respected no limits and swept away everything."

Robow touched Yusuf's arm. "My losses made me a warrior. Yours made you a pirate. We are not so different."

Yusuf stopped their walk. He glanced back at the roof of his compound, where Suleiman kept watch. This Islamist did not come to Qandala alone. He certainly had men in the alleyways, perhaps in pickup trucks with mounted machine guns. Yusuf did not want to stroll too far from his own gate and clan.

"How may I help you, Sheikh Robow?"

"The opposite. I have come to help you."

"With respect, because you are my guest, that would be a first."

The Islamist laughed, a barking trill that made Yusuf suspect he was unaccustomed to laughter.

"I was told you are a blunt man, Yusuf Raage. I am no diplomat myself. So, with respect as your guest, I will be plain."

"*Cad iyo caanaa lagu noolyahay.*" We live on meat and milk. The plain things.

Robow held his hands apart, to show they were empty and the offerings of a friend.

"The town of Harardhere has fallen."

"I know."

"We did not take it. We visited the elders and pirate chiefs and asked, frankly, for a share of the pirate income. And for them to stop interfering with our shipments from Yemen. Harardhere was quite the pirate stronghold."

Yusuf licked his lips, to speak carefully. "But you've declared piracy anti-Islamic."

"Yes, we have. You are lawless. We are Allah's law. But Allah's battles may not always be fought by the righteous. Pirates can have a purpose."

"I assume this includes me."

"Of course. But I will come to you in a moment. We were turned down by the pirates of Harardhere."

"It cannot be easy turning down al-Shabaab."

The sheikh stayed sanguine. "The ways of man are many. This is why the fewer ways of Allah are preferable. In any case, the militants of Hizb al-Islam took advantage and came in with guns. To be honest, this was done before we could do the same. They are now in control of Harardhere and impose the law. Many of the pirates fled north. Some have already relocated here. I saw the ship at anchor offshore. I know it is not yours."

"No."

"But in the end, even for Allah's warriors, pirate money was too much of a lure. Hizb al-Islam has made a deal with the pirates of Harardhere to split their ransoms in return for not driving them out completely."

Yusuf knit fingers in front of his robe to keep from balling his fists.

"You are coming to Qandala?"

The sheikh grinned, hiding his hands in his dangling white sleeves. "This is not in our plans. But I ask you to understand. Al-Shabaab and Hizb al-Islam are rivals. We are fairly similar in our beliefs. This is more of a sibling squabble than over Wahabbist doctrine. We have taken the ports of Barawe and Kismayo. Hizb al-Islam has set their sights on the pirate den of Eyl next, so we will make a move there first. Both of us need access to shipping. We require supplies, not unlike your own operation."

Yusuf and the sheikh walked in the waning sun. Robow smiled at the pebbles underfoot; Yusuf strode, impatient for the dangling threat to fall.

"What are you offering me?"

"A bargain."

"I'm listening."

"How large is your militia?"

"I pay fifty men. I can get a thousand of my clan in two days."

"Even if you can't, your point is taken. You pirates are getting more difficult to uproot."

"We didn't become pirates to share. We all know about Harardhere."

"Good. Then I bring you an offer the pirates of Harardhere were denied. We will not come to your town. And we will protect you from Hizb al-Islam should their interests turn to Qandala. You may continue to stay pirates in your little *rer manjo* village."

Yusuf drew himself to his full height. "If?"

Robow did not release his grin. "You are like a fish yourself, Yusuf. You see a bait and you go straight for it. Though you know there is a barb. Yes, if. If you do me one favor. A favor, by the way, which will benefit you, also."

Yusuf looked to his cousin on the roof of his home.

"What is it?"

"I understand you have hijacked five ships so far."

"Six."

"Excellent. I want you to hijack one more. A very important ship to us."

"What is on it?"

"Consider it empty for now. Capture it, and bring it to me here in Qandala. Once we have our hands on this ship, the West will pay a great deal to buy it back. More money than you have ever seen. We will, of course, split the proceeds. Each of our shares will be magnificent."

"Why me? There are a thousand pirates."

"Because you have a reputation, Yusuf Raage. You are greedy but reliable. And more importantly, you are a blood-soaked man. Walk with me. I'll tell you the rest."

—•—

Yusuf pulled Suleiman from the party, into the house. Aziza shot the two a dour glance, unhappy to have her brother waylaid from the festivity. Yusuf closed the door solidly to leave no doubt that she should make no objection.

In the study, he unrolled a nautical chart across a table. He stabbed a finger on the sheet between Abd al Kuri and Cape Guardafui, where the Indian Ocean flowed into the mouth of the Gulf of Aden.

"Robow says the freighter will be right here."

Suleiman smoothed a curling corner of the chart. "So will a hundred other ships. Why this one?"

Yusuf pointed to a chair. "Sit."

Yusuf's home had been built with pirate money. Others used their gains to buy property in Kenya or the Emirates, often driving up prices. Yusuf Raage kept the villagers of Qandala employed when the monsoons held them off the water. Let Mombasa and Dubai men care for their own. Three years back, when his house was done, he'd ordered a school constructed for the village, boys and girls alike. What would happen to it if Sheikh Robow came back, or the guns of Hizb al-Islam?

"I don't like it," Suleiman said, taking his seat.

Yusuf stayed at the table. With a story to tell, he needed his hands and legs.

"The ship will enter the gulf in twenty days."

"What's on board? Why do the Islamists care?"

"Robow says the freighter is empty. But there are armed guards."

"That makes no sense."

"What does it matter? When did we start caring about cargo? We take ships and crews. We hold them for ransom. Tankers, freighters, fishing boats. Empty or not, all the same, they have men running them. We'll take this ship and crew, bring them to Qandala, drop anchor, and sell them back. We've done it before."

"I don't like it."

"You've said that."

"I stand by it. Let this go, cousin. *Maya*." No.

Yusuf put fingers inside his beard to find the right words.

"After this, we're finished. We'll be rich enough to quit."

"I'm rich enough now. So are you. The monsoons have been over for two months. We haven't gone out once. I figured we were finished already. And I don't mind."

Yusuf sat across from Suleiman. The two were *tol*, cousins through brothers. They'd grown up together, as children here in Qandala, then as young teens in Plumstead, East London, when their fathers left war-choked Somalia for the West. They'd attended public school together, and in the Somali gangs committed crimes shoulder to shoulder. Suleiman was never comfortable in the English mist. He longed for his desert homeland and the blue ocean. He'd stayed long enough to learn English, read the Qu'ran in that language, then, twenty-five years ago, at age eighteen, came home to Qandala. He joined the rebellion against the Barre government, then became a fisherman. Yusuf followed five years later. Now Barre was gone, the fish too, and the cousins were thieves again.

"Yusuf…" Suleiman tapped fingers together before his face, thoughtful with his words. He was the older cousin, but no one disputed Yusuf as chieftain. "Have you considered that our day has passed?"

This was all Yusuf had thought of for the two months since the monsoons. He'd paced behind his walls, watching other crews go out on the hunt. His investors in Kenya and Dubai had sent messengers to ask when he might lead another venture onto *bad-weyn*.

Yusuf gave them no answer, because Suleiman was right. The Somali pirates' day was fading. He'd seen the signs gathering, like rising wind and whitecaps.

In years past, even last year, freighters plowing the Gulf of Aden had been vulnerable and slow, somewhat careless. Full oil or chemical tankers lumbered low in the water, heavy container ships lacked speed; fishing boats were the easiest of all—a pirate could almost step on board. International crews would not fight to defend someone else's cargo; captains lacked experience and preparation for hijackings. Ship owners had not spent enough money to protect their sailors and ships, and insurers made a windfall, tripling their rates to cover vessels passing through pirate waters. Governments around the world had turned a blind eye, deciding that moderate Muslim pirates who demanded only money were a lesser evil than Islamist radicals. Hundreds of millions of dollars in ransom had flowed into Somalia, a fractured land that had no other way to bring in that kind of wealth. The pirates had known to preserve this balance: do not kill hostages or steal cargos, never become so greedy that the insurers and owners feel the scales tip away from them.

Now the pirates were suffering from their own successes. It was inevitable. Silently, Yusuf had watched it happen. Impoverished shepherds and farmers from the mountains and plains, drawn to the coast to make what seemed easy money, brought with them no knowledge of the ocean or boats. The poorest of fishermen, though they knew *bad-weyn*, came to piracy with desperation and anger over their stolen livelihoods. These men and unschooled teenagers took low-paying positions in pirate gangs or formed their own. They went to the sea as hijackers; they failed time and again. Many died on the water. It was not uncommon to hear of pirate crews actually attacking naval ships by mistake. Whenever these miserable men did manage to capture a tanker or freighter, they often behaved in barbaric or violent ways. Chewing *qaat* was giving way to gin and cocaine. More merchant seamen and yachters were being wounded or killed in the hijackings. Some captured crews had begun fighting back, mounting ambushes to retake their ships, costing more lives both Somali and foreign. The cost of ransoms had skyrocketed, and the delicate balance began to unravel. The money these new pirates gained made them more vulgar, and villagers began to resist their presence. This opened the door for Hizb al-Islam and al-Shabaab, fundamentalists who brought with them guns and the laws of *sharia*. Village elders simply exchanged devils, and pirates up and down the coast were being run out of town.

More and more, pirates like Yusuf also became warlords, hiring private armies to provide order in their villages and protect against the creep of the Islamists in Somalia.

On the Gulf of Aden, coalition warships took up their mission with more intent and danger. They escorted freighters traveling in convoys, staying close enough to respond in fifteen minutes to a distress call. At the first sign of a speeding skiff or a loitering dhow, the warships closed in, launching helicopters armed to the teeth. The pirates usually veered off, but if they did not, if they pressed the hijacking, more and more of them were shot to pieces. When they did manage to climb on board, they often found ships equipped with panic rooms, strongholds where the crews could lock themselves away from pirates. This left the Somalis with no hostages, wide open to commando assaults to retake the ship. Shipping companies had begun to explore deterrent technologies like sonic or water cannons and blinding laser guns. Less commonly, but growing more frequent, the hijackers encountered men armed to defend the cargo.

Warships, even submarines, prowled the gulf for pirate mother ships towing skiffs, doing no fishing, rusted, suspicious, sometimes with ladders blatantly in sight. These dhows were increasingly boarded by the navies, even in international waters. When guns or grapples were found, they were thrown overboard.

For years, most pirates had been released when caught. Who would try them in court, who could punish them, when the Somalis, from a lawless land, assaulted a freighter owned in one country, flagged in another, sailed by citizens of two and three countries, captured by another nation's navy in international waters? Jurisdiction was a stew. The warships usually chose to disarm the pirates and put them back to sea with a stern warning. Today, the patience of the coalition nations was at an end. Kenya and the Seychelles received huge stipends from maritime countries to take charge of prosecuting pirates in their courts. Pirates swelled the sweltering jails in Mombasa, Victoria, Puntland, and Somaliland.

But prison bars were for the luckiest of captured pirates. Yemen was now sentencing hijackers to death. Every day, stories flew up and down the coast of mother ships that never returned to land, sunk by the warships, crews gunned down by armed guards on freighters and tankers. Speeding skiffs were being sent to the bottom by helicopters. Some shipping companies had even begun to hire their own navies, private mercenaries to protect their shipments. While Yusuf did not disregard these tales, he suspected that the dead and missing pirates were probably victims of their own poor seamanship as much as the violence of guards and warships.

Still, with hunger and poverty driving them, legal ways to provide for themselves and their families dwindling, and no government to secure them, the pirates' attacks on shipping continued to grow. The year before, over four hundred ships had been attacked, fifty captured and ransomed. More than $400 million had been paid for their release. The pirates had expanded their hunting grounds far beyond the Gulf of Aden. Freighters, tankers, and commercial fishing boats were being attacked a thousand miles from the Somali coast into the Indian Ocean, as far south as Madagascar and Mozambique, east to the Maldives, west beyond Bab-al-Mandeb into the Red Sea. Yusuf had spent weeks bobbing in sun, star, and storm on his dhow, immense distances from his home waters, stalking prey that was increasingly expecting him and ready for him. He wanted no more of it. He was rich now; he preferred to die in a feather bed. He wanted no more of the blood of poorer men on his hands. The stakes were being raised every day. The bleakness in Somalia drove an ever-degrading quality of man to piracy, men who increasingly threatened to kill hostages or blow up ships, even sell off the organs and eyes of hostages when ransom demands went unmet or were too slow in negotiation. Torture of hostages remained rare, but was no longer unheard of.

Hijacking had become the province of the most reckless.

Suleiman had said it. Yusuf had no more taste for these risks and this life. He was finished. Until the visit today from Sheikh Robow.

Yusuf could not hold his older cousin's eyes with his half-truth.

"It's not about the money."

Suleiman let fall a palm on the arm of his chair. The gesture said this much was obvious.

Yusuf related Robow's thinly veiled threat. Either al-Shabaab or Hizb al-Islam would sooner or later make a move on Qandala and the other pirate strongholds. They'd already captured Harardhere, and they had designs on Eyl. The two factions' rivalry and religion dictated it. Hijacking this one ship would keep them at bay from Qandala.

"Let them come." Suleiman did not flinch in his chair. "When did we ever run? We have men and guns. We can get more."

"I knew that would be your answer. That's why I told you about the money first." Yusuf pressed a hand on his cousin's knee.

"Listen to me. They'll come here. They will. These groups work with al-Qaeda. They want control over both sides of the gulf. They're in Yemen, and now they're making moves in Somalia. You and I don't want them here—fair enough. So we'll stay and fight, our clan with us. If we win, how many will die along the way? If we lose, even if you and I survive, we will run. And that will be like death. Let's take the damn ship."

Suleiman scratched his beard. "Do you remember your mother's story about the man who bargained with the shark?"

Yusuf was touched by the recollection of his mother. She'd died in England soon after he'd returned to Somalia, proud that he'd come home. She believed he might right his life here among his people, fighting to restore some dignity to their homeland. She didn't live long enough to know if he had.

"The shark ate him last."

"That's all you've agreed to with these Islamists. You know this."

"Yes."

"Maybe that's the best we can do for now. It will give us time to prepare for when they break their bargain. But, cousin, think. This ship is not empty."

"I know."

"Robow is lying. Or he doesn't know what's on it. Neither pleases me."

Yusuf looked out a window at a serpentine and complex world. Secrets, power, treasure; what was so valuable, or dangerous, aboard this freighter that al-Shabaab came to pirates to grab it for them?

In twenty days, the ship would sail through Somali waters. Yusuf, to protect his village, would hijack it.

Suleiman asked, "This doesn't worry you?"

"I save my worries for when I have choice. I have neither in this case. Whatever's on the ship, we'll take it and we'll ransom it along with the crew. Then we retire. You have my word."

"Tell me what little you do know about the ship."

Yusuf related Sheikh Robow's information. The freighter was French-owned and flagged, built in 2003. Fully loaded, she could handle 2,200 containers, with a crew of twenty-six. Two hundred twenty meters long, thirty meters wide. She had three cranes on deck that allowed her to load and unload herself.

"This won't be an easy one to take," Suleiman said, glum again. "Aside from the guards, she'll be fast and riding high if she's really empty. The bulbous bow will be above the surface. The prop will be out of the water at the stern. Her wake will be rough. The captain will be good. They'll be on the lookout."

"You'll figure it out." Yusuf smoothed his robe.

Suleiman tapped the map on the table, already planning. "I know a trick the Malaccan pirates use when there are guards on board. One of the Indians on the *Bannon* told me he'd seen it. I don't know how well it will work if the ship's running empty."

"And if it doesn't work?"

"We'll fight our way on. Like always."

"That's for later. Let's go back to the party. I don't want a knife fight with Aziza this time."

Suleiman kept his seat. "One last question."

"Yes."

"Why does an al-Shabaab sheikh come ask you to hijack it? There are other pirates. Other villages they can threaten. Why visit Yusuf Raage?"

Yusuf held his hands out from his sides to put himself on display. "He says I am known to be a bloody man."

Nothing Yusuf had said caused Suleiman to laugh, but this.

Chapter 6

Camp Lemonnier
Djibouti

Jamie cradled the phone in both hands, one palm flattened over the receiver to mute it.

"Hey, hey, hey!" He waved the phone over his head. "Everybody, quiet! It's the PRCC!"

LB set down his Ping-Pong paddle. He was winning 10–3 over Mouse, the smallest PJ in the unit, who claimed that back home he had an Oakland Raiders cheerleader for a girlfriend. After four years of playing, Mouse could not say the last time he'd beaten LB.

"Dude," Mouse called after him. "You quit, I win."

"I don't quit. We start over later. There's a mission."

Mouse clapped down his paddle.

Everyone around the big table and on bar stools watched Wally Bloom stride to the phone. Jamie held it out with excitement for this first call from the Personnel Recovery Coordination Cell since they'd arrived in Lemonnier three weeks ago.

Wally took the receiver. Jamie backed away, but not enough. Wally shooed him off a few more steps before answering.

"Bloom here." Wally listened only for a moment before responding, "On our way, ma'am," then returning the receiver to the eager Jamie.

"LB," Wally called, "Major Torres wants me and you at the JOC, stat. Let's roll."

"What've we got?"

Wally headed for the Barn's door with LB trailing. He used his length to take long strides and put LB in a semi-jog.

"Dunno yet."

This first mission had come two weeks into their deployment in Horn of Africa. The unit from Long Island they'd replaced had waited two months for their first call. In combat theaters, the action ran in a more steady current, sometimes a mission a week. For years in Iraq and Afghanistan, the United States had kept plenty of aircraft going, plus long-range patrols in remote, inhospitable, and denied terrain, tangling with an insurgent enemy, advising and supporting the local militaries in remote locations. Isolated personnel included downed air crews, troops cut off by severe weather, and small covert actions behind enemy lines; all these kept the phones ringing.

Here in HOA, the IPs were very different, the rescues quieter and more infrequent. The American military presence in Africa was primarily threat assessment. The United States needed to catch the next hot spots in the world while they were just sparks, and chances were good they were smoldering somewhere in Africa. Yemen, Somalia, Eritrea, Libya, Egypt, down to Uganda—LB could throw a dart at a map of the eastern half of the giant continent and hit something or someone America was keeping an eye on. The PJs' rescue missions were most often ODA teams, CIA, Special Forces, SEALs, direct action commandos, or any covert operative engaged in recon and intel, counterterrorism, or unconventional warfare. When these black operatives found themselves in sudden need of rescue from a blown cover, unexpected resistance, wounds, dangerous weather, even fatigue, they called for the PJs.

In their two previous tours in HOA, LB and Wally had effected rescues in deserts, mountains, plains, and jungles. They'd dropped in fast and silent, bringing teams with enough muscle to fend off an enemy and extract their isolated personnel. If the IPs were hurt, the PJs stabilized them. If they couldn't run anymore, the PJs carried them. They'd exfilled wounded enemies, recovered the bodies of American battle dead, plucked natives off hills ahead of floodwaters and contractors off roofs ahead of mobs.

When the phone rang in HOA, the mission could be anything.

———

LB hadn't been inside the Joint Operations Center since his last stint at Lemonnier three years ago. Outwardly, little had changed. A wall of video screens, banks of computers, a windowless intensity, and icebox air conditioning greeted him and Wally. Across wall monitors, the Falcon View program displayed a rolling map pinpointing the target's location, distance, and weather.

Major Torres stepped forward with hand outstretched. Black hair in a bun, dark eyes over a smile, she was the warmest thing in the JOC. LB had sat with her and Wally at a few meals in the Bob Hope mess. He found the PRCC smart and focused. Here, in her electronic element, she looked even crisper, prettier. She shook Wally's hand first.

"That was fast."

Wally grinned. "You're my reason for living, Major."

Torres shook LB's hand next. "This one's a milk run."

Deadpan, LB said, "Milk gives me gas, Major."

She nodded with her smile intact, still shaking hands, but blinked.

Wally stepped in. "Okay. Let's brief."

LB let go of her hand. Torres turned to the Falcon View. Behind her, LB nudged Wally. He mouthed, *She likes you.* Wally did the same. *She hates you.*

"Gentlemen." Torres moved close to the wall display. Using a finger as a pointer, she indicated the target, a ship entering the mouth of the Gulf of Aden from the east.

"The captain of the *CMA CGM Valnea* has put out a distress call. It was received by a Canadian warship who forwarded it to us. The Joint Force COs have discussed it. We've decided to respond as a humanitarian mission. We're not busy with anything else right now, and nothing's on the horizon. Early this morning the vessel had an accident on board. They require medical assistance. We're sending it."

Wally asked, "This got anything to do with a hijacking? That ship's smack in the middle of pirate waters."

"No pirates. There was a mechanical explosion belowdecks in the engine room. Before dawn, the second engineer and a cadet were inspecting the ship's pistons. Something big blew. A blast of steam out of the gasket knocked the engineer into a rail, breaking his back. He's got paralysis below the waist. The cadet took second-degree burns over half his body and face. The captain reports that the injuries are more than they can care for. The medical officer on the ship is also the first mate. He's handy with first aid. Nothing more. They need medication and advice."

"How urgent?"

"The burn case is bad. The back patient is stable but in a lot of discomfort. Don't know if the paralysis is permanent or temporary."

LB said, "Sounds like pain management, mostly. Infection control for the burns. Anti-inflams for the spinal. They asking for a medevac?"

"Yes."

"Can we land on deck?"

"No."

Torres motioned to the conference table. Waiting for them were bottled water and stapled reports. Torres handed out the pages.

LB and Wally flipped quickly through the sheets. On top lay company photos of the *Valnea*, a stock-looking container vessel. Three high cranes, aft, mid, and fore, gave the *Valnea* the ability to load and offload herself. The cranes presided over an empty white cargo deck, spiked with tall metal lashing bridges where the containers would slide in to be secured, so that it resembled a vast field of barbed wire fences. The big ship was clearly designed to run empty only on rare occasions; everything about her said beast of burden. She rode high; her dull red hull paint rose a good fifteen feet above the water. The gigantic bow bulb, used to break through the water, was also halfway exposed. *Valnea* didn't look comfortable without a couple thousand containers strapped to her back.

Below the company photos lay several black-and-white satellite pictures taken hours ago in the Gulf of Aden. As in the brochure beauty shots of the *Valnea*, the ship ran empty, not one container visible anywhere. The lashing bridges would prevent a chopper from landing.

LB flipped to peruse the rest of the collected info—a schematic of the freighter, its dimensions, capacities, power supply, architecture.

Torres tapped the satellite shots on her report. "As you can tell, we won't be landing on the ship. And we can't hoist the injured up to the choppers."

LB shrugged, frustrated not for the first time with the inability of the MH-53 copters to recover personnel from a hover. In other theaters, the MH-53 was a combat platform loaded to the teeth with rockets and guns. The ones at Lemonnier were cargo choppers, used to lift and carry immense weights, deliver and pick up soldiers and vehicles. On all of the MH-53s, even in combat theaters, the feeble door hoist wouldn't support the weight of a full Stokes litter. The starboard door wouldn't even open far enough to haul the basket in. In HOA, the PJs didn't have their own air force helicopters, the HH-60 Pave Hawks built for CSAR. The Guardian Angels of Djibouti were stuck using the marines' machines and pilots.

LB raised a hand, a schoolboy gesture. Torres didn't call on him, expecting him to speak without the formality. LB didn't budge.

Wally made a sucking sound, then said, "Just ask."

LB lowered the hand. He could tell Wally wanted to kick him under the table.

"We can fast-rope in."

"That is what I'd intended to suggest, yes."

"Okay."

Torres continued. "You take two PJ teams, drop in one. Carry enough meds for forty-eight hours, to get them to shore. Give the medical officer all the guidance you can in forty minutes. Then you head back here."

"Roger." LB checked the Falcon View for an update. The *Valnea* was located 20 miles northwest of Cape Guardafui, 510 miles away.

"Speed and heading?"

Torres answered. "Twelve knots. Bearing two sixty. En route to the French hospital here in Djibouti."

Wally screwed up his face at this. "Twelve knots? That's a big, modern freighter running empty. It should be doing over twenty coming into the gulf. Why's it going so slow?"

"The skipper reports he's got seven pistons working, not eight. He can't keep the speed up, not with his engine out of balance. The vibration would wreck the rest of the engine. Twelve knots is all he can do."

LB snorted. "Does the guy have a map?" He aimed his chin at the Falcon View and the icon for the ship limping into the Gulf of Aden, into the thick of Somali pirate waters.

Torres said, "The ship's well protected. Three armed guards are on board, and the captain's experienced in the route. They set out two and a half weeks ago from Vladivostok. Port of call Beirut."

Wally asked, "What about the crew? Who are they?"

"Russian skipper and officers, except for a Romanian chief engineer. The ratings are all Filipino. The engineer with the busted back is Russian. The burned cadet is Ukrainian. The three guards are Serbian. They all speak English."

Wally said, "Sounds like a floating UN."

LB held up a satellite photo. "Excuse me. Why are there guards on an empty ship?"

Torres considered LB's question. She addressed her answer to Wally.

"The CO left here just before I called you. The word's come down to him, and now I'm giving it to you. This is a high-value shipment."

LB's eyebrows went up, piqued. "So it's not empty?"

The major continued speaking to Wally, as if to say, *I'm expecting you to curb your dog.*

"We don't know, and we don't ask." Now Torres looked at LB. She was no-nonsense, all officer. "Understand something. Your stay on this ship will be short. While you're on board, you limit your attention to the injured. Let me repeat myself. Regarding any cargo, you show no interest."

"Understood."

For the next five minutes, LB and Wally took notes on sea, wind, and air conditions, current and approaching weather, water temperature, all in case one or both of the mission choppers had to ditch along the way. They calculated where the *Valnea*, headed their way at twelve knots, would be after three hours of chopper flight time at 150 miles per hour. LB allowed for forty minutes of hover over the ship to assess the situation, then rope-ladder up to the choppers for the return trip.

Wally closed his notebook first.

"LB, go on back to the Barn. Spin up two teams—you choose. Two PJs each. No need for me or Robey on this one. You'll take two copters and a refuel. Wheels up in thirty. The major and I will brief the pilots."

LB stood, so stocky he hardly seemed to rise out of his chair.

Wally kept his seat. Torres got to her feet to extend her hand and send LB on his way. She didn't need to, but she was trying to be polite. The instinct lasted only a moment. With LB's mitt in hers, eye to eye, the major shook her head, chuckling.

"You are a bowling ball of a man, Sergeant."

"Yes, ma'am. You deliver me right, I'll do the job every time." LB nodded at Wally, then the major. "You kids behave. Daddy's got to go to work."

Torres patted the back of LB's hand in mock sympathy. She spoke over her shoulder. "I'm just glad he's yours, Wally. If he was mine, I'd kill him."

Wally laughed, said nothing, and returned to his notes. LB let go the major's hand. He backed away.

"No offense, Major. But if it was that easy, someone would've done it by now."

"Go."

"Yes, ma'am."

Chapter 7

——·——

Qandala
Puntland
Somalia

Yusuf's dhow had rusted during the winter monsoons and his seven months of lassitude. His crew had done a poor job maintaining the boat; it sat neglected at a salty berth in Bosaso, fifty miles west. He'd stolen the sixty-foot trawler two years ago from a Pakistani crew, and there was little pride in its ownership among the Somalis. The two long skiffs, built of wood by local hands, had been kept in better shape, out of the water, painted and oiled, their twin outboards protected and ready. Yusuf sent for the dhow to be motored from Bosaso and then anchored off Qandala. For the next three days he had the boat painted and fumigated, and all engine oil, filters, and belts changed. He found a skinny black cat in an alley in Qandala, named it Sheik Robow, and made it one of the crew, in charge of rats.

When the word went out that Yusuf Raage was taking to *bad-weyn* again, two hundred men arrived at his gate. He allowed them all inside the adobe walls and let Suleiman choose twenty-four of the most experienced. None of them were teenagers except for cousin Guleed, all of them *rer manjo*, coastal men, and Darood. Everyone had gone to sea with Yusuf and Suleiman at least once before. There would be no *qaat* on this venture, nor alcohol. Because the voyage was to be short, Yusuf contacted none of his foreign investors. He and Suleiman would finance this hijacking.

The two cousins told the selected crew nothing of the truth. They provisioned the boat as they normally would for a longer stay at sea, with water and food to last two weeks, plenty of fishing poles. Neither mentioned this was not to be a hunt on open waters; they would not prowl the gulf or Indian Ocean for prey but wait for only one ship no more than 150 miles from Qandala.

Every man in the crew provided his own weapon. Suleiman inspected each gun, found half unreliable. With Guleed he traveled in a technical to Bosaso for a dozen additional Kalashnikovs, two dozen RPGs, and ammunition. While there, they bought five hundred meters of rope and new aluminum grapnels. The cost came to less than three thousand American dollars.

On the morning of departure, Yusuf walked through Qandala with his men around him. All wore loose *khameez* tunics or Western-style T-shirts and shorts. Weapons strapped across their shoulders, they jangled and stirred up dust. Yusuf led the men past the schoolhouse he had built, so the boys and girls could set aside their books to wave good-bye to him and his pirates. At the end of the road of shanties, he knocked at a door. Yusuf handed the old man who answered, Hoodo's grandfather, a packet of $10,000.

"In three days," he whispered. "Maybe four."

With Suleiman and two dozen Darood beside him toting guns and rocket launchers, Yusuf marched his crew the mile to the beach. There the skiffs waited to take them out to the anchored dhow.

Along the way, Yusuf looked for signs. Lizards would be lucky, and several scurried away from their sandals. Circling gulls meant success, but Yusuf saw none yet. The cat, a happy animal to have been found and adopted, purred on Guleed's arm.

As he approached the gulf, the sky and water made Yusuf wince, they were so blue together. His decade in London as a boy and young man had not made him Christian, nor had it deepened his Muslim roots. Even so, Yusuf sensed that Allah favored him today. The children had cheered, he was wealthy, and Hoodo's grandfather had smiled. Nothing dead lay along his path to the sea, no poor omens.

At the beach, he passed the spot where he'd knifed Madoowbe. No mark showed in the sand; none was expected. Nor had there been any mention of the killing in the village since it happened, seven months ago. Bold Boy was gone. The earth and man alike cleaned themselves of blood when the act was righteous.

No farewell had been arranged for Yusuf's armed crew. No families or elders saw them off; three black skiffs waited alone on the beach. Only Yusuf and Suleiman knew the true purpose of this quick voyage. They would protect Qandala. And if in doing so they became the wealthiest pirates in Somalia, so be it.

The crew dragged the skiffs into the shallow, lapping gulf, then climbed aboard. Yusuf stepped into the sea last, but did not put his wet feet into the skiff. He waited. The crew scanned the sky with him. None saw a gull anywhere.

———•———

Yusuf stuck his head into the cockpit. Old man Deg Deg stood at the wooden wheel helm, where he'd been for the first five hours at sea. Deg Deg was the oldest of the crew. His name meant "hurry." Even at fifty he had a spry speed about him. His right ear had been sheared off by an exploding shell twenty years before in the long civil war. He'd been the helmsman for Yusuf's six previous hijackings.

Yusuf said into the little hole in the side of the old man's head, "Come with me."

Deg Deg looped a noose around one of the wheel's pegs. The dhow would motor straight northwest.

Suleiman gathered the rest of the pirates at midships. Barrels of extra diesel were tied to the rails, mixing their smell with the odor of fresh deck paint and the breezy salt gulf in the afternoon. Fishing nets and floats had been scattered over the deck to camouflage the pirate ship as a fishing boat. All weapons were stowed below and out of sight. Behind the dhow trailed the trio of towed skiffs.

Deg Deg joined the crew. Gold-toothed Suleiman spoke first. "You should know what we're going to do."

With that, Suleiman moved to stand among the men.

Yusuf smiled at his Darood crewmen and two cousins. "A man who has not traveled," he said, "has no eyes."

He told the men everything. Sheik Robow's threat to Qandala. The sheik's report that the French ship would be running empty, even with armed guards on board. Yusuf's shared belief with Suleiman that perhaps when they found her, she would not be empty at all. This made no difference. The pirates would take her and save their village from al-Shabaab, if only until another day would come. But until then, they would not flinch.

"The freighter," he announced, "will be in the Internationally Recognized Transit Corridor. Warships will be close. Suleiman has a plan to trick the guards. If that doesn't work, we have two dozen RPGs to convince her to slow down." The men all nodded; this was the only way any of them had ever taken a ship, by violence and intimidation. None of them had ever boarded an armed vessel before.

Yusuf raised a hand, as if in blessing. "This may be the most dangerous hijacking any of us have done. But believe me, the ransom will make each of you a king."

The men stood silently with hands at their sides. They were not the sort to question. If Yusuf Raage said they would be kings, they would follow and be kings.

Deg Deg was the first to break ranks, headed to the pilothouse. He released the wheel from the rope to take the dhow in hand. The others returned to their chores, chipping away rust, painting, or boiling rice or tea and rolling *subaayad* patties for lunch.

Suleiman and Guleed stayed behind only long enough to pat Yusuf on the shoulder. They moved to the stern to sit on weathered crates. With a blade, Suleiman showed the boy how to cut and tie cords of the new hemp rope into ladders.

Deg Deg motored toward the protected corridor that ran the length of the Gulf of Aden. Yusuf stepped to the bow with binoculars and a handheld GPS, tracking the dhow's speed and course. The two thin men scraping rust left him alone.

Yusuf did not scan the horizon. It was too soon; the transit corridor lay thirty more miles ahead. He saw no great cargo ships on *bad-weyn*, just smaller Somali and Yemeni craft truly fishing, or trafficking in refugees or guns, or other pirates. He could not discern these ships' business and had no wish to.

Yusuf lay on a warm, bunched net. He closed his eyes to rest and wonder about the secrets of the freighter that, in a few hours, he was going to seize, then sell.

Chapter 8

——·——

Jamie clapped when told he was coming on the mission. Doc went straight to work. Mouse grumbled about his losing streak at Ping-Pong.

The four set out their med rucks on the riggers' table. Each PJ's pack was laid out the same way: three large pockets, A, B, and C, airway, bleeding, circulation. On this op they had the advantage of knowing the injuries in advance. The issue on the ship would be to determine the severity of the burns and the extent of the paralysis, then instruct the crew how to treat them.

LB and Jamie raided the medic's closet. LB stocked up on nonstick dressings, IV fluids, antibiotic ointment for the burns, and two catheters. Jamie filled his ruck with bags of Solu-Medrol, a corticosteroid anti-inflammatory, plus extra vials of morphine and fentanyl. Both those sailors had to be in considerable pain.

As team leader, LB belted himself into his Rhodesian vest, satellite and team radios snug to his ribs. All four PJs grabbed flight helmets, shouldered their packs and carbines. Before heading out to the choppers, LB told the team what Torres had said: that this was, in fact, a milk run. They were not headed into an isolated zone; there were no combat nor enemy lines to drop behind, no severe weather. None of them wore armor or carted extra magazines. This was not an extraction but a humanitarian mission.

"These are the jobs," he said to Doc, Jamie, and Mouse, "the milk runs, where shit happens. Stay focused. Do the job. Get back. Let's roll."

They headed for the Barn door, held open by Robey. When LB passed, the young lieutenant put out a hand.

"Hoo-ya, LB."

LB shook firmly. "If I can't handle this one, you come and get me."

Robey grinned. "I'll bring hell."

"Hoo-ya, LT."

Quincy waited for them in an ATV cart. He smacked each on the helmet, a throwback to his football days, then drove them to the airfield and the warming MH-53s.

The tarmac radiated morning heat. Wally waited between the two choppers. LB tapped Jamie on the shoulder to come with him in *Detroit 1*; Doc and Mouse would follow aboard *Detroit 2*.

Wally approached.

Detroit 1's jet engine whined louder, the blades flipping slowly. Wally took down his sunglasses. LB pulled off his helmet.

Over the chopper noise, LB shouted, "What?"

Wally shook his head. "Nothing."

"You came out here to tell me nothing?"

"Torres doesn't want you on the boat. She says send Doc."

"What'd you tell her?"

"I said I don't make that call. She doesn't either. You do."

LB grimaced at the sun blazing over the gulf. He screwed on his helmet. Wally stepped away. Before climbing into the bay of *Detroit 1*, LB faced Wally, standing outside the wash of the propellers, racing now and building lift.

Haphazardly, LB saluted.

In the vast cargo bay of the MH-53, LB divided the ride over the gulf into thirds.

For the opening hour he talked with Jamie about how they would diagnose and treat severe burns and a spinal injury. Jamie, in three years as a pararescueman, hadn't yet seen a bad burn case. LB described the changes heat could work on human flesh and reviewed the distressing effects on the body's functions. The Ukrainian cadet had been blasted by steam, so they could expect red, swollen, blistering dead skin and a raw, repellent smell. The broken back would be hard to analyze without an X-ray. They'd try to reduce the swelling in the sailor's spine to see if his symptoms eased. Both injured would need pain relief. Neither would have control of his urine or bowels.

Lying on the vibrating floor of the big chopper in smooth air, head on his ruck, LB slept through the second hour. Jamie, always eager, stood behind the cockpit, watching the pilots and the streaking water below.

In the third hour, LB wondered about the *Valnea*. Torres said the ship was empty but guarded. Steaming at twelve knots instead of twenty. Operated by Russians, Romanians, Ukrainians, Filipinos, guarded by Serbs, an odd mix. And why the blatant command to ignore the ship's cargo if it had none?

This was obviously a spook ship bound for Lebanon. No question, something big and under the radar was going on with her, big enough for word to come down through the chain of command that the PJs were to show no curiosity.

When *Detroit 1*'s pilot finally announced he had the freighter in visual range, LB joined Jamie behind the cockpit to peer out the windshield. The *Valnea* swelled out of the distance to appear just as she had in the color brochure photos, riding high, her three cranes with no cargo to loom over, baring much of her painted hull that would be below the waterline if she were running loaded. At the bow, the great bulb should have been under the surface, too, but raised a pretty wake pushing the gulf aside.

Valnea seemed effortless, cruising on the vast blue. She did not look wounded.

The two copters circled the ship while *Detroit 1*'s pilot hailed her. In lightly accented English, the *Valnea* answered, taking instructions for the chopper's approach. The vessel would maintain course and speed.

Jamie and LB climbed into their med rucks and M4s. *Detroit 1* leaned back to slow and match the freighter's speed. The chopper crept up from behind while *Detroit 2* kept pace a hundred yards to the right. LB tested the fast rope, tugging hard where it attached to the MH-53's frame.

The pilot bled off altitude, closing the distance to the peak of the ship's great superstructure, a six-story white building. LB peered into the sooty maw of the *Valnea*'s smokestack behind the wide pilothouse. Left and right, steel wings extended from the superstructure. *Detroit 1* descended, settling in above the starboard wing.

The chopper's pilot murmured in LB's helmet, "LZ is below."

LB answered, "Roger that." He and Jamie unhooked from the intercom to plug into their team comm. Both PJs radio-checked.

Jamie kicked the fat green rope out the door. The line snapped taut, with its bottom half coiled on the wing's deck twenty yards below. The wheelhouse door struggled to open against the prop wash; two sailors pushed their way out to watch the giant helicopter hover beside the smokestack. The MH-53's downward gale pushed them back against the door.

LB gave *Detroit 1*'s pilots an okay signal. He gripped the rope with gloved hands, pinched it between his boots, and slid down to the *Valnea*. On deck, he held the line taut for Jamie. When both were down, the rope was reeled back in by the chopper's flight engineer. LB and Jamie knelt to keep from being blown overboard while *Detroit 1* backed away.

With the big chopper beating into position to join *Detroit 2* alongside the ship, the two sailors walked forward. The shorter one, blond and pasty, sported a potbelly. The taller man approached lean and blackbird dark, a white captain's hat on his head.

The tall one reached out in greeting. LB shook hands, struck by the firmness of the clasp, the sinews in the arm. This was a scrawny but strong Russian.

"*Pazhalusta*. I am Captain Anatoly Pavelovich Drozdov." The captain beamed down on LB, pleased. His face crinkled around a knobby, veined nose. Drozdov was, or had been, a prodigious drinker. "You are welcome aboard the *Valnea*. And such a dramatic arrival."

Drozdov motioned to the heavyset sailor beside him. "This is First Mate Grisha Mikhailovich Pravdin. It was his notion to call for help."

LB took the mate's hand, also a memorable grasp.

"First Sergeant DiNardo. This is Staff Sergeant Dempsey."

LB took a moment to glance around, high above the waterline of the great freighter. Forward, the boat had the length of one and a half white football fields; to the stern, another fifty yards. From the helicopter, the ship had seemed easy in the water; here on her deck, she felt anxious, tippy, missing the two thousand containers that would normally stabilize her.

A brisk breeze nudged at LB, cooler than on the tarmac at Lemonnier. Out to sea on all sides, no other vessels studded the horizon—no convoy, warship, or pirate.

Before LB could ask Drozdov to take them to the patients, Jamie tapped at his elbow. With his chin, the young PJ indicated the distant bow. There, a pair of dark figures walked the rail.

"Two of the guards we have been given." Drozdov spoke with obvious distaste. "I do not like guns on my ship."

LB jerked to hear a new voice at his back.

"Nor do I."

He spun to a man taller than Drozdov, paler than the first mate, swathed in black from head to toe, an odd choice under a stark sun. The man's torso widened to shoulders broader than LB's. What made his statement ominous was the Zastava M21, heavy and lethal, the assault weapon of the Serbian army, hanging off his shoulder.

"This sneaky creature," said Drozdov, indicating the guard, "is Bojan. Mr. Bojan, these are American sergeants—"

"I will take your weapons." The Serb extended a big hand.

Jamie hooked a thumb inside the strap of his own M4. "No."

Bojan's hand did not waver.

"I must control all weapons on this ship. I have been given that order."

LB stretched an arm to silence Jamie. "Mr. Bojan. Sergeant Dempsey and I are in the United States Air Force. We were invited aboard this ship, weapons and all."

"I have no instructions for exception. Not for US Air Force. Not for no one."

"We don't surrender our weapons to civilians."

"I have not been civilian very long." Bojan lowered his meaty palm. "Please, Sergeant. The two sailors are in great pain. I do not want to put you off this ship without your help. But I will. The captain knows I have this authority."

Drozdov bobbed his white captain's hat to grant the point.

LB considered what he was facing. Guns in the hands of others was why Bojan had been put here in the first place. While LB didn't embrace the notion of turning over his M4—no soldier would—he'd surely do the same in big Bojan's place. And the Serb was right. The two injured sailors needed his and Jamie's help and the medicines they'd brought. How could he go back to the Barn and report to Torres and Wally that he'd left a couple of Russians in agony because he refused to give up his weapon?

"It's cool," LB told Jamie. He unslung his own carbine, holding back only the four-inch blade under his pants leg in the holster above his boot. No one got that.

Jamie followed suit with his own M4. From his med ruck, he pulled a stashed 203 40 mm grenade launcher and a Beretta 9 mm sidearm.

LB's jaw hung. "Dude."

Baby-faced Jamie glared at the Serb. "I'll want these back."

The captain flattened a hand to his own breast. "I will be accountable for your weapons, gentlemen. You have my word, they will be returned to you."

Bojan collected the arsenal. With a nod, he pivoted for the wheelhouse and, hardly encumbered by the guns, was gone.

Jamie spread his hands at LB. "What?"

"Nothing, Rambo."

First Mate Grisha affably patted his belly. Neither he nor the captain gave any hint that they were the officers of a massive, seagoing puzzle.

Grisha spoke into the wind. "Mr. Bojan and his Serbs have not added personality to our long voyage."

Jamie asked, "Are the wounded in the infirmary?"

Drozdov replied. "Come."

Stepping inside the superstructure, both PJs shivered to a jolt of air conditioning. These former Soviets liked their air chilly. The captain sealed the door, throwing two watertight handles to stop its whistling.

The wheelhouse spread into an expanse of radar screen, dials, toggles, compasses, and monitors. Two padded leather chairs oversaw the controls. Between them the steering wheel was comically small, as if for a child's car. A wide windshield of shaded impact glass provided a cool panorama of the distant bow and seas ahead. Behind, a map table and wooden shelves gave the bridge the feel of a library with an ocean view.

In one leather chair sat a pale, long-limbed woman. When she turned to LB, she moved with an uncoiling grace. She swung down her legs to stand and greet LB and Jamie. Her face was all angles and circles, black eyes and prominent nose, bangled earlobes, heavy eyebrows to balance a sprawling smile. She was dressed in a white linen cargo shirt over khaki pants, the clothes of a traveler. She wore her jet-black hair close to the scalp.

Drozdov escorted the two PJs to her. LB and Jamie pulled down their helmets, and the woman extended a lanky arm, striding to meet them. Her long fingers enveloped LB's. She stood at least three inches taller.

Drozdov said, "This beautiful woman is counter to Mr. Bojan. She is our passenger. Iris, these are air force Sergeants DiNardo and Dempsey. They are pararescuemen."

She withdrew her hand from LB's, offering it to Jamie.

"*Dobriy den'*, gentlemen."

Both PJs said, "Ma'am."

"I very much liked your *entrez*. Like gods."

LB and Jamie exchanged looks. Jamie muttered a shy "Thank you," and let go of her hand.

LB said, "You're Russian?"

"Yes. You have spent much time there?"

"Obviously not enough."

"Wonderful." She almost loomed over him. "I know you must go attend to the men. I understand they are very hurt."

LB liked her version of English better than Drozdov's. All the hard edges of the language were smoothed on her lips.

Jamie poked him in the back to reply.

"Yes. Yes, ma'am."

The captain removed his billed cap. He mussed his own hair, short and black as Iris's. He motioned both PJs to follow Grisha, then took one of the leather chairs. Iris slid into the other.

The first mate led them past the map table, into a down stairwell. One floor below the bridge, he punched the button for an elevator. The rotund officer's eyes widened with mischief.

"She is pleasant, no?"

LB nodded. "Pleasant, yes. What do you know about her?"

"Iris Cherlina? Very little. She is passenger."

"That's it?"

Grisha tapped a finger to his lips. "I know what I am told. And that is nothing."

Over his shoulder, LB raised eyebrows at Jamie.

The elevator arrived, and the door hissed aside. Inside, Grisha patted Jamie on the shoulder affably.

"Thank you, both of you, for giving your weapons to Bojan. I know this was uncomfortable. But on cargo vessels, there is a long tradition against guns. They are not wanted."

The elevator descended slowly from F deck five floors to A. LB shrugged.

"You got pirates all over the place. Why not arm yourself?"

"We are at sea for months. Ten, twenty thousand ocean miles. We are family on this ship. We argue, make errors, like family. What does captain do with crewman who drinks too much or misses shift, who is unhappy he must be disciplined, if there are guns on board? What does captain do with crew who decides they want to take cargo for themselves and mutiny? What if man cannot stand argument with shipmate and wants to fight with gun? These are not first-time questions here in twenty-first century, you understand? These are asked by captains for many centuries."

The elevator arrived at A deck. Grisha led them into a long wood-paneled hall without windows. The floors had been mopped spotless; every shiny surface gleamed under fluorescent lights. Captain Drozdov ran a spick-and-span ship.

Leading them to the infirmary, the mate continued, "As for pirates, listen. If we shoot at them with rifles, they will come with cannons. If we use cannons, they will use missiles. If we kill one, they will kill two. Who would want to get into bidding war with such people? We are merchant sailors. We train for seas, not guns."

LB asked, "What about the warships?"

"Yes, if there is time to call. But understand, countries with warships in the Gulf of Aden are not coordinated. They meet once a month in hotel in Bahrain, they cooperate through online chat room. This is not proper approach to pirates."

Jamie spoke up. "So hire guards instead. Like Bojan."

Grisha stopped in the hall to shake a pudgy finger.

"And what will you do with Bojan when your ship wants to enter waters of a nation that does not allow guns into their harbor? This is commercial vessel. That port is closed to us. I tell you, around the world every maritime nation has different rulebook. For guns, you would pass these nations by? You make no money this way, young man."

Grisha moved down the hall. He spoke over his shoulder, wanting to finish his thought on the matter. "I will be glad to put them off my ship when we arrive."

The first mate halted at a door marked by a red cross against a white field, the infirmary. With a hand on the knob, he paused.

"But today I am going twelve knots on a broken ship. In these devil's waters I must be glad to have the guns of Bojan. The pirates, they make people crazy. They have made Anatoly Drozdov crazy." The first mate stopped himself from saying more about his captain. He cracked the infirmary door. "And I am glad to have you here for these two hurt boys. *Spasibo*. Now, before we enter."

"Yeah."

"I am not doctor. I am sailor. You understand?"

LB rolled his med ruck off his shoulders. "No worries. Let's see what we got."

With Jamie at his back, LB entered the small sickbay. He did not recoil at the smell of urine because he expected it.

Grisha raised his hands. "I am sorry." He flustered quickly with the apology. "They cannot control. I cannot—"

"Hey, Grisha. It's all right. We got this. Listen to me. Either of these guys got allergies to drugs?"

"I have checked records. They do not."

"Good. Now, can you find some disinfectant?"

"Of course."

"We'll take a look at your boys. You start mopping. Okay?"

The first mate hurried out to fetch a bucket and mop, uttering again that he was sorry.

The infirmary held two beds. On the closest lay a smallish man in a T-shirt. Straps held him down to a stiff board, tightened across his forehead, chest, waist, and legs. A foam brace circled his neck. A sour-smelling sheet covered him below the waist. LB moved to his bedside, standing without care in urine that had dribbled there. The seaman grimaced, raising one arm off his chest to take LB's hand. LB squeezed to say he had arrived and there was to be no shame in this room.

Jamie stepped to the second bed, where a young man, the cadet, moaned. The boy had been stripped; his torso and right leg were swaddled in white gauze bandages. The skin left bare had flushed a fevered pink. The boy's rib cage rose and fell in a fast pant. Around his scalded mouth and brow, bubbled flesh wept. Jamie waved a hand over the boy's bandages, as foul with urine as the engineer's sheet and the infirmary floor. The young PJ dug into his med ruck for rubber gloves to start peeling away the cadet's gauze.

Jamie checked the IV in the cadet's arm. He'd been plugged into a bag of saline. The bag was empty, the burns were thirsty.

LB let go the engineer's hand with a pat on his chest. "You'll be okay, pal. Hang on, I gotta do something for you here."

He opened his ruck to withdraw the catheters he'd stashed. As soon as he'd heard the victims had suffered paralysis and burns, LB knew that neither man would be able to hold his water. The engineer couldn't sense anything below the waist, and the cadet was in so much pain he couldn't stay conscious.

Jamie unwrapped all the cadet's bandages. He stuffed them, the cadet's sheet, and their stench into a trash bag. The boy's skin glistened with fluids weeping out of his tissues, as the cells of his body tried to cool themselves.

LB handed Jamie one of the catheters, then set to work on the engineer. The insertion went quickly; The man couldn't feel a thing he was doing. LB slid the small sterile tube into the engineer's penis, threading the tube deeper into the urethra until urine flowed. This meant he'd reached the bladder. A quick injection of fluid swelled the inserted end to hold it in place. LB hooked the plastic collection bag to the bed, and it was done.

Right behind him, Jamie finished with the cadet.

The first mate returned with a mop and a bucket slopping with sudsy water. The pungency of the bleach added to the urine stench.

"Prop the door open," LB told him.

Grisha did so, then began to mop.

"That is Nikita. He is dear friend. When piston blew he was thrown against railing. Broken back. Broken rib. The rib causes him pain."

Nikita whispered something in Russian. LB bent closer. The sailor cleared his throat, then repeated himself. He could not turn his immobilized head.

"*Chyort.*" Damn.

LB asked Grisha, "What've you given him?"

"What I have. Fluids. Morphine."

"How often with the morphine?"

"Every hour when I check on him."

"He needs to be checked every ten to fifteen."

LB moved next to the bed. He leaned over so Nikita could see his face.

"Nikita. Buddy, how you feeling?"

"Like *blyadischa*. Tired whore. Nothing in the legs."

LB patted the engineer's shoulder. "That's funny. Good. Now listen to me. You might have a broken spine. You might not. Maybe what you have is some bad swelling in your back, a couple of bruised vertebrae pressing on your nerves. That could be where the paralysis is coming from. We're gonna hook you up to a high-dose anti-inflammatory, see if we can get the swelling down. That might help. You'll be at the hospital in Djibouti in two more days. Can you stay calm?"

"Could you?"

LB moved his eyes directly above the sailor's. "If I had someone as good as me looking me over? Yeah."

Frightened Nikita tried not to be amused. "Americans."

Together with Grisha and Jamie, LB pulled the damp sheet from beneath the engineer, then stuffed it into the garbage bag. Grisha found clean linens to lay over Nikita, then returned to his mop.

LB joined Jamie beside the cadet. Together they wrapped fresh bandages over his burns, tenderly lifting the boy's limbs. The cadet's face twisted with every movement, eyes sputtered open, lapsing in and out of awareness. His breathing came in fits between groans from his blistered mouth. Fingers clenched at nothing and released.

LB curled a finger for Grisha to stop mopping and come beside the bandaged cadet. Jamie stacked bags of Solu-Medrol and set out vials of morphine.

LB laid a hand across the cadet's unwrapped forearm. The boy's temperature felt dangerously high. At the end of the tube in his arm, the liter bag of saline hung empty.

Barely audible, Grisha said, "His name is Alek."

"You check on him every hour, too?"

Grisha recoiled at LB's tone. "Yes."

LB took down the drained IV bag. "Well," he said, not looking at Grisha, "Alek is dying. His kidneys are shutting down from lack of fluids. You see these bubbles?" He circled a quick finger around the cadet's mouth, cheek, and brow. "He's got these over half his body. He's using up all his water. We've got to stay ahead of what he's doing. If he runs dry, his kidneys shut down and he's dead."

LB guessed the cadet's weight at about 170 pounds.

"He gets a liter of saline every twenty minutes until he stabilizes. Then eight liters over the next ten hours. You got this kid on the same morphine schedule? Every hour?"

"Yes."

LB pulled from his ruck one of the vials of fentanyl, stronger than morphine. This needed to be injected every thirty to sixty minutes instead of the morphine's five to ten. LB drew a few cc's of fentanyl into a syringe and pushed the needle into the port of the IV line, slowly injecting the painkiller. In moments, the kid's unconscious clenching relaxed, his muttering quieted.

LB drew the four-inch knife from his leg sheath. He slit one of the saline bags and handed it to Grisha.

"Every hour, you check his bandages. Make sure they stay wet. Pour nothing but sterile solution on them."

Grisha grew red-faced, and glistens rimmed his eyes. Carefully, he sprinkled fluid over the fresh gauze wraps. He was ashamed to have done such a poor job as medical officer for his shipmates.

LB eased off. Grisha had done the best he could with his first-aid training. He'd called for help. That call had probably saved the kid's life. Maybe they'd get lucky and the steroids would take some pressure off the engineer's spine, put some feeling back in his legs.

Just like Grisha had said, these were sailors, not medical men, not soldiers. No reason to get mad at the guy. Grisha was already kicking himself pretty good. LB drew his first deep breath since entering the infirmary. His hope for these two patients, his patience for Grisha, sweetened on the odor of disinfectant.

"Hey. You did great. They're gonna be fine."

The stricken mate nodded without looking up from the chore. "I will stay."

"All right. You know what to do."

"Yes, Sergeant. Please inform the captain what you have told me."

LB and Jamie emptied their rucks of saline, painkiller, and Solu-Medrol. Heading for the door, LB passed the strapped-down engineer. He rapped an easy fist on the sailor's chest.

"I'll be back. Don't move."

Nikita raised a backhand as if to slap at LB. He muttered, "*Idi na khui.*"

LB replied, "*Idi nyuhai plavki.*"

In the hall, Jamie asked, "What was that?"

"He told me to go to the penis. I told him to go smell underwear. I've rescued a few Russians. Love how they curse."

"I mean, why'd you say you'd be back?"

"C'mon."

The two rode the elevator up to F deck. They climbed the stairwell into the cold bridge. Captain Drozdov and Iris sat where LB had left them, in the chairs facing the windshield and controls. Drozdov was in deep conversation with a graying, lanky man. Iris listened intently. Outside the starboard windows, keeping a steady distance, *Detroit 1* and *2* waited for word from LB.

The man between Drozdov and Iris spoke with his hands, drawing circles and little explosions in the air. Noticing the PJs near, he lowered his arms, snapped into a shallow, military bow. Before he opened his mouth, LB had recognized the training and discipline of an old-school Soviet.

"Gentlemen. I am Chief Engineer Razvan Utva. How much damage has my engine done to those two?"

LB let Jamie make the report. Both patients were stable for now. Nikita was on a strong anti-inflammatory; the cadet was getting a heavy regimen of fluids. The first mate would stay with them in the infirmary for now.

"Perhaps," the engineer asked, "they may both recover?"

Stone-faced, Jamie said, "We'll see."

Razvan chewed his lip, waiting for some other statement. The young PJ stayed tough and true, and said no more.

The chief dipped his head again, accepting the judgment. He seemed to be taking the accident as his personal fault. His engine had done this.

Drozdov asked him, "Do you know the cause?"

"No, Captain. But I will. I am not resting. And please. No more than fifty rpm. She cannot take more. Gentlemen. Miss Iris."

The chief excused himself. He pivoted away, his face set.

Drozdov addressed LB and Jamie. "So, you will be leaving now. That is too bad, but I thank you for coming. You have educated my first mate what must be done, yes?"

LB raised a finger. "Gimme a moment." To Jamie, he said, "Step over here."

He towed Jamie through the portal, outside onto the starboard wing. The day's heat slapped at him after thirty minutes of Russian winter inside Drozdov's superstructure. *Detroit 1* and *2* hovered a hundred yards away.

"I'm thinking we should stay."

Jamie waved this off. "No. We did our time. We go back."

"You saw how that guy Grisha was caring for those two. Piss everywhere. Not checking the fluids. He hasn't got a clue, and he isn't gonna get one. We leave, that burned kid might not make it. The engineer needs to be monitored. You know what I'm saying."

"I'm not arguing that point. We just don't have orders to stay."

LB dug the radio out of his Rhodesian vest. "Let me get some orders. Go inside. Flirt with the Russian lady. I'll be right in."

Jamie threw up his palms in peevish surrender. LB called *Detroit 1* on the aircraft common frequency. He asked for a sat patch to the PRCC, then waited while the chopper relayed his message.

In a few minutes, his radio peeped.

"Lima Bravo, Lima Bravo. Torres here."

"Major, LB."

"What do you want, Sergeant?"

"Major, request permission to stay behind on the ship. The condition of the injured exceeds what we expected. The quality of care on board is not sufficient. We can do the job. The ship's crew can't."

"Denied. Return to base."

"Major, with respect, why send us out here if you're not gonna let us do the job the way we see fit? One of the injured might not last to Djibouti."

"I can't leave the PJ team down two men. You're on a humanitarian mission. We could spare you for eight hours, not forty-eight. That was the deal."

"Major, I don't think the burned kid who can barely stay conscious for the pain cares about the deal. He's fighting infection and dehydration. The paralysis case needs monitoring to see if we can reduce his injuries. He's scared out of his mind. He don't care either."

"My hands are tied. Come back."

"Major, a compromise. Let me stay by myself. I can do this. I'll send Sergeant Dempsey back."

"No."

"I'm asking you. We'll only be down a single PJ for two days. I'll stand alert here twenty-four/seven. You need me, come pick me up. I'll be ready. But I can't leave these two guys in the state we found them. The mission was bullshit if I do, pardon my French. Ma'am, please. You got my word."

The sat link buzzed while Torres considered.

"All right. You know my conditions. No curiosity about the crew or the cargo. Press the mission. Take care of the injured. Get back here in two days. And if something comes up, I damn well will come get you."

"Thank you, Major."

"Out."

LB stowed the radio. He entered the bridge. From the copilot's leather chair, Iris smiled to see him.

LB focused on Drozdov. "All right. Call Bojan. Have him bring back Sergeant Dempsey's weapons."

Jamie tugged LB's arm. "Whoa, hang on."

LB excused himself again from Drozdov and Iris. He walked Jamie to the starboard windows with a view of the copters keeping pace.

Jamie spoke first. "You're staying alone? What the hell."

"Listen to me. Torres wouldn't go for both of us staying. It's okay. There's no good reason for two of us to hang out here. It's gonna be two days of this."

"This is a surprise. We work in teams."

"Yeah, when there's work to do. This is a one-man job. If a real mission spins up at Lemonnier, Torres will send a chopper for me. Go get your weapons. It's okay. Help Wally keep an eye on Robey. I got this."

"I know what you got. A freaking boner."

"Hey, careful. I'm your elder. By a lot."

"That's why it's a surprise."

"A mouth like that, I know why you carry so many guns. Go."

LB threw the chocks on the watertight door to return to the starboard wing. He waved to the two choppers, both sideslipping to keep watch on the *Valnea*. LB toggled his radio to the aircraft freq.

"*Detroit 1, Detroit 1*, this is Hallmark."

"Go, Hallmark."

"Pickup for one."

"Everything okay?"

As the chopper pilot spoke, *Detroit 1* broke formation to slide behind the freighter. *Detroit 2* held position.

"Juliet Delta's going back to base. Lima Bravo is staying. All good. Confirm."

"Five by five."

In minutes Jamie joined him on the wing, his ruck and M4 in place. The other weapons were stowed away. No one came out to watch him depart.

With *Detroit 1* tucking itself closer to the ship's great chimney, the wind on the platform mounted. LB shouted, "I'll see you in two days."

"Let me know if the guy moves his legs."

"Will do."

The copter eased overhead. LB and Jamie knelt under the intense prop wash. From the open door the MH-53's engineer tossed down a rope ladder, and LB moved to anchor it. Jamie took a running leap and launched himself athletically several rungs up the ladder. With LB holding the ladder taut, the young PJ scampered up to the thrumming copter.

LB ducked away while the ladder was reeled in. The giant MH-53 lifted its nose to fall back from the ship. The chopper peeled to its side, gaining quick distance.

"Have fun, Hallmark. *Detroit 1* out." *Detroit 2* moved up. Both copters beat away low, whipping up froth on the flat, vacant sea.

———

LB did not go back into the wheelhouse but walked the exterior stairway down the side of the superstructure. After six stories, at deck level, he looked overboard, down the ship's hull, another three stories to the water.

Making his way to the door for A level, he passed three crewmen in blue overalls and construction hats. The men worked to sand away chipped paint from the gray steel floor and rail. On the opposite side, across the thirty meters of the freighter's broad beam, another team did the same.

These men, all Filipinos, came to greet LB warily, pointing at the sky to indicate that he was the American soldier from the helicopter. Some spoke enough English to ask how the injured crewmen were: Would they be okay? The deckhands were short and wiry; their work required nimbleness and stamina. When the *Valnea* was loaded, they stacked her 2,200 containers, locked them in place, then cleaned and maintained the ship under way. LB wanted to ask what they thought of armed Serbian guards on a ship carrying no cargo, but he'd been told not to snoop.

Inside the superstructure, he poked his head into the infirmary. The second engineer and cadet both slept under blankets of morphine and fentanyl. Grisha kept vigil from a stool beside his friend Nikita. LB checked the progress of Nikita's anti-inflammatory drip, then the cadet's bandages. The boy's exposed skin had cooled slightly and its crimson cast had faded, marking progress in lowering his core temperature. His saline bag ran low. LB considered changing it but gave the task to Grisha. The man needed badly to be helpful. The first mate hung the fresh bag and flipped open the petcock. The cadet moaned, deep in narcotic, but did not wake.

LB held open the infirmary door for Grisha to follow into the hall, to talk without waking the injured.

"I'll be staying on board with you to Djibouti. That all right?"

"Yes. That is excellent news."

"So, how'd this happen?"

The first mate rubbed the bridge of his nose, tired. "This morning before breakfast, Nikita inspected engine with cadet. On catwalk along the pistons. No warning, cylinder seven blew. The boy was closest, burned by steam from gasket, then blown into Nikita, who hit rail with his back. And *derr'mo*, here we are."

"I heard the chief say he didn't know what caused it."

"I do not know this Razvan much. He is Romanian. Shipping company normally puts Russian officers together. He seems clever. I think he will find. He is always in engine room. Go ask him. But you know what I think?"

"No."

"*Eto piz`dets.*" This is fucked up.

In the elevator, LB punched the button for the engine control room. The doors opened into a room without windows, only rows of computer screens above a lengthy desk and a massive bank of fuse panels, switches, gauges, and LCD readouts. Chief Razvan sat chin in hand, staring into one screen, a sheaf of computer printouts in front of him. The room pulsed with a low, droning burr from the great engine behind the walls.

"Chief. May I come in?"

"Enter."

LB took the swivel chair beside him. The Romanian worked off three computer screens at once, each with different schematics. The one in front of LB depicted the eight pistons of the ship's engine, all rising and falling in rhythm except for number seven, which stood inert and bathed in red.

Razvan made notations on his papers. The information on all sides of LB was indecipherable. He sat in the belly of a modern cargo ship, a miracle of electronics, mechanics, girth, and power. The chief engineer on this freighter had to be a whiz kid in several fields.

LB waited until Razvan finished his scrutinizing and note taking.

The chief looked up. "The second engineer and cadet. Their condition."

"We've got the cadet on fluids; he's stable but in and out of consciousness. Nikita's on steroids. We'll have to wait and see where things go."

"The boy. He looked bad." The Romanian shook his gray head, tongue stuck behind his lips. "Thank you, Sergeant."

LB tapped the image of the dead cylinder seven on the screen in front of him.

"That why we're going twelve knots?"

Razvan blew out his cheeks. "*Pfff.* This captain. He would go twenty-five if I turn my back."

"Why?"

"These are pirate waters. You are soldier; you know this."

"Yeah."

"We are sitting like ducks going this speed. Drozdov is nervous. But we cannot go faster. Seven pistons cannot balance. Vibration will damage bearings, shaft, other pistons."

"What about the guards?"

"Ah, yes. You may sleep well being guarded by Serbs. I do not."

LB didn't inquire; the antagonisms of Central Europe were ancient and as inscrutable to an outsider as the machines around him.

"Can you tell me what happened?"

"What do you know about engines?"

"Compared to you, or a kid from Sacramento?"

"Me."

"Nothing."

"Good. I don't like opinions."

"I'm the same. My motto is, when in doubt, I go with me."

Razvan cracked his first grin. "Okay. This accident. It was an untimed injection."

"I've done that before."

"You can stop now, Sergeant."

LB raised a hand to yield. Chief continued.

"The engine runs on heavy fuel oil. In normal operation, piston comes up, goes down. Every second revolution, at specific point, fuel is injected into top of cylinder. Pressure increases as piston rises, until fuel ignites. At this exact moment, when piston is pushed back down by explosion, exhaust portal at top of cylinder opens to release waste gases. But…"

Chief laid a long finger to the screen in front of LB, where an animation showed seven of the eight pistons still pumping. He selected one tall cylinder.

"If fuel comes into cylinder at wrong time…" Chief knocked the computerized image. "Now! When the piston is in wrong place, explosion happens too soon. Exhaust portal is not open. Too much pressure builds up in cylinder, and boom."

LB had worked on enough engines to know what *boom* meant. "The head gasket blows."

"Yes. Cylinder cracks. Water flows into cylinder."

"Steam."

"Then accident. Two men standing in front of discharge from broken gasket."

"The call goes out, and here I am."

"With our happy crew."

"What time did it happen?"

Chief flipped to find the proper computer sheet. "Oh-four-forty-eight hours, thirty-five-point-oh-nine seconds."

"Exact."

"Right now, time is all I know. Cause is not so easy. I am compiling data. Voltage records, alarms, pressure, injector rates." Razvan flopped a hand on the stack of papers. *"Duten pula calului."*

"What's that mean?"

"Go to horse dick."

"Man. I love how you guys cuss."

"An odd thing to love."

"Can you show me where it happened?"

Chief cocked an eyebrow, quickly suspicious. LB wondered if growing up under secret police had made the crew on this boat itchy. Or if this unexplained voyage from Vladivostok to Beirut was doing it.

"You are investigator now?"

"No. I'm stuck on this ship for two days. What else is there to do?"

Chief hunched. "Okay."

He handed LB ear protection headgear. Sliding on his own muffs, he opened a thick door. A fleet, warm gush of air greeted them on a suspended platform. They looked down over a massive room, a collection of steel blocks, rods, trusses, pipes, every hard bit of it adding its bawl and whine to stir the roar rattling

LB's chest, rapping on the pads blocking his ears. He lifted one earpiece for a moment to hear the real, deafening din.

Razvan led him down the stairwell. The floor under this hive of machines did not tremble as LB thought it might. It felt concrete. Even with a ruined piston, Chief's engine ran balanced and tuned, just as he said.

Without turning to see if LB followed, Chief strode purposefully through a warren of equipment and apparatuses, all interconnected by cables, ducts, and miles of electric wire. The primary color was a mute yellow, with interruptions of battleship gray. The bolts and nuts holding everything together were the size of LB's fists. He recognized nothing; not a piece resembled anything in a regular car or boat motor. The scale of the freighter's engine beggared any machine LB had seen, even on naval ships. The *Valnea*'s engine was dazzling, even chugging at half speed.

Razvan ducked into the maze, beneath a web of catwalks and beams, conducting the tour at a long-legged gait without pause or explanations. Along the way, LB stayed lost. He could not find his way out if Razvan took a powder on him down here. He made out only one recognizable thing: a spinning black shaft the size of a tree trunk, horizontal, disappearing into the hull. Attached to the other end must have been the gargantuan propeller to push this ship.

Rounding a final corner, Chief mounted a platform running beside the heart of the engine, the row of oversize pistons. He strode down the line of chrome and copper cylinder housings, setting a hand to some to feel for the enemy in this room, vibration. At the seventh, he finally faced LB. Beneath the raging sounds of the engine room, he mouthed, "Each one weighs four tons." Then, unexpectedly, he playacted the moment of injury for the second engineer Nikita, slamming himself into the railing in slow motion.

The quiet piston casing was not blackened or warped by the incident, though its housing, gears, cables, dials sat motionless.

Razvan laid hands on the casing to draw forth the sense of its failure. Chief showed no disdain or anger for piston seven; nothing in his engine room lost value just because it was out of order. LB, who saved broken men, admired this.

Chapter 9

——•——

Somali dhow
Gulf of Aden

In late afternoon, a helicopter flew their way to investigate the dhow.

Yusuf shouted for his crew to look like fishermen. The men quickly dropped lines without lures, climbed into the skiffs to cast and trail nets; one-eared Deg Deg steered a wide circle as if trawling. By the time the copter arrived, bearing the markings of the Chinese navy, Yusuf and his pirates looked engaged and innocent. They waved madly and stupidly until the hovering copter and its guns veered away.

Within the hour, a convoy of freighters and low-riding tankers appeared over the horizon. Six ships in a line, all making fifteen knots, filed past Yusuf's dhow two miles away. Like a herding dog, the brute Chinese warship kept a steady distance from the ships. Deg Deg slowed the dhow; they would drift here on the rim of the transit corridor and watch the parade of commercial freighters and their bristling escort.

Six hours remained to sundown. Bobbing on gentle swells, ready to take up make-believe fishing at a moment's notice, Yusuf and the crew marked the passing of every vessel plying the path to and from Suez. Gigantic container ships more than three hundred meters long scudded past, loaded with mountains of cargo. From miles away, Yusuf and Suleiman could read the company names painted in huge letters across their hulls: Maersk from Denmark, Hapag-Lloyd of Germany, Switzerland's MSC, COSCO of China, Israel's ZIM. These ships employed the latest designs—bulbous bows, immense length, and tremendous engines. They sailed without the protection and bother of convoys, lone fortresses made impregnable by their speed and high freeboard.

Automobile haulers cruised by, leviathans from Korea and Japan headed to European or Saudi markets. Ponderous, high-walled, and ungainly as they looked, with all their cargo shielded belowdecks, they were nevertheless among the fastest freighters on the water.

Humbler ships, flagged out of Liberia, Panama, the Marshall Islands, Portugal, were more common on the gulf—brown-hulled chemical and oil tankers, rust-bucket cargo ships, commercial fishing vessels with arms spread wide, trawlers, net seiners, longliners swarmed by gulls when catching. Indian or Pakistani dhows, trawlers manned by Yemeni smugglers. Even a sailboat in the far distance, likely some insane and intrepid white people trying to sneak through these dangerous waters.

Yusuf and Suleiman sat alone on the rolling bow, sipping cool tea, bearing down through binoculars on every freighter as soon as it grew visible in the distance. Yusuf lifted his black-and-white-checked *keffiyeh* to hood his head from the sun. Over five hours, they let three dozen westbound ships slip by; the same number headed east. Whenever a likely vessel passed too far away to be identified, Deg Deg steered them closer, until Yusuf waved him off; not the right ship.

The cousins watched until two more hours of sunlight remained on the gulf. If their target did not appear in the next sixty minutes, the plan was to turn west and motor through the night at top speed toward Bab-el-Mandeb, that mile-and-a-half-wide passage connecting the Gulf of Aden and the Red Sea, a 350-mile sprint. That way they could stay ahead of the coming traffic, wait for their prey at the narrow strait through which every ship going to or from Suez had to pass.

Sheikh Robow's description of the freighter made Suleiman and Yusuf expect she would not be part of a guarded convoy; those clusters were for older, slower boats. She'd be off on her own, running twenty-plus knots. Her captain wouldn't feel the need for naval protection or a gaggle of other ships around her, not with that kind of speed and guns aboard.

With an hour left, eyes worn down by binoculars and the water's late-day glare, Yusuf stood from his wooden crate. His knees ached. In the west, the sun lowered onto a cushion of fiery clouds. Light polished the water as the day eased away and the low-lying mists melted. The bending horizon grew razor sharp against the sky.

From belowdecks, the smell of fried meat and *maraq* soup wafted to the bow. The rest of the crew had eaten earlier. Bowls of food sat untouched beside both cousins. Yusuf stuffed a cold slice of seasoned goat into his mouth. Chewing, he picked at a bit of gourd dipped in yoghurt.

Suleiman did not lower his binoculars from the east. Yusuf spoke to the black top of his head.

"Eat. I'm going to tell Deg Deg we're moving."

Suleiman had elbows on his knees, steadying the glasses. "Wait."

Yusuf licked his fingers. "Why? What do you see?"

"I can't be certain. Dolphins. We have luck coming. Good or bad, I can't tell. But luck."

"We have night coming. We need to go."

"Sit."

Yusuf wanted to raise his own binoculars, but he left this to Suleiman, who seemed to be trying to conjure the freighter.

Long ago Yusuf had learned to trust Suleiman's instincts. His older cousin studied the ways of spirits and animals and their signs. Dolphins were indeed an omen of change approaching, like clouds. There was magic on the earth, a strangeness outside man's world. Suleiman could put his finger on it. But this was not magic; this was the sea, where nature ruled alone. The two of them were searching for one ship out of a passing hundred on a wide water, on the word of an Islamist who'd threatened them, a man not of their clan. Their best chance now was to hurry to Bab-el-Mandeb, arrive at noon tomorrow, and wait there. Even then they couldn't be sure their target wouldn't pass them in the night, or that it hadn't already come through here and they'd simply missed it.

Yusuf lowered his weight again to the crate. He set the cold dinner plate across his lap. He thought of Hoodo across his lap instead, warmer than this goat and curd, surer than this goose chase for al-Shabaab.

Without pulling his eyes from the glasses, Suleiman asked, "Do you remember what you said before we took our first ship? Seven years ago?"

Yusuf swallowed tea. He gazed toward the stern, where the crew smoked along the rails or watched the setting sun. Some toyed with the cat. Inside the wheelhouse, Deg Deg needed a decision. Instead, Suleiman wanted a memory.

Yusuf tamped down his impatience. He spoke to the side of Suleiman's narrow face.

"Of course."

"Tell me now."

"I said that you and I would die on the same day."

Suleiman nodded behind the glasses. Twenty minutes earlier, a convoy had passed the dhow, plowing to Bab-el-Mandeb. The eight vessels, European and Asian, guarded by a German war cruiser, had not yet sailed out of sight. Yusuf eyed the fading ships and their trail of smudges in the air.

Suleiman lowered the binoculars. "Are you sure you want to do this?"

"I said that out of loyalty. It was not a prediction."

"Do you want to do this?"

"Yes."

Suleiman handed Yusuf the binoculars. He aimed a hand due east, at a white sliver alone on the blue rim of the world.

"I believe it may be this day, cousin."

Yusuf bore down through the lenses. Quickly he found the ship. Even seven or eight miles out, in the slanting light of the failing sun, he read the tall, pale letters writ across the blue hull: CMA CGM.

A French ship, moving west on her own.

Not a single container stood on deck below her three cranes. She skipped high over the water, the brown skirt of her bottom paint visible. She sailed where, when, and how Sheik Robow had said she would.

Her name: *Valnea*.

Chapter 10

———

The engineer Nikita wiggled a big toe.

He could not shift his strapped-down head to see. He groped for LB on the stool beside him.

"*Vot edo da*! Did you see? Look! Look, Sergeant! Is moving?"

LB confirmed the toe did flinch.

"I am not cripple! *Gospodi*! Sergeant, I am not cripple!"

Nikita spread both arms to celebrate in a hug. LB hung back; the man would not stop shouting. On the next bed, the cadet groaned, waking to find pain. To quiet the engineer, LB bent over him for a quick embrace but could not wrap his arms around the board or the cot. Nikita clamped him tight, pounding the back of LB's rib cage. He sobbed, "*Spasibo, bolshoe spasibo.*"

LB wriggled loose. "Okay, okay. That's great." He patted Nikita on the chest. "Let's keep it down; the kid needs to sleep."

"*Da, da*," the engineer panted, sniffing back tears. "But this is good, yes?"

"It's a good sign. The anti-inflams are working. You still might have a break in your spine, but it doesn't look like paralysis. We'll know more in Djibouti. And you're staying on that board till we get there."

"Of course, of course." Nikita kept his voice from climbing again. "Go. Find Grisha. I will wiggle for him."

LB checked the cadet's bandages for moistness. He headed for the door. Behind him Nikita whispered, "Thank you, *svóloch.*"

"You're welcome, *hui.*"

The first mate Grisha was not in the wheelhouse, the only place LB knew to look for him. He found Drozdov in his captain's chair. To the rear, the third officer sat at the map table, filling in the logbook.

LB told Drozdov of Nikita's progress and the request to see Grisha. The Russian captain received the news with a long sigh of relief. Picking up the intercom phone, he found the first mate in his quarters.

"Nikita has moved a toe."

Drozdov set down the receiver. LB imagined chubby Grisha bolting for the stairs.

LB climbed into the empty leather chair beside Drozdov, facing the broad tempered-glass windshield. Far ahead, a convoy steamed toward Suez. The *Valnea* sailed into an afternoon that had aged while LB kept vigil in the infirmary. The dropping sun shone into the ship's westbound face.

On both large, round radar screens in the command dash, a red line swept out of the center blip that was the *Valnea.* The distant klatch of freighters showed as dark arrowheads, their speeds and headings digitized beneath each mark. To the north, a warship shadowed them. Above and below the convoy, two east–west electronic lines displayed the bounds of the IRTC, five nautical miles wide. Yemen lay a hundred miles to the north, Somalia an equal distance south. The *Valnea* plowed down the middle of the lane. She sailed alone.

"We cannot keep up," Drozdov said. "The ships in the convoy are making sixteen knots. I have reported damage to UKMTO Dubai. That is all I can do."

"When exactly do we get to Djibouti?"

The captain rolled a track ball. The cursor on one radar screen zoomed ahead, scrolling the distance from the center blip.

"Three hundred eighty miles. At this *chërtov* speed, dawn day after tomorrow. Perhaps."

"Perhaps what?"

Drozdov laughed a grave chuckle that wrinkled his pocked nose. He gazed forward to the lowering sun.

"What do you think of my ship, Sergeant?"

LB patted the leather arms of his chair. "She's a beauty."

"*Fah.* She is *govnó*. Shit." Drozdov turned dark eyes at LB. "Twenty years ago I am master on ships that are at sea even to this day. I see them, I talk on radio to them. Those were made of thick steel, good material. I worked on ships half this size with crew of thirty. Today I have just twenty men. Is all about money now. Companies care nothing for men, for metal, only money. This *Valnea*, she will have life of maybe ten years. Then she will be scrap. The steel will melt, then go into another ship, then another. You watch, look around. Every day, crew is grinding, painting to stay ahead of rust. Razvan is fixing breaks in something all the time. Two boys are hurt bad because engine explodes. Now we are limping to hospital. *Da*, I am captain of shit. I have become man to do this only for money, like owners, like insurance company. I am no better."

LB hadn't sat with Drozdov for any of this; he'd just meant to report on Nikita. The captain didn't break his gaze from LB, inviting comment.

"You're not happy, so quit."

Drozdov's temples folded into creases etched by decades of ocean winds and shadeless light. Even grinning, his face dimmed.

"No. I drink too much on land."

LB let the statement linger; it wasn't the sort of remark to leave on.

"So tell me about Iris Cherlina."

Drozdov's narrow chest shook to a private, dour chuckle. LB's question seemed to have struck another nerve in the captain.

"I know nothing about Iris Cherlina."

"How can that be? I mean, she's your passenger. She was sitting right here when I came on board. You don't talk to her?"

Drozdov tapped a finger on the arm of his chair, the way Grisha had done against his lips. Iris Cherlina made these sailors twitchy.

"You have curiosity, Sergeant?"

"No more than any regular guy would for a good-looking woman."

"I will tell you what I know, since you are regular guy. Iris Cherlina eats alone at all meals. In the day, she sometimes sits on the bridge to watch the seas go by. The rest of the time, she stays alone. At nightfall, she disappears into her cabin. Or she walks forward into the dark. That is what I know. This is cargo ship, not cruise liner. I do not talk to her. My crew do not talk to her. We do what I suggest you should do. Look."

This wasn't very friendly on anybody's part, but LB kept that to himself.

LB had two days on this ship. He wasn't going to take Drozdov's advice and just look. He kept that to himself, too. And he'd been told by Torres to show no curiosity about the *Valnea*'s crew and cargo. Iris Cherlina wasn't a sailor, and she wasn't in a container.

Drozdov pivoted his attention to his instruments and radar, releasing LB from the leather seat and the conversation. He slid from the chair with no more notice from the captain.

LB left the air conditioning of the bridge to step out on the starboard wing. In the dusk, Iris stood with a cigarette between her fingers. She leaned against the rail when she saw him, the gesture implying that she would stay in place for his company. The woman was the counterpoint to Drozdov, slim and unruffled, not worn by sea and weather, pummeled by long labor, or pitted by liquor. The wind and the tinted light suited her. The breeze carried a puff of tobacco off her wide, smiling lips. She flipped the cigarette overboard. She did not look unapproachable, or off-limits.

Iris Cherlina spoke first. "I understand you are staying on the *Valnea* until we reach Djibouti."

"Yes, ma'am."

Iris Cherlina appraised this development, which seemed suddenly to please her. She put forth a manicured hand—red nails against linen skin, a broad palm. She had the handshake of a musician, an artist, something where the firmness of her touch mattered.

"Let's meet properly. I am Iris Cherlina."

LB felt the urge for a hat he could remove, or a better suit of clothes than his uniform and communications vest to bow in.

"First Sergeant Gus DiNardo." He held her hand for an extra shake, as if he were introducing himself twice. "Everyone calls me LB."

"LB. What does that stand for?"

"It's just a call sign."

"For?"

"All right. Little Bastard."

"Honestly?"

"Who would lie about that?"

"Fair enough. How on earth did you come by it?"

"I spend my summers as an instructor at the PJ School. It's called the Pipeline. Some call it Superman School. It's pretty tough."

"What is a PJ?"

"Pararescue jumper."

"You jump to the rescue, Sergeant?"

"That's a good way to put it."

"Exactly how tough is your Superman School?"

"One in ten make it through. It's the hardest training regimen in the American military."

"Impressive. Is this the only place where you are a little bastard?"

"Yes, ma'am. Absolutely."

"Forgive me. I think that is a half truth."

"It might be. I guess it depends on which half you need at the moment."

"I like that."

Iris Cherlina blinked again, long and languorous, as if savoring. LB did not consider himself a man of charm, but he was making this woman stay in place to talk, work her eyes. Was this what Drozdov feared about her, that she might agitate some of his crew, start some fights?

LB hooked a thumb over his shoulder. "The captain. That's a piece of work."

"Yes, poor man."

"How's it going, being the only woman on a ship?"

"*Mne pó figu.* I don't care."

"So, what does Cherlina mean in Russian? 'Dear,' like in French?"

"Yes. But also, it means expensive."

"Nice. Wow."

"And you? DiNardo?"

"It's Italian. Means I'm related to Nero. He burned Rome and killed Christians. So you definitely win the name thing."

"I do."

LB checked his watch. Every hour he had to wet the cadet's bandages, change out his saline bag, keep him dopey on fentanyl. He had forty more minutes to spend with Iris Cherlina.

Gazing at her, LB thought she was as much a collection of question marks as this entire voyage. He didn't know what to ask first, what might lead to more conversation, what might make her walk away alone. Silently, he toted up what he knew about

Iris and the *Valnea*. Iris was a Russian passenger on a freighter carrying a highly secret cargo—so secret his own government had told him to put on blinders—guarded by gun-toting Serbs. She had the run of the ship and stayed pretty much to herself, either because she wanted it that way or because Drozdov had gotten the same orders as LB—no curiosity. Early this morning an accident had injured two crewmen, making the *Valnea* cut her speed in half. The captain was an alcoholic who disliked his ship, who the first mate claimed had been made crazy by pirates. The Romanian chief engineer had no idea why his engine had failed. And this morning LB had been choppered in, an unexpected witness to whatever intrigues were on board.

LB figured, too, that a lot of what Iris Cherlina would say, if she talked to him, would be lies.

"Hey, I haven't seen much of the boat. I figure you've been here for two and a half weeks."

"Yes."

"Give me a tour?"

"You do not strike me as a tourist. But whatever you wish."

"So, you got on board in Vladivostok."

"How did you know?"

"You just agreed you'd been here for two and a half weeks."

"Of course."

"Lead the way."

Iris opted for the stairs down the side of the superstructure. LB followed. Descending, he asked her back, "What do you do in Russia?"

"I'm a scientist."

"What kind?"

"Electrophysics. My specialty is heat resistance."

"You don't look like an electrophysicist."

"No?" She pouted. "And I try so hard."

"It's awful cold in Russia for someone interested in heat."

"I worked at a research institute."

"Which one?"

"I'm afraid that's off limits, Sergeant."

"LB."

"LB, then."

The two wended down more staircases. The late daylight purpled. The wide water lost its blue shades, inking toward gray.

"You said 'worked.'"

"I have retired from that institute. I've left Russia. For warmer climes, as it were."

"You look young to retire."

"Thank you. I have taken employment at a lab in Lebanon."

"Is there a lot of money in electrophysics these days?"

"Untold."

"Government?"

Iris Cherlina waggled a finger at another question she would not answer. LB switched gears.

"You like falafel, I hope."

"Better than cold beet soup."

He and Iris rounded another metal corner of the six staircases. He allowed a gap in their talk, letting their shoes on the steel steps be the sound of their company. They descended two more floors.

"So why'd the lab in Russia shut down? If there's that much money in heat resistance in Beirut, why not in Russia?"

"We'd gone as far as we could go there. My government has lost interest, and we lost funds. I'm taking the research in a new direction."

"So you booked a three-week passage on a commercial freighter from Vladivostok."

Iris Cherlina stopped on a landing between stairwells. Without dropping her smile, she turned.

"Yes."

She held her ground, waiting for him to choose whether she could stay in his company or would have to leave him if he pressed.

He clapped. "Looks like a great idea. No crowds. See the world. How's the food?"

Iris beamed, a toothy beauty. She strode to LB, slipped her arm inside his so they could walk linked down the last stairs.

"The Filipino cook has no touch. I do not eat the heads of fish."

"I'll see if I can't whip you up something special for dinner. Some pasta."

"Are you a good cook?"

"I'm better than fish heads."

She laughed and patted his forearm. This was his reward for letting her lie. It seemed fair pay. She took his arm down the steps.

At deck level, Iris released him. "Let's walk to the bow. It's my favorite place."

She led him along the starboard rail. They moved single file through the skinny passage, more tunnel than walkway. Here on deck, the ship seemed livelier than from the cool vantage of the bridge or the high perch of the wings. The water sloughing off the great hull whispered a constant shush. Under LB's boots, the floor vibrated. The huge engine, even hobbled, murmured in the steel. Thick walls suggested the mammoth weight this ship could carry. All the angles were sharp, the passage studded with ladders, beams, low-hanging lanterns. The *Valnea* had been designed and built every inch for cargo, not comfort. According to Drozdov, she was also disposable.

LB followed Iris Cherlina past a large red lifeboat hung on davits, and smaller life rafts packed into plastic barrels along the rail. The stroll to the bow and back would cover a quarter of a mile.

As they stepped onto the open bow, the night's first stars appeared behind Iris's head. The crimson sun had been doused only minutes before. One of Bojan's Serbs strode the opposite rail, black-clad. Spotting them, he reversed course and approached, keeping his weapon slung but laying an obvious hand on it.

"Dr. Cherlina. He is not allowed here."

Iris held up a palm to halt any further comment. Despite her imperious raised hand, the guard parted his lips to say more. She stopped him again.

"He is with me."

She tucked her arm inside LB's to turn away from the Serb. LB didn't like having his back to a gun, any gun, but Iris towed him away, and the guard returned to his patrol.

Iris Cherlina was no passenger on this ship—that much was plain. She had authority the guard couldn't top, and she wasn't shy about showing that to LB.

The bow offered more room to move than elsewhere on the ship, though it was cluttered with large hawsers, a pair of oversize windlasses for raising and dropping the twin anchors, rusty chains with links big around as LB. In the center, a high mast rose, topped by an unlit beacon. He looked back the length of the ship to the pilothouse, over the vast and vacant container deck that resembled a no-man's-land for giants, with its rows of fences and steel cables.

Straight off the bow, at the foot of the slumping sun in a rippling red pool, the silhouette of a small ship lay miles ahead.

Iris leaned over the rail. LB copied her. Both looked far down to the bulbous bow cutting high out of the water. Several dolphins swooped on either side, cruising in the breaking crest. Iris waved at them.

Over the slapping wash, his shoulders touching hers, LB asked, "Why'd you say 'poor man' about the captain?"

Iris did not straighten. The dolphins kept her bent over the rail. LB pulled himself erect, fixing on the dim outline of the small ship, bobbing without running lights in the *Valnea*'s path.

Iris came up, flushed. She considered him a long moment.

"You do pay attention, don't you?"

"I'm in a life-and-death profession. It's what I do."

LB liked her long blinks, as she retreated behind her lids to make a plan. She looked sexy when she closed her eyes, smart when she opened them.

"All right," Iris Cherlina said. "This comes from Grisha, but it is also painfully obvious. The captain is a troubled man."

"Check."

"A few years back, he was hijacked in these waters. His ship was anchored off the coast for eight months while the insurance company negotiated with the Somalis. The crew was treated well enough, but the captain didn't take well to captivity. He fought with the pirates, and they beat him. After the ransom, Drozdov went home to Russia. He became a drunkard. He was dismissed by the company. His wife left him. This year he became sober, and they took him back."

"For this voyage."

Again Iris blinked like an owl.

"Yes. How did you know?"

Because it made sense. Find a captain so down on his luck that he'd accept a cargo he knew nothing about. No curiosity.

"Just a guess."

He glanced at his watch. Time for him to head back to the infirmary.

"Tell me something."

"That's what I've been doing, Sergeant."

"Yeah. Why're you okay with talking to me?"

Iris Cherlina withdrew, playacting as if hurt. "Do I seem standoffish?"

"No. But Drozdov says you don't talk to anyone, and they don't talk to you. You eat by yourself, wander around by yourself. How come?"

"I don't know. I'm an outsider; they are busy all the time. We just fell into mutual silence. But after two and a half weeks of scant attention, to be honest, I am very glad to have a man show some interest in me."

"Sounds like you talk to Grisha."

"Some. But he...well, he is not you."

He dipped his head to the flattery, even though her explanation didn't square with what Drozdov said, that she kept mostly to herself.

The shadow ship in the *Valnea*'s path loitered, one mile bigger in the twilight.

"Let's go back. I've got to check on the infirmary. Then dinner. I'll have a chat with the cook."

He led the way into the narrow passage. Again LB swung his shoulders to avoid bumping into the hard pillars supporting the overhang. Far below the rail, in the faint light, phosphorus twinkled in the foaming wake.

They passed another strolling Serbian. The guard backed out of the way, wordless. LB wondered how good Bojan's guys would be in a scrap. In his long experience, the ones with the attitude most often came up short. Doc and Quincy were plain Nevada cowboys, Jamie was shy, Wally was clean-cut, and LB had seen every one of them dive into whatever hot or freezing hell the job threw at them. LB would take Mouse, even young Robey, every PJ or CRO he'd ever known, over these arrogant Serb security guards any day.

Reaching the superstructure, Iris stayed with LB in the infirmary, bathing the cadet's bandages while LB checked the pace of the saline IV and the fentanyl drip. The boy's urine flow lagged behind the input of saline, meaning that his body was still holding fluids in its tissues and blisters. Iris was unfazed at the boy's bubbled, boiled skin, unmoved by his half-awake moan, raised no eyebrows at the catheters. She had a scientist's easy detachment. Nikita had added another toe to his wiggling.

Grisha agreed to stay in the infirmary through dinner if he could share in whatever meal LB would prepare for Iris. The first mate got a peck on the cheek from the departing Iris.

Down the hall, LB stabbed the elevator button. When the door slid open, Chief Engineer Razvan stood inside, clutching a brace of folders and loose printout sheets. LB let Iris step in first. The engineer nodded curtly to them both.

Iris lit the button for F deck, explaining she needed a rest before dinner. When the elevator stopped, LB spoke as she exited into the hall.

"See you at dinner."

"I expect genius," Iris called around the closing door, "from a relative of Nero's."

The door slid shut on Iris turning away. LB would check in with Drozdov on the bridge, have the captain assign him quarters, then head back down to the galley to introduce himself to the Filipino chef.

The elevator continued its ascent. Chief Razvan appeared agitated, finger-tapping the thick sheaf of sheets in his arms. LB made quick conversation, telling him that Nikita might recover; the cadet showed improvement but wasn't out of the woods. The Romanian nodded, staring at his shoes. He seemed to want to burst out of the elevator.

Rising to the top floor, before the door opened, LB quizzed the engineer. "What've you got? Your eyes are bugging out of your head."

Chief raised a finger. "You." He stuck the digit into LB's chest. "You are a reliable person."

"Yeah?"

Before LB could question him further, the elevator stopped. Razvan charged out, up the steps to the pilothouse, leaving LB to walk in his wake.

"Captain," the chief called the instant he entered the cool, broad pilothouse, "a word."

From his chair, Drozdov presided over the array of controls and screens. Outside the ship's wide windows, the steaming white light glowed in the dusk above the faraway bow.

Without turning from his instruments, Drozdov said, "In a minute."

Razvan hurried to stand beside the captain's chair, hefting his bale of pages.

"I am sorry, Captain, but now."

Drozdov pivoted a taut face. Something else had been bothering him before Chief exploded into the bridge.

"Yes."

Razvan slapped his papers. "The accident was no accident. It was deliberate." Chief glanced around the wheelhouse, though only the three of them were there. "Somebody on this ship. Sabotage."

LB was jolted. The secrets on the *Valnea* were starting to become oppressive. He kept silent, but suddenly, badly, he wanted off the ship. Stuck here for another thirty hours. He thought of calling Torres on the satellite radio in his vest, telling her to come get him.

Drozdov stayed icy. "How do you know this?"

"I have searched every record of the engine. I found this." The Romanian plopped his stack of papers on the console.

Before he could dig in, Drozdov said, "Just tell me."

"Yes, all right. At oh-four-thirteen this morning, voltage for cylinder seven dropped off one instant before the accident. The injection timing signal to the cylinder was interrupted. This caused fuel to come in the wrong time to piston stroke. That blew the gasket. Then, poof, like magic, the voltage returned to the cylinder."

"Tell me why you think this is sabotage. And be quick, Chief." Drozdov pointed at one of his radar screens. "I have another problem."

Chief leaped to his explanation. "In computer records, when there is short in the power, I will see two alarms. The first is pre-alarm. It tells me where to look. It is like skid marks in front of car wreck. The second alarm is actual power interruption. In this case, Captain, I only have alarm, not the pre-alarm. No skid mark. This says the power failure did not come from failure of engine but from outside. This was human hand."

"How was it done?"

"Simple. Anyone with knowledge can go to fuse box for cylinder seven. Pull the correct fuse. Two seconds. Put it back."

"You are sure?"

Chief gathered his computer sheets off the console. "Of course. I am sure also that only cadet, Nikita, this American, and I did not do it. The rest of you, I watch now."

Drozdov turned his weathered face to LB. He asked, "Who would do this?" as if an outsider to the ship might have the best idea.

You, for one, Captain, LB thought.

"Chief," LB asked, "can you see the pistons from the fuse box?"

"No. Whoever did this could not see Nikita and cadet. Perhaps that was mistake. But I do not forgive."

Drozdov's chin dropped to his chest. After a quick moment, he raised his gaze to his controls and the radar sweep.

The small ship off the bow lurked only a mile away, and dead ahead. The blip faded in and out, its radar signature on the water small and sketchy.

LB asked, "What's that?"

"That, Sergeant, is my other problem. Right now, the greater of the two."

"Is it pirates?"

Drozdov answered by bringing a walkie-talkie from his lap to his lips. He thumbed the talk button. "Mr. Bojan, this is bridge. Bojan, bridge. Respond."

Before the Serb guard could answer, the captain unclipped another microphone from the console. In clear tones, he said, "All hands, all hands. This is the captain. Officers to the bridge. Crew prepare to take secure position. This is not a drill."

Razvan pivoted with his papers for the stairs. Drozdov said at his departing back, "Chief, please tend to the engine."

LB was left alone with Drozdov. The captain's face was set hard. LB looked for a crack in the man's composure, some flashback to captivity, thirst for a bottle, a wince, a lick of the lips.

Drozdov locked eyes on the radar screen, measuring distance and time, calculating the next move, staying captain.

LB asked again, "Pirates?"

In a low growl, Drozdov said, "I do not know. I have never seen this from pirates. One vessel at dusk, sitting in the path of a freighter. This is new. The Somalis come at sunup. In two or three skiffs. They race in from both sides, shoot their rockets, threaten on the radio until we stop. This ship ahead"—Drozdov pointed again—"this one is quiet. We will find out shortly."

He put his chin into an open hand, pulled down on his jowls. Drozdov was not panicked. The gesture spoke instead of calculation.

"And someone I trust has disabled my ship so these *mudaki* may hijack us more easily." The captain turned his head to fake a disgusted spit. "Disloyal *zhopoliz.*"

Who would want to be hijacked? It made no sense.

One of the officers rushed from the stairwell into the pilothouse. Instantly Drozdov ordered, "Go to manual. Starboard five."

The mate positioned himself between the leather chairs, standing at the console. He punched a button and set hands on the tiny steering wheel. He came starboard five degrees. Moments after, the ship ahead moved to stay in the *Valnea*'s course.

Drozdov leaned forward to tap the radar screen. He said to LB, "I have seen mornings after storms where containers have been opened and emptied. Leather jackets, Dom Pérignon, motorcycle parts. In storms, Sergeant. Pirates are desperate men. They cannot be predicted."

Grisha chugged in, huffing. Drozdov instructed him, "Hail the vessel in our path."

LB had no role on the bridge. If pirates were coming, he belonged where he could do some good.

"I'm going."

"Where?"

"To get my gun back from Bojan."

"He will not give it to you. He has orders."

"Then give him different orders."

"Bojan does not work for me on this ship of wonders."

LB stepped back from the console. He flung both arms over his head, swung a boot at his own frustration, infuriated and diminished. "Shit," he barked through clenched teeth. "Son of a bitch."

"Yes!" Drozdov sang. "Yes, Sergeant. That's the spirit!"

Chapter 11

———

Pirate skiffs
Gulf of Aden

Yusuf raised a fist.

In the center, Suleiman did the same. To his right, young Guleed hoisted his balled hand.

The three cousins stood in the bows of three black skiffs lashed together. They signaled to one another: Courage.

The boats idled their engines. Along with Yusuf and Guleed in the left and right skiffs, one helmsman and one gunner waited in each. Seventeen more pirates crowded behind Suleiman, standing in the bow of the middle skiff. All were armed with Kalashnikov rifles. A dozen rocket-propelled grenade launchers were secured to the floorboards of each of the three skiffs, along with rope ladders and new aluminum grappling hooks tied to long tethers. At Yusuf's feet lay two hundred meters of coiled hemp rope. The line ran past Suleiman in the middle to an equal coil at Guleed's bare feet.

Every eye was turned to the enormous bow of the freighter bearing down on them. Yusuf could not understand why the *Valnea* moved so slowly. A vessel of this class was capable of twenty-five knots, even more running empty. The ship wasn't in a convoy; she ran alone. Why? Was she wounded? Was this a trap? Yusuf had brooded over these questions, moving to stay in the freighter's path, skulking to spring his own trap. He had no more time to ponder; the white steaming light on her forward mast charged closer, high in the air like an approaching comet.

Over the skiff's VHF radio, the freighter repeated its hail on Channel 16. The voice was very matter-of-fact. "Unidentified vessel, unidentified vessel, *CMA CGN Valnea*. Please respond."

Yusuf said, "Cut that off."

Water sprayed off the huge bulbous bow that would ram them in another thirty seconds. With the immense ship almost on top of them, her twelve knots didn't seem so sluggish to Yusuf. The noise of the bow cutting through the water and the rumble of the propeller beneath the surface vibrated under his soles. He held his fist higher, to be seen by his men in the dim light. Twenty-three narrow Darood faces locked on him. Yusuf looked once to the stars—still a moonless night—to take a bit of peace with him into the hijacking.

The freighter charged so close that it blocked the stars to the east, and the walls of the hull echoed the splashing, bulbous bow. Yusuf nodded to his two kinsmen. He dropped his fist.

Instantly, the lines tying the skiffs together were let go. The trio of helmsmen blared their engines. Yusuf and Guleed peeled away left and right, playing out the coiled rope between them, straining to hold the line taut above the water. Suleiman's skiff dodged left, barely escaping the slicing bow, almost swamped by the ship's wash. Suleiman's helmsman quickly regained control. Hugging the *Valnea*'s painted skirt, the skiff slowed, slipping along the hull back toward the stern and out of sight.

Yusuf's and Guleed's skiffs sped just ahead of the bulbous bow, avoiding the wake that nearly tipped Suleiman. The cousins leaned against the rope, stretching it above the surface. The bulb rose three meters out of the breaking water, over their heads. When Suleiman had first told Yusuf of this tactic weeks ago, it had sounded like an excellent ploy, a way to fool the ship and its armed guards. Now, attempting it, Yusuf wasn't so confident. He was more sure with an RPG in his hands against a Goliath freighter than with a rope.

Both helmsmen nudged the cousins as close to the dripping steel as they dared. The surge and sound of the freighter here at the leading edge were overwhelming, so much force split the sea. Yusuf bellowed to Guleed, "Ready?" The boy could not possibly hear over the roaring water and skiff engines, but Guleed jerked his head to show that he knew what Yusuf wanted.

Yusuf gave his helmsman the order, and Guleed did the same. Both skiffs, twenty meters apart, eased their throttles to let the *Valnea* creep slightly ahead. The cousins yanked hard on the rope, nearing the nose of the bulbous bow. If the line hit the water, the freighter would run over it, Yusuf would have to cut the rope, and this tactic would fail. Then they'd untie the rocket launchers and hail the ship with threats. With grappling hooks and ladders, they'd attempt to board, the more usual tactic of Somali piracy. If the armed guards resisted, Yusuf, Guleed, and Suleiman in their skiffs would harass and beat the ship until she submitted, or until the pirates managed to board under fire, a violent and deadly option.

Yusuf pulled hard against the rope, hoping Suleiman's gambit worked.

Mist off the bow clouded his vision. With no free hand to wipe his eyes, his tunic soaked, he lost focus. The line took slack and bounced on the surface, almost snagging under the bow. Yusuf and opposite him Guleed leaned back with all their strength to lift the rope free.

Yusuf's hands burned around the thick hemp. The pain honed his will. He jutted his chin at his helmsman to ease the skiff's speed a little more, to touch the rope to the front of the bulb. Opposite him, Guleed disappeared behind the bow and spray.

Yusuf hauled on the line through the assault of water, the bounding of the skiff over the chop. Slowly, the rope neared the bulb until it touched its tip. Now the trick was to lift the rope over the bulb to bridle *Valnea* so they could ride her.

Yusuf nodded to his clansman at the wheel. He envisioned Guleed on the right side of the ship doing the same, nudging closer.

The skiff angled in, shortening the distance to the colossal hull. Yusuf raised the rope high over his head. The wash from the bulb splattered his eyes, and he blinked fast to clear his vision. The helmsman fought to keep the skiff steady so Yusuf might not lose his balance.

Yusuf let a meter of slack into the rope; at the same moment, he flicked his arms and wrist to send a loop into the line. He tried this several times, hoping to nurse the rope to the top of the rounded bulb. Yusuf stumbled to his knees, unable to use his hands to catch himself.

"Closer!" he yelled to the helmsman. The man shook his head, afraid to take on more of the ship's wake. The other in the skiff, the gunner, leaped to shove the frightened driver away. He took hold of the wheel and throttle. Like all the pirates in Yusuf's crew, he, too, was a man of the sea. The displaced one took a seat at the center of the skiff, angry.

The rope stayed bent over the bow's bulbous nose. Leaning against the line, Yusuf moved to the bow of the skiff. He climbed onto the short crossbeam, lifting his arms as high as he could. This risked a slip off the skiff shimmying on the *Valnea*'s wake, the deluge of spray shoving him off his perch. To fall in the dark water would be to drown, sucked under the freighter, chopped by the propeller. To fail to take this ship would be to invite another visit from Sheikh Robow, only a slightly better fate.

Yusuf raised his arms their highest. He pulled against the rope, sensing Guleed on the other end in the same struggle. He wavered on the bow, unable to hold his stance on the shuddering skiff, in the cataract all around him.

The disgraced pirate, the displaced one, leaped forward to wrap his arms around Yusuf's knees, propping him in place.

"Take it!" the man shouted.

With his stance steadied, Yusuf snapped the rope upward as hard as he could. A ripple whipped into the line; when it reached the bow, the rope slid upward.

Yusuf had snared the *Valnea*.

Keeping pressure on the line, he stepped down to cleat the rope at the skiff's bow. On the starboard side of the freighter, Guleed would be doing the same. Yusuf gripped the shoulders of the pirate who'd held him, turned him, and put him back behind the skiff's wheel, redeemed. The gunner, no longer at the helm, scrambled to untie a rocket launcher from the floorboards.

The skiff bled off speed, letting the freighter pull ahead while the coils of rope slithered into the water. The side of the skiff skimmed against the ship's hull, gliding backward beneath the giant white letters CMA CGM. No more than a minute had passed since the start of the attack. No reaction had come from the *Valnea*. If Suleiman's plan was working, the ship's captain hadn't yet figured out where they were.

The long rope continued to spiral into the gulf as the bow gained distance forward. With his Kalashnikov, Yusuf scanned the freighter's rail far above, three stories high, ready to discourage anyone who might gaze down. The night's calm, barely begun, remained unbroken by the *Valnea*.

After one more tense minute, the skiff had slipped 150 meters astern of the ship's bow. The vessel remained silent and dark, no lights or alarms. The last of the rope skipped overboard. Instantly the line jumped out of the gulf, taut between the two skiffs, looped across the ship's nose. Yusuf's helmsman idled the twin outboards, leaving only the freighter's deep drone and hissing wake. Yusuf and Guleed were now being towed by the freighter, running at her sides like jackals. The *Valnea* could not outsprint them or shake them off.

Yusuf did not have to wait longer for the freighter's reply. A searchlight flared from the port wing. The beam scanned forward to the bow, then out to sea, until it panned down the long hull to find Yusuf standing in his skiff. The light warmed his neck.

The vibrations of the great freighter trembled against Yusuf's little boat, pressed to her ribs; her engine and propeller throbbed into the skiff's wooden frame. The *Valnea* bellowed at Yusuf, glared at him with one hot white eye, demanding he release her. Instead, Yusuf loosed a half dozen rounds toward the searchlight, though he had no chance of hitting it, just to fix the attention of the sailor manning it. Beside Yusuf, the gunner lifted an RPG, aimed at the wing where the light streamed down. Yusuf waved him off. The *Valnea* had not fired on them. The rockets were to be used only then.

Overhead, a klaxon rang. The skiff squealed, tilting away from the ship. Yusuf and the gunner quickly sat, hanging on to keep from being pitched overboard. The *Valnea* reared out of the water, lifting herself, the helmsman gunning his engines to free the skiff from the rolling leviathan.

The *Valnea* careened sharply to the left toward Yusuf, turning as though to address him, to say what Suleiman had said weeks ago.

Let this go, cousin.

The helmsman could not budge the skiff; one of the propellers was lifted out of the water.

Yusuf reached out to stroke the freighter's rising steel torso.

"*Maya*," he told her. No.

Chapter 12

—•—

On the radar sweep, the *Valnea*'s large blip swallowed the smaller signature lying in its path.

"That ship," Drozdov said. "It has disappeared."

LB asked, "What the hell? Did we hit it?"

Grisha stopped hailing the mystery vessel. The VHF microphone hovered at his lips. "I felt nothing."

"It was not radar shadow," Drozdov said. "It moved to stay in our way."

LB agreed. "I saw it. Dead ahead."

"Steady on." Drozdov gestured to the second mate, who had both hands on the tiny wheel. In the captain's lap, the walkie-talkie squawked.

"Bojan here."

Drozdov answered. "We have possible intruder off the bow. Perhaps a collision."

Bojan paused before replying. "Which is it?"

"I don't know. I expect you to tell me. Out."

Drozdov set the walkie-talkie aside. "Sergeant, Grisha. Man the searchlights. Find that boat. Wreckage, something."

LB rushed to the left wing, Grisha ran right. Throwing open the chocks on the watertight portal, LB raced to the tip of the wing. He flicked the switch on the back of the spotlight. The beam came alive, aimed into the open air.

The searchlight, bulky and powerful, needed both hands to swing. Heat off the bulb sizzled inside the round casing. LB aimed forward to the bow, then out to sea in case of flotsam or survivors. Finding nothing but foam and black swells, he played the light down the side of the freighter.

Froth sparkled on the water, sea mist drifted through the beam. No evidence of a ship entered the circle of the spotlight—nothing, until he aimed straight down. There, nine stories below, an intact wooden skiff hugged the *Valnea*'s hull.

In the boat stood one black man gripping a Kalashnikov, another with an RPG across his shoulder. A third sat behind the wheel. The skiff, long and sleek, looked fast, with twin outboards.

Why only three men?

They were armed men. The big one with the submachine gun made the point by raising his muzzle at the searchlight. The gun flashed and chattered. Bullets struck sparks around LB. The pirate missed the light but beat the steel close enough to make LB dive out of the way.

"Son of a bitch!" Staying low, he skittered for the wheelhouse. Flinging open the door, he shouted, "Pirates!"

Across the pilothouse, Grisha crawled in, hollering at Drozdov from his hands and knees. "Three pirates! They're shooting!"

LB ducked in the doorway. "Same here."

"That's all? Six pirates?"

"You come count 'em."

Drozdov beckoned to them both. "Inside." A young officer and a Filipino crewman darted to replace them at the searchlights.

LB moved behind Drozdov, and Grisha skittered into the second seat.

"General alarm," Drozdov ordered. Grisha flipped a switch on the console. A bell rang through the freighter. Above the bridge, the ship's whistle blew. Seven short bursts, then a long blast. In two corners of the wheelhouse, red lights flashed.

"Helm, evasive maneuvers."

"Aye, Captain."

The Russian manning the wheel spun hard left. *Valnea* responded ponderously, taking a long moment to urge her massive girth into the turn. Once the pivot began, she proved nimble, surprising LB, banking enough to make him brace against Drozdov's chair. Outside the wide windshield, the starlit horizon tilted. The earsplitting alarm cycle began again.

"Grisha?"

"Captain."

"Activate SSAS."

"Aye."

The first mate reached under the radar dashboard to push a hidden button.

LB asked Drozdov, "What's that?"

"Ship security alarm. Now home office and warships in area know we are under pirate attack. We have sent position, speed, and course."

"What about the crew?"

"They have orders to barricade themselves in engine room. Crew will not fight; it is not job of seamen. If we see pirates climbing on board, that is where we will go. You will make sure the wounded are moved properly. We will deny the pirates hostages and leave the heroics to Bojan and the warships. That is their pay. We have ours."

"What about Iris Cherlina?"

"She has heard the alarm. I expect her any minute."

Drozdov took up the walkie-talkie. "Bojan, Bojan. Bridge."

"Go, bridge."

"We have two pirate skiffs. One port, another starboard. Three men each. They are armed."

"I see them."

"Mr. Bojan, I want to be plain. I insist there be no shooting, repeat, no shooting without my permission, or unless they shoot at you and your men. I have alerted warships. They will send assistance. We need only fend off the pirates until then. If pirates attempt to board, I will activate fire hoses. We will reserve lethal response for last resort. Do you understand?"

"I will protect this ship, Captain."

"See that you do only that, Mr. Bojan. You know my mind on this."

"I do."

"Bridge out."

The captain set the walkie-talkie down hard. The helmsman continued to drive the *Valnea* into her sharp left-hand pirouette. When Drozdov turned to LB, he had to look uphill. He shook his head in small tremors. He let slip a short, rueful laugh.

"There are only six pirates. This seems infantile."

"These guys are probably chewing on a pound of *qaat*. They haven't got a clue what they're doing. They didn't look very clever."

"Perhaps. Do you know why I will not allow Bojan to shoot them? Not unless they set foot on my ship. Grisha, you understand."

From his chair beside Drozdov, the portly mate dipped his head, knowing and saddened by it.

"I can guess," LB said. "But tell me."

The captain poked a finger into his own chest. "I have been the guest of Somali pirates before. I did not have a good visit. Because of that time, I want two things very much right now. A drink of vodka and revenge. *Dat' pizdy*. To beat the shit out of someone. Both would feel very nice to me. And the desire for them would become addiction again. I do not like being prisoner of anything. So I will not drink. I will not hate. And I will not kill unless there is no other way. This emblem on your arm, sergeant. I think you have made this choice yourself."

"Not the drinking part. But yeah. I have."

The general alarm completed its third circuit. Drozdov cut it off. "Everyone knows."

The loudspeaker in the dash crackled. A hail came through. "*CMA CGN Valnea, CMA CGN Valnea.* Coalition American warship USS *Nicholas.* Do you copy? Over."

Drozdov snatched the microphone from Grisha. To LB, he whispered, "Your countrymen." He clicked the talk button. "*Nicholas, Valnea.* Captain Drozdov. Go."

"Captain, we're received a distress signal from your vessel. Are you under attack?"

"*Nicholas,* yes. Two skiffs, six pirates. Armed and firing on my ship. No injuries."

"Have they boarded?"

"Negative. They have made no attempt yet. They are staying alongside. I cannot outrun them; we have damaged engine. Twelve knots top speed. Taking evasive maneuvers. Can you send help? Over."

"*Valnea.* I'll have a chopper in the air in five minutes. ETA your position twenty minutes. We are turning your way. ETA my vessel at your position one hour. Copy?"

"*Nicholas,* yes."

"Hold 'em off, Skipper. Cavalry's coming. We will monitor this channel. Out."

"Thank you, Captain. *Valnea* out."

Drozdov communicated this development to Bojan. The Serb guard had both skiffs under observation. "The Somalis," Bojan said, "they are like children. They are intoxicated. We will watch them until the American helicopter comes. They will turn and run."

Grisha widened the sweep on one radar screen, locating USS *Nicholas* thirty-three miles to the west. The warship's radar signature showed *Nicholas* already pointing east, sprinting to the rescue.

Drozdov's helmsman twisted the small steering wheel to the right. The deck evened out, then began its tilt in the opposite direction as the hull swung into a zigzag.

LB analyzed the situation. A couple of skiffs cruising at *Valnea's* sides. Six pirates. A few wild potshots at the searchlights. The pirates had RPGs but hadn't used them. No effort to toss up grapnels or mount ladders. Attacking just after dusk. And that odd tactic of waiting in the freighter's path, skiffs lashed together to look like a single ship on the radar. Then splitting up at the last second to fake a collision, an attack Drozdov had never seen before. Were these Somalis so high on *qaat* they couldn't mount a proper hijacking, as Bojan implied? Why were they just hanging out alongside the ship's hull? What was the purpose? Confusion? Stalling?

Ah, hell.

Stalling.

LB grabbed the walkie-talkie off the console. Drozdov shot him a raised eyebrow.

"Bojan, Bojan. Sergeant DiNardo."

The Serb swiftly answered. "Sergeant, this is private communication with captain only."

"Shut up, Bojan. Listen to me. Those two skiffs might be a distraction. Repeat, they might be a distraction. There could be another boat. Go look for it."

At this, Drozdov's chin fell to his chest. He lapped a hand over his brow, muttering, *"Dolboyob."* LB knew this one, too. Stupid.

Bojan snapped his response. "I have situation under control, Sergeant. Bojan out."

The Serb would not answer LB's hail. He tossed the walkie-talkie to Grisha.

"Keep calling him. Tell him I'm on my way."

Drozdov said, "Go quickly."

LB broke downhill for the left wing. Exiting the portal, he snared a flashlight and made his way down the rail to the Filipino manning the spotlight. The lit-up pirate skiff far below no longer snugged against the great hull but kept pace twenty yards off. LB instructed the Filipino crew to wait one minute, then take the searchlight beam off the skiff and move it forward along the hull, then back.

He flung himself at the exterior stairs.

LB could not fly down the six staircases. The *Valnea* tilted harder as she curved to the right, making the stairs treacherous. He moved as fast as he could, suspecting that every tick of the clock worked for the pirates.

Bojan greeted him at the last step. The Serb held his Zastava M21 ready at his waist. Behind him, the white girder of light from the wing shone down.

"Go inside, Sergeant."

"Look." LB showed the flashlight. "I'm unarmed, thanks to you. I just need to see something up close. I think we're being deked."

"I do not know this word."

"Fooled, Bojan. Tricked. I don't think these pirates are children. I'm betting they've got another skiff. Let me take one look."

"You are medic. Please restrict your efforts to that."

Ten years in Special Forces; LB wanted to bellow this in the Serb's face. Instead, he said again, "One look."

"One. Then back to the infirmary."

LB leaned over the port rail, flicking on the flashlight. The skiff held its position off the hull, pacing the freighter's speed exactly. The pirates made no menacing moves at the *Valnea*, only gazed into the dazzling searchlight with weapons up. No one fired. It looked like a standoff. LB feared it was not.

The *Valnea*'s big searchlight panned forward as instructed to the ship's bow. No more boats lurked in the darkness against the hull where they might hide too close to reflect on *Valnea*'s radar.

Something stirred in the foam beside the hull. A slash broke the water, then dipped back into the black gulf, splashed again, skipped, and disappeared.

The searchlight returned to the skiff. There it was, a rope faring off the bow into the dark water.

LB's balance shifted as *Valnea* continued her careening course, swaying back to her left. As the ship rose into the turn, the pirate skiff closed the distance to the hull.

LB bolted from the rail, downhill across the ship's beam to starboard. Behind him, Bojan ran, shouting.

Reaching the gunwale, LB looked down behind the flashlight before the guard on starboard could intercept him. Another rope ran forward off this spotlighted skiff's sharp bow. The long boat angled away from the hull just as the skiff on the opposite side bore in.

Bojan caught up. LB whirled on him.

"I got to go forward."

"Inside." Bojan motioned to his arriving guard. "Take him inside."

"Listen to me. We're on the same team here. Come with me. I got a hunch."

Bojan moved closer. "Take your hunch and your ass inside, Sergeant."

LB raised a hand into Bojan's chest to stop the big man from laying hands on him first.

"Or what?"

"For your own safety."

LB dropped the hand. He backed away.

"Yeah. That's not really what PJs do."

He spun on his boots, breaking into a sprint through the corridor. Bojan cursed and followed him, as LB wanted.

LB dashed into the dark and slanting companionway, dodging the many steel pillars, ladders, hydrants, and lashings in the way. While not nimble, LB was faster than the Serb with the heavy Zastava bouncing against his chest. He did not slow for the full length of the *Valnea*, did not look back at Bojan or over the night sea. LB ran flat out until he popped from beneath the long overhang, onto the bow, and under the first stars.

Weaving quickly between fat hawsers, he rushed to the tip of the bow. Leaning out with the glowing flashlight in hand, LB found what he'd come looking for.

Bojan grabbed him by the collar to yank him backward.

"Before you say anything"—LB held the flashlight out to the panting Serb—"take a look."

"I will"—Bojan mustered the breath to finish his threat—"put you in brig."

"Look first. Then brig."

Bojan slung the Zastava over his heaving shoulders. LB bent over the rail to watch him train the flashlight on the rope looped around the *Valnea*'s nose above her giant bow bulb. The Serb played the beam left and right, following the cord along both sides until it disappeared into the breaking water.

"Impossible."

LB patted the big guard on the back to return standing on the deck.

"You get it now? That's why they were waiting in front of us. One skiff on each side—they let us go right between them. They strung that rope around the ship's nose. Drozdov is zigzagging, but all he's doing is flinging them around. We're not gonna shake these guys."

"We are towing them." The Serb bared his teeth. "*Sranje*," he cursed, then lifted his chin to LB to say, Go ahead, speak.

"They're not trying to climb up. They're not shooting. Those two pirate skiffs are keeping our attention on them, that's all. There's another boat."

Bojan curled his upper lip, an angry, sour face. He thrust LB the flashlight, burdened enough with the Zastava. "Sergeant, come." Bojan rammed a finger toward the port corridor. "The stern."

Bojan took off barreling through the narrow companionway, twisting his shoulders to fit. LB reached instinctively for the M4 that was not strapped across his shoulder.

The two bolted single file. The unlit passage tilted more with Drozdov's useless evasion, making both men balance against the rail as they ran. Bojan jangled with weapons, LB's jump boots clomped.

Somali pirates. LB had always considered them the same way Bojan described them, as ignorant and rash, not much more than simpleton villagers with guns. He had to rethink that now. From the look of things, these guys were clever. And no question, they had balls. But what were they after—why so much trouble and violence? What was inside this damned ship?

LB had no time to mull this over, darting behind Bojan down the hard corridor. The big Serb, already winded from chasing LB to the bow, couldn't keep the pace for long. He reached the ladder below the forward crane before slowing to a jogging walk.

"I'll meet you there."

With that, LB dodged around Bojan, who did not move to stop him. He ran the rest of the way to the stern, rounding the last steel corner to the fantail. He bent over the rail, catching his breath. The wake behind the *Valnea* was intense, choppy, ghostly. One black-painted skiff crowded with dark men joggled on the foam.

Bojan skidded to a stop beside him. He looked, then spat over the rail at the pirates.

"So. No brig for you, Sergeant."

Two thin men wearing loose white tunics and Kalashnikovs across their backs worked their way up a pair of rope ladders strung from grapnels. The hooks had been flung over the rail of the mooring deck below, fifteen feet closer to the water. The Somalis were only a few rungs from boarding the freighter.

Bojan braced the stock of the Zastava under his armpit.

"You have knife?"

LB was already on the move. He sprang for the down staircase, hopping for a moment to grab the four-inch blade out of the sheath around his calf. Behind him, Bojan ran uphill to the center of the rail, directly above the rope ladders. He halted and fired a burst. LB couldn't gauge the result, already lunging the first steps down to the mooring deck to slash away the ropes. This close, the Serb had to hit somebody. The answering blast of bullets halted LB on the stairs. Bojan stood as if in the center of fireworks, sparks and ricochets in the steel all around him. He jerked, raked by many rounds. Bojan staggered from the rail, then stepped up to fire another volley. More bullets answered from below, another corona of sparks lit him up. Bojan stumbled backward, the Zastava too high when he pulled the trigger again. He fired uselessly over the gulf, then collapsed against the wall.

LB reversed, vaulting back to Bojan. The slumped Serb held up a shaking hand to stop him. LB ignored it. He skidded to his knees at the guard's side.

Blood dribbled from the corners of the big man's mouth. Pale skin and wet wounds peeked through a half-dozen rips in his sweater. He breathed with a grating noise, the holes in his chest burbling. One squeeze of his hand in LB's came strong and pained.

"Uh-oh," Bojan wheezed.

"We gotta get you out of here."

"Too late. Here." Bojan unclipped the walkie-talkie from his belt. He handed it quavering to LB. "Warn Drozdov."

LB stuffed the radio in his vest, then lifted the Zastava's strap from around Bojan's shoulders to loop it over his own. He raced through his options. He could trade shots with the pirates scrambling on board, probably take a few rounds himself, and die next to Bojan. He could run for the other two guards or wait to see if they heard the gunfire and ran this way. In either case, by the time LB managed to mount any kind of defense, a dozen pirates would already be over the rail below and spreading over the ship.

This would become a running firefight against superior numbers on a roller-coaster deck. Or he could get Bojan to safety, warn the captain, and rescue the wounded, plus maybe his own neck.

Gripping the Serb by the wrist, he dug his other arm between the man's splayed legs. He drew his knees in close for the fireman's carry.

"Never too late, pal. This is gonna hurt."

Bojan hissed when LB hoisted him. The Serb lay on his wounds across LB's shoulders. Standing under the weight, LB broke into a jog. Each step drew another Serbian curse. Below, one Somali had already cleared the grappling hook and dropped to the mooring deck. The other rope ladder had no barefoot pirate on it. Bojan must have taken that one out. Two more climbed onto the first rungs. The others in the skiff held the ropes taut or kept gun barrels searching over their heads. The *Valnea*'s dodging did nothing to dislodge them. They, too, were being towed.

LB freed a hand for the walkie-talkie. He hit the talk button.

"Drozdov, DiNardo. Copy?"

"Yes, Sergeant."

"A couple dozen pirates at the stern. At least one already on board, the rest on their way."

"What about the guards?"

"Bojan's down. The other two are watching the skiffs. Get your people to the engine room."

"*Yebanat.*"

"I know. Get moving."

"Where are you going?"

"The infirmary."

"I have not heard from Iris Cherlina."

"Shit."

"Yes, I know. Out."

LB crab-walked down the skinny passageway with Bojan astride his shoulders, careful not to bang the Serb's head. The deck leveled out and did not swing the other direction. LB pictured no one at the wheel now.

He prickled with the advent of action. This was a container ship; not a jungle, desert, or ice storm, it was unfamiliar territory. One man had already been shot. The warship's helicopter was going to arrive too late. LB didn't know the protocols of the *Valnea*, barely knew her layout. He had no plan. All he could do was protect the injured, kick himself for giving up his weapon, then letting Jamie go home on the chopper, lock himself in the engine room with Drozdov and the crew, then leave the rest to the cavalry.

He made it through the passageway, figuring he was no more than a minute ahead of the pirates. He reached the guard stationed on port. The Serb fumbled his weapon, alarmed at the sight of Bojan across LB's shoulders.

"What has happened?"

"There's pirates on board. We gotta move. Now."

"Bojan."

"He's been shot. There's no time. Go get the other guard. Meet me in the infirmary. Fast."

"Is he dead?"

"Not yet. But we're all gonna be if you don't hump it. Move."

The Serb tore across the ship to the starboard rail to collect the other guard. LB ducked Bojan into the superstructure, bumping him on the steel portal. Bojan grunted, "Sergeant, I hurt enough. Really."

LB lurched past the infirmary, running out of steam nearing the elevator. He stabbed the down indicator, then shed Bojan to the floor.

Lighter by two hundred pounds, Serbian blood on his shoulders, LB raced back to the infirmary. Nikita, unable to turn his strapped head toward LB bursting in, reached wildly.

"What is going on? I heard general alarm."

LB pushed down the engineer's hands. "Listen. We're gonna move you to the engine room. Pirates are on the ship."

LB ignored the engineer's spurt of questions. The man's feet quivered while he fought down his shock. LB unclipped Nikita's bag of anti-inflammatory, then stacked three more on his chest. He loaded the engineer with two boxes of bandage wraps for Bojan and four bags of fluids. The last thing he slapped on Nikita was the half-filled catheter bag. "Hang on to these, buddy."

The two black-garbed guards surged in. LB was glad to see both keeping their composure. He instructed them: "Lift this one outta here. Get him to the elevator. Take Bojan and him down to the engine room. Stay with the crew. Protect them. Got it?"

Both nodded. One asked, pointing to the unconscious, bandaged cadet, "What about him?"

LB held open the infirmary door, hitching a thumb down the hall at the elevator and the sagging Bojan. "I'll bring him. You go. Go. Send the elevator back to A deck."

The guards lugged Nikita on his board, trailing the sheet that covered him. LB shut the infirmary door. By now, pirates were definitely crawling over the mooring deck and headed up the stairs.

With no time to be gentle, LB stacked the remaining bags of saline and fentanyl on the cadet's bandaged chest. The kid seemed unaware except for a flinch of the fingers. Unclipping the catheter bag from the bed, he noted that the cadet's urine remained brownish, a sign of continued dehydration. He might not survive a long siege in the engine room, the hottest and least antiseptic place on the ship.

LB rolled the cadet and the medical supplies in the blanket. The boy stiffened against LB's arms sliding under him. A deep groan crossed his rounded lips.

LB lifted the kid. He turned for the door to see it opening, with no hand free to reach for his gun or knife. He could not drop the cadet.

Drozdov flew into the infirmary, leaving the door open.

"Put him down, Sergeant."

"What?"

"I will take him to engine room. You must go."

"Go where?"

"Iris Cherlina is missing. If they find her, they will have their hostage. She is not in her room, not in accommodation. She may be again on the bow. I don't know. But find her. Hide her. You are not on ship's manifest. Pirates will not look for you."

The captain dug fast hands into the cadet's clothes hanging on a hook. He dug out a key on a ring. He slapped this on the cot where the cadet had lain.

"This is master key. Every lock on the ship. If you must hide, this will take you places. Now."

Drozdov stepped forward to extend his arms next to LB's beneath the wrapped cadet. Tugging the cadet out of LB's arms, he held the boy well enough, though he turned red with the burden.

"I must speak quickly, Sergeant."

"Go."

"I do not know the secrets on this ship," the Russian urged. "I do not know the lies of Iris Cherlina. *Wed'ma*, she is not just passenger. You have guessed this?"

"It wasn't tough."

"I was told, no questions."

"Maybe you should've asked a few."

"Too late for that. Now listen to me. The people who put her here, and Bojan, me, all the bullshit on this ship, are not going to let it stay hijacked. They will come. You have radios. You have gun. Help them. And remember."

"What?"

"Someone has sabotaged the *Valnea*. Trust no one. They may do same to you."

"All right. Get bandages on Bojan fast. And make sure the kid—"

"Grisha knows."

"All right, all right. Be safe."

"*Otyebis* safe. Run."

LB swept the master key off the cot, pocketed it, and flew out of the infirmary. He lapped his finger over the Zastava's trigger. The elevator waited at the long end of the hall for Drozdov. Bojan, the guards, Nikita, were gone. Behind him, the captain staggered under the cadet. LB wished them all luck, and himself.

He moved to the door leading out to the main deck. He swung the heavy portal as quickly as he dared, judging time more important than stealth. Outside, LB flattened his back to the wall, listening. High-pitched voices flitted over the ship's hum.

He squatted to present the smallest profile. Stepping onto the open deck, LB swerved eyes and gun together, left and right. In the narrow, dark passageway, men crept his way, Kalashnikovs at their hips. LB could take a knee and drop the first two or three, framed in the passage with nowhere to hide. That would leave a dozen more flowing up both sides of the *Valnea*. In a gunfight, he'd be flanked and finished in seconds. Somali pirates weren't soldiers, but they weren't known as cowards, despite Bojan's disregard. The big Serb's blood on his shoulders told him the Somalis would shoot back.

Iris Cherlina. Where was she that she didn't hear the alarms? Had the woman gone to the bow, like Drozdov said, or had she been on the stern for some reason? Did the pirates already have her—was that why she'd gone missing?

There wasn't time to figure any of that out now. He had to keep himself on the loose, or he'd be no help to Iris or Drozdov.

The pirates bore down on LB's position. Only one way to go. He drew a deep breath and came out of his crouch.

He lit out across the open steel deck, momentarily exposed until he reached the starboard rail, banked hard left, and pelted forward. He heard nothing but his own hurtle and the ever-present whisper of the ship's wake. LB braced for a bullet in the back. After a hundred meters, halfway to the bow, he slowed, bringing the Zastava around to check if he was pursued.

His eyes adjusted better in the dim passage. More by motion than shape, he discerned Somalis behind him. They came his way without hurry or caution, thirty meters back, calling to each other, confident in their weapons and number. LB was maybe twenty seconds ahead of them.

He scurried forward to the bow, not sure if the pirates had seen him in the long passageway. He stayed low, below the glow of stars across the rail.

Reaching the open bow, he hissed Iris's name, running beneath the steaming light past every place she might hide. He kept an eye on the rail where the pirates would emerge in moments. He considered again squaring them up in the Zastava's sights and standing his ground. If he had Jamie with him, he'd do it. The two of them back-to-back could hold off the pirates for twenty minutes until that chopper arrived. One more time, he damned himself for being in this mess on his own.

Iris wasn't on the bow. LB had no more time. If the pirates had her, he was already too late. If not, she was holed up somewhere better than he could find in the next ten seconds.

He needed to get off the open bow. Dodging hawsers, anchor rodes, and life-raft barrels, darting in and out of the shadows, LB dashed along the port rail, scanning for hiding places. The *Valnea* had plenty of dark crannies he could cram himself into, steel dead-ends with no back door. He needed a secure place to regroup and think, make a plan, move if discovered, not a spot for a siege.

He couldn't stay in the passageway. Even if he managed to keep ahead of the Somalis behind him, another pack was sure to come hunting from the other direction. He'd be caught between the two. Six more pirates waited in the pair of spotlighted skiffs roped around the ship's nose. In minutes there'd be twenty-plus armed bandits on board, more than enough to ferret him out.

LB had to duck out of sight. Now.

He stood in front of the short ladder leading up to the empty cargo deck beneath the forward crane. Other than jumping overboard, the ladder was the only way out of the corridor. LB strapped the Zastava across his shoulder, then leaped up the rungs.

On the broad cargo deck, he took in his surroundings and chances for cover. In the wide spaces between the lashing bridges, the bare deck was not a place he could hide for long. He'd be spotted minutes after the pirates got the same idea and climbed up to tramp around. LB needed a better lair.

The answer lay just ahead, an access hatch leading down to the cargo hold. Hurrying to it, he dug into his pocket for the master key Drozdov had thrust at him a minute ago. Torres had said no curiosity. This wasn't a violation of that order. This was survival and evasion.

LB braked to his knees, reaching for the door's padlock with the key.

The lock was not there.

In the dark, on the white deck beside the hatch cover, the lock stood opened.

Was this where Iris was hiding, belowdecks? Did she have a master key, too?

LB had no more time to ponder. He heaved open the hatch cover to swing his legs onto the ladder leading down. Once his head had dropped below deck level, he pulled the hatch down against its spring hinges, then spun the watertight wheel to dog it shut.

LB flicked on the flashlight. He dropped the rest of the way down the steel ladder to a narrow metal catwalk. Working the light, he was greeted by a gigantic catacomb of rails and beams, columns, platforms, and more ladders stretching forward and aft, many stories down. A grottolike quiet reflected every step and rustle of his creep along the catwalk high above the hull.

A second pale glow filtered from below, deep in the steel cells of the *Valnea*. LB found the next ladder and, shielding his flashlight behind a cupped hand, descended into the freighter's secrets.

146

Chapter 13

——•——

Pirate skiffs
Alongside CMA CGN Valnea
Gulf of Aden

The cargo ship stopped swerving. Yusuf's skiff closed against the great hull behind the long rope, jostling over foam.

Minutes later, the searchlight went out.

Yusuf and his gunner kept weapons in hand, sights on the rail above. The *Valnea* drove ahead, droning and deafening. Yusuf's night vision, spoiled by the spotlight, reasserted itself. Stars emerged. He left his gunner to guard the skiff and admired the constellations.

The helmsman gunned the skiff's engines, bending Yusuf's knees to make him sit. The skiff angled away from the hull, away from the long gangway dropping where the boat had been. Yusuf moved to the skiff's bow. With his onyx-handled blade he slashed the tow rope. Guleed on the other side would be cut loose. He would know they had taken the ship.

On the descending staircase Suleiman stood, arms raised in triumph. He looked foolishly pleased with himself after so much reluctance to take on this hijacking. When Yusuf stepped onto the platform, he embraced his *tol*.

"Are you all right?" he asked close to Suleiman's ear.

"Yes, of course. Why?"

"All those teeth. I thought you might be in pain. I see it's a smile."

Suleiman shouted, "We did it, cousin."

"You did it. All I did was hang on and ride."

"We lost only one. There was shooting. It's safe now."

"What about the ship's crew? Do we have them?"

"We have enough."

On the black gulf, a white wake carved from behind the *Valnea*'s stern. Guleed's skiff motored their way. The two waited on the platform for the third cousin, to circle him in their arms, then climb the stairs to the captured ship.

Yusuf led them up the gangway. The long walk winded him and amazed him, that they had taken this massive freighter. If she'd been steaming at flank speed, Yusuf might only be nipping at the *Valnea*'s heels right now, flinging grappling hooks that fell short, firing rocket grenades at her, and screaming threats over the radio. They might be drowned after flipping in the vessel's much bigger wake. Maybe shot dead by her guards or a warship's helicopter. Or fleeing.

Yusuf let the mystery of the *Valnea*'s speed go unsolved for now. He stepped onto the deck, out of his sandals, to feel her under his soles. She was his, if only until daybreak, when he anchored her off Qandala. Robow would be waiting there. The sheikh had his intentions for her, as well. But tonight, plowing the sea, Yusuf was her master.

Suleiman took him by the arm. "I have five men on the bridge. Guleed will turn us for Qandala. I have six others out searching. Someone's loose on the ship."

"Who, a guard?"

"I don't know. So far he's done nothing against us. We'll find him. I have eight more waiting in the engine room."

"Is the crew locked in?"

"Most of them."

Suleiman sent Guleed to the pilothouse. Then he led Yusuf not to the engine room but into the accommodation. They stopped at a door with a red cross on it. Suleiman nodded to the guard he'd posted there.

Inside sat a raven-haired man. Standing, his dented face rose as high as Yusuf's. The man winced; some pain shot through him. He seemed unhurt. Was it a thought?

Behind him on a cot lay a naked lad wrapped in bandages. The unconscious boy looked bad, cooked red and blistered. One bag of clear fluid fed into him, another, of dark urine, led out.

Suleiman motioned with the introductions. "Yusuf Raage, this is Captain Drozdov. We caught him carrying this boy to the elevator."

Drozdov eyed Yusuf, pushing his tongue behind his lips. "Yusuf Raage, the pirate. I recognize this name."

Yusuf inclined his brow. "How do you know me, Captain?"

"How do the Americans say? This is not my first rodeo."

"I am flattered."

"Don't be. You are *svoloch'*."

Yusuf folded his arms, leaning against the infirmary wall to wait.

Drozdov translated. "Bastard."

"Keep that in mind. Now come with us to the engine room."

"No."

Yusuf stepped closer, assessing the captain. Drozdov seemed of Yusuf's age, a slighter build, but alcohol kept a man thin. Powerful hands, a dark eye.

"You have seen misery, Captain."

"From the likes of you, yes."

"Then you understand what I have to do. Suleiman. The boy."

Yusuf's kinsman stepped to the cot. Before he could slide arms under the young sailor, Drozdov shoved him away. Suleiman backed off and drew his pistol.

Drozdov asked, "Why?"

"My cousin here can put that gun against your head outside the engine room, or this boy's head. I prefer the boy only because he will stay quiet. But you, we do not have to carry. Your crew will come out either way, and we can go about our business. Besides, one of your guards shot one of my men. It seems fair."

Drozdov did not shift his defiant posture.

"It's just a ship, Captain. Someone else's ship, not yours. It's not worth lives. Only money."

Drozdov stormed past Suleiman's outstretched gun, to fling open the infirmary door. In the hall, the guard jumped in surprise. The captain walked the length of the hall, headed for the stairwell. Yusuf kept pace.

"Captain."

"What?"

"May I ask a question?"

"So polite. Where did you get manners, pirate?"

"In England. Where I grew up."

Drozdov made a spitting noise.

"Ask."

"Why is your ship going so slowly?"

Drozdov stopped in the hall. Face to face, he growled.

"You know why."

"Tell me so I can see if you know."

"Sabotage."

"You're sure of this?"

"*Vali otsyuda* sure. Positive! You have put someone on my ship! You are worse than bastard. You are *govnosos*. Shit sucker."

Drozdov stomped away. Yusuf held his ground, gesturing for the guard to stay with the captain to the staircase. Suleiman sidled close.

In a low voice, he asked, "Do you have someone on this crew?"

"No."

In a second, all the victory of the hijacking leaked out of Suleiman. His head sagged to his chest, gold teeth bared.

Yusuf asked, "What does this mean?"

"It means everything I was afraid of has happened. We are being maneuvered by someone. It means we are puppets."

Yusuf set a hand to Suleiman's shoulder. He recalled this narrow, older shoulder at his side fighting in Plumstead alleys, plucking fish from the Somali sea, shaking and angry at sickness and civil war. Suleiman had stood with Yusuf on the bridge of six captured ships, had divided millions of dollars. Both had put blood on their hands for each other and for their clan. At every step, they had never been puppets.

"Lift your head, cousin. We are kings of this land. Come."

———

The window framed a blue-eyed face in earmuffs. The glass was shatterproof, the door a steel watertight portal. The crew behind this door was impregnable.

Suleiman pushed his pistol against Drozdov's temple. The Russian set his mouth hard, staring into the window and the head gaping back. Believing his life was on the line, Drozdov seemed to will his crew to stay locked in the engine room. What sort of man was this? Yusuf put this aside, another mystery to be untangled later. He stepped in front of his eight pirates holding automatic weapons ready.

Yusuf waggled the walkie-talkie he'd taken from Drozdov. The man in the window nodded, then pulled aside one earmuff to press a similar radio to his ear. The noise in the engine room was surely intense.

"Can you hear me?" Yusuf called into his handset.

The face nodded.

"I do not need you to come out. I have my hostages. The captain and the burned boy. The warships will not come to your rescue. You may all stay in the engine room."

The blue eyes widened.

"But hear me. If you touch the engine, if you disable one system on this ship, I will bring the captain back down here in pieces. Then the boy. Do you understand?"

The face licked lips. He turned away, glancing to someone behind him. It seemed he got no guidance. He looked back at Yusuf without defiance or strategy.

"If you come out, we will feed you and keep you safe. I know you have wounded with you. They will get care. Do you have weapons?"

The face nodded.

"I want every armed man to walk out first. Then the crew. I need an answer now."

The man lowered the walkie-talkie. He turned his back to the window. Yusuf imagined him shouting to the gathered crew: They have the captain. They have the boy. What should we do?

The discussion inside the loud engine room concluded quickly. The blue eyes returned and bobbed agreement.

The steel wheel of the door turned from the inside. Yusuf's pirates lifted their weapons. The locking chocks spun. The door edged open.

A swell of engine clatter emerged first, then the man in the window, sheathed in black. He offered his automatic weapon to Yusuf. At his back came another guard, also surrendering his arms. The third, the largest of them, dragged himself propped on the shoulders of two Filipino crewmen. Gauze wrapped the man's bare torso, scarlet seeped through the layers. He carried no gun.

Suleiman stopped him. "You were the one shooting."

The big guard shook slowly, his laughter agonized into a cough.

"So were you."

"Where is your rifle?"

"I dropped it in the water."

Suleiman pushed a finger against the bandages to hold the big man in place. The two eyed each other, stopping the line, scowling as men who had traded bullets.

"Do you mind?" the guard rasped. "I prefer to lie down."

The guard hobbled to the elevator. Both smaller Filipinos struggled to support him.

Yusuf counted the seamen leaving the loud engine room, all of them shedding earmuffs. Twenty-seven filed past, including one strapped to a backboard carried between a pair of Russians. Adding the captain and burned boy, that accounted for all the crew and officers, plus three guards.

One of them was the saboteur. Whose man was it? Al-Qaeda, CIA, Mossad?

When the last sailors had been escorted up the stairs, Yusuf and Suleiman were left with Drozdov. Suleiman sealed the heavy portal, restoring quiet.

Yusuf asked the captain, "Is that everyone?"

"Yes."

Suleiman seemed more galled by the minute. He shoved his gold teeth close to Drozdov, holding the pistol high beside his own head to show that it was asking, too.

"Then who did my men chase?"

Drozdov gave no inch. "My passenger. Iris Cherlina."

Yusuf eased his cousin back from the Russian.

"A woman passenger?"

"Yes."

"She is on the manifest?"

"Of course."

Yusuf turned Drozdov for the stairs. The captain walked off, muttering in Russian, surly as Suleiman.

"Just a woman, cousin." Yusuf linked his kinsman's arm. "Let her go."

"At this speed," Suleiman whispered, "it won't be four hours to Qandala. It's eight."

"I know. We'll make it. We anchor at sunup." Yusuf towed Suleiman to the stairs. "Then we get off this damn ship."

Chapter 14

CMA CGN Valnea
Gulf of Aden

LB lowered himself by a series of levels and ladders. Surrounded by steel, he became conscious of every noise he made, boots on the rungs, Bojan's jangling gun, his breathing. His combat sense told him to sneak down until he knew what he was headed into.

Reaching the bottom of the hold, he gazed into a vast honeycomb. The size and complexity of the ship belowdecks stunned LB. The diffuse glow from his flashlight did not reach its limits. But only strides away from the bottom of his ladder, on the canyon floor, two rows of railroad cars looked puny and alone.

Here were the first of the *Valnea's* secrets.

When Major Torres sent him on this mission, she hadn't counted on pirates, gunplay, a saboteur. If LB's life and the safety of others were at risk, he needed to find out everything he could about the terrain, the players, and the stakes.

Time for curiosity. If he got in trouble for it later, that'd be good news. He'd be alive for it.

The first line of nine railcars supported long, rounded cargos covered by tied-down tarpaulins. The nine beds in the second row held rectangular loads, also hidden by tarps. LB crept to the nearest car. When he was standing close, the shipment no longer appeared small. It dwarfed him.

He sliced his knife across the tarp, cutting a slash big enough to stick in his head and flashlight.

"Holy…" LB clamped his teeth, or he might shout.

He trained his flashlight along the frost-colored fuselage of an unmanned aerial vehicle. The drone's long wings lay bound to its sides. Inert and dismantled, the thing still looked deadly and blindly robotic. He'd seen plenty of UAVs on runways in Afghanistan. Always they gave him the same chill, knowing and disliking what they were, drone hunter-killers, the faceless future of warfare.

He scanned the colossal length of the plane, not recognizing the shape. This was no Predator or Reaper. It wasn't American.

On one wing, close to the root, his light passed over a label. LB withdrew his head, shielding the flashlight. He moved to cut another slit in the tarp.

He aimed the light to read the label. IAI. Israeli Aircraft Industry.

LB sliced into the eight other tarps in line. He found identical UAVs.

Why were Israeli drones being shipped to Lebanon?

He cut through the tarps on all the railcars in the second row. The first four held CCS mobile bunkers. These were hardened nerve centers, C4I stations for command, control, communications, computers, and intelligence. The last five cars were packed with ground radar arrays, aerostat dirigibles, remote video terminals—every persistent surveillance sensor an army needed for detection, identification, and targeting.

Like the drones, all of it was Israeli.

This didn't add up. Israel shared a border with Lebanon. If all this heavy hardware was bound for Beirut, why not ship it overland a hundred miles instead of loading it onto a freighter in one of the remotest reaches of the world, Vladivostok?

As he stared at the radar arrays under his flashlight, a few bits and pieces of this mystery ship began to fit for LB.

Why did the *Valnea* run empty, except for these railcars, for ten thousand miles?

Simple. She was calling into only one port. This wasn't a commercial voyage but a charter, meant to ferry the drones and electronics straight to Beirut.

Then why load up so far out of the way in a far corner of Russia? And why protect the drones with Bojan?

The obvious reason was secrecy. This shipment wasn't just sensitive. It was probably illegal. The customer was bound to be on a UN watch list. Russia couldn't ship military technology this advanced to just anybody. In the Middle East, that list of banned parties was long, and it included Lebanon. The *Valnea*'s cranes would let her unload the drones anywhere along the Lebanese coast, self-sufficient and secretive.

To pull it off, the ship needed a captain who wouldn't pry. Drozdov was perfect, an experienced but retread officer who would shut his mouth and click his heels to get back on his feet. The rest of the crew would follow his orders. Drozdov seemed angry with himself, and his ship, for it.

The size and expense of the operation were considerable. Drones, C4I stations, and battlefield radars would easily top several billion dollars. Major Torres had been real clear that LB should keep his nose out of exactly where he'd stuck it. This indicated pressure from above. That spelled government—LB's government.

So Russia, the United States, and Israel were in bed together. That put a lot of horsepower in play. Who else?

Who was getting the shipment? Too soon to know. Chances were, the stuff wasn't destined for poor Lebanon, not for $5 billion anyway. Because it was being delivered in secret, the customer was somebody who could afford it but couldn't get military hardware like this above the table.

No surprise. Prisoners, technology, weapons, information; this sort of back-door, black-op swap was done all the time between nations who were at each other's throats in public, in each other's pockets under the table.

What was at stake this time? What was being traded for drones and radar? Surely more than just money.

Also too soon to know.

Just as vital to LB's survival: Who on board the *Valnea* was trying to stop it? Who had the know-how, motive, access, and sheer stones?

If the saboteur's purpose was to keep the ship from reaching Beirut, why foul just one piston? Why not pull a bunch of fuses and shut down the whole engine?

LB clicked off the flashlight, closing the flap he'd cut into the last tarp. He scratched his ear, mulling all this over.

What if the intent wasn't to stop the ship? What if the saboteur wanted only to slow her?

Why? To delay arrival in Beirut?

But if the point was to get to Lebanon later, the sabotage could have been done anytime over the past two weeks. Why wait ten thousand miles to do it here, in the middle of the Gulf of Aden, pirate central?

Drozdov said someone had slowed the ship so she could be hijacked. Someone on this ship was working with the pirates. If this was true, incredible. Again, why? Who?

Too many open-ended questions. LB centered on the one thing he could be sure of. Drozdov was dead on. Very powerful interests had a lot to lose here. If the *Valnea* got hijacked and her secrets hauled into the light of day by a bunch of ragtag Somalis waving AK-47s, heads would roll in Tel Aviv, Washington, and Moscow.

Drozdov had sent the signal that the ship was under attack. Now that pirates were aboard, someone, somewhere, was sure to come gunning to get the *Valnea* back. Maybe if Drozdov and his crew made it to the engine room, that American warship could drop a marine assault team on board. To keep that from happening, the pirates would have to get their hands on a hostage. They needed Iris Cherlina. As soon as they checked the ship's manifest, they'd know she was on board and at large.

What role did she play in all this? Iris claimed to be an electrophysicist. She likely hadn't been lying—who picks that for a fake career? But how did that figure in with several billion dollars' worth of illegally transported military electronics? Iris, the drones, and the radar were all bound for Beirut. How was she linked to the big undercover deal in the belly of this ship?

He hoped she had nothing to do with any of it, and in the same moment cut that wish loose as foolish. Iris Cherlina was plenty good-looking. She'd played up to him to chump him. Drozdov called her a liar. Plainly the captain was right. If there were vast amounts of money involved, as she claimed, Iris was likely in this mess up to her pretty ears. Along with who else on board?

In the middle of all this uncertainty, one fact stood rock solid. If the *Valnea* wasn't freed by someone in the next several hours, she'd be anchored off the Somali coast by sunup. After that, no one would get her back, not before the pirates stamped her secrets all over the world's front page.

If LB wanted answers, and he did, he needed to find Iris Cherlina. He was going to ask her one more time what she was doing on this ship.

He headed for the bow and the muffled light.

Chapter 15

The ship's crew huddled beneath the long windshield in the ship's bridge. The Filipino deckhands sat one way, legs crossed under them. The taller Western officers sat with knees pulled to their chests. The Serb guards hunkered beside their wounded, bandaged comrade, who lay on his back, his head in one of their laps.

Suleiman read names aloud from the ship's crew list. Guleed guarded the sailors with his Kalashnikov, waving it slowly back and forth across them. The rest of Yusuf's men had been given thirty minutes to loot the crew's quarters, before they would take up positions around the freighter, guarding her beam, bow, and stern.

Suleiman mangled many of the Filipino and Slavic names. As he worked down the list, some crewmen did not know to raise their hands. Suleiman's voice rose in frustration when a hand did not go up with every name. Yusuf quietly reminded his cousin to stay calm; they were in control, and anger did not help the situation.

Drozdov sat stiff in his captain's chair, Yusuf beside him in the copilot's seat. Outside the windshield, behind the crew's heads, a searchlight from the warship's helicopter washed back and forth across the broad cargo deck. The *Valnea* drove ahead at twelve knots, on autopilot for the Somali coast and Qandala eighty miles off.

Suleiman closed the manifest. Every crewman, officer, and guard had been accounted for, including the pair in the infirmary. The only name unanswered was Iris Cherlina, the passenger. She hid somewhere in the dark crevices of the ship. Iris Cherlina was not worth sending men to look for her.

Yusuf hoped she stayed out of sight the rest of the night. He didn't need the distraction of his men being around a foreign woman. They were *rer manjo*, good seamen and pirates. But they were mostly poor Somali men, and a man's poverty rarely remained in his pocket. It wore down his soul. Yusuf could not guarantee her safety.

A woman would be useful, but not now. Later, in the ransom negotiations.

"Captain."

Drozdov turned a weary head. The man had collapsed into himself in the ten minutes Yusuf had been on board. His face, pocked and weary, looked like a moonstone.

"Yes."

"Hail the warship. Tell them to recall their helicopter. Or I will shoot a hostage under that searchlight."

Drozdov did not move. "Is that how it will be? Everything you want you will get, or you will shoot a hostage?"

Yusuf took the VHF microphone from the dash. He held it out to Drozdov.

"Help me get through the next seven hours, Captain. We can judge each other another time."

The *Valnea*'s crew beneath the flashing windows watched their captain refuse to take the microphone. One, a heavyset officer, unfolded from the floor. He raised both hands to tell Guleed that he was no threat, that he wanted to come forward.

Drozdov waved the officer down. Lethargic, as though moving through water, he took the microphone.

"USS *Nicholas*, USS *Nicholas*. CMA CGN *Valnea*."

The loudspeaker piped. "*Valnea*. Coalition warship USS *Nicholas*. What is your status? Over."

"Captain, we have pirates on board. They have taken ship and have my crew hostage. The pirates demand you to recall your helicopter." Drozdov spoke directly to Yusuf, a seething wince of his eyes. "They will shoot a hostage."

"Roger that, *Valnea*."

Yusuf took back the microphone. He held it until the spotlight washing over the freighter shut off and the helicopter's blinking lights moved away west, back to the warship that was visible on both the radar and the dark horizon.

"*Valnea*. Is the pirate captain nearby?"

Yusuf brought the mike to his lips.

"This is he."

"Sir, you speak English?"

"Very well."

"Sir, do not harm any hostages. We have complied."

"Thank you. Captain, what is your name?"

"Goldberg, sir."

"Captain Goldberg. I have two more demands. First, keep your vessel at least five miles away from me at all times. Do you understand?"

"Affirmative."

"Next. I want you to send a skiff alongside my starboard beam. I want no more than two men in it. Unarmed."

"Sir, I can't promise that."

Yusuf spoke facing Drozdov.

"I have wounded on board, Captain. I don't have time to care for them. You will take them off my hands. I have hostages enough."

"Sir, I have the safety of my own crew to look out for. You understand. I need a guarantee."

"You have my word, Captain. Your people will not be harmed."

"All right, I'll have to accept that. We'll reach your position in fifteen minutes."

DAVID L. ROBBINS

"Good."

"If you cut your speed, we can make that ten."

"Fifteen will be fine. *Valnea* out."

The Russian strapped to the backboard cursed from the moment he was carried out of the infirmary to the main deck. Suleiman, still impatient and anxious, pressed the barrel of his pistol into the grousing Russian's groin where the urine bag attached. This shut him up.

The scalded boy was bundled into a bedsheet like a hammock and hoisted outdoors. The pirates pitied his condition, blistered and moaning, conscious enough to be in agony. They tried to be careful hefting him down the long, lowered gangway.

At the bottom of the stairs, waiting on the platform, Yusuf stood in the same spot where his skiff had ridden beside the *Valnea*'s great flank. He bathed again in the warm searchlight from above. Foam licked his bare feet skimming just above the water. Along the starboard rail three stories up, all the hostages stood in line, including Captain Drozdov. Behind them, a dozen Darood held Kalashnikovs.

Bathed in the spotlight, Yusuf could not see far over the black gulf or any stars. The turning of the freighter's screw, the hiss of the wake—these blotted out other sounds. He did not hear the warship's inflatable raft arrive out of the darkness until it had motored very close, blinking a flashlight only fifty yards away. This worried him, that the American boat could approach so near without discovery, without even trying to be stealthy. What if this had been a raid? Wasn't the plodding *Valnea* just as vulnerable to commandos as it had been to Yusuf's pirates?

Seven hours to Qandala.

The beam shifted away from Yusuf to the closing raft. As Yusuf had ordered, only two sailors manned the craft. They held no weapons. The one at the helm was dressed in camouflage and

162

body armor, probably an American marine. The sailor in the bow wore a naval officer's uniform.

The raft motored alongside. The officer tossed a painter caught by Suleiman, who tied it off. The marine stood, a big man, showing empty hands, then tied a stern line to snug the raft close. The officer, well tanned with an older seaman's creases, saluted.

He asked, "Permission to come aboard?"

Yusuf reached down to help him onto the platform.

"*Salaamu alaykum.*"

The American held on to Yusuf's offered hand to shake it. "I'm Captain Goldberg, USS *Nicholas*."

"Yusuf Raage. Thank you for coming personally, Captain."

"We got ourselves a situation here. Maybe we can figure it out, the two of us."

"First, the wounded. Please take them aboard."

"Aye, sir."

Goldberg motioned for his hefty marine to help load the two injured Russians. The burned and bandaged boy on the sheet was placed gingerly into the raft. His eyes were open, round as coins, his pain easy to see. The one strapped to the backboard grabbed his testicles to shake them at the pirates handing him over, shouting, "*Poshol nahuj!*"

Yusuf said to the captain, "As I said, I haven't the time."

"I understand. Can I have a private word with you?"

Goldberg took a step closer to Yusuf. Suleiman set a hand on the pistol stuffed in his waistband. The marine, even unarmed, rose in the stern of the raft.

"I would keep my distance, Captain. My cousin is very protective."

"I still need that private word."

Yusuf gestured for his six pirates who'd hauled the Russians down the gangway to climb back to the deck. Suleiman held his ground.

"Speak."

"All right. Listen, I don't know what's on this ship, and I don't want to know. But you kicked a hornets' nest when you took it. My phone has not stopped ringing. And the calls I'm getting are from very important people in my government. Very. Military and civilian both, if you get my drift."

"Make your point, Captain."

"I'm telling you to walk away. No harm done. Get back in your skiffs and go hijack yourself another freighter. You got my word: I'll wave and let you go. See you another time. But not this time. This is bigger than you want and more than you can handle. That's a heads-up for your own good."

"For my good."

"Yes, sir."

Yusuf turned to his cousin, listening behind him. Suleiman kept his face blank, out of deference for Yusuf as leader. Both knew the American had just spoken everything on Suleiman's mind.

Yusuf lapped a hand behind his kinsman's neck. He squeezed in fondness and loyalty. His cousin would share whatever fate was his; that was their long-standing pact.

Yusuf raised his hand high into the spotlight. At the signal, the beam swept away, plunging the platform and raft into darkness. The light leaped up the *Valnea*'s tall hull, to the hostages gathered along the starboard rail.

Guleed's single gunshot clapped loud enough to be heard at the bottom of the gangway. One hostage went limp; arms and shoulders flopped overboard until the legs were lifted from behind, dumping the black-clad body into the air. The searchlight followed the long, awkward somersault into the water.

The corpse splashed into the wake, then bobbed to the surface facedown. This was the large guard, the one wounded during the taking of the ship. The searchlight stayed on the body surging past the platform, beneath Yusuf's bare feet, under the gaze of the warship captain. The body drifted quickly behind in pinkening foam, swallowed into the indifferent gulf.

Yusuf spoke to the side of the captain's head. "The man was an armed guard. He shot one of my clansmen."

Goldberg pivoted slowly to glare at Yusuf. He barely hid his anger.

"When your phone rings again, Captain, tell them if anyone attacks this ship, I will kill every hostage. You asked for the guarantee of Yusuf Raage. Tell them you have it."

Suleiman did not lift his hand from his weapon until the American had stepped into the raft, slipped the lines, and motored away with the wounded. The spotlight tracked the boat deep into the night, until it became small and the beam blinked off.

Chapter 16

Through the honeycomb of steel, beneath the moan of the freighter's engines, LB crept forward. He hid behind pillars, pausing, edging forward toward the source of the light. The glow did not waver, and the shadows it cast didn't shift.

When he rounded the last corner into the cargo bay, he saw the source. A flashlight lay abandoned on the deck.

Instinctively, LB raised Bojan's Zastava. He advanced slowly into the rim of light.

The spilled beam played across one more railcar standing alone, its large rectangular face wrapped like the others in a tarp. LB swept the Serb's gun in a circle, scanning the blackness. He backed toward the railcar.

"Stop right there." The voice bounced around the hard cargo bay, sounding as if it came from several mouths. LB quit backpedaling. "I've got a gun pointed at your head. Drop the rifle."

He did not comply.

"Iris, it's me. LB." His own voice flew into the gloom, rattling in the dark.

"LB? What are you doing here?"

"I figure to ask you the same question. Come on out."

Echoed footsteps preceded Iris. She emerged in her khakis and linen blouse. She carried no gun.

Iris Cherlina walked fast right at him. LB lowered the Zastava so she could walk into his arms.

"I'm so scared," she whispered.

He wasn't sure of the right pressure to put around her waist. She was a beautiful liar, and involved in something sneaky and international, way past his pay grade. He squeezed once, said, "Yeah," then let her go. Iris backed off when he did.

"I'll go first," he said, "since I'm the one who really has a gun. What are you doing down here? What's going on?"

Iris Cherlina picked up the flashlight she'd laid on the deck. She turned the light away from his eyes. "I went to my cabin to rest for dinner, like I said. But I was curious about that ship you and I saw off the bow at sunset. So I walked forward. I looked over the side and saw the pirates. It was incredible. Frightening. When I heard the alarm, I climbed down here to hide. I was lucky."

"Why didn't you tell somebody?"

She blinked at him, indulgent. "That defeats the purpose of hiding."

"Where'd you get a master key?"

Around Iris, the engine hummed while, high above, pirates swarmed the ship.

"LB. You're not supposed to be here."

"Too late." He dropped the question to point at the mystery railcar behind her. "That's yours, isn't it? And all that back there. The drones, the radar."

Iris didn't nod, nor did she need to for him to know he was right.

She covered her mouth. "Is that blood on your shoulders?"

"Bojan's been shot. I had to carry him."

Iris spoke behind her fingers. "Oh my God. Are we safe? Did the pirates follow you?"

"They don't know I'm down here. Last I saw, Drozdov and the crew were headed to the engine room to lock themselves in. I'm not sure if they made it. If they didn't, the pirates are going to check the manifest and find out you're missing. They might come looking. They'll need a hostage."

"And if they do?"

"If they come down here, they're gonna find your Israeli hardware and whatever you got behind door number three over there."

"What will you do?"

"Me? Haven't got a clue. You're gonna help me figure that out."

"How can I do that, Sergeant?"

LB shouldered the big Zastava. He flicked on his own flashlight to spotlight a circle of the bare steel floor.

"Iris, sit."

"Why?"

"Because we're going to talk."

"I can't tell you anything. It's all classified."

LB firmed his tone. "Lady, do you understand what I do for a living? Everything I do is classified. I shit classified."

"Not like this."

"Sit."

Iris folded her legs onto the carpet of light. With less grace, LB settled beside her. He laid the Zastava across his lap. While he spoke, he kept one ear trained into the darkness. If he could find Iris, the pirates could.

"Listen to me. I just looked at a few billion dollars' worth of Israeli surveillance gear that I'm told is headed to Beirut. That makes no sense. I'm going to look under the tarp of that last railcar there, and I'm pretty sure that's going to make no sense either. I find you standing in the middle of it all. I need to know what's going on, and you're gonna tell me."

"Why should I do that?"

LB kept a rein on his voice, though he wanted to shout.

"Because it's all been hijacked."

Still, his volume made echoes, a chorus to tell him to quiet down. Barking at Iris wouldn't help.

"Look at me. I'm a soldier. My country's involved in this somehow. I need to know what I should do here. I'm operating way outside my orders. I have to decide whether or not to defend these railcars or just save my own ass and yours. So give it to me quick. And make it easy to understand." LB pointed. "What's under that tarp?"

"I'm sorry. That information is secret."

"I'm looking at it, so it ain't a secret anymore."

Iris mulled this over too long. LB rose off the deck.

"Fine."

He strode away from her voice calling for him to stop. Iris did not follow, which was smart.

LB cut a long slash in the tarp to make the point that he was aggravated. He stuffed his upper body in with the flashlight, blocked by the solid side of a wooden crate. He played the light over the labels spray-painted there in Cyrillic. This cargo wasn't Israeli, but Russian.

He pulled himself farther inside the tarp, hopped up to climb above the wall, and sliced more tarp to give himself room. Outside the stuffy confines, Iris had come alongside to shout for him to stop. She would tell him what was inside. LB ignored her, figuring he'd have a stronger chance of getting the truth out of Iris if he saw firsthand what was inside.

With one more long zip of the blade through the roof of the tarp, he clambered over the side, to balance on a wooden cross-beam. Beneath his boots, packed tight, padded by foam, lay what looked like a thirty-foot-long engine block.

The thing was rectangular, gray steel, four feet high by three feet wide. The sides were solid plate, but the top featured twin rows of fist-size black bolts clamping it down like the head on a motor, maybe a hundred of them.

"Come down." Iris hit him with her flashlight beam while he stood to consider what he was looking at. He kept his place above the machine.

The thing was bound to have a military application, judging by the drones and radar that accompanied it. It was long, straight, and seriously held together.

"It's a gun," he guessed.

"Yes." Iris Cherlina cast her beam to the deck to light the way for him to climb down. "It's a gun. Now get off it."

LB eased down from the crate. He sat on the deck, setting his back against the railroad wheels to face the dark expanse of the hold. He patted the floor for Iris to join him; she folded neatly down, laying her flashlight inside the ring of her crossed legs so she glowed as if beside a campfire. LB rested the Zastava across his knees.

"Tell me. Plain terms. What is that? And who are you?"

Iris Cherlina lifted both palms. LB was no scientist, and she seemed unclear where to begin.

LB had little patience for her hesitation. "Just start."

"All right. I'll answer the personal question first. I am, as I told you, an electrophysicist. I worked at the Molniya machine-building plant in Moscow."

"That's weapons research. Nuclear."

"Yes, it is. I am a weapons engineer. Molniya does more than nuclear."

"So what are you doing on this boat?"

"I am merely accompanying this." She tapped the back of her hand against the railcar. "I will assist in its installation. That is all. Then I really will take a position at another lab."

"And what, exactly, is this?"

"An electromagnetic launcher."

"Okay"—LB nodded—"okay. That's a railgun. I've heard of that. The navy's doing a lot of R&D on them."

"Yes, I know. Your US Navy is not alone. Nor are they in the forefront." Iris almost sniffed when she said this.

"You're about to say Russia is."

"And China. Our weapons research is not so strapped as yours with budget cuts, verification and safety issues."

"Especially that safety thing. That can be a pain in the ass."

Iris blinked. "Don't behave like a child."

"So the Russians haven't lost interest in electrophysics, like you said."

"That was a lie, Gus." She patted his arm indulgently.

Iris Cherlina continued smoothly, not slowed by her admission or his attempts at wit. "Do you know how an EML works?"

He rummaged for some insight, something to speed the conversation, but dredged up nothing.

"Go ahead."

"It's a simple concept, really. Two rails of conductive metal are laid parallel. An electric current is introduced into one. This creates a positive magnetic field around that rail. The current crosses an armature sabot, to flow down the second, negative rail. The armature is designed to slide along the rails. The opposing magnetic fields generate a Lorentz force. This repels the armature in the direction away from the power source."

LB whisked his hand into the air to imitate a launch. "That pushes out the shell."

"With immense power."

"How much?"

"That depends on the electricity applied. Your naval research lab expects that within ten years it will be able to fire a projectile over three hundred nautical miles at speeds up to Mach 8, with an accuracy of five meters. The power needed for this will be in the millions of amps. But imagine what will happen when the first nation's warship puts out to sea equipped with a railgun. It will control a diameter of six hundred miles, sit at invincible distances, and pound targets on sea and land. Troops onshore won't need to take their own artillery. This weapon will revolutionize warfare. And it gets better."

LB finally recalled something he'd heard about railguns.

"No powder."

Iris Cherlina smiled broadly, pleased.

"No explosive propellants. Railguns use only electricity. Ships will be safer. EM projectiles are more powerful. They're smaller, lighter, even cheaper. And since there's no chemical or thermal trace from firing an EM weapon, the rounds will be harder to track by an enemy."

"Will it really work as well as all that?"

"Oh, yes."

"Then what's the holdup? Why's it ten years off?"

"Because in its current form, the EM gun can only fire once. Then it has to be rebuilt."

"What happens?"

"When you run that much current through a conductive metal, a fraction of the electricity is turned into heat. The power needs of a railgun are so great, the heat generated is enough to melt the rails. Also keep in mind that the magnetic fields of the rails are opposing, so they push at each other with enormous force. Add the friction of the armature passing over them at such speeds, and you have a pitted, warped, ruined railgun after one shot. Maybe two."

"So cool the rails somehow."

"Your navy is experimenting with cryogenics, and redirecting the heat energy into the ocean. They've also played with liquid and vapor metals. They're still ten years away."

LB regarded the railcar at his back, the cut-up tarp over the bland-looking machine.

"But you Russians," he said, pointing at the crate, "you're taking it a different direction. That's what this is."

She smiled, a little ghastly in the flashlight spill but still very pretty.

"Very good. What else can you guess?"

LB brought the finger around to Iris. "Metals. That's why you're here. You're working on better metals for the rails."

"Among other things, but yes. Nanocrystalline structured composite powders of copper, titanium, and boron to improve the superconductivity of the metals. But even after we solve that, there are other obstacles. Guidance systems for the projectiles must be designed to survive the g-force loading with that kind of acceleration."

"What is it, a couple hundred Gs?"

"A couple thousand."

LB whistled.

"And the electricity required to launch a projectile at such distances and speeds is immense. Miniaturizing the power source is a huge challenge in making an EML deployable. Right now, the generators are the size of a car. And a wall of them is needed. So at the moment, only naval ships and static installations are possible."

LB stood to stretch his legs. He walked away from the glow rising from the circle of Iris's crossed legs, to gaze off into the blackness of the cargo hold.

"Lady, everything you just told me I can get off the Internet. That's not classified."

"That's as far as I can go."

"What about the drones? The radar?"

She dismissed the other railcars with a flick of her wrist. "I know nothing about them. I've never even looked under the tarpaulins."

He walked another step away from her light. "You're gonna have to do better." LB spoke into the darkness, implying he might just keep walking. "Where's it all going?"

"That's the real secret, Sergeant."

LB spun to stamp back to Iris Cherlina.

"You see this blood on my shoulders? One guy's already taken a bullet for that secret. He didn't know where this stuff was going either. But I'm not Bojan—it's not my job to defend these machines. Mine is to defend my country. I got a suspicion the US is involved here somehow. But until I know for sure, I'm not sticking my neck out for somebody else's undercover deal. Tell me who's getting all this crap, or I go worry about myself and you're on your own." LB had bent at the waist to speak. He straightened to glare down at her. "Try me."

"You won't like the answer."

"Big surprise there."

Iris Cherlina steepled fingertips under her chin, considering. After moments, she clapped once and decided.

"Did you know Mahmoud Ahmadinejad was once the head of Iran's electromagnetic research program?" She gazed up at him. "Close your mouth, Sergeant. You're gaping."

LB clamped his teeth before speaking. "Iran?"

"Yes. He's actually an engineer. He wants this machine very badly."

"You're not ten years away, are you?"

"No. I am not."

LB sat back down beside her. "Holy shit."

Iris laid a hand on his knee while LB came to grips with sending this kind of technology to Iran under the table.

She asked, "You've heard of the Stuxnet worm?"

"Yeah. Sure."

Stuxnet was a computer cybermissile developed by Israel and the United States in 2009 that knocked out almost a fifth of the centrifuges, almost a thousand of them, at Iran's Natanz uranium enrichment facility.

Iris continued. "There have also been assassinations of nuclear physicists in Tehran, and so on. Iran has finally realized they will never be allowed to develop a nuclear device. Israel and the West will prevent it. So Iran has accepted a deal."

"Whose deal?"

"Who else but your United States could drag along Israel and Russia into such a thing? They have persuaded Iran to trade in their nuclear weapons program for the contents of this ship. Iran has entered the EML sweepstakes to see who can develop and deploy a railgun first."

"They're going conventional. That explains the radar and drones."

"Yes, it would seem. In return, an announcement will be made later this year that the embargoes on Iran have been lifted. It's bare-knuckle politics at its best, really."

It all made sense. The whole reason Iran was trying for a nuke was to get a seat at the table, show the world they were someone to be reckoned with. But Iran was never going to be allowed to have a nuclear weapon, period. Letting them in on the race for a railgun in trade for standing down their nuclear research? That was clever. Iran could puff out their chests on the Arab street, and the West and Israel would breathe easier for a while with a non-nuclear Iran. They'd find a way to beat them out of this deal later, when the time came.

Even though it added up, the whole trade was just kicking the can down the road. If somehow Iran actually developed the first deployable railgun, what country in the Middle East could stand up to them? No one. LB bit back his aggravation that, in the revolutionized warfare of the future, America's warriors would likely be on the front lines again, sorting all this out.

For now, his duty was clear, if unsavory. Protect these machines. The United States was driving this deal, and though it was supposed to be a secret, now that he knew, he had no choice. LB took a long exhale to stay collected.

"So you're going to Tehran."

"Yes."

"Okay. We got two problems. One, there's pirates on board. Two, someone else knows about your toys. Whoever it is slowed the ship on purpose to get it hijacked."

Iris drew back in surprise. "You're saying the accident was sabotage?"

"Yep."

She continued to shake her head, disbelieving. "Impossible. No one in the crew knows what is down here."

"Yeah, well, obviously you're wrong. It's someone who knows how this ship works, and has a stake in the pirates taking it."

"How do you know this?"

"The chief engineer figured it out. But that's for later. Right now I gotta go topside."

"Why?"

"To make a call."

"I'm coming with you."

LB shook this off. "Stay. You can hide better down here. I can move faster."

He struck up the beam to his flashlight.

Iris Cherlina moved into the sallow light around LB. She lapped a hand on his arm.

"I don't want to be down here in the dark. I need some fresh air. And I'm frightened. I'm safer with you. Please let me come."

"All right, only up to the deck. But be quiet. Can you do that much?"

"Watch me."

"I have been. Did you tell me everything?"

"Most of it. Enough for you to make up your mind, yes?"

"Yeah. Maybe later. You're buying the beers. It'll be expensive."

"I can afford it."

"You'll need to. Let's go."

Chapter 17

—·—

11 Degrees North
Camp Lemonnier
Djibouti

Wally tossed his second dart, sticking in the triple 17. Dow threw up his hands.

Eleven Degrees North was packed tonight. Any time a northerly breeze slipped across the gulf, the Djiboutian heat and humidity eased, the mosquitoes were blown inland, and Camp Lemonnier's rec facility got busy. Outside on the wide patio, marines, sailors, airmen, soldiers, and DoD contractors sipped, smoked, chatted, and watched *The Blob* on the big projection screen. On the airstrip just beyond the wire fence, a night-flying HC-130 rumbled in the cool evening, doing a pretakeoff run-up. Inside the former French legion hangar that now held the bar, TVs showed delayed sports and the nonstop military channel. Wally lined up his next toss, aiming for the bull.

Though Wally'd missed by an inch, Dow reacted as if the dart had hit him in the eye. Wally was too far ahead. The lanky staff sergeant had been the last PJ to arrive for this rotation at Lemonnier, showing up at noon today after a TDY climbing Kilimanjaro. Dow was the third youngest in the unit after Robey and Jamie, but looked older than Doc. He claimed he'd gone prematurely gray because he'd had LB at Superman School. Dow was the best Ping-Pong and darts player in the squad, but he'd been on a plane all day and was off his game against Wally.

Before stepping forward to tote his score on the chalkboard, Wally lifted his beer for a swig.

A large hand stopped him.

"Captain. How many beers have you had tonight?"

Wally turned to the blocky MP sergeant, who kept a solid grip on his forearm. Another of equal size and bearing stood close behind. Both men's chests looked wide enough to project the movie on.

Wally lowered the bottle.

"This is my first." He aimed his chin at Dow. "He's about to lose and buy me my second. I'm not on alert."

"Sir, we need you to come with us. Pronto."

"Time for me to finish beating him?"

"We've got a cart outside."

Dow asked, "What about me?"

The MP said, "You can walk." He turned, expecting Wally to get moving.

Dow headed to pay the tab. "I'll see you at the Barn."

Wally fell in behind the pair of MPs, the crowd making way as the sergeants strode straight for the door. Wally made their manner his own, striding with purpose past a hundred men and women in all the services who gaped at his hurried, escorted exit from 11 Degrees North. Wally slid on his sunglasses.

———

The MPs drove Wally through the camp at a speed that would have gotten anyone else in trouble. They conducted him to the door of the JOC, held it open, saluted, and stayed behind.

Torres did not greet Wally alone this time. Seated at the table were base commander Colonel McElroy and Air Force CO Colonel Flinger. On the wall, the Falcon View monitors were centered on the same freighter as this morning, the *Valnea*. The ship's direction was way off, bearing not to Bab-al-Mandeb but southeast for Somalia. An American warship shadowed the freighter.

Wally had a sinking feeling even before McElroy and Flinger rose from their chairs. The two officers stood long enough to shake his hand and say only, "Wally." Torres motioned him to a seat at the head of the table. A file folder and a cell phone rested in front of his place.

McElroy stabbed a finger at Torres. "Sit rep, Major."

Torres indicated the Falcon View monitors. "Forty-five minutes ago at twenty-ten hours, the Maritime Op Center and CTF 151 received a distress signal from the freighter *CMA CGN Valnea*. The ship was under attack by pirates. The pirates have since taken control and turned the *Valnea* south for the Somali coast. We believe the destination is Qandala, a pirate stronghold. An American frigate, the *Nicholas*, is in the area. Ship CO Captain Goldberg has had direct contact with the pirates. Thirty minutes ago, the pirate chief Yusuf Raage called for an evac of the two wounded sailors we responded to this morning. Goldberg and a marine arrived on-site in a Zodiac. In front of Goldberg, Raage had one hostage executed. Raage claims the hostage shot one of his men during the hijacking. Goldberg is convinced he'll shoot more if we move against the ship."

Wally pushed aside everything Torres had said except for the killing of the hostage.

"LB's on the *Valnea*."

Colonel McElroy spoke. "We know. We've had no contact from Sergeant DiNardo. We can't confirm whether he's still on board."

Wally would not believe LB was dead. Simple as that. "He is, sir. I've known him a long time. He's still at large."

"I hope you're right, but until we hear otherwise, we're assuming he's not. We'll keep our fingers crossed, but we're on a short leash here. Major, continue."

Torres touched Wally's wrist. The gesture was hopeful and fleet, before she became the PRCC again.

"For reasons that will remain classified, the *Valnea* is not a ship the United States government will allow to stay in the pirates' hands."

"Who's going to take it down?"

Colonel Flinger, Wally's CO, reached across the table to push the cell phone directly in front of Wally. "Pick that up and dial oh-three-one-oh."

"Sir, what are you saying?"

"I'm saying pick up the phone and dial."

Together the three officers folded their hands to lean back in their seats.

Wally dialed. The phone did not ring. A voice, deep in timbre, commanding in the first syllables, answered.

"Hello, Captain Bloom."

"Sir."

"This is General Madson. You know who I am."

Wally stiffened his spine. "Yes, sir." This was the four-star CO of AFRICOM.

"I might have a job for you. I don't like it. You won't like it."

"Hoo-ya, sir."

Madson made a quiet, approving huff.

"I assume by now you know the raw facts."

"Yes, sir."

"I can't tell you what's on that ship. I will share with you that the president has been very clear with me. He will not allow the *Valnea* to be anchored off the coast of Somalia. Reporters from every Arab news service are not going to crawl over it. There's secrets on that ship that will stay secret."

"I understand, sir."

"Good. We have limited options here. I can't find a special-ops unit anywhere in your theater that can spin up in the time frame we're dealing with. This ship is seven hours from the

Somali coast. The president has given me less than that. SEALs, Delta, Special Forces—none of them can do it."

In his own head, Wally sped through the inventory of options. SEAL teams were based in Norfolk and San Diego, both on the other side of the world. An SF group sat on alert in Stuttgart, an eight-hour flight away. Some SEAL, Delta, and SF teams might be close enough in Afghanistan or Iraq, but they were all deployed and engaged. No way they could be pulled off the line, briefed, and transported in time to take down a moving, hijacked freighter in the Gulf of Aden before dawn.

"Sir, what about Mossad? Spetsnaz?"

"Same problem. No one's close enough."

"You've got the *Nicholas* on-site. Why not send in a marine team?"

"I've thought about that. They're my second choice for two reasons. First, I can't come up with a way to maintain surprise. These pirates know they're being watched. They'll see a Zodiac or a chopper coming. I don't want a big shootout. I want a surgical strike. A black op. Second, the fewer people who know about what we're doing, the better. *Nicholas* has a couple hundred crewmen on board. That's too many eyes on. I want no press, no medals, no letters to Mom and sweethearts. So I need you to do something for me."

"Yes, sir."

"Your unit is sitting alert with planes and choppers on the tarmac two hours from the target. I know you PJs can move fast. I need you to convince me I can send a Guardian Angel unit to capture that freighter back from the pirates. So sell me."

Madson wanted to send the Eighty-Second ERQS on a combat mission! To recapture a mammoth moving freighter in the dark, four hundred miles away, hijacked by an unknown number of Somalis holding thirty hostages, in under seven hours.

Torres and the two colonels gazed at Wally with a mix of admiration and sympathy, as if he were unfortunate somehow.

They'd given up on LB. They seemed about to do the same to him.

Wally opened the file folder. The first pages were a series of satellite infrared close-ups of the ship under way, taken eleven minutes ago. The first showed the green signatures of reflected light off four pirates staked openly on the bow, and at least ten more along the port and starboard rails, partially hidden. In the next, one man each guarded the port and starboard wings beside the pilothouse, looking over the vast cargo deck. The next image displayed one pirate and possibly another at the stern. The last page was a detailed schematic of the *Valnea* with all her dimensions.

On the Falcon View, the freighter steamed toward land with *Nicholas* riding five miles off her beam. What did she carry that was so important? Wally attended the question only a moment, then set it aside for the mission. The brass wanted to send PJs on a strictly combat op. They weren't designed for that.

Wally knew his men, knew himself. He imagined the jump, the assault, planned it in his head before speaking.

"General, we can do this."

"Go on."

"We save lives, yes sir. But every man on my team is a highly trained combatant. Sergeant Quincy was a SEAL, Doc Holliday came over from the marines. Sergeant Dow's a weapons specialist. Mouse Turner's done two tours in Iraq with LRP squads." Wally almost mentioned LB's formidable background but stopped. "We've got every skill this job needs, sir. And we can fight."

Madson listened, mumbling, "Mmm-hmm." When Wally finished, the general said, "You left yourself out. A pretty good Ranger officer. A good man to follow out of an airplane, I hear."

"Yes, sir."

"What about the rest of your team?"

"Everyone in my unit will do whatever you order. We'll do it to the best of our abilities, and we won't fail. Breaking it down one man at a time is not what we're about, sir. No disrespect."

"None taken. Good answer. Still not enough. Tell me why you won't fail, Captain Bloom."

"Because one of my men is on board the *Valnea*. Sir."

"I know. First Sergeant Gus DiNardo."

"Yes, sir."

"He still alive? Your folks haven't heard from him."

"No doubt, sir."

"He's that good?"

"Better, sir."

"Friend of yours?"

"Yes, sir."

Silence dangled while Madson considered Wally's answers. Electronic warbles in the background marked the line as scrambled and secure.

"All right, Captain. You've got the job."

"Thank you, sir."

"Don't thank me yet. You got four hours."

"Sir?"

"The leaders of four countries do not want that ship anywhere near the Somali coast, under any circumstances. It will not be allowed to get within thirty miles. The Russians and the Israelis in particular have been exceedingly clear in expressing this to the president. That means in four hours and one minute, I am going to order the *Valnea* destroyed unless you have control of her. We won't be delegating this to the Israelis or anyone. This is our operation. You understand?"

"Yes, sir."

"I have a Reaper locked and loaded en route. The drone will be over the target by oh–two hundred hours. The president and I are well aware of the consequences. There are twenty-seven civilians on board. You and your team may be, also. If it has to be done, we'll do it while she's still in deep water and out of sight of land. We will clear the area of the USS *Nicholas* and simply blame the pirates for the sinking."

Wally almost lowered the phone from his ear.

Madson prodded. "Captain?"

"Yes, sir."

"You will share this information only with your team. Got it?"

"Yes, sir."

"I suggest you come up with an exit strategy. In case. Have a way off that ship."

"I hear you, sir."

"There's more. Only for your team's ears."

"Yes, sir."

"I cannot describe this as a hostage situation." The general paused. "I'll be plain. Freeing the ship's crew is a secondary objective. Your primary directive is to liberate that ship from the pirates. In four hours."

Madson allowed another gap, longer than the first. Wally listened to him breathe. The general cleared his throat, and continued.

"I don't know how many others can live this time, son. We'll see. You still want the job?"

"Yes, sir. Sergeant DiNardo's still on board."

"That remains a good answer."

"Yes, sir."

"You're a brave soldier. I'll make sure people know that."

"Thank you, sir."

"No curiosity about the cargo, Captain. Look the other way, if you can. Once you're on board, do not disable the ship to gain more time. We don't want it towed to some port for repairs; we don't want it on the news or on anybody's radar. Understood?"

"Yes, sir."

"After you gain control, you're to stay in place until relieved. We'll send helmsmen over from the naval escort. Now, I got one more order. This one's for your ears only. Repeat, your ears only."

Wally turned from the Falcon View to the officers at the table, eyeing him. He flattened his voice to imply nothing with his response.

"Yes, sir. I understand."

"The president does not like the idea of a Somali pirate taking his ship. This was supposed to be a quiet little piece of diplomacy, under the radar. Now it's a cluster fuck. The president has looked into the dossier of this pirate chief Yusuf Raage. He has determined this is a dangerous man. A sadistic man, who may have al-Qaeda contacts. I am authorized to order you to terminate Yusuf Raage, with prejudice. Understood?"

"Affirmative, sir."

"Questions?"

"No, sir."

"All right. Good luck. I'm going to say a prayer for you. I will look forward to shaking your hand."

"My whole team, sir."

"Hell, we'll have a party. Hoo-ya, Captain."

"Yes, sir."

Wally set down the cell phone. Torres, McElroy, and Flinger all cocked their heads, inquisitive.

Wally pointed at the pad and pen in front of Torres. "Major, may I?"

He scribbled while he spoke.

"I need a complete schematic of the *Valnea*. Copies of those photos. All the intel you've got on the pirates, strength, arms, whatever Goldberg saw. Weather forecast for the flight route and over the target fifty miles out. Have two planes ready, one rigged for a RAMZ drop, the other for a HALO."

Wally planted the pen in the middle of the pad. He skidded them back to Torres. He stood too fast for the others to rise with him.

"I'll brief my team in ten. I want to be loaded in twenty. In the air in thirty."

Torres said, "I'm on it."

Colonel McElroy raised a palm. "Slow down, Captain."

"Sir?"

"I don't like being in the dark. Brief us first."

Wally slid the cell phone over to the camp CO.

"No disrespect, sir. Dial oh-three-ten. I've got my orders." Wally stayed in place only long enough to smile at Torres. "Dinner when I get back."

Chapter 18

CMA CGN *Valnea*
Gulf of Aden

Drozdov sat with his officers and the Filipinos beneath the long windshield of the darkened wheelhouse. Yusuf came for him, asking that he take the captain's chair.

"Please," Yusuf said.

"*Spasiba*. No. I will sit with crew." Since Yusuf had come aboard twenty minutes ago, the Russian, already thin and angular, had grown more pallid. Duskiness deepened his eye sockets.

"But you are the captain."

Drozdov mimed spitting on the floor. "And you are murderer."

Suleiman was on the ship's deck, putting guards in place. Guleed, younger and more hot-tempered, took a stride forward behind his Kalashnikov.

Yusuf said, "Then, with that in mind, please come to your chair."

A chubby, whispering officer prevailed on Drozdov to rise from the floor. The Filipino crewmen approved with nods that he retake his place while they sat herded and hostage in front of Yusuf's guns. Drozdov stood, and Yusuf ushered him around the wide dash to the leather chairs.

The two sat side by side. The bridge remained gloomily lit to preserve night vision, the only radiance coming from the gauges and radar screens. The ship coursed darkly across the gulf, save for red and green running lights fore and aft, and a white steaming light atop the bow mast. Amber glows off the dash made Drozdov appear even more cadaverous.

From the copilot seat, Yusuf surveyed the ship's instruments. Compass heading 110° SE, engine turning rpms at twelve knots. The radar showed the *Valnea* with her naval escort *Nicholas* holding off the port beam. Eighty miles of empty sea stretched ahead to the Somali coast.

"Captain."

"What?"

"I want to ask you for *waawaan*. A truce."

"Not possible."

Yusuf leaned into the space between the pilots' chairs. He lowered his voice.

"I was not born into a violent world. I had parents who taught me stories and poems. I'm sure you understand, Africa is a changeable land. In the last twenty years, Somalia has changed more than others. We have seen civil war. We've been invaded by foreigners, driven them off, and fell again into civil war. We are torn apart. Little men have become lords of little lands. The greed of greater nations has made us beggars. Some of us cannot beg, so we chose instead to become thieves. I have no course but this, Captain. I cannot choose what I do, only how. I do not wish for more violence, but you must know it is a tool at my command. I want your cooperation to be willing. But I will force it."

Drozdov listened without looking at Yusuf, fixing his gaze forward into the night.

"Yes, I know begging."

"Do you."

Drozdov nodded, solemn.

"Three years ago, I am captain of MV *Stanislaus*. Crew of twenty-two. Malta to Mombasa, five thousand containers, famine relief. We carry nothing but food for starving people. Somali skiffs came at dawn, rockets and guns. They took half hour to get on board, not so good as you. We were taken to Somali coast, to Eyl."

Drozdov swung his head heavily, sadly, to Yusuf.

"We anchored there eight months. Pirates and shipping company, insurance, negotiators, all bosses, played games with ransom. The crew, we wait on *Stanislaus* with hunger, illness"— Drozdov tapped a finger into his temple—"a boredom that could kill a man. And the Somalis? Our hosts? They chewed *qaat* and slaughtered animals, entertained themselves by pretending executions of the crew. They said to me your company will not pay. We must convince them. A dozen times, I am put on my knees with gun to my head." Drozdov set his finger to the middle of his forehead, crooking the thumb to mimic a pistol. "Click. The last few times I begged them to put a bullet in the fucking thing. I could not stand another day. Then, surprise. I had to stand one more day. For eight months."

Yusuf leaned onto his elbow, closer, eye to eye with Drozdov. "What kind of dogs do you have in Russia, that you can beat them for years and they will not bite you? We do not have those dogs in Somalia."

"You have lost, Yusuf Raage? Yes? *Eto mnye do huya.* I have lost! Three years, I lose my family, job, my health. And never did the begging stop. I had to beg for this damn ship."

Folding his arms as if closing a door, Drozdov sat back.

Yusuf leaned away, returning the span between them. He'd known of the *Stanislaus*. The pirates were Abgaal of the Hawiya clan from the south. The eight-month negotiation in Eyl showed that they were poorly organized; to Yusuf's knowledge, that crew took no more ships. Yusuf believed Drozdov's story, if for no other reason than the ruin of the man sitting beside him in the captain's chair.

"Yes," he said mildly to ease the temper of their talk, "this damn ship. In seven hours, you will be anchoring again, Captain, this time off the coast of my village, Qandala. You have my word the ransom will be arranged quickly. Under my orders you and your crew will be treated as *misafir*, guests, so long as your own conduct warrants. I promise you also I will not blink to execute you or anyone who challenges me. I will not apologize for the pirates of the *Stanislaus*. As you say, they were not as good as me."

Drozdov glowered, silent and set against Yusuf. The dim wheelhouse was hushed, marked only by the drone of the engine and the hostages shifting beneath the windshield. Guleed paced their length.

"I want to confide something in you," Yusuf said. The captain shot him a glance, keeping himself upright. "If you'd been going twenty-four knots, we might not have been able to board you without a fight. You should know I did not sabotage this ship. I had nothing to do with it."

Drozdov's head snapped around. "This is true?"

"Yes, Captain. I wish I could take credit; it would have been a brilliant move to have someone on board working for me. But I am not so clever." Yusuf aimed an accusing finger at the sitting seamen but locked his eyes on Drozdov. "One of them is responsible. One of your crew wanted me on this ship."

Yusuf pushed out of the copilot's chair.

"I do not like being manipulated. You do not like being betrayed and hijacked. In this, we have a common interest. Stand up, Captain."

Drozdov got to his feet. Silently, he moved around the dash to stand in front of his men. All of them had heard Yusuf's words. On the floor, the Filipinos looked to each other, to find someone among them with an explanation. The officers shook heads

190

THE DEVIL'S WATERS

at their wrathful captain glaring down on them; they all denied guilt.

Behind him, Yusuf said, "Let's find out who is working against us. For this, again, I ask a truce."

"*Da.*"

"Cousin." Guleed stepped up. "Watch them."

"Where are you going?"

"The captain and I are off to see why this damn ship is so important."

Drozdov tried with his stare to burn a confession from the crew. Yusuf turned him away.

"We are going to have a look belowdecks."

Chapter 19

Camp Lemonnier
Djibouti

Wally charged through the Barn, beneath the tall shelf where Doc and LB lived.

"Everybody!" He jogged into the common area where the entire PJ team was assembled. "Briefing room. Now."

All nine filed into the small room used for briefings and movies. Wally shut the door. Quickly the team spread onto the two tiers of beat-up sofas and leather chairs. Wally stayed in front.

"We got a mission. Set alert thirty."

Dow said, "Whoa," at the thirty-minute notice. Jamie whistled. Every man hardened his posture in his seat.

"One hour ago, Somali pirates hijacked a freighter out in the gulf. The ship is the *CMA CGN Valnea*."

On the back row, Jamie's feet shot under him. He gripped the arms of his chair. Wally motioned for him to stay down.

"That's right, it's the same ship LB and Jamie boarded this morning. LB's still there. That hasn't been confirmed, but we all know him, and we know he's pissed off. The freighter's carrying some kind of highly classified cargo. The bottom line is, these pirates have taken the wrong ship. I've just come back from the JOC. I spoke with very high brass on the phone. We've been given the order to take the *Valnea* back before she reaches the Somali coast."

Dow asked, "They're sending a PJ team? Where are the SEALs?"

"We got the job for two reasons. First, there's a tight window on this one. We're sitting alert four hundred miles from the target. There's no combat-capable team in range but us. We can get there faster than SEALs, Special Forces, anyone else. Second, one of our own is on that ship."

The team stirred. Each looked at another, bonds of training and action asserting themselves. They showed each other balled fists. We'll do this. You, and you, and you, and me.

"Yep." Wally addressed this to Robey. "LB needs rescuing."

He explained the situation. The pirates were lethal, that much was known. There'd already been one acknowledged killing. He made no mention of the concern that the victim might have been LB. He gave the location, speed, and direction of the freighter, one hundred miles from the Somali coast. A US warship was tracking her. The number of pirates on board was still indeterminate, but they could expect at least twenty armed targets, likely more.

Doc asked, "What about the crew?"

"Hostage."

"How many?"

"Twenty-seven. That includes a couple guards and one passenger."

"Passenger? Who gets on a freighter as a passenger?"

"Don't know. It's odd."

"Where're they being held?"

"Don't know that either."

"Got to have that."

Wally tapped the knuckles of one hand into the palm of the other. Unease filtered among the team. Most of them knew Wally well enough to notice anytime he pulled up short.

Big Quincy asked, "Now's not the time to dance, Captain. What's up?"

"This is where it gets tough."

Mouse said, "Okay."

"Our orders are to regain control of the ship."

"And?"

"According to the orders, freeing the hostages is a secondary objective."

Jamie spoke first above the buzz in the room. "That's dicked up."

"I know."

"They're civilians."

"They are."

"The brass don't care if they die? What the hell?"

"They care. Just not as much as they do about the ship."

Doc asked, "What about LB?"

"Settle, everyone. I don't know. We'll do everything we can to find him and limit casualties. But the orders are clear. There's something on that ship that can't be left in pirate hands, pure and simple. Our priority is taking the Somalis down. Retake the ship. At all cost."

Dow piped up. "At all cost. I hate that fucking phrase. You notice nobody going on the mission ever says it?"

In the front row, without turning, Robey said, "Wally's going."

Wally stopped the dialogue. "We'll brief on the plane. Wheels up in twenty-five. We'll go in two teams. Team One, with me, will assault the ship. This'll be a HALO jump. Eighteen thousand feet. Open at three thousand. Team Two will drop with the RAMZ at five thousand to an LZ two miles downwind. Anybody on Team One who misses the ship, Team Two picks them up. Pack extra rounds. Weapons suppressed. Lighten your med rucks."

Doc shook his head. "I'm taking all of mine." Jamie, Mouse, and another PJ, Fitz, agreed.

Wally backed off. "All right. But we stow 'em at the LZ. This is close quarters."

"Roger."

"The target's a cargo ship moving twelve knots at night. The freighter's under guard. The LZ is a wing to the left of the pilothouse. We won't have a lot of room. Who's had anything to drink?"

Wally lifted his own hand first. Doc, Robey, Mouse, and Jamie, the team on alert tonight, did not lift theirs. The rest put hands in the air.

"Who's had two or more?"

All hands went down.

"I need straight answers."

Fitz and the only PJ on the team as big as Quincy, a Tex-Mex named Sandoval, stuck their hands back up.

"How many?"

"Three."

Fitz and Sandoval were well inside their tolerances, but not for combat.

"You're both on Team Two. Man the RAMZ with Robey. Coffee before you kit up."

The pair said, "Roger."

Robey stood, a muscular kid.

"Let me go with Team One."

"No. I need CQB experience."

"I can do it."

"And you will. But not tonight. Sit down."

"Sir."

"I don't have time, Lieutenant. You've got your team and your orders. Sit down."

Robey took his chair, reining himself in.

Doc asked, "Why HALO? It's a tough jump to be opening low. Let's go HAHO, get some more time to line it up. It's a moving target."

"We don't have forty minutes to spend under canopy. That's the next thing I have to tell you."

Quincy muttered, "Uh-oh."

Wally pointed to the big PJ. "That's about right. We got three and a half hours from wheels up. With a two-and-a-half-hour flight, that leaves a sixty-minute window for us to take the ship down." Wally consulted his watch. "That's oh-two-ten hours. That means we move fast, every step of the way."

Jamie asked, "What happens at oh-two-ten?"

Wally removed everything from his voice but the words.

"The United States government is going to sink the *Valnea*. There's an armed Predator en route."

On the chairs and sofa, every head jerked.

"Sink it? With us on it?"

"If they have to. Yeah."

"The hostages, everybody?"

"It's got to be before the ship gets in view of land. No witnesses. Deep water. They'll claim the pirates blew it up."

The team grew quiet. Their excitement for the mission changed. It didn't disappear but turned inward, where each man reminded himself privately of his pledge to serve as called upon.

"If it gets to that, jump overboard. Robey will pick you up."

Quincy asked, "You gonna jump overboard? Leave the hostages with the pirates?"

"No."

"Then don't fucking bring it up. Sir."

Doc snapped, "Quincy."

Wally waved it away. "It's okay. Anything I missed?"

The elder PJ wiped a hand over his crown. "What the hell is on that ship?"

"Don't know."

Doc rose. "I'll bet LB knows," he said to the team. "Let's go ask him."

Wally opened the door. "On the tarmac in ten."

The Barn became a hive. Loadmasters drove in a forklift to snatch a RAMZ package and haul it to the flight line. Doc, team leader in LB's absence, stormed among the lockers, checking every man's preparation. In shouts he repeated Wally's orders for suppression tubes on all weapons, extra mags, counted down the minutes until wheels up. Robey's team changed out of their cams into wetsuit shorties and dive gear. Doc tugged straps, checked gauges, weapons, packs. He growled at the men to do this now, do that later on the plane, move it.

"Everyone! Remember to take whistles, buzz saws, strobes, extra water. The LZ is a moving goddamn ship in the middle of the night! We'll inspect chutes on the plane. Quincy, grab an extra."

Doc visited each locker with a smudge can to grease up every face.

Wally geared up. He clamped the suppressor tube to the barrel of his M4, checked the charge on his radios and night-vision goggles. He stuffed four extra ammo magazines into his backpack, made sure he had all water survival items. Doc stopped last at Wally's locker to black his face.

When Doc finished smearing the grease, Wally reached for his helmet.

"Get the men together."

"Roger."

Wally took a moment before stepping away from his locker. Putting a pen to the notepad he kept handy, he wrote a fast note to his mother and father in Nevada, another to his sister in San Francisco, and lastly an apology to Major Torres for being late to dinner. He set his Air Force Academy ring on top of the pages. He shut the locker door.

The team waited for him in a semicircle. Wally stepped to the center. Over a dozen years, in the minutes before a hundred missions, he'd never said these words. He swallowed once to make sure he didn't choke them back.

"Before we head out, each man go to your locker. Leave behind something your families will want from you. A note, wedding ring, picture, you figure it out. Take two minutes. Go."

Turning away, Dow made the team's only comment. He breathed, "Holy shit."

Wally stood alone with Mouse in the suddenly quiet Barn.

"What about the cheerleader?"

Mouse grinned. "She knows."

Wally let a few seconds pass.

"You really have a—"

"Yeah, I do. With the Oakland Raiders. Jesus, Wally. You think this is a good time?"

From his locker, Doc said, "Shut up, both of you."

Mouse mimicked an annoyed swing of a Ping-Pong paddle, mouthing how he was going to kick Wally's ass when they got back.

Chapter 20

CMA CGN Valnea
Gulf of Aden

Yusuf left the wheelhouse with Drozdov, unarmed save for a flashlight and the onyx-handled blade tucked in the waistband under his *khameez*. They walked onto the wing past Suleiman's gunman. The young guard started when they emerged, as if he'd been drowsy. Yusuf wondered if it might have been a mistake stopping the pirates from chewing *qaat*. The leaf would keep them awake. Dawn and Somalia were still six and a half hours away.

In starlight he led the Russian down the six metal staircases. Yusuf strode in front to prevent Drozdov from surprising any of Suleiman's guards. He didn't worry about the captain behind him; this man would do nothing heroic.

Reaching the deck, they walked the starboard rail. Yusuf was again taken by the size of the ship. Yusuf and Drozdov approached one guard, then another forty meters later, in the long and narrow companionway. Neither pirate heard them coming out of the dark. Both were caught gazing out to sea, weapons across their backs, elbows on the rail. The first snapped to a foolish, eager attention at Yusuf's arrival. Clattering, he brought the RPG across his belly. Yusuf led Drozdov on. The second, a younger one, turned a slow glance to Yusuf's advance. The boy slouched closer to the rail to make room for Yusuf and the Russian to get by.

Two-handed, Yusuf gripped the thin Darood by the tunic, lifting him out of one sandal. Yusuf bent the boy backward across the rail. The pirate's white eyes flitted from Yusuf's nose to the foaming wake three stories below.

"Stay awake," Yusuf growled in Somali. "Watch the water." He shook the boy, scooting him inches farther over the rail. "Or I'll give you a closer look."

Without hauling the pirate back in, Yusuf released his tunic. The boy scrabbled to gain his balance, windmilling to put his feet back on the deck.

Yusuf pivoted to the wall and the ladder. He climbed ahead of Drozdov up to the cargo deck. He'd never been on an empty freighter. While Drozdov clambered behind him, Yusuf admired the white expanse, the posts and cables to hold a thousand containers. He imagined the cranes loading and unloading this giant, the faraway places she and her crew had traveled and traded, the globe made small enough to view from such a life on board.

Yusuf Raage could never captain a vessel like this. He came from a land ruined by avarice and bloodshed, rained on them by outsiders. Yusuf wanted Drozdov, ashen under the half-light of constellations, to say he was sorry.

He said to the Russian, "Move."

Drozdov led the way now, down an aisle between lashing bridges. He halted at a hatch in the deck plates, producing a key to open the padlock. The captain lifted the hatch door. Yusuf invited him down the ladder first by shining the flashlight onto the yellow rungs.

The two descended into the empty cargo hold. Drozdov proved nimble on the ladders and catwalks of the ship's hidden interior. Yusuf directed the light mostly to guide his own steps; Drozdov seemed to know where he was going.

After six levels, they arrived at the hull's bottom. Yusuf shone the beam along the open floor.

"This way," Drozdov said. His words fled into the great chamber, echoing deeper than the light could reach. Yusuf followed toward the bow. They climbed across railings in their way like hurdles, passing beneath other tiers of catwalks. Yusuf shone the light in all directions, admiring the structure and expanse, imagining it filled with containers. Drozdov tramped in front, Yusuf strides behind. He fixed the light in the Russian's path, leaving the darkness intact on the sides.

After two more tiers of catwalks and pillars, the beam fell on two ranks of nine railroad cars stretching the width of the hull. In the first row, the loads were irregularly shaped; the rest were large rectangles. All had been strapped down and covered by tarpaulins.

Yusuf led Drozdov closer. Quickly, his flashlight beam found a slit in the tarp of the first railcar. Someone had been here before them, probing under the covers. Slits were cut in every one. Who would have done this?

The two peered inside the loads. The cargo was all military hardware, aircraft and technology, marked as Israeli-made.

With his head beside Yusuf's inside the last tarp, examining the ghostly wings of an oddly shaped aircraft, Drozdov mused.

"All these Israeli machines. Picked up in a corner of Russia, going to Lebanon. Why? And someone on my ship trying to stop it. Why?"

The riddles did not unravel for Yusuf any more than they did for Drozdov.

The saboteur knew the answers.

And Sheikh Robow. There was little chance the sheikh's interest in hijacking these machines was only ransom. He must have known what the cargo was. Did he want this equipment for his own cause? Or was his purpose deeper?

"They are not going to Lebanon anymore, Captain. They are going to Somalia."

The two withdrew their heads from the tarpaulin.

"This is illegal shipment," Drozdov muttered. "Super secrets, armed guards, Iris Cherlina. Someone wrecked my ship. Fuck. This is big monkey business. I knew it."

"Cherlina. Is that the passenger?"

"I don't know what she is. *Oslayob*, I cannot believe I am captain of this ship."

Yusuf stepped behind the flashlight, headed for the bow to see if any more cargo waited belowdecks. "I can't believe I took it."

They passed through another six-story tier of pillars and platforms. Yusuf quit imagining the vast hold packed with containers. He filled the void now only with himself, Drozdov, and whatever mysteries were down here with them.

Climbing over a railing, Yusuf walked into the open floor of another empty bay. Drozdov closed beside him, pointing.

"There is final tier. Beyond that is last bay, then bow."

Shuffling across the empty floor, Yusuf cast the beam past the vertical structures ahead. On the other side, at the farthest reaches of the light, squatted one more long railroad car, loaded and masked by a tarp. Yusuf slowed. Drozdov bumped into him from behind.

They crossed the floor cautiously. Yusuf held the flashlight at arm's length. Drozdov stayed to his rear, a hand on Yusuf's back. Approaching the last tier, Yusuf halted before clambering over the rail into the final cargo bay. He cast the beam through the opening.

Twenty meters ahead, the light played over one more railcar, isolated here in the bow. Yusuf lifted himself over the rail, keeping the beam on this tarpaulin as he approached. The covering had been shredded more than the others.

Drozdov, never taking his hand from Yusuf's back, followed.

"Someone is very curious," Yusuf said. He whirled with the flashlight, casting past Drozdov. The jumble of steel in the hold gave up little, only more shadows.

Yusuf slid the onyx-handled knife from under his *khameez*. Drozdov spoke from behind.

Drozdov asked, "You could not bring a gun?"

"It seemed unnecessary."

The Russian made a spitting noise. "Very confident."

Yusuf drifted the light across Drozdov's face. The captain's features were as hard as his ship, no sign of fear. Yusuf considered turning around to come back with more than this knife, with a few extra men.

"Come," the captain said. "I suspect that one is big secret."

Yusuf followed the light forward. Drozdov moved to his shoulder, side by side.

The cargo strapped to this final railcar was a mystery. Yusuf hoisted himself up inside the cut-up tarp to climb over a crate wall painted with Cyrillic characters. Inside, the flashlight showed him nothing he could recognize, just a long block of steel plates bolted together. It could be anything.

Yusuf put his head outside one of the slices made by another's knife. "Captain."

"Yes."

"Read the side of the crate."

Drozdov inserted his head into the slit. Yusuf leaned the flashlight over the edge to light the wall for him.

"It is Molniya machine plant. In Moscow."

"Do you know it?"

"No. Move over."

Drozdov shimmied under the tarp to climb beside Yusuf over the unnamed device.

"*Zdayus.* What is it?"

Yusuf cared less about what the machine was than who'd made these cuts to look at it before him. What did Sheikh Robow want with it?

The thing was ugly. Yusuf leaned down to lay a hand on it. The machine felt terrible under his fingers, like a bone from the last man on earth. Suleiman would surely sense it to be a bad sign.

Chapter 21

Four stories below, a large Somali approached behind a flashlight beam. He'd spotted the last railroad car bearing the railgun. LB followed him down the open sight of the Zastava. At the pirate's side walked Drozdov.

LB and Iris had been lucky. They'd been on the parapet, climbing up to the open night to make LB's call, when they caught the first glimmer of the pirate's approaching light. But that luck was fleeting, and seemed to have run out already. The Somalis had Drozdov. That was very bad news. It meant the pirates had at least one hostage, maybe more. Perhaps Bojan and the wounded. What if the rest of the crew had never made it to the engine room and were now captive? This development was going to make an already dangerous rescue even more dicey for whoever was on their way to shoot it out with the pirates.

Drozdov and the pirate examined the railgun together. They made note of the slashes LB had cut in the tarp, and the pirate whirled with his flashlight to check the dark hold behind him, spooked that someone else had been there. The pirate and Drozdov held a hushed conversation LB couldn't make out for the distance and echoes. They looked like a team.

LB had an ugly thought. Was Drozdov actually the saboteur? Was he the one working with the pirates?

The Russian certainly had no love for this ship. His life was in shambles, and hijacking was a high-stakes game; this multibillion-dollar cargo could make him rich if they got away with it. And Drozdov had been hijacked before. Had he been recruited then to partner up with the Somalis?

That was all difficult to believe. Drozdov seemed to be passionate about his damaged career, fiercely loyal to his crew. Even under the drink and bad luck that weighed him down, he appeared a decent, strong man. But Drozdov certainly had the knowledge to do damage to the engine; Chief Razvan suspected everyone. It was hard to ignore the sight of the Russian captain calmly exploring the railgun with the big pirate. Was Drozdov under threat? Or was he just one more bad guy in a world full of them? More quandaries for later.

In the dark, on the catwalk beside him, Iris Cherlina nudged LB. She whispered, "Shoot the pirate."

LB shook his head. Iris elbowed him. It made no sense to shoot the Somali. If LB hit him, what would happen down here when other pirates came looking for him and Drozdov—an Alamo by flashlights? If LB missed and the pirate got away, his own presence on the ship would be blown.

Besides, Iris Cherlina had no idea how hard it was to shoot a man in the back. If she could imagine it and it didn't bother her, that was scary.

Drozdov and the pirate crawled up inside the tarp, examined the gun, then walked off. LB wondered if Drozdov and the Somali even knew what the thing was, were aware what it could do, and that it was headed to Iran.

LB and Iris watched Drozdov's and the pirate's voices and flashlight cross the open bay, then under the tier where they knelt. The two men worked their way far forward, to the ladders they'd climbed down. Iris and LB stayed motionless in utter blackness, to stir no sound in the cargo hold.

Hearing the clang of a closing cargo hatch, LB waited to let them clear the deck above.

After five silent minutes, he struck up his own flashlight.

"Stay close. Don't make a move I don't tell you to make."

Asking Iris to lead him to the ladder where she'd entered the hold, he cut the flashlight and climbed. He lifted the heavy cover only inches, to scan the cargo deck. Seeing no lights or Somalis, he clambered out. Before Iris could follow, LB opened a palm, warning her to stay belowdecks.

He bent low behind the cover of the lashing bridges fore and aft. To the stern, Drozdov and the pirate walked behind their flashlight. At the top of the superstructure, the broad windshield of the bridge remained opaque.

LB tugged the satellite antenna from his vest. Hollow rods telescoped into two tiers of umbrellalike branches, plugged into his sat-comm radio at the base. He put on the headset, then leveled the small compass latched to his vest. In the thin light, he found his azimuth, 110 degrees.

Aiming the antenna southwest over the stern port quarter, he tilted the rods to the stars at his best guess of 55 degrees above the horizon, where his satellite ought to be, and pushed the PTT button on his vest.

"Hallmark ops. Hallmark ops. Lima Bravo. Over."

He repeated the call twice, switching the antenna's direction each time to a different star, before his headset rustled.

"Lima Bravo, Hallmark ops. Been waiting to hear from you."

"Roger that, Hallmark. I've been busy."

"Hang on for Major Torres."

In the seconds before the PRCC came on the line, Iris poked her head up from the open hatch. She asked, "Why do you call them Hallmark?"

"When you care to send the very best."

In his ear, "Lima Bravo, PRCC here."

"Major, Lima Bravo."

"Good to hear from you. We were worried."

"You were right."

"What's your status?"

"My status is, I'm hijacked."

"Are you safe?"

"For now. That can change."

"We're aware of the pirates on board. *Valnea*'s distress signal reached us an hour ago. What intel can you give me?"

"Estimate twenty to twenty-four targets. All armed with AKs. Plenty of RPGs on board, too. Be advised the pirates have at least one hostage, the captain. Probably more."

"LB, they've got the whole crew. There's a US warship nearby, the *Nicholas*. The CO saw them execute a hostage in exchange for one of the pirates being shot. We thought it might have been you."

Bojan.

"He was a Serb guard."

"All right. Are you armed?"

"Affirmative."

"Do you know the location of the hostages?"

"Negative."

"What other intel can you provide?"

LB kept his mouth shut about the drones and Iris's science project.

"Nothing else."

Torres paused, likely conferring with others in the JOC.

"Recommend you stay secure."

"Until when?"

The PRCC paused again.

"Repeat, Sergeant. Recommend you stay secure."

"And I repeat, Major. Till when?"

A second voice on the line cut in.

"Break break."

Torres said, "Go ahead, Juggler."

"Until I come get your ass."

LB almost dropped the antenna in surprise. He had to lift it before the connection was broken.

"Wally?"

"Affirmative."

"Where are you?"

"We're on our way."

"We?"

"The team."

LB couldn't believe this. Not Spetsnaz, Mossad, SEALs, SF, but his own pararescue unit had been handed the ship takedown. How the hell did that happen?

It didn't matter. His PJ team was flying to rescue him. Never, ever, would he live this down. His own boys were coming for him. He stood with the mike to his lips, stymied.

"Will explain later," Wally continued. "Can you recon? I want exact number and location of targets."

LB gathered his wits to respond. "Major? You want me secure, or you want me recon?"

Torres reentered. "It's Juggler's mission."

Wally said, "Recon."

"Roger."

"Still got your team radio?"

"Affirmative."

"ETA your position oh-one-ten hours. Copy?"

LB checked his watch. Just over ninety minutes.

"Roger."

Wally said, "PRCC, recommend we continue as fragged."

Torres answered. "Agree. Press mission. Will monitor this freq. You boys chat. Good luck. Out."

Iris Cherlina stood at the top of the ladder, listening. LB glanced around the cargo deck to be sure he'd stayed unheard and unseen. Starlight glanced off the white steel field and tall lashing bridges. Forward, the running light on its mast cast a pallid sheet over the bow. LB expected a quarter moon soon after midnight.

"Juggler."

"Yeah."

"Thanks for not giving me any grief over this."

"That comes later."

"I figured. Look, I'm in a dicey spot right now. So be quick. What's the plan?"

"Two jump teams. One HALO assault, six-man. One RAMZ, three-man."

"Where's your LZ?"

"RAMZ will be two miles behind the ship downwind. Assault team on the port wing, next to the bridge. Backstop team on the starboard wing. Take control of the wheelhouse and defend. Hunt down the pirates. Secure the ship."

"Sounds tough."

"You got a better idea, now's a good time."

"I'll get back to you after I look around."

"Can you do it? There's a lot of pirates on board."

"You remember all those times in South America? When you were still at the academy?"

"Yeah."

"What did you think I was doing in the fucking jungle?"

"Roger."

"Juggler."

"Yeah."

"What about the hostages?"

LB waited. He hardened his gaze at the star far beyond the reach of the antenna, as if speaking to Wally behind his sunglasses.

"Why didn't you ask me to recon the hostages?"

"Need to know, LB."

"What does that mean?"

"Get me the intel. Be careful. Juggler out."

The line went cold. LB held the antenna in place for more seconds before folding it away.

"Go down," he told Iris.

"Why?"

"I've got a job to do."

"Is someone coming?"

"Yeah. My unit. They're coming to get me. It's humiliating."

"How is that possible?"

"I'm supposed to be the rescuer. I'll take some shit over this."

"But you're not from an assault unit. You said you were pararescue."

"We do what we have to."

Iris Cherlina seemed troubled. "I didn't know."

"Most people don't. Anyway, don't worry. The boys are good. A lot of combat vets on the team. We'll be okay."

"When will they get here?"

"About an hour after midnight." He handed her his spare flashlight. "You stay down there. You hear or see anything that's not me, you go dark and find someplace to hide. I'll be back in under an hour."

"What was that about the hostages?"

"Dunno. Something's up. I don't like it, but it's not my call. We'll know soon enough. Go on."

Iris Cherlina reached a hand out of the hatch to pat his boot. "Don't leave me down here long."

"Don't be scared. Go." He grabbed for the hatch cover to lower it in place. Iris stopped him.

"Wait."

"What?"

"That's odd."

"What is?"

"Look. The padlock is gone."

"Was it there when you came down?"

"Of course. I always leave it next to the hatch so I can lock behind me."

"Drozdov and the pirate. They know where you come and go now."

"I suppose that's right."

"Great. Hide, Iris. Go."

LB pushed on the top of her head. He lowered the hatch, spun the watertight wheel.

He rose only to a crouch, staying out of sight.

Chapter 22

Yusuf climbed the last rung. He aimed the flashlight behind him to light Drozdov's way. The Russian clambered up on deck, then locked the hatch cover. Yusuf kept the light aimed downward. Drozdov's features, already sagging and pale, seemed even more sapped.

"Captain, I am ignorant of those machines. What do they mean to you?"

"For a pirate and a bastard, you are not an ignorant man, Yusuf Raage."

"My patience is already thin. Do not strain it. Tell me what we saw."

Drozdov laughed quietly. Perhaps he recalled pushing the patience of his previous captors. Yusuf's threats meant little to this sad man. That might have to change.

Drozdov removed his cap to run a hand over his cropped white hair.

"The first railcars, those were nothing. Radar, drone aircraft. *Pff.* Israeli and top of the line, maybe. But nothing big weapons buyers cannot get and sell. That's why Vladivostok. Those are Russian black market. Untraced."

"What about the last car?"

"Yes. That one is bad."

"How bad?"

"It is technology I do not know. It looks simple, but that only means it cannot be. My guess is that it is a weapon of the future. If so, it means the future was going to Lebanon. Now it is going to Somalia. Either one, I do not like."

Drozdov waited while Yusuf weighed this. Without question, Robow had known what was on this ship. With lies he'd sent Yusuf here to the center of a web. Yusuf was snared in it. He sensed the spider coming. If Yusuf lived to the morning, Robow's price for acquiring this ship would be much higher than he'd predicted. Perhaps his life.

"I believe we are someone's pawns, Captain, you and me."

Drozdov turned his head to again make the sound of his empty spit.

"Then we believe the same." The Russian pointed to the open dark sea. "They are on their way. You will not be allowed to keep this ship. You know that."

"Yes."

"Then why don't you go? Get in your skiffs."

"Because the moment we leave, I have no doubt the American warship has orders to shoot us out of the water. If we take hostages with us, we'll be boarded and arrested as murderers. No. We are trapped here with you, Captain. Until we reach Somalia or we die. Together."

"Again, I don't like either one." Drozdov extended a hand. "For now, give me the flashlight. Let's see if we can find some answers, eh?"

Yusuf handed over the light.

It did not take long to walk the alleys between the tall lashing bridges, beneath the towering midship and forward cranes. Drozdov kept the flashlight beam to the deck as if on a scent, searching for his own sign of the saboteur.

Drozdov was right. They would not be allowed to keep the *Valnea* easily. The rest of their crawl back through the gulf to the coast was going to be more dangerous than Yusuf could have guessed. Yusuf would not tell his pirates what he'd seen below; that would serve no purpose but to spook his men. He'd tell only Suleiman, his lieutenant.

Drozdov stopped at every hatch cover to shine the light on the padlocks that secured them. Four times he rattled the locks, testing their hold. At the fifth hatch, the padlock lay beside the hatch cover. He put this lock in his pocket.

Yusuf followed him aft, to check the rest of the hatches. They found no more opened locks.

Drozdov handed the light back to Yusuf. "Now I know."

Yusuf led the way off the cargo deck, down the ladder to the narrow companionway. Yusuf moved in front, again to prevent the captain from startling one of Suleiman's gunners along the rail. Down the long steely hall, through the dark hum of the ship, Drozdov simmered.

They took the elevator up from A deck to F. Drozdov passed Yusuf on the flight of stairs leading to the wheelhouse. The captain shoved the door open. Yusuf trailed him into the bridge. Suleiman, Guleed, and four gunners with Kalashnikovs at their hips spun at Drozdov's hurried entry. Yusuf came quickly behind, motioning them not to be alarmed.

Drozdov's crew sat where they'd been left, herded beneath the windshield. He faced them.

He held high a key out of his pocket.

"All of you. Show me your master key."

The Filipinos and officers dug into their trousers. They held their keys aloft to match Drozdov's. All except one, the pudgy Russian.

Drozdov tossed this one the opened lock.

"Grisha." The captain said this sadly, like a verdict.

The officer got off the floor. Guleed's gun tracked him approaching Yusuf and Drozdov.

The officer said, "May we speak in private?"

Drozdov led this Russian out of the wheelhouse, to the port wing. Yusuf followed close behind.

Outside, a warm headwind riffled past. Drozdov turned on his officer. The chubby man retreated until his back came up against the rail. Drozdov closed in.

"This is why you recommend me for *Valnea*. To make a fool of me."

"No, Anatoly."

"Yes. To destroy me."

"No."

"*Sooka*, yes! This pirate, he has knife, big knife. He is not happy to be here, trust me. I will let him ask questions if you do not answer me. *Da*?"

"*Da*."

"Good. Who has your key? Iris Cherlina?"

The chubby officer bobbed his head.

Drozdov spat at her name, this time for real. "You are loadmaster. Do you know what she has brought on this boat?"

"Israeli radar, drones. Electronics."

"Yes."

Drozdov snatched the flashlight again from Yusuf. He struck his officer across the face with the butt of it.

"What else? A weapon?"

Grisha raised his hands in defense, not to be struck again. The mark of the first blow marred his cheek.

"I don't know any weapon. Only radar. Drones."

Drozdov yelled through the mate's cringing hands, "What is it? Where is it going? And who is this *shalava* Iris Cherlina?"

Grisha lowered his hands only enough to answer over them. "In Vladivostok, we load nineteen railcars. The pier is deserted, police clear everybody out but me and her."

"So it was you running the crane that night."

"Yes, Anatoly. I did what I was ordered to do."

"Lower your hands, Grisha. You look like a coward. Stop making me sick and tell me. Or I will let the pirate give you reason to fear. What did you do?"

The mate straightened and dropped his hands, Drozdov's challenge putting some steel in his spine. Yusuf had found the man's cringing disturbing, as well.

"All the cars were covered in tarps. Iris Cherlina comes, she has papers from company, from government. There is no manifest. She is scientist, she tells me she is going with the cargo to Beirut, she is in charge. Okay. She tells me load those eighteen together. One she wanted separate in the bow. I don't ask. I don't look under the tarps."

Yusuf leaned his own girth in on the frightened Russian.

"Why didn't you ask?"

"She said they are electronics. No word of guns. Why would I ask more?"

"Yes," Drozdov snapped. "Why wouldn't you ask? Why does she have your master key? What is Iris Cherlina to you?"

"Nothing. I swear, nothing. She paid me."

"Ahh, there we are. Paid you to be a traitor. How much?"

"Anatoly, I have a family."

Drozdov roared back. "I have a family! How much?"

"Fifty thousand dollars. For a key. To run a crane for thirty minutes."

Yusuf inserted a hand between the Russians to ease Drozdov back. He asked, "How much did she pay you to sabotage this ship?"

Grisha was slow to answer. Yusuf made as if to reach at his back under the *khameez*.

"Two hundred thousand dollars. But she was the one to pull fuse. I only showed her how. She could not see piston row from the fuse box. She did not know engineer and cadet were inspecting. I asked her. She is sorry."

Drozdov's hands flew up. "Sorry? She is sorry for almost killing two of my crew? *Blyad*."

Yusuf leaned in. "Did she slow the ship to bring me on board?"

"Yes."

"Why?"

Yusuf's asking was not enough. Drozdov lunged past his restraining arm to grab his officer by the lapels. Drozdov shrieked in the sailor's face, his eyes bulging with rage.

"Why?"

Grisha blinked; his lips groped for words.

Drozdov released the mate with a shove against the rail. Suleiman's gunner, standing at the end of the wing, watched with casual interest, weapon strapped and not ready. The night wind gusted, then backed down.

"She is patriot," Grisha said, mustering a tone almost proud.

Yusuf laughed in shock. "A what?"

"*Da*. The Israeli machines, they are top secret, paid for by America and Russia. Iris Cherlina says after Beirut, they are going overland to Tehran."

Yusuf found this impossible. "Israel would never allow that. Iran will use them against Israel."

The mate shrugged, accepting that he knew only his part of a much larger tale. "Some kind of big trade. Under the table with Iran. This is all she told me, I swear. Iris Cherlina is big scientist in Russia. She does not want these machines going to Iran. Who would? That is crazy for the world. She said we will slow ship in the Gulf of Aden. Pirates will come. They will hijack and tell the world what shit is going on. Everything will be exposed. Pirates will do it all. She will be safe."

Drozdov growled, "So for money, you became patriot, too."

Grisha plainly wanted to say yes to this, but could not for the pain on his captain's face.

So much made sense to Yusuf now. The bloody hand of Iran was mingled with those of Israel, America, and Russia in all this. These were the games rich nations played, and the back of a fist for the rest of the world. Guns, secrets, immense sums of money and power. You schemed with them, shared in the plunder and lies, or you were made like Somalia. Like Yusuf, Drozdov, and their men. Pawns.

There wasn't a chance Robow was going to let Yusuf ransom this ship back. No, if the Sunni Islamists got their hands on it, they were going to wield this ship like a sword to cut at their enemies. A shame. To keep this cargo quiet, to sell it back to America, Israel, and Russia with no fanfare, the ransom would truly have been astronomical.

Behind Yusuf's restraining arm, Drozdov continued to berate his mate. "For money, you turn your back on your crew, your captain." Drozdov's voice crumbled with each item he listed of Grisha's treacheries. "You almost kill Nikita and cadet. You bring me on *Valnea* to think I am returned to respectable captain. You bring pirates on my ship. Now we go to Somalia. When we are done there as prisoners, you are rich man. I am lost again."

"Captain," Yusuf said, "I gave you my word."

"You are pirate. Bojan died on your word."

Drozdov, bent by betrayal, turned away. He shambled across the dark wing to the bridge.

"Captain?"

Drozdov stopped at Yusuf's voice. "*Da.*"

"Give me your master key. I may want to go look for this Iris Cherlina."

Yusuf took the key. Drozdov went into the bridge. Yusuf remained behind with the fat officer. He drew the knife from under his *khameez*.

"I'm not as angry as your captain. I understand what a man will do for money." Yusuf rolled the knife in his fingers to let the Russian see the red-crusted edge. "I've done hard things for money. Also for an ideal. I don't care which describes you. I don't care if you knew about the weapon. I want to know one more thing."

Grisha fixed on the blade rotating inches from his nose. "Yes."

"An Islamist came to my house to make a deal with me. He wanted me to take this ship. This particular ship. How did Iris Cherlina do this?"

"She is scientist. Brilliant woman."

"I see that."

The Russian spoke eagerly, as if he were part of an accomplishment.

"The Chechens. They are in Vladivostok; they have Mafia. It was simple thing to contact them. Pay them to pass the word to Somalis. She says, hey, *Valnea* takes big illegal shipment to Iran. A science fiction gun? I don't know. But Israeli electronics? A secret cargo to Iran, bought by Russia and America? The Chechens, they do not love Israel, Iran, Russia, America. A shipment like this, hijacked? The embarrassment to those countries? Come on, Mr. Pirate. This is easy. For Iris Cherlina, it was child's play."

Child's play was that woman lying to this fat, greedy sailor. But something more, something murky, lay beneath the surface. Yusuf looked forward to meeting this scientist and prying the truth out of her personally.

"And she was willing to be hijacked to stop it?"

"Strong woman."

"That *qumayo* will need to be. And you, my friend. You are Russian. You would do this to your own land?"

"I am poor Russian. That is different land."

"So you were willing to be hijacked and bring your entire crew along. For money."

"Yes."

"Believe me, I understand what a poor man will do."

Yusuf set the point of the knife beneath Grisha's chin. He tilted the officer's head backward, making him stare down his own cheeks out of scared eyes.

"You will ransom yourself. You will pay me two hundred and fifty thousand dollars."

Yusuf lifted the tip, putting the officer on tiptoes. A crimson drop ran down the blade.

"Go back inside and sit with the men you've deceived. I will let you go for money. I don't know what they will ask."

Yusuf lowered the dagger. The officer staggered to the wheelhouse.

Suleiman came out of the bridge. Yusuf sent the guard inside. He would speak with his cousin privately.

"The captain," Suleiman said, "has found his traitor. What did you find?"

Yusuf explained what Grisha had revealed about the passenger Iris Cherlina. Her bribe, the Chechens and Islamists, the intrigues between Iran and the other nations, the drone aircraft and electronics deep in the cargo hold. The strange machine, perhaps a cannon, alone in the forward cargo bay.

Suleiman sucked his gold teeth. "We should find this woman." He nodded to himself, a private image perhaps of questioning Iris Cherlina.

"I want to speak with her too, cousin. But nothing she'll tell us will change in the next five hours. Let her hide. Right now, we need everyone on guard." Yusuf lapped a hand over his cousin's thin shoulder. "I fear this night."

Suleiman nodded. "We have their balls. I suppose they will want them back." He turned to go back to the wheelhouse. "We'll kill a goat in Qandala."

Yusuf stayed outside with the stars, admiring the velvet depth of the dark. He gazed south for land and east for the sun. Both lay long hours away. He would trade all the money he had for both right now.

Chapter 23

———

On board HC-130 Broadway 1
6,000 feet above the Gulf of Aden

The team cheered LB's call with fist pumps. Just as important as his survival, they all liked their chances better now with him at large under the pirates' noses. LB was—Wally could describe him only one way—LB.

Wally propped a whiteboard across his lap. He drew a bad facsimile of a cargo ship, resembling a spearhead. He made stick figures for pirates.

Around him in the rumbling bay of the HC-130, Doc put the team through a final op check. Communications were tested, weapons function okayed. He dug into fanny packs and rucks for flotation devices, 228 mm lights, tourniquets, med supplies, flashlights, night-vision goggles. Doc pounded on body armor and counted ammo magazines. The target was ninety minutes out.

Doc shot Wally a thumbs-up. Wally gathered and seated the team. He pulled off his headset to shout the briefing, trusting his own voice more than the team intercom to be sure every word was heard.

He began with the dimensions of the freighter. Two hundred meters long, thirty meters wide. Nine meters in height from the waterline to the rail, twenty-seven meters from the top of the superstructure to the surface. Her max speed was twelve knots because of a busted piston.

He handed out the brochure photos of the *Valnea*.

"She's got no containers on deck. Lots of room for the targets to spread out, but expect them to be along these corridors, here at the stern, on the bow, and flanking the bridge. LB's going to get us better intel on number and location of the guards."

Jamie shouted, "Any info on the hostages?"

Wally answered quickly, to be definitive. "No."

The team nodded unhappily.

"Listen up. We are not on a CSAR op. This is search and destroy. I want clarity on this. We'll do what we can for the hostages. But we'll follow orders, and we'll get home. Any questions, ask them now." No mouths opened. "All right."

He continued into the mission brief. Weather over the target remained clear. Seas one foot, water temperature 75°F. Winds at sea level seven knots southwest.

The HC-130 would go black sixty minutes out. Zero hour approximately 0110. Chutes on at zero minus thirty. The stack would be Wally at the bottom, then big Quincy, Jamie, Dow, Mouse, and Doc as team leader. Fifteen-second intervals between them on landing.

Wally propped the whiteboard on his knees for the team to see. He set a finger on the port wing beside the pilothouse.

"This is our LZ. It's thirty feet long, ten feet wide. Nine stories above the water, and it's moving at twelve knots."

Quincy carped, "That's a shit Z."

The team chuckled. That broke some ice.

"Anyone who misses the ship will get picked up by Robey. He and his team will be in the water with the RAMZ five minutes before we jump."

Doc called out, "At least his team'll be there. Can't speak for Robey."

Quincy barked, "All the more reason to hit the shit Z, guys."

Wally didn't laugh with the team. The LT was green, and this was a tough first mission. Wally had more hope than confidence in the young CRO.

Doc leaned forward to stab a finger at the port wing, on the stick figure there.

"That a guard?"

"Yes."

"That a problem?"

"I'm at the bottom of the stack. I'll secure the LZ."

"How?"

"I'll kick him in the head."

Doc settled back. "Oh."

Mouse raised a hand. He shouted, "I missed that. Did you just say you're gonna kick him in the head?"

Wally drew a small circle on the whiteboard. He tossed the panel on the deck between him and the team.

"To be a member of the jump team at the academy, you had to cover a three-inch dot with your boot ten times in a row." He planted one heel over the circle. "To run the team, you had to do it twenty times. I ran it. I'll kick him in the head."

He plucked the board off the deck. "The moon won't be up when we land, so it'll be plenty dark. If we're lucky, we'll be on station before anyone inside the bridge spots us. Quincy, when you get down, help the others behind you. There's gonna be wind on that wing. Dow and Jamie, the moment you're out of your containers, you take defensive positions here and here. As soon as we're all down, Dow, you lead Mouse by this catwalk"—Wally trailed a finger behind the bridge, along a platform running beneath the smokestack—"around to the starboard wing. You're the backstop. Doc, Jamie, and Quincy stay with me on the port wing. We're the assault team."

Doc, Jamie, and Quincy knocked fists. Mouse and Dow did the same.

"When everyone's in position, on my signal, we move on the bridge. If the doors are locked, we shoot out the windows on my mark and unlock them. Dow and Quincy throw flashbangs, then we enter. Doc heads for the exit in the rear of the bridge, behind the chart room. Cut off retreat to the stairs. Dow and Mouse handle any targets who head for the starboard wing. Pirate strength inside the bridge is unknown. We'll wait on LB for that. We don't know who else might be inside, so take down only armed and identified targets. When you do, shoot to kill."

Once control of the bridge was established, the team would take up defensive positions to hold it. Wally would pull back on the throttle and stop the ship's progress toward the Somali coast.

"That should keep the Reaper off our backs."

Next, two teams would fan out over the ship to locate and free the hostages, then mop up pirate resistance. Once the ship was secure, Wally would radio the trailing warship *Nicholas*. A pilot would be sent over to turn the freighter around and guide it to Djibouti.

Jamie asked, "If any pirates surrender, can we take prisoners?"

"Yes."

Every PJ looked relieved. Wally made no mention, per his orders, of his lone task to eliminate the pirate chieftain Yusuf Raage, whether he surrendered or not.

"That's it. Rest up." Wally checked his watch. "Zero minus eighty."

Chapter 24

CMA CGN Valnea
Gulf of Aden

Short-legged and thick, LB was not built for scrambling in tight places. The rows of lashing bridges across the cargo deck made for great cover if he stood still, but he couldn't.

After clambering over and through the first two sets of gates and cables, LB paused to gather himself. He remembered what it was like to be younger and leaner, when he could have slung himself over this landscape, leaped and landed, leaped again. There was a time he was so quick that even if he was spotted, no one would believe they'd seen a man, not just a trick of the eye.

He squatted in an alley between two lashing bridges, at the base of the forward crane, stuck with a beat-up, squat forty-two-year-old soldier's body. If he continued to stumble over the obstacles every twenty feet on the cargo deck, he'd be a sitting duck for anyone watching from the bridge, even in starlight. His camos and clumsiness would mark him against the white-painted field.

If he was going to get a count of the pirates, their weapons and positions, no other way presented itself. He'd need to take a closer look. If possible, without compromising himself, he wanted a peek, too, at the location and condition of the hostages.

Why had Wally skipped over the hostages? What did he mean, "need to know"? LB didn't like where that pointed. He was out of the loop, but accepted that was how it should be. If the pirates captured him, it'd be best if he didn't know the whole plan.

Twenty years in the military; this was his first time on the wrong side of the PJ equation. Being the one waiting for the cavalry, on the ground, on the run, in danger and scared, he blessed every man on those HC-130s rushing his way, taking his peril for their own. LB hoped all those times he'd been the one blessed added up, and paid off tonight.

He slung the Zastava to his back. He didn't expect to use it; with more than an hour until Wally and the team dropped in, he stood no chance of surviving a gunfight with dozens of pirates. He tugged his pants leg out of his boot to take in hand the quietest weapon, his four-inch blade.

LB had a few things in his favor: it was the darkest part of the night, the Somalis didn't know he was here, and he knew what he was doing. With a deep and uneasy breath, he crept to port for the ladder off the cargo deck.

He approached the opening on hands and knees. Slowly, he dropped his head first, glancing both ways along the narrow steel corridor. LB would recon only one side of the ship; logic indicated the pirates would assign guards equally left and right.

Ten feet away, the outline of a single pirate shuffled toward the stern. The path to the bow looked clear. LB eased down the ladder, lay flat. When he was sure he could move, he coiled into a low crouch.

Carefully, he coaxed every corner and crooked line of the passage to hide him. He kept watch forward and aft, should the guard behind him come back his way. The Milky Way cast enough light to betray him, so he crawled in the murk beneath the rail. Far below, the wake water made enough noise to hide his small jangles and footfalls.

After forty yards, LB emerged from the companionway, stepping from under the cover of the cargo deck. He stopped to rest his legs, on fire from the long walking squat. Ahead, high on its mast, the steaming light glowed over the open bow. With many places to hide, he hurried behind a hawser meant to hold docking lines thick as his arm. Along the rail, four pirates kept watch over the broad gulf. LB slunk back into the portside companionway.

Immediately he ducked into a dark nook, kneeling behind a life raft canister. The guard he'd avoided minutes before strolled his way. LB peered from behind cover until the Somali ambled back toward the stern. Softly, careful to stay in the shadows below the rail, LB followed the pirate for thirty meters, as far as he dared, before scampering up another ladder to the cargo deck. There he waited, getting a sense of the distance this guard covered and the pace of his patrol.

Waiting a minute, LB poked his head through the ladder opening. The Somali had passed, returning to the bow. LB crept down the ladder, hunched low, and made his way toward the stern, head on a swivel, until he caught sight of the next target in the passage.

Twice more, he stole up ladders to lay low on the cargo deck, keeping an eye through the opening until the pirates sauntered past. LB descended to move sternward, invisible and soundless.

Nearing the foot of the superstructure, the glowing red dot of a cigarette sent him scuttling behind the nearest cover, a metal staircase. One more Somali came his way from the corridor behind the superstructure. The pirate paid more attention to the cigarette than to his vigilance. He walked past LB to the port rail, dropping his spent butt on the deck. LB huddled in the shadows, watching through the louvers of the stairs while the pirate tried to light another in the breeze.

The Somali could not get his cigarette going. He moved away from the open wind that snuffed his matches to the cover of the superstructure. With his back only five feet from LB's hiding place, the pirate managed to light his smoke. With a deep drag, he took a seat on the stairs.

LB tightened his grip on the knife. The pirate's blouse hung loosely around him; he was thin and young, redolent of the odor of days without a bath. He enjoyed his cigarette as a luxury, a poor man's savor. LB concentrated on his own balance, the pirate's rib cage under the blowing tunic, and a heartsick prayer for him to go away.

Someone had put LB in this position—Wally and the team, too. Somebody very high up had decided that politics and schemes were bigger than the PJ oath. LB was going to have to kill, probably a lot, before he got off this ship. He made himself a promise to square that up with someone, first chance he got.

The Somali tipped back his head to finish the cigarette. When he'd drawn it down to his fingertips, he tossed the glowing nub under the steps.

The butt bounced off LB's shoulder, showered sparks, and landed out in the open.

LB came out of his crouch.

The pirate looked down.

LB surged forward. He shot his left arm between the open stairs, wrapping the pirate's waist to lock him in place. His right hand drove the knife into the Somali's back, aiming for a lung. The pirate's legs and arms heaved, he shrieked in shock. LB hauled him down harder, pulled out the knife, and rammed it again to the hilt between the pirate's ribs. In wounded panic the Somali found the last of his strength, jammed his feet and hands under him to push off the steps. The sudden move lifted LB hard into the stairs, slamming his face and chest against the metal edges. The pirate flailed to get away.

LB's grip slipped around the pirate's waist. The man pivoted, straining away from the reaching arm and blade. He twisted fast, wringing his torso from LB's grip. Still at close range with his knees on the stairs, not yet mortally wounded, he reached with shaking hands toward his dangling Kalashnikov.

With no other choice left, LB flung himself against the stairs, extending his arm as far as he could. His fingertips found the fabric of the pirate's blouse. LB grabbed, yanked the Somali off balance, chest down into the steps, and plunged the knife. The pirate lay on the Kalashnikov, unable to bring it to bear. His last gasp came in LB's face.

The man had screamed, only once but enough to alert any other pirates in earshot. LB drew out the knife. He skittered from under the steps, swinging the Zastava into his hands. He shoved his back against the superstructure to check all directions. Nothing pricked his senses. The headwind must have blown the pirate's shout backward. The stern, right over the propeller and wake, would be the noisiest spot on deck. Maybe the guards there hadn't heard their mate's killing.

LB approached the corpse splayed on the stairs. The man's heart had spilled over LB's hands. Wiping blood on his pants legs, he stood over the pirate, whose blood oozed onto the stairs, dripping where LB had hidden.

He rolled the Somali over. The dead man's features had relaxed from their last spasm on the point of LB's knife. The mouth and eyes had shut, slack and final.

He whispered, "Can't leave you here, pal. Sorry."

LB hefted the corpse across his shoulders. Keeping to the shadows between the stairs and port rail, he checked for any trace of other pirates. The way was clear. He dumped the body overboard, throwing away the Kalashnikov too. LB didn't watch the corpse and rifle tumble but stooped to hustle into the passage. He found a cranny there. No one came his way. The pirate's thin body had landed unseen in the froth three stories below; the splash it made didn't rise above the sounds of the freighter under way. Except for his blood, dark in a dark corner, he was gone.

LB crept to find three more Somalis at the stern rail. That made three targets on port, three on the stern, four on the bow; he supposed another four down the starboard rail. He checked his watch. The recon had taken forty minutes. He returned to the base of the superstructure and the steps, but could not consider going up them. He had valuable intel for the operation. Wally and the team would need to incorporate the locations of the guards on deck into their assault plan. There wasn't time to hunt for the hostages.

LB picked his way forward along the companionway, stealing as far as he guessed the dead pirate might've had as his patrol. He hoped the man's absence wouldn't be noticed for another hour. Even if it was, it would take the others a while to figure out he wasn't just off sleeping somewhere.

LB mounted a ladder to the cargo deck. With Iris's master key, he unlocked a cargo hatch and lowered himself into the utter blackness below.

Standing on the top step, he donned his headset, spreading the sat-comm antenna, found his satellite, and reported to Torres what he'd found. Fourteen Somalis, plus their locations, all with AK-47s. He estimated five or six more somewhere in the superstructure, possibly on the bridge or guarding the hostages. She asked if he knew the location of the hostages. He had nothing.

Torres inquired whether he was undetected. He told her about the pirate he'd taken down, dumping the body overboard. She mentioned her regret and commended him. LB told her to stow it, then added, "Ma'am."

He folded the antenna and closed the hatch. Behind his flashlight, he descended six levels to the bottom of the ship. Putting his boots on the hull, he worked his way forward through the maze of pillars and railings.

Walking in the buttery glow of the flashlight, LB came to the first railcars. He glanced ahead; no light came from the forward cargo bay. He called out to Iris. She answered from high on a catwalk with her own flashlight beam.

Chapter 25

Past midnight, young Guleed paced the length of the pilothouse, Kalashnikov at his hip. A pair of gunmen stood at either end of the posts he padded between. A third made coffee, while a fourth stood idly beside the long dashboard.

Yusuf in the captain's chair leaned to Suleiman in the other seat.

"Will you ask Guleed to stop that?"

"No. He's nervous. Let him walk."

"He's making me nervous."

"Sitting still makes you nervous, cousin."

Herded beneath the windshield, the sailors eyed Guleed, who menaced them with his gun at each pass. Or they slumped and slept. Sad Drozdov hunkered in the center of his crew. Yusuf had not installed him again in the captain's chair. He let the Russian pout, dealing in his own way, like Guleed, with the dragging minutes. Grisha the traitor curled alone at the end of the group. Yusuf would not bother to make this man's captivity any more miserable than the others. His shipmates would see to that.

Yusuf imagined arriving in Qandala at first light. As quickly as he could, he'd ferry a hundred armed Darood on board, pay them well, put Suleiman in charge. If this freighter ever saw Somali waters, money would be Yusuf's last concern.

He mused for a moment about how to negotiate for a ship like this, wrapped in secrets no government could openly acknowledge. Who would speak for it, who would pay? But there was going to be no ransom for the ship. Without question, Robow and his *jihadi* guns would be waiting on the beach to take control of it. Yusuf and his Darood would be handed Drozdov and his crew to hold and ransom, but the freighter and its secrets would go with Robow. Ah, well. Even the scraps from this hijacking would be sufficient, if Yusuf survived until morning to receive them.

These worries gave rise to more, like thorns under Yusuf's seat. He stood to tug on Suleiman's *khameez*.

"Walk with me."

Suleiman lowered his sandals to the deck. He shouldered his weapon.

Yusuf took Guleed aside. "We're doing no good sitting behind you. Watch them. Stay calm."

"Stop protecting me. What did you see in the cargo hold?"

"*Quruxsami*," Yusuf said. It is beautiful.

Lifting his gun and a flashlight off the control panel, Yusuf surveyed the dials and radar sweep. The *Valnea* held at twelve knots, autopilot bearing for Qandala. The seas lay open on all sides save for the American warship steady to the west. The coast waited sixty more miles south.

Yusuf stepped around the dash to stand in front of the crew and Drozdov. The captain showed him only the black top of his mussed hair. Drozdov would not lift his eyes from his crossed legs.

"I have grabbed the ears of the tiger, Captain. I cannot hold on. I cannot let go."

Drozdov lowered his chin farther—no sympathy for Yusuf's dilemma. Suleiman guided Yusuf away.

They left the bridge for the starboard wing. Suleiman's guard shifted elbows off the rail, displaying his alertness. An arid southerly breeze greeted the cousins. Yusuf tasted the red dust of Somalia. Five more hours until he set his feet on it. The first place he would walk in that dust with the sun climbing over his shoulder would be to the door of Hoodo's grandfather.

Suleiman led the way down the outside steps. Yusuf followed his cousin's Kalashnikov, poked ahead as they rounded each dark corner. At each turn, they did not know if they might see some commando or flash of gunfire.

Reaching the deck, the two stood shoulder to shoulder at the starboard rail. Across the dark water glowed the running lights of the warship. Would the raid come by sea or helicopter?

Suleiman wondered the same, because he asked, "Will we kill the hostages?"

"You're the one who reads signs. You tell me."

To choose his words, Suleiman pulled back his lips, gold teeth without sparkle. "This ship, the moment you told me, I hated it." He wrapped a hand over the steel rail, reading the pulse in it. "We are part of it. We will not choose. We will do what this ship demands."

Yusuf bent over the rail. They stood at the spot where the big guard had been shot by Guleed and tossed overboard. Yusuf pondered a bullet in the brain and the plummet. What awaited afterward? In his youth, Islam had taught Yusuf one afterlife, the Christians in England another. War in his native land had left him believing that nothing lay beyond the bullet. Wealth and piracy had caused him to stop thinking of heaven altogether. The machinations of Sheikh Robow and Iris Cherlina had brought him back around. What followed death?

Over the moonless water, Yusuf cast his thoughts to his time in England. He recalled the strong British faith, not just in themselves as a people and in their rights to justice for their living bodies but also for their souls. They built churches on every corner to give each man his chance at redemption, to repent his faults and transgressions and so enter heaven. Yusuf wished to believe in that way, that after this ship he might live correctly and be forgiven, awarded paradise. This was better than Suleiman's reading of telltales, his Somali belief in the unchangeable.

Suleiman led the way to the stern. He let his weapon dangle across his chest, did not scan the sea. For the first time since stepping on board the *Valnea*, he appeared calm, resolved.

On the stern they spent time with the guards there, three of Suleiman's best, all alert men. Below, Suleiman's skiff trailed the freighter, bounding on the white wake, still strung by rope ladders. The other two skiffs bounced alongside. Yusuf tugged on one ladder's grappling hook. He ought to snip the lines, cut all temptation to sneak away. He told the men on the stern they would get extra shares of the ransom. They bowed to him as their chief.

Suleiman raised an eyebrow and asked, "*Waad walantahay?*" Are you crazy? Suleiman asked if Deg Deg and the rest would get the same.

Yusuf answered, "Yes." He bit his tongue to stop from saying, Take it all.

Chapter 26

On board HC-130 Broadway 1
6,000 feet above the Gulf of Aden

On the whiteboard, Wally drew new stick figures. Three on the stern, four at the bow, four more along the starboard rail, three on port. Across the torso of each he marked a slash for a Kalashnikov.

Doc gathered the men. Again Wally addressed them without the team intercom.

"I just got off the horn with the PRCC. LB checked in. Here's his recon on the targets around the main deck. Everyone's got an AK."

Jamie pointed at the gap on the port rail beside the super-structure.

"No one there."

Wally tapped a fingertip on the blank space, imagining what had happened there.

"LB neutralized him. He says he wasn't seen."

The engine drone in the back of the aircraft covered any mumbles from the team. Torres hadn't relayed LB's situation, nor had she indicated she knew anything about it. LB must have been left with no choice. Wally set the board aside, put elbows on his knees, and waited.

He had no doubt that the PJs could pull off this mission. The team had all the jump and combat skills needed. A Reaper was going to blow the freighter out from under them if they didn't secure the ship fast enough—that was surely motivation. But to take life—for most of them, to return to killing after rejecting it; for Jamie and Dow, to do it for the first time—after years of training and missions, going all out to find every way to reach a threatened and isolated life, then save it. This had been Wally's chief concern. With all their bravado, these men might yet hesitate to kill.

The news that LB had done so ahead of them sent a wave through the team. Wally watched as what he hoped for happened. The men blinked, looked down and inward. Slowly, each raised his eyes to nod curtly at Wally, accepting the job laid out for them. The PJs took from LB's kill the full realization that this mission would spill blood, and it gave them the license to do so themselves.

With no more words, the unit dispersed. They spread out across the HC-130's cargo deck, lying with heads on their jump containers or rucks. Doc moved among them, talking with each, cementing their resolve.

Wally slouched in a mesh seat along the fuselage. With sixty minutes to the target, he stuffed in earplugs and shut his eyes.

What if the pirates figured out one of their men was missing on the port rail? Would they think he was off in a corner getting high on *qaat*? That he'd fallen overboard by accident? That there was an enemy on board? What would be the pirates' alert level when Wally and the PJs touched down?

Wally had no way to know any of this. Everything lay ahead. He sank back into his honed instincts. He had clear orders. Ready, trusted men around him. He needed only one more thing. The green jump light.

Chapter 27

On board CMA CGN Valnea
Gulf of Aden

Iris Cherlina lit her way down the ladders, four stories. When she arrived beside LB, she squeezed his arm.

"Did you get everything you needed?"

"Most of it."

Iris sniffed, curling her nostrils. She washed her light over LB. Brown crust discolored his nails and the creases of his right hand. Iris backed away to play the beam across his smeared camo pants and shoulders.

"More blood?"

"Don't worry about it."

"Whatever happened, I'm glad you're all right."

"Thanks."

"Is your team still coming?"

LB checked his watch. "Forty more minutes. I couldn't find the hostages."

"They could be anywhere. The mess room, rec hall, any of the offices, up on the bridge. A dozen places. You didn't have time."

All along he'd believed the bridge was the most likely spot. He would have done it that way. Guard the nerve center of the ship and the hostages at the same time. LB couldn't be sure, so did not make that suggestion when he spoke to Torres. Besides, Wally had made it clear: the hostages weren't a priority. The powers behind this ship wanted her back or sunk. They were prepared for a body count in return.

LB clicked off his flashlight. "Cut yours off. Let's sit."

Iris Cherlina did not douse her light. "I'm tired of the dark."

"We're safer in the dark."

Iris moved closer, folded her long legs near him. She flicked off her flashlight. Blackness swept in. The drumming in the ship seemed to swell.

Iris Cherlina said, "Talk to me."

"About what?"

"Your team. You almost dropped your radio when you found out they were coming to get you."

"Yeah."

"Why?"

"Okay. You're a scientist. View this like one."

LB clicked on his flashlight and handed it to her. He stood to loosen his BDU belt. Iris Cherlina followed his movements with the light and a surprised look.

"What on earth are you doing?"

LB tugged down his waistband just enough to show Iris Cherlina the pair of green footprints tattooed on his buttocks.

"I...um..." She searched for words. "I'm speechless."

LB hoisted his pants, redid his belt, and sat. He took back the flashlight to cut it off.

"It's the Jolly Green Giant's feet. Jolly, that's the nickname for a helicopter. Every PJ and CRO gets that tattoo."

"Lovely."

"You don't get it. I mean *every* PJ and CRO gets that tattoo. And there's one rule for all of us. You never, ever put yourself in a position to jeopardize another PJ. Right now, that's me. Wally's not going to let me live this down."

"But it's not your fault."

LB laughed loudly enough to make echoes. He reeled himself in. "You have no idea how little that's going to matter."

"Wally is the one I heard you call Juggler."

"I've known him a long time."

"Tell me about Wally."

"I met him fifteen years ago when he was a cadet at the academy. Kid was the best jumper at the school—he ran the student jump competition team. I was a lieutenant in the Rangers then. We were tasked to the academy one summer for a month of high-altitude jump training. Cadet First Class Wally Bloom was our instructor. Thirty, forty jumps, every one dead on. Time came to move on, but I kept thinking about how damn good he was. So I put in a request for him to jumpmaster a special-ops mission my team was making into Honduras. The commandant approved it. We jumped on O2 from eighteen thousand, stuck the LZ. I left Wally behind with a guard for a couple days. We went into the jungle, did whatever, and came back for him. We all walked out at night to a covert airfield in the bush. A blacked-out plane picked us up. We dropped him off at the academy."

"It sounds exciting."

"Yeah, Wally loved it. He wanted to do more missions, and I said sure. He missed fifteen weeks of classes. The commandant put out the word that so long as he did the work, he was excused from class. The kid read a lot of textbooks by flashlight in the back of an HC-130. He was gone so much, he got himself kicked off the jump team."

Iris elbowed LB. "No. You got him kicked off the jump team."

"Probably."

In the dark, Iris nudged closer. LB did not slide away but let the pressure of her shoulder lie against his.

"Did he join the PJs because you did?"

"Yep. Even became a Ranger like I did. With one big difference. When I decided to become a PJ, I was a captain and quit my commission. Wally wanted to stay an officer. Now he's made captain and I'm a first sergeant."

"So you compete with each other."

"Nah."

In the darkness, facing an uncertain hour racing closer, with the warmth of a woman leaning against him, LB saw little use in posturing.

"Yeah."

Iris slouched more of her weight against LB, as if in reward for his candor.

"You said there was one rule for every PJ. But that's not true. There's two rules, aren't there?"

"Yeah."

"That others may live. I saw it on your sleeve."

"Yeah."

"LB, tell me something."

"Sure."

"You said you were a captain once. You quit to become a PJ. Why did you do that? What made you change?"

In the dark, he brushed a hand over his bristle haircut.

"You don't want to know what it's like, taking a man's life. If you got anything going on at all, family, friends, job, you figure the next guy does, too. I spent a lot of years killing some bad dudes in some hard-to-reach places. At first it was simple, duty and country, you know? But after a while, I started thinking of the life I'd just stopped, the whole life. Was there a gal somewhere who hoped to change him? Was there a kid waiting for his old man to come home and play catch? It goes on and on while you're washing blood off a knife or crossing a name off a list or writing a report. I'd had enough of killing long before I quit. Then the PJs came my way."

"And you jumped to the rescue."

LB wanted to chuckle at Iris's pun but could not. In the humming dark, memories crept up on him like jackals in those many jungles. Surprising Iris, LB switched on the flashlight for no reason but to chase them off.

Chapter 28

—.—

On board HC-130 Broadway 1
12,000 feet above the Gulf of Aden

Sixty minutes from the drop, the HC-130 went black. A pair of green bulbs cast the only light over the PJs to preserve their night vision.

Thirty minutes out, Wally ordered them to don chutes. The navigator came down from the flight deck to brief him and Doc on the drop zone and his DKAV release point calculation.

Winds aloft had been measured at up to twelve thousand feet. Averages had been taken on the direction and velocity of the winds at four different altitudes, coming out to eighteen knots at 210°. The HC-130 would climb the last six thousand feet ten minutes from the target and take a final measurement. Since the LZ was a moving platform, *Valnea*'s speed and direction had been factored in, as well.

The navigator spread a map for Wally and Doc. In the emerald glow of the cargo bay, he set a finger to an X drawn over the Gulf of Aden, forty-four miles north of the Somali coast. This was where the freighter, if it did not deviate, would be when the PJs popped their canopies. Another mark a quarter mile downrange showed where the LZ would be when the jumpers landed.

The navigator ticked the release point 2,800 meters ahead of the ship, heading 215°. Doc and Wally checked his figures and agreed.

The navigator folded the map to return to the cockpit. He shook hands, shouting, "Good luck. O2 in fifteen." The plane would soon be climbing to jump altitude, where the team and flight crew would switch to oxygen.

Wally strapped into his own chute. Doc conducted his jumpmaster inspection, tugging on every container's belts and buckles, confirming the route and security of all lines. When he was done, Wally checked Doc's rig.

The team conducted a last test of their communications. Every PJ broadcast loud and clear to the others. Weapons were secured, NVGs turned on and off, helmets thumped like footballers. To maintain surprise at the LZ, the night jump would be made without chem lights. Ten minutes out, the signal came from the cockpit to switch to oxygen. The team strapped masks across their noses and mouths, twisted open their bottles. They settled in the seats along the fuselage. Staying on his feet, Wally thumbed the intercom talk button.

"Any questions?" He checked his watch. "Robey's team is under canopy."

No one wisecracked about the young LT.

Wally looked over Doc, Quincy, Dow, Mouse, Jamie, all seated along the fuselage. They were laden with weaponry as much as medicine. His gut clutched to think he was commanding a search-and-destroy op, something he'd not done in over ten years. He put hands to his hips and could figure nothing to say. These men were all professionals, capable and committed. They needed no pep talk to do the job. But what if something happened, and later he recalled how he'd stood here silent? What if there were things he should have said, and didn't?

"Let's focus, stay cool, and do what we can. One thing I know for sure. We can do a shitload."

It wasn't eloquent. It would have to do.

"Anybody want to pray, let's take a second."

Wally watched his team's eyes above their oxygen masks, glad to see everyone's lowered brows. He left them to it. The green bulbs went out, leaving the cargo bay lit only by the red ready light marking the final minutes before the jump.

"Hoo-ya."

The team belted out, "Hoo-ya!" maxing the intercom.

Behind Wally, the loadmaster punched a button. The HC-130's ramp whined, parting from the fuselage at the top. The panel descended until it leveled with the floor, opening the rear of the aircraft to the air. Wally walked closer to the edge, taking handholds against the jiggling floor and whipping wind. Beyond the lowered door, beneath the silhouette of the HC-130's tail, the night spread spangled and clear. Far below, somewhere on the water three and a half miles down, the *Valnea*'s pirates ran for home. Hiding somewhere on board, LB watched the sky.

Bathed in red, Wally gave his PJs the thumbs-up to rise and join them.

Chapter 29

On board CMA CGN Valnea
Gulf of Aden

Yusuf and Suleiman spoke to every man on the starboard rail. They handed out cigarettes and talked disparagingly of the American warship tracking them. Yusuf did not know these men well; Suleiman had been in charge of picking them. From each Yusuf collected name, village, subclan, and family. The pirates bowed to him when Suleiman shared the news of extra shares for all from the ransom.

Reaching the bow, four men gathered in the white glow of the steaming light. Yusuf leaned over the rail to look down at the bulbous bow skipping over the sea, carving the great crest that had almost thwarted them four hours ago. The frightened helmsman, the one who'd grabbed Yusuf's feet to steady him in the skiff, came forward sheepishly. Yusuf shook his hand.

"*Mahad sanid.*"

The pirate lowered his forehead to touch Yusuf's knuckles.

All four were grateful for the quiet of the night and the ease of the hijacking, though one of their original number had been shot during the boarding. While they appreciated that man's sacrifice, he was not of their village. When Suleiman mentioned the added shares, they asked if the dead pirate's family would also benefit from the bonus. Suleiman asked what they thought about it. They said no.

Yusuf kept his face to the wind. The horizon lay bare, with no trace of land. He wished, only for a moment, his destination was not dark little Qandala but Mogadishu, Jeddah, Aden, some city with lights visible from fifty miles out. He wanted a glow earlier than the sun, something to see and push for, some bit of this night finished. The freighter's bow heaved forward into blackness, toward more blackness.

Yusuf led Suleiman into the passage along the port rail. In the east, the moon had not yet risen. They stopped to talk with the pirates on guard there, each forty meters apart. Yusuf learned more names and homes. He gave out his last cigarettes.

They strode the rail to speak with the pirate stationed beside the superstructure. Halfway there, from behind, Suleiman asked, "What are you doing?"

Yusuf stopped. "Speak."

"You're nervous. I haven't seen you like this."

Yusuf wished he'd kept a last cigarette for himself. Lighting it would settle him.

"Perhaps. I don't like so much unexplained. The woman, the cargo, Robow, Iran, all of it. And I don't like waiting. If they're coming, I want them here. Let's fight."

Suleiman nodded in the dimness. The older cousin took a grip on Yusuf's arm firmly, to anchor him.

"I have little to tell you. Except this. If you are going to be frightened, do it privately."

Suleiman turned away to have Yusuf follow.

At the superstructure, no pirate stood along the port rail. A cigarette stub and matches littered the deck. Suleiman walked alone to the stern, then returned with no information about the guard who should be posted here.

"What do you think?" Yusuf asked.

Suleiman's gold teeth clenched before speaking. "This is Farah's post. I know him. I've fished with him. This is strange."

"Is he off somewhere sleeping?"

"Not this one."

The two poked around, turning up nothing. If Suleiman was wrong, if the man had wandered off, then he'd gone far from his station. Had he sneaked up on the cargo deck to curl up out of sight?

Suleiman continued to poke in the shadows. Yusuf stopped at another cigarette butt lying beside the stairs.

Was Farah the fisherman napping somewhere up the stairs, on one of the landings? Was he inside the superstructure, tucked into some crewman's cot?

Yusuf set his foot on the bottom step, to climb and search after him.

A stain, like rust, blemished the tread before Yusuf's next stride. Odd. Drozdov kept an immaculate ship.

Yusuf dipped a finger to it. The blot had dried. It was not corrosion. Rust would not drip. Yusuf backed away to peer beneath the steps.

"Come here."

Suleiman hurried over. He scratched a nail through the dark mark under the stairs, then tasted it.

"Blood."

Both took Kalashnikovs in hand. Instinctively, the way they had done as younger men, the cousins put themselves back-to-back.

Yusuf whispered, "What does this mean?"

"Quiet."

Suleiman tuned his senses to the night. Yusuf could not silence himself enough to hear or see beyond what he conjured out of the blood. An enemy was on the ship. Where? How many? When did they board? How?

"Quiet," Suleiman repeated.

Yusuf took hold of his breathing.

Over his shoulder, Suleiman muttered, "It might have been a quarrel. Among the men. Farah was a gambler."

"Who did this? Why didn't someone hear it?"

Suleiman pivoted to face Yusuf. "Listen to me carefully."

"Yes."

"I know you rely on me. And I would repay that reliance with my life. But you're making it very difficult. I am not confident right now. Do you understand? "

Yusuf pulled his eyes from his kinsman's slim face. Out to the sea, into the steel passageway left and right, the dotted dark sky, even below his feet into the hold, in every direction lay the threat of an enemy. Who had spilled this blood? A pirate, a commando? What could Yusuf do? Raise an alarm? Run around the ship shouting a warning, about what? If raiders were here, he had no idea where they were; he might run into their guns yelling the alarm. Then what could the pirates do—fight phantoms? How could the commandos have gotten on board? No one had seen a boat, helicopter, plane. If Farah had been killed over a debt, it could be dealt with better in Qandala than here and now. Above, six stories tall, the white superstructure remained silent. On top, inside the bridge, Guleed and his gunners held the hostages. Not a sound or flash had come from up there, no battle to free them. The great ship continued to plow at twelve knots toward the coast and sunrise.

What was going on?

Yusuf had one course open to him. He turned again to lay his back to Suleiman's back, and aimed his weapon into the dark.

Chapter 30

———•———

On board CMA CGN Valnea
Gulf of Aden

LB lit the face of his watch. "Oh–two hundred hours. Ten minutes."

Iris Cherlina lifted her head from his shoulder. "Are you going up?"

"Yeah."

She stood with him in the flashlight glow. After not seeing her in the dark for twenty minutes, only listening to her breathe and feeling the easy weight of her head against his ear, her long arm beside his, LB had lost track of how appealing Iris Cherlina was, and how unsettling.

She tapped fingertips, uncomfortable. "I have a question."

"Okay."

"How will they do it, do you think? The attack. Your friend."

"Wally."

"How will he do it?"

"He'll bring them in on the port wing."

Iris Cherlina screwed up her face, disbelieving. "There's not much room."

"Not much choice. They can't land on the cargo deck—too open, too many obstacles. The bow's out because of that light on the mast. They could try on top of the bridge, but there's radar arrays and the smokestack up there. Lots to get hung up on. Plus it's visible from all sides. That leaves the wings."

"Can they do it? Honestly?"

"Like I told you, Wally Bloom under a parachute is a rat; he can squeeze in anywhere. Trust me, he's scared the crap out of me more than once following him in."

"There'll be guards on the wings."

"My guys have guns, too."

Iris Cherlina covered her mouth behind both hands. "I didn't imagine this."

LB had to get climbing. He needed to be on deck, plugged into the team radio frequency and ready when Wally touched down.

"It ain't your fault. Like you said, you're a scientist. You're doing your job. The pirates brought this on themselves."

Iris Cherlina reached for his sleeve. "How long? The attack— how long will it take before your team gets control of the ship?"

LB shrugged. She slid her fingers to the back of his hand.

He said, "Don't worry. You'll be safe down here."

"How long?"

LB played the raid out in his head. Hit the LZ, stash the chutes, take assault positions, attack the bridge. Wally would have the whole team with him. With surprise on their side, if they could keep it, and some luck, that could take thirty to ninety seconds. Even after they got control of the wheelhouse, fourteen more pirates were still posted around the main deck. If the Somalis counterattacked and the bridge became a stronghold, the battle could get nasty fast. The pirates had plenty of guns and RPGs. Killing wouldn't dissuade them; they'd shown that already. Wally couldn't just sit with his back to the wall and let the pirates pummel him. He'd have to go on the offensive some- how. And what about the hostages? Still a wild card.

"I dunno," LB said. "I haven't got enough info."

"Can you guess?"

LB wanted to ease Iris Cherlina's fear. He made up an answer. "An hour ought to do it."

"Thank you. Then what?"

"Iris, you okay?"

"Please. Then what?"

"There's an American warship nearby. I suppose they'll come alongside and take over."

"How close are they?"

"Five miles."

"Good."

"Listen. You don't fret about any of this. My guys can handle it. They'll come loaded for bear. I'll be up there to help. You stay below. Same deal as before. Don't come out of hiding until you see me come back for you."

Iris smiled bravely. The wind seemed back in her sails. LB checked his watch: six minutes to zero hour.

"Go." She touched the bloodstain across his shoulder. "Be safe, Gus."

LB paused long enough to suppress the urge to do something foolish like kiss her. He swung the flashlight around, headed to the first ladder.

Chapter 31

On board HC-130 Broadway 1
18,000 feet above the Gulf of Aden

Doc, Jamie, and Mouse put their backs to the night, heels on the edge. Wally, Quincy, and Dow faced them.

The red ready light lit the team. Night vision goggles on, O2 masks up, jump containers, rucks, weapons, armor, gloves—nothing of each man was exposed in the seconds before the leap. The feel for each flowed through their hands holding one another in place on the windy open ramp.

Framed by stars, Doc nodded first. The others, Wally too, dipped helmets.

The red bulb extinguished. In Wally's hands, Doc relaxed. The green go light flicked on. Doc hopped back into nothing.

Wally dove after him.

The HC-130 bolted away. Wally and the team were flung forward by the speed of the plane, hurled into a torrent of wind. Wally spread his limbs, arching his back to control the accelerating fall.

Gaining control of his descent, he counted five electric green figures through the NVGs. The team maneuvered with precision into a wide circle, all facing inward, dropping at the same rate.

Five seconds into the jump, at 220 feet per second, the altimeter strapped to Wally's wrist passed 17,000.

From three and a quarter miles up, the fleeing freighter was easy to spot. The bow light gleamed in Wally's goggles like an emerald sparkler, and the starlit deck made the *Valnea* radiant against the darker waters.

In the plummeting circle, big Quincy fell faster, pulling ahead a few meters. Wally and the less bulky others, especially Mouse, lowered their profiles against the rushing air to keep pace. The digital readout on Wally's wrist clicked off altitude.

The assault team streaked downward in their ring formation, uniforms rippling. In fifty seconds of freefall, they plunged two miles. The cargo ship grew larger by the moment. Wally wanted to say something like, "Here we go," but no one would hear him over the radio for the roaring wind.

At four thousand feet, the men rotated away from the center to put more space between them. Executing the moves together, each waved and checked the airspace around him. Wally reached back to his container, gripped the pillow handle. Two seconds later, at three thousand feet, he and the PJs threw out their pilot chutes.

Six gray silks unraveled into the rushing air, lines played out at the fantastic rate of their descent. Jamie's chute blossomed first, plucking him up and away. A split second after, Wally's canopy filled. The whiplash snatched a gasp from his lungs, stretched his organs, tongue, every muscle downward for a heartbeat. Instantly the plummet slowed, everything snapped into place, and he floated gently down.

Wally grabbed the uncoiled toggles left and right. He found the green images of all five PJs drifting around him. He unclipped one side of the oxygen mask and shut off the oxygen bottle.

Team leader Doc called over the radio, "Sound off. PJ one up."

Mouse, second in the stack, responded, "PJ two up."

Wally answered last: "Six up."

The team guided their chutes into a vertical stack. Wally spiraled to the bottom. The rest stalled and banked until Quincy was in position above and behind Wally, then Jamie, Dow, and Mouse, Doc riding at the top.

They glided down and forward on the southwest wind. Wally's altimeter read 2,300 feet. They approached the freighter out of the west, gliding at eighteen knots. Still a mile off, the ship plowed from left to right, her phosphorescent wake glowing in the NVGs. Wally figured he had three more airborne minutes to intercept her.

He bored in straight for the starboard beam. His goggles highlighted pirates around the deck. Four spread out along the starboard rail, four at the bow, one on each of the wings. Wally had no line of sight on the stern or port rail. There'd be another three Somalis guarding each, just like LB said.

On the water two miles behind the *Valnea*, a small craft paired itself to the ship's speed: Robey, Sandoval, and Fitz in the inflated RAMZ.

High overhead, Doc issued clipped orders to keep the stack in line, maintaining two hundred feet vertical separation between them. "Come left two; speed up four." Wally latched his focus to the wind, calculating how far and fast he needed to fly.

A half mile out from the ship, another glowing silhouette appeared in the center of the freighter. It popped out of a hatch in the cargo deck, then ducked fast behind cover.

Wally thumbed his PTT.

"Lima Bravo, Lima Bravo. Juggler."

The team freq scratched, then cleared.

"Juggler, Lima Bravo. Right on time. Where are you?"

At a thousand feet altitude, Wally and the team would be visible only if someone knew exactly where to look and tracked them blacking out stars.

"Off the starboard beam, fifteen hundred feet out, one thousand altitude."

LB's green image raised hands. "Nothing."

"Good. You secure?"

"Ready."

"Winds on deck?"

"Five to eight headwind."

"I'll cross over your position in about thirty seconds. I'll bank left and come up from behind."

"Is there a guard on the wing?"

"Yeah."

Wally worked the right toggle to counter a crossbreeze. Altitude was down to 750 feet. In ten more seconds he would cross over the *Valnea*'s starboard side. This close, the deep hum of her engine and the slicing bow matched the buzz of the radio's silence. Between his dangling boots, Wally lined up the image of a crouching LB.

LB said, "Do what you gotta do. All of you."

"Roger that. Look straight up."

"Nothing."

"Over you now."

"I can smell Quincy."

The big PJ answered. "Bite me, LB."

"Come get me outta here and I will."

Doc spoke. "Clear the line."

Wally stepped back in. "Roger. LB, monitor."

"Will do. Good luck, boys."

Wally's canopy kicked him left, tugged on a gust eddied by the great ship passing beneath him. He adjusted, staying on course across the freighter's midsection. His altimeter read six hundred feet. Wally subtracted ninety feet; the LZ stood at the top of the superstructure, nine stories above the water.

The NVGs gave Wally his first clean look at the Somali on the port wing. The pirate faced into the headwind, elbows on the rail. The pirate looked thin, with arms and shoulders typical of an underfed villager in Africa. His blouse ruffled around him; a scarf covered his head. Wally was glad for the glimmering image of the man, just an amplified light signature, no memorable features.

He cleared *Valnea* below and flew another hundred meters past her port beam. Behind him, the freighter kept pushing ahead at twelve knots.

"Doc."

"Go."

"Ready?"

"Get 'em, Wally."

Wally hauled on his left toggle. The ram chute responded, banking him counterclockwise. On the left harness strap across his chest, he unclipped the Stevens lanyard. This would stop his reserve chute from deploying when he landed, because he was going to hit the LZ without his main canopy. Last, Wally flicked off the safety on his M4.

Completing the turn, he shortened the distance to the *Valnea*. A hundred yards out and two hundred yards up, Wally braked to let the freighter slide completely by. The NVGs highlighted the guards on the port rail just as LB described, with one exception: below the superstructure, where LB claimed he'd taken out a Somali, there now stood two green figures.

Wally had thirty more seconds under canopy before he either landed on the ship or splashed. The pirate on the port wing made no movement to show he was aware of Wally hanging in space, circling in behind him.

The ship was now four hundred feet below. Wally put on speed, zooming down from behind, chasing her. Accelerating, he bled more altitude. The freighter whipped up a five-knot headwind as LB had predicted, mingling with the ten-knot crosswind out of the southwest. Diesel exhaust and a wave of heat rising from the smokestack washed across Wally's glide path, fouling and stirring the air. The freighter ran away from him at twelve knots. Wally worked the chute's airfoil for all the velocity and lift he could squeeze from it, holding his line behind the freighter.

He had only moments left. Quincy, two hundred feet above him, was lining up on the same track. The Somali in Wally's goggles kept his focus forward.

Wally drifted down, coming level with the belching smokestack. Without warning, hot exhaust smacked his chute, sheering him left, away from his target.

With no time to spare, he yanked hard on the right toggle, correcting so quickly the chute stalled. The violent maneuver bucked him outside the wing's railing, over the dark water. The approach was going wrong. Twenty feet out and ten feet above the wing, Wally was close enough now to shoot the guard but couldn't spare his hands from the toggles; he might manage to take out the Somali just before slamming into the side of the ship—not an option. His nerves spiked. Wally clamped his teeth, stuck with the plan, and fought the chute in its final seconds.

He flew the last ten feet forward as fast as the chute could carry him. A southwest gust gave him one last jolt of lift. The canopy loomed above the rail. The pirate tilted back his head to catch the sudden dark whoosh above him. Instead of sneaking up on the guard from behind, Wally by accident and fortune swooped in from the side. His boot had a clean shot at the pirate's temple.

He cocked his leg to time the kick. The canopy swept him down and in, fast. Wally flared the chute, hitting the brakes. The tip of his boot struck dead in the center of the pirate's head scarf. The man was bowled over, buckling to a heap on the deck.

Wally sailed over the flattened pirate, reaching back for the handle of the main chute cutaway. He yanked out the pillow grip. Instantly, the long lines separated from the container, the toggles beside his shoulders sprang away. Wally dropped the last few feet to the floor, spreading his legs to straddle the pirate, a final flourish. Behind him, the freed canopy, snared on the breeze, blew across the wing's rail, tumbling into what he hoped was enough darkness.

Wally slung the M4 into his hands. Bending at the waist, he shoved the suppressed muzzle into the dazed pirate's chest and punched two rounds through the heart. The Somali spasmed as if shocked, then lay still.

Wally stood above the body, pausing to read his own reaction. He'd known this kill was coming and could not predict what would come after. A shaking hand, bile in his throat, dry mouth—he needed to adjust and continue. He wanted to feel nothing, and that was what he got. He sensed only luck and the wind.

"Okay," he whispered as if to someone else. "Here we go."

He thumbed the talk button on his vest.

"LZ secure. Five?"

Quincy answered, "Five. Go."

"Watch out for turbulence from the smokestack. Come in wide."

"Roger."

"One, you copy?"

From the top of the stack, Doc said, "PJ one. Roger."

The dimly lit wheelhouse stayed dark. Wally's NVGs showed the green heads and shoulders of two men standing in the middle of the wide room, another pacing between them.

Wally ditched the empty container. He folded the night-vision goggles onto his helmet to get a fuller view of Quincy coming in. The big PJ drifted out of the blackness, invisible until the final ten feet. He nudged his gray chute left, giving the ship's chimney a wide berth to slide in without a whisper. Quincy touched boots down in the center of the wing, then dropped to his knees. Before the wind could drag his canopy back into the air and him with it over the rail, Wally gathered in the lines to collapse it. Quincy unclipped his harnesses, dumping the container. He thrust his weapon at the wheelhouse door while Wally finished securing the silk.

Wally took a knee beside him, M4 up and ready, infrared sight on. He clicked the NVGs down over his eyes.

Quincy cocked his brow at the dead pirate. "I fucking saw you kick him in the head. Nice."

"Go help Jamie."

"Mouse owes me fifty."

"Fifty?"

"He bet against it. I couldn't get him to lay out the cheerleader's phone number."

"Go."

Wally would discuss that lack of faith with Mouse later, maybe over the Ping-Pong table.

He scooted out of the way to make room. Quincy moved to help the next jumper in line. Descending, Jamie had trouble negotiating the crossbreeze and the headwind together while dodging the smokestack, leaving himself too little altitude closing in on the wing.

The radio buzzed. "I'm gonna miss it."

Wally could not turn to watch or help; his weapon had to stay trained on the wheelhouse.

Quincy stayed calm. "Brake left. Left. More."

"Too late."

"Stick out your arm. Now."

A scuffle sounded at Wally's back, a grunt in his earpiece.

"Jesus," Jamie heaved, "you're strong."

Moments after, Jamie crouched next to Wally, gun to his cheek, breathing hard.

Dow drifted down next. Judging by the lack of radio chatter, he landed without a problem. One by one the PJs hit the LZ, and Quincy collapsed their chutes. Each shed his container and med ruck. They took positions on the wing, suppressed barrels in a row at the dark wheelhouse. Dow defended the approach from the staircase. Once Doc was down, Quincy rolled all the chutes in their lines to stash them in a corner.

Doc settled next to Wally. He, like all the PJs, stole a look at the pirate's corpse.

Doc asked, "You okay?"

"Mouse bet against me."

"Dow did, too."

"Did you bet?"

"No. I got mouths to feed in Vegas. But I would've bet on you."

Wally didn't delude himself. These were LB's guys, no one questioned that. But Quincy had bet on him. And Doc would have. That was something.

He folded the NVGs over his eyes to read his watch: 0112 hours. The team was on the LZ, on schedule. Wally gestured to the catwalk running behind the bridge.

"Stay low. Go."

Doc waggled a hand for Mouse to follow to the starboard wing. The pair stooped and disappeared around the corner, beneath the smokestack.

Quincy, Jamie, and Dow flanked Wally, M4s fixed on the pilothouse door. The night breeze mixed with low throbbing hums out of the radar array rotating above the bridge. Wally crept to the white pilothouse wall. He pressed his back under a window.

Oh-one-fourteen hours.

The radio clicked.

"Juggler, Doc."

"Go."

"Starboard wing secure."

"Roger. Assault positions. On my mark."

Wally let seconds pass to test if the pirates were still oblivious. Slowly, he lifted his head above the bottom of the window.

Inside the control room, the glowing radar and computer screens were more than enough to light up Wally's NVGs with the green figures of humans. Two armed pirates stood at opposite ends of the wide bridge. Another paced between them, plainly nervous, weapon at his hip, finger on the trigger. Two more leaned against the long dashboard. Gathered on the floor below the main windshield, huddled against each other, sat the two dozen hostages.

Wally whispered into the mike at his lips. "Doc, hold."

"What's up?"

"The hostages are in the control room. There's five guards with AKs."

"What do you want to do?"

"Gimme a sec."

"Holding."

Wally tamped down a spur of anger with himself at not preparing for this possibility, that the hostages would be front and center for the firefight. He'd been ordered not to consider them his prime directive, so had left them out when planning the raid, focusing only on regaining control of the ship. Now, faced with twenty-four helpless men menaced by armed pirates, Wally knelt at the brink of the actual and inevitable body count, the blood on the floor General Madson had barely mentioned.

What could he have done differently? Even if he'd planned for the hostages to be right where they were, he still had to assault the control room. He had less than an hour to do it. There wasn't time for both a hostage negotiation and a siege.

Wally dropped below the window, sliding down the wall. He lifted the NVGs from his eyes.

"Doc."

"Go."

"I got orders."

"I know."

"What do you think?"

Doc paused before answering. "I think we got orders."

The gun barrels of Quincy, Jamie, and Dow dipped while Wally sat in front of them. All three PJs, men he admired, shrugged behind their weapons. Orders.

"Doc, how much med supply we got?"

"Not enough if it goes bad."

"Damn it."

"What next?"

"We press the mission. Check your door. See if it's locked."

Keeping his arm out of sight, Wally twisted the higher of the two watertight chocks. He waited to be sure the motion was unseen, then rotated the lower chock. With both seals undone, he put pressure on the door handle. It moved. Wally stopped before it clicked.

"Port door unlocked."

Doc responded, "Starboard unlocked."

"Flashbangs, on my mark."

Quincy scurried next to Wally, flashbang in hand. Dow and Jamie, the team's youngest and best shooters, readied to be the first ones in. Both lowered NVGs over their eyes to see through the smoke after the blinding light of the grenades, and to read the infrared targeting beams off their M4 scopes.

Wally reached for the door handle.

"Break break!" The radio sizzled. "Break, break! Juggler, hold!"

Wally dropped his hand. "Go, LB."

"Don't do it, Wally. Don't do it."

Beside Wally, big Quincy laid a hand over his arm, making LB's radio plea physical.

"I don't have a lot of time, LB."

"You've got hostages in there. You can't raid the bridge."

"This isn't your mission. You stay secure. We don't have any choice."

"You do. Listen to me. There's another way."

Leaning close, Quincy nodded.

Doc cut in. "Give him a chance."

"Okay. Tell me, fast."

"Even if you take the bridge, you might not hold it. There's fifteen more targets out here on the ship. They got AKs and a bunch of rocket grenades. If they try to take the bridge back, they might do it. They might not, but either way it'll be bloody. You're holed up on exposed high ground with twenty-four civilians, or however many you'll have left. They're gonna panic. A lot more of 'em are gonna die. You're outgunned and outnumbered."

From the other wing, Jamie spoke for the first time. "Let's cut the pirates' numbers down first."

LB said, "That's what I'm thinking. Juggler."

"Go."

"I know where they all are. I know the ship. If we take down the targets around the deck first, the ones in the wheelhouse might give up without a fight. Look, I can guess at your orders. Believe me, I know we have to take this ship back. But we gotta try to do it without sacrificing the hostages. I think we can."

Wally checked the time: 0117.

Quincy, Jamie, and Doc waited to charge into the bridge on his order. On the opposite wing, Dow and Mouse crouched, ready.

If they stuck to the plan, they'd have control of the bridge in under a minute, plus the likelihood of several dead and wounded hostages. They'd deal next with the casualties. Before he could clear the rest of the ship, Wally would have to leave three men behind to deal with the wounded and defend the bridge. That left only three plus LB to go after the remaining fifteen Somalis. And he couldn't call off the Predator, that ticking bomb, until the ship was secure.

What if the pirates below heard the battle for the bridge? The team's weapons were suppressed, but AK-47s would make a ruckus. If the guards and their guns and RPGs decided to retake the bridge, the mission would become a siege, like LB said, with a countdown to a missile.

In LB's plan, they might save a lot more lives. But could they really clear the freighter first, then negotiate with the five Somalis inside the control room, all in under fifty-three minutes? What if the pirates started killing off hostages? What if the deadline got too close? At that point, whatever was left of the team would have to assault the bridge anyway.

"All right, everyone. Listen up."

Wally crawled away from the pilothouse wall. He stood just enough to peer over the rail to the main deck six stories below. The two figures there stood back-to-back along the port rail.

"Doc."

"Go."

"Look down to the main deck. How many targets you see?"

"One."

"All right. LB, you copy?"

"Go."

"We're going to do both plans. Dow and Mouse stay on the starboard wing. Quincy and Doc hold on the port wing. Jamie and me link up with LB at the foot of the starboard stairs. The three of us will neutralize the pirates on the main deck. Once it's secure, we come back up here, either to negotiate with the pirates inside the bridge or to press the assault. We'll make that call when we get to it. If things go south on the main deck, or we run out of time, Doc leads the assault on the pilothouse. Questions?"

Quincy, Jamie, and Doc shook their heads.

"Juggler."

"Go, LB."

"Who handles the target at the bottom of the starboard stairs?"

Jamie spoke again. "I will."

LB replied. "Roger."

Wally pointed at Jamie. The young PJ looked back through night goggles and fell in behind him. Quincy put his back to the rail, weapon leveled at the bridge door. Dow took position guarding the stairwell.

Wally led Jamie over the catwalk behind the bridge. A soiled, sooty warmth from the smokestack grazed his cheeks. Reaching the starboard wing, Wally patted Dow and Mouse on the shoulders.

Dow said, "Good hunting."

Mouse added, "Fast hunting."

Wally put Jamie in the lead descending the first of the six staircases. His watch read 0121. Forty-nine minutes.

Jamie led with his gun barrel down the metal stairs, pausing at every corner, close-quarters technique. Wally let the young PJ set the pace, and watched their tail.

Out on the gulf, a shimmering key of silver lay on the ripples, the first touch of the rising quarter moon.

Chapter 32

On board CMA CGN Valnea
Gulf of Aden

"What is that?"

Yusuf spun his cousin by the shoulder, quickly, before the shade disappeared.

"Where?"

"There." Yusuf pointed over the rail, up and toward the stern. "See? The stars black out. Something floating away."

"Yes, I think. Yes."

A piece of the night twisted around itself as though in agony, then was gone. Yusuf brought up his flashlight, too late.

"What was it?"

Suleiman put fingers into his beard before he spoke. Yusuf scanned the sky east for more dark swirls. Now he had blood on the boat, ghosts in the air.

Suleiman dropped the hand from his beard, keeping his gaze skyward. He waited, measuring what he had seen.

He asked, "Have you been to Qardho?"

The town lay on the road south to Eyl, in a bleached riverbed.

"I've been through it."

"Did you visit the stone hole?"

"No. I don't know what that is."

"Outside town, in a limestone hill, the rock is split wide enough for a man to walk. Inside, where the stone is cool, there is a pit so deep the locals say it reaches hell. At night, *jinn* appear above the pit. Sometimes they are like beasts, hairy and hideous. Or they take the shape of ostriches and run into the desert."

"Have you been there?"

"Yes. Many times."

"Have you seen this?"

Suleiman sighed, the indulgent manner of an older kinsman. "What does it matter that I have not seen a *jinn* when the Qu'ran says they exist?"

Suleiman eyed the night where the black flutter had been and disappeared.

"They are real. They are *ayat*." Miracles. "So was that."

In the tales Yusuf's mother told, the spirits were always beautiful. They looked like men, they loved or hated men. Even the evil *jinn* in her tales were never horrible to behold, not like the beasts and ostriches Suleiman described. She schooled him as a child that *jinn* could be killed with a date or a plum stone shot from a sling. He had none of these.

In the east where the moon would rise, a pearly blush crept along the horizon. Time did not pause to worry over Yusuf or to recall the stories of his mother. Another minute of silence carried him closer to whatever this long night was going to be.

He said, "They will not send regular soldiers to take this ship back. There will be killing."

Suleiman held his gaze into the stars. "The *jinn* has come to watch."

"This is what the signs say? That the soldiers are coming?"

"No, cousin." Suleiman lowered his eyes to the ship. He shrugged his Kalashnikov into his hands. "They are not coming. They are here."

Yusuf leveled his own rifle to the dark corridor at the base of the bloodstained steps.

Behind his gun, Suleiman whispered, "I should like to see a *jinn* before I die."

Yusuf would not ignore his cousin's portents or the memory of his mother's tales. But he let Suleiman watch for signs.

Yusuf watched for men.

Chapter 33

———•———

From the cargo deck, LB monitored the short exchanges between Wally and Jamie. Doc and the others surrounding the bridge would be listening too.

"Clear." Jamie had just arrived at the next landing down, checked it, found it empty.

"Go." Wally moved on his tail, watching their backsides.

As he'd done an hour earlier, LB slipped in and out of the companionway, forging his way toward the stern. He dropped down off the cargo deck, lay flat, then crept in shadow below the level of the steel rail. LB gained as much distance as he could, then scurried up another dark ladder until the next guard had passed or turned away.

He reached the aft corner of the cargo deck, ducking behind the last lashing bridge to catch his breath. The gray face of the superstructure seemed a giant tombstone. The radio buzzed in his ear.

"LB. In position?"

"Roger."

"Hold."

Moments later, Jamie spoke.

"Target down."

LB hustled to the ladder. Landing on the deck, he spun the Zastava across his back. Jamie had detached the magazine from the dead man's Kalashnikov to drop it overboard. He dug hands under the pirate's armpits. LB hurried to take hold of the sandaled feet. Hefting the body, he noted the callused heels. The Somali's blouse bore twin punctures in the chest. Black blood seeped into the linen.

"Over here," LB whispered. They lugged the body to a gloomy corner. No need to risk dumping it overboard. The corpse didn't have to stay hidden for long. It was going to be one of many very shortly.

LB shook hands with Jamie. "Sorry about this."

"Me, too. Later. Hey, did the engineer move his legs?"

"A couple of toes."

"Nice."

"Hey, kid. Next time I say I got it by myself, kick me."

"I'll let Wally do it."

LB didn't follow the reference. It didn't matter. Wally crouched, waiting in the companionway. LB and Jamie took knees beside him.

"Which way?" Wally asked.

"Good to see you, too."

"I know. Which way?"

"Hit the stern first. Lock down our six. Three targets. The wind'll carry the sound backward."

Wally tapped the Serb's unsuppressed weapon hanging off LB's shoulder. "Keep that quiet as long as you can. Jamie, take point."

The young PJ entered the narrow passage to the stern, coiled and athletic, holding the M4 ready. Wally gestured LB to the center, then took the rear.

They moved quickly, keeping close and low. Nearing the corner of the stern, Wally whispered to LB, "Hold."

LB stopped. Wally edged past in the narrow corridor.

Jamie eased the final distance to the corner, Wally tight behind him. Jamie dropped his NVGs over his eyes and lay flat.

He edged his face forward. Directly over him, Wally hugged the wall, ready to step out and fire. Jamie murmured into the radio, "I got the far one. You take the close one. We'll both get the middle."

Jamie skittered back. He gathered to a knee, night goggles down to rely on the IR beam of his weapon.

Gun barrels tilted up, Wally said, "Now." The two whirled around the corner, Wally high, Jamie bent low, M4s leveled into the open. They found their targets fast. Both guns jerked in tandem. The suppression tubes cloaked any flashes; reports were dulled to pops and the clacks of chambering rounds. The wind blew most of the sound out over the water. Jamie fired three times, Wally four. Without lowering their carbines, the two slipped around the corner. LB scurried behind them in support.

Wally and Jamie hastened along the stern rail, the only two silhouettes in motion. Wan moonlight dusted the three downed pirates. Wally leaned over them to fire once into each. He heaved two AKs and an RPG overboard. Three towed skiffs bounded on the *Valnea*'s wake, attached to grappling hooks over the rail. Jamie trained his M4 on the starboard corner while Wally mopped up. LB pivoted away to do his part and guard the starboard passage.

Six pirates were dead so far. One Serb. More to come. No one and nothing could stop the tempest of this night. Jamie, the youngest of the PJs, was handling himself well in close combat. This underscored how foolish LB had been to separate from him. There was no such thing as a milk run.

Wally and Jamie moved beside LB. Wally checked his watch. Even in the poor light, blood dotted the rim of the suppression tube on his M4.

LB asked, "Something you said before. On the radio."

"What?"

"You said Doc assaults the bridge if we run out of time. What'd you mean?"

"I should've told you earlier."

"Told me what?"

"We got forty-four minutes. At oh-two-one-oh, a Reaper's going to sink us if we haven't secured the ship."

"Us? You mean, like, us?"

"Hostages, pirates, us. Presidential order. It's got to be done in deep water and before we get in range of the coast. They'll blame the pirates for blowing up the ship. All very neat."

That it was. With a drone locked and loaded, invisibly high, the PJs had no choice down here on the ship. They were locked in, too, along with the Somalis. Neither side had any way out but to kill the other. This was worse than combat. It was gladiatorial.

Jamie asked LB, "You know what's on this ship?"

"Yeah. I do."

"Don't tell me. But does this make sense to you? To blow it up rather than let the Somalis keep it?"

"Yeah."

"Well," the young PJ said, "at least that's something."

Jamie flipped the NVGs over his eyes. He crouched, facing the bow, instantly ready. "Where's the next one?"

Chapter 34

Wally kept his mouth shut about it, but LB was useless.

He couldn't fire the Serb weapon; one burst from the loud Zastava, and their position would be compromised. He wore no body armor. Creeping along the corridor, Wally had to keep him in the middle, protected between himself and Jamie. LB knew where the Somalis were, but Jamie's NVGs showed him better than LB's whispers what lay ahead.

LB had little stomach for the killing. He had bloodstains on his pants and shoulders, and maybe that was enough for him. LB winced at the blood Wally was taking on, splashed on the muzzle of his suppressor, sprayed over his boots. Wally couldn't be sure all the distance shots he and Jamie took were lethal. He had to put the Somalis down to stay, couldn't risk a wounded pirate sounding the alarm or sneaking up on them from behind. Killing was terrible work, but it was the mission.

They crept past the starboard stairwell where Jamie had made his first shot, a clean takedown. Since then, Jamie, younger than LB and Wally by more than a decade, had held himself in check. He could've moved faster without the two of them in tow, but PJs didn't operate alone. LB had known this when he sent Jamie back on the chopper.

Thirty yards along the narrow passageway, passing the crane towering over the ship's midsection, Jamie flattened to the deck.

"Down."

LB and Wally dove for the steel floor.

The next pirate to die trod their way, lit well in the goggles.

Jamie set up the shot, propped on his elbows, eye pressed to the infrared sight. The thin emerald rail that only Jamie and Wally could see reached out to the pirate's heart. Wally couldn't bring his own weapon into play without sitting up straight, couldn't back up Jamie's shot because of LB lying in front of him.

"Let him come," Wally whispered into the radio. "Wait till he reacts."

The pirate closed to ten yards before his arms moved to bring up his Kalashnikov. His sandals skidded a backward step. Jamie's single round continued the Somali's reversal, lifting him off his feet and dropping him faceup.

Wally pushed off the deck, careful to stay below the rail. LB leaped to his feet and beat him to the pirate. Kneeling, LB pushed two fingers into the man's carotid for a pulse. His hand was there when Wally drove the M4's barrel into the Somali's chest and pulled the trigger.

"Goddammit," LB whispered from his knees. "He wasn't dead."

Wally threw the pirate's AK over the rail. He answered LB with a fresh glance at his watch.

"Oh-one-twenty-nine. Let's go."

Jamie resumed inching along the starboard passageway, and LB turned to follow. Wally bit back the urge to bicker.

Forty yards later they killed the next pirate the same way, Wally finishing the downed Somali after Jamie's shot to the chest. LB stayed flat on the deck until Wally pitched the pirate's weapon overboard.

The ship coursed over a flat and empty sea. The closer to the bow Jamie led them, the louder grew the noise of the hull carving the water. The young PJ quickened his pace, counting on the masking breeze and sea.

Wally checked with Doc. Nothing had changed inside the bridge. The pirates and hostages rode the freighter into the night, nervous but unaware. Dow cut in to remind Wally of the time.

The next Somali, the last one on starboard before the bow, came into view thirty yards away. This one leaned out over the rail, quietly studying the wake or the heavens. He exposed only his waist and legs to Jamie's IR beam, his torso obscured behind a steel support. Wally couldn't wait on the man's reverie to finish. He had no time to indulge this pirate looking longingly for home or into the magnetic sky. Wally stood above the rail. He hoisted the M4 to his shoulder and strode past the kneeling Jamie and LB.

The pillar blocked the pirate's view of Wally stopping ten feet away.

"Hey."

The Somali, thin like the others, a short man and darker than the horizon, brought his attention around the pillar. He faced Wally, hands lifted from his sides. Wally shot the pirate twice in the chest before he could complete the gesture of surrender.

Wally did not fire into this one again. He'd been close enough to know.

Seven down.

He dropped the Somali's gun over the rail, then lowered into the shadows beside the body. LB and Jamie skittered to him.

LB wore no helmet or goggles, nothing to conceal his conflict over the carnage, no matter how necessary. Like the pirate, Wally gave him no chance to do more. He addressed Jamie.

"There's four on the bow. How do you want to handle it?"

"Maybe we should back up. Go around the stern and clean up the port side one at a time, like we've been doing. Then hit the bow."

The time was 0132. Thirty-eight minutes left. By the time they'd backtracked two hundred meters around to port, staying out of sight the whole way, they'd have lost at least four minutes.

"LB?"

Wally made ready to cut him off if he brought up anything but a tactic. LB pulled his eyes from the corpse.

"The whole starboard rail is bodies. Some Somali goes looking for a cigarette, we're screwed. There's nine left around the deck. We got four of 'em in one place. I say we go to the bow. After that, if things go bad, the numbers are a lot better."

Wally agreed. "We press the bow. Jamie."

The young PJ stayed on point, leading them the last twenty yards along the starboard rail. The overhang ended, and the bow opened to the night sky. Jamie halted at the corner to peek. He lifted his NVGs, motioning Wally forward.

Wally nudged past LB to ease his head around the steel wall.

From the top of a mast, a white beacon bathed the bow in garish light. Night-vision goggles would be useless here.

Wally whispered, "There goes our advantage."

The bow was a wide but jumbled space. The business of anchoring and mooring the freighter took place here. Thick chains, lines, the metal stubs of hawsers—nowhere was there ten clear feet without an obstruction. Lit from above, the maze of gray steel was a warren of shadows and cover. A running firefight here could last a long time, longer than the Predator would give them. If the five pirates left on the port rail got involved, Wally, Jamie, and LB could get bottled up, probably until they were killed by either the pirates or the drone. Wally would have to put the call in for Doc to take the bridge.

Wally leaned his head out farther.

One Somali ambled along the starboard rail, tunic and head scarf fluttering in the gusts. He carried an RPG. Another, with an AK, walked the rail on port.

"LB."

"Yeah."

"You said there were four up here."

"There were an hour ago."

Wally let LB replace him at the corner. LB raised his head slowly to get a better angle across the cluttered bow. After seconds, he reeled himself in. Jamie took his place to keep watch.

"Two of them might be sleeping, or sitting down. There's a lot of places to hide up here."

Wally pushed his M4 around so it hung across his back, where it would jangle less.

LB asked, "What're you doing?"

"Gotta go find them." Wally rolled off his knees to his haunches. To Jamie, he said, "Stay ready. We'll move after we know where they all are."

LB blocked Wally's path. "What's gotten into you?"

"Move."

"No. PJs don't work alone."

Mirroring Wally, LB swung the big Zastava to his back. From under his pants leg he pulled a blood-sullied blade.

LB shrugged. "Okay, I admit. I kinda forgot that."

Wally unsheathed his own knife.

⸺•⸺

Wally lost sight of LB quickly. Squat and thick, LB disappeared into the jumbled terrain like a cat, shadows gathering across his back. Wally jackknifed himself as small as he could, bending at the waist and knees, and sped from cover to cover, the breeze and sea sounds shrouding the scuffles of his boots. LB scoured the right half of the bow, Wally the left. Around the corner, Jamie kept an infrared eye on the two pacing Somalis. Every few seconds, he murmured to the crawling LB and Wally about where the pirates walked or looked.

Wally crabbed sideways, pausing in pools of shade made crisp by the harsh light overhead. He checked for places a tired pirate might loaf on a warm hijacked night. Maybe away from the light, or near the rail so his mates could wake him if a boss came near. Where was a soft place on this hard bow?

Wally stole between hawsers. He scurried into the open to hide behind the bulk of a giant spool, one of two windlasses for hauling the great anchor chain. The machine had a broad shadow, and there he found his pirate. The napping Somali was sprawled on a heavy nylon line laid out in switchback rows to make a bed. Beside him lay a rocket grenade launcher.

"Got him," Wally whispered. "Sleeping on a pile of rope. Next to the left windlass."

"Roger," Jamie uttered. "You're clear so far."

"LB?"

"Hold." Moments passed, then LB came back. "I see the ropes on this side. No one on them."

The reek of corrosion dripped from the iron chain. Wally slunk deeper into the shadow of the links.

"LB. Anything?"

"Nothing. This side of the bow's clear."

"Sit tight. Jamie."

"Go."

"Looks like there's only three targets up here. You still have visual on two?"

"Roger."

"Can you make both shots?"

"The one close to me, yeah. The one over by you, that's forty yards. He's moving. There's too much stuff in the way."

"Can you make the shots?"

"Clean? Negative."

Wally tapped the blade against his gloved palm. The plan formed fast for him, and he saw no other way.

"LB?"

"Go."

"Can you get over here?"

"Yeah."

"Okay. I know you're hating this."

"Shut up, Wally. I'll do him."

"All right. Move."

Wally raised his head to get a fix on the pirate twenty yards away, strolling the port rail. The quarter moon had slipped above the horizon, gilding the waters where the Somali cast his attention.

Wally could take him. He slid away the knife and shed the M4 from his back into his hands. This pirate was chubby, with a protruding belly under the dangling Kalashnikov. How could that be, from such a poor country? The man walked barefoot with a lazy gait.

Wally detected a rumple in the shadows. LB emerged to sidle next to him in the shadow of the windlass, knife in hand.

"Jamie. LB's in position. On my mark."

"Roger."

The shadows altered LB's face. He looked younger, the crevices smoothed. Wally laid a hand on LB's crusted shoulder.

"I'm sorry. Go."

LB stayed under Wally's touch for a moment before pivoting away.

On his toes, agile for his girth, LB appeared to float to the sleeping pirate. Moving into a patch of light, he did little to attract the eye, creeping ahead, doubled tightly. He held the blade tucked like a talon behind his wrist to prevent a flash. He slipped into the carpet of shadow where the Somali lay.

Wally alerted Jamie. "Ready."

"On my target."

LB did not pounce on the pirate but knelt beside him gently, as if to anoint rather than kill. Wrapping both hands around the knife's handle, he raised the blade above the pirate's torso. Wally needed to take his gaze away, to put them on his own target, but a realization glued him to LB. The missions he'd jumpmastered for Gus DiNardo long ago hadn't been just recon.

LB hovered a last moment, then rammed the knife in two-handed. He fell forward behind the blade, driving it down under his full weight. The knife sank up to the hilt in the pirate's chest. LB spread-eagled across the man to keep him from thrashing. He clapped one hand over the Somali's mouth, with the other turning the blade like a clock key to widen the wound. The pirate's limbs flogged but life ebbed from them fast, to a weak flop and release.

Wally flexed his grip on the M4.

LB, not lifting his head from the dead man, breathed into the radio. "Go."

Wally popped up from the cover of the windlass, out from the shadows. In the light of the beacon, he sped the rifle to his shoulder. Fifteen yards away, the Somali did not turn to him. The pirate had heard with Wally the cry of the guard on starboard taking Jamie's bullet. Wally's target moved a step in that direction, raising his Kalashnikov. He presented only his profile.

Wally fired once into his gut to slow him. The second round spun him by the shoulder. The third backpedaled the Somali until he tripped and slumped against the rail.

Wally stepped forward to make the kill certain.

The fat pirate fired back.

Chapter 35

———

The Somali's bullets blew Wally backward and down.

Before the pirate could shoot again, LB swung the Zastava off his back. Without time to aim, he loosed the big gun, nailing the pirate against the rail. The Somali shook like a doll on the end of LB's burst, then stilled.

The explosions of the Kalashnikov and the big Serb gun echoed across the freighter, driven toward the stern on the headwind. LB yanked his knife out of the dead pirate and leaped to Wally.

He dragged Wally out of the open, behind cover of the great windlass. Wally kicked to help, a good sign. A ragged tear in the left biceps and a neat hole in the center of his Rhodesian vest were the marks of the AK. Jamie skidded to his knees beside them into the shadows, just in time to duck a blast from a pirate rounding the corner of the starboard companionway. Bullets pinged against the iron anchor chain, chewing off sparks.

Jamie answered fire. The Somali retreated.

With his M4 up and waiting for the pirate to stick out his head again, Jamie muttered, "There's your fourth pirate. Off taking a piss or something."

On his back, Wally sputtered, catching his breath. He panted through blown-out cheeks. His legs scrabbled as if on fire.

"Shit…the guy was supposed to be dead."

LB's bloodied knife cut into the sleeve of Wally's camo tunic. "Sit still."

He tore the opening wide enough to probe the channel in Wally's biceps, pushing Wally to a sitting position to get a better look at the entire wound. The Kalashnikov's round had grooved the inside of the muscle, missing bone and major vessels. It surely stung like hell.

Sucking in his lips, proving LB right, Wally dug a finger into the tear in his web vest, over his sternum. The 7.62 round had pounded a Kevlar armor plate, knocked Wally over, then bounced away. This one should have killed him.

Wally blinked, restoring himself.

"You're not bleeding too bad. We'll get that wrapped later. You good?"

Wally worked his left hand. He gritted his teeth and shifted to his knees. The M4 returned to his grasp.

Wally swung his vision around the bow, as if taking in the situation for the first time. He'd been out of it for the last fifteen seconds. "What have we got?"

"Three of the four targets on the bow are down. The fourth one was in the passageway. He got a look at us. Probably heard the AK. He definitely heard me."

"Yeah. LB, thanks."

"No fun being rescued, is it?"

"No fun."

Over the stock of his carbine, Jamie spoke. "I think he went to get his buddies."

"Ten down," Wally said. "That leaves six more on the deck. Plus the five inside the bridge."

LB pivoted the Zastava to the starboard rail, should the pirates try to bracket them.

"What do you want to do?"

Wally checked his watch. "Thirty minutes. Halfway."

Jamie hoisted his rifle barrel. "Lemme shoot out that damn light."

LB thought this a good idea. Darkness would restore some of their advantage with the night-vision goggles. Wally pulled down Jamie's aim.

"Don't. They can see that light from the bridge." Wally thumbed his talk button. "Doc. Juggler."

"Juggler, go."

"We've been spotted."

"We heard the shots. What happened?"

"I screwed up. Any change inside the bridge?"

"Negative. They didn't hear it, I reckon. Everybody okay?"

"All good. Listen. Six targets left. They might come your way."

"That'll suck. What's your move?"

"We're gonna chase them, make our way to you. We'll keep them off your back, if we can."

"Roger."

"If we get stuck, you take the bridge without us."

"Roger. Don't get stuck."

"I hear you. Hold."

"Holding."

LB swiped the knife and his palm across his bent thigh, adding more smears to his uniform. He slipped the blade into its sheath around his calf. Wally checked his watch again, calculating. A red glisten seeped onto his wrist, under the watchband, into his glove.

The stench of rust off the anchor chain blended with the tang of so much loose blood. The combination was heady for LB, tempting his nausea. He was relieved when Wally led him and Jamie away from cover under the white light, into the open wind.

They approached the port corridor the same way they'd shot their way to the bow along the starboard rail: Jamie on point, LB in the middle, Wally covering their six.

Chapter 36

——

The claps of gunfire reached Yusuf first, then the sound of sandals flapping on the deck. Next on the wind came the metal clatter of a gun rattling against a running man's chest.

"It begins," Suleiman said.

The pirate ran out of the dim corridor, up to Yusuf's leveled weapon. Suleiman caught the man by the shoulders, as if he might run past.

"Jama, slow down," Suleiman urged. "What has happened?"

The pirate's blouse had slid off one shoulder like a woman's. His rifle hung askew. He'd run for all he was worth. He nodded excitedly at Yusuf and Suleiman, catching his breath, too much to say.

"Jama, tell us."

The man looked up from his feet. "Soldiers."

Yusuf stepped away from this news, putting Suleiman between himself and Jama. He turned his back to drink in a last look into the night, the stars above the gulf no different than in the desert. The thin moon rose like a scimitar tonight. There must be a place for peace inside a violent man, or he is too dark and lost and he cannot make violence do his bidding.

Suleiman asked, "How many?"

"I saw only three."

"Where?"

"On the bow. Ahmad, Beni, and the fat one, they are dead."

Soldiers. Not omens or ghosts, but men with guns. Suleiman was right.

Yusuf spoke above his cousin. "How did they get on board?"

Jama rattled his head. "I do not know. There was no ship, no plane. Nothing."

Suleiman adjusted the man's *khameez*. He straightened the Kalashnikov by its strap. He pushed the gun into Jama's belly until the pirate's hands took it.

"You are Darood. These soldiers, they have killed your clansmen. There are only three. Can you fight them?"

"Yes."

"Good. Go tell the rest what I have said. Surround them and kill them."

Even with his firm answer, Jama did not turn away on his own. Suleiman spun him to push him back into the corridor.

Jama ran off. Suleiman watched him go. "As you say. These are not regular soldiers."

"We have to warn Guleed."

Suleiman gazed up the side of the superstructure. Far on top, the bridge remained without gunfire or lights. "There's no fighting anywhere else."

Yusuf moved for the stairs. "I'll go."

Suleiman stopped him. "Guleed is always ready. No, cousin. We should stay on deck. We have enough to handle three soldiers, even these. But I know our men. They'll need to be commanded."

"Why only three? How did they get on the bow?"

Suleiman did not pause with the questions. He rushed past Yusuf to the stern.

—•—

All three lay dead. Each bore the same signs of their killing. A bullet to the body, then two more like fang marks into their hearts.

They found none of the men's weapons.

Suleiman lagged among the bodies, standing in blood. Yusuf eyed the skiffs trailing behind the freighter in the roar of the wake and propeller. He could shimmy down a rope ladder, awaken an engine, and chance an escape. Only fifty miles to the coast.

He spat into the water. These men had followed Yusuf to this ship, for wealth and Qandala. In the end, it was for Robow and secret machines. For two holes in their hearts.

Somewhere in the ribs of the freighter hid the passenger scientist Iris Cherlina. Was she behind this as well? Had she brought down the soldiers the same way she'd beckoned Yusuf? Did these dead bodies stack at her door? She would do well to stay in hiding.

Yusuf wanted to make a vow. He'd done this in the war when comrades fell, had sworn to fight on. The war became a folly, and he became a pirate. There were no oaths for pirates. Now, with dead clansman at his feet, all he could do for vengeance was hold this ship.

"Come," he called to Suleiman.

Yusuf turned the corner to the starboard rail. Suleiman caught up with him. Hurrying, both held their Kalashnikovs ready. No guard waited beside the superstructure. Yusuf slowed his approach.

His sandals skidded on the deck. He found no corpse or weapon, only two spent brass cases rolling in the blood pool. Suleiman hastened forward.

Forty meters on, the next pirate lay like the ones on the stern, shorn of his gun, bullets through the heart. Yusuf lent a finger to the cheek of this one. The flesh flexed, still warm. The soldiers were only minutes ahead.

Nearing the bow, another corpse plus the three Jama had reported dead made Suleiman ask, "Three soldiers did this?"

"It seems so."

"What sort of men can these be?"

Brutal men who could rip a heart when called for. Yusuf was such a man; he'd done it. Suleiman too.

Gunfire erupted from the port side. The crackle of automatic weapons streaked across the base of the forward crane. Jama and what few living pirates he could find had engaged the soldiers.

Yusuf lumbered into the open range of the bow. Under the stark glow of the steaming light, another dead pirate greeted him, slumped at the rail. This one had been shot only through the head; one side of his skull was missing and gruesome. He'd been allowed to keep his weapon, a rocket launcher. Yusuf took it.

Suleiman led him to two more bodies. A fat one lay against the rail, Kalashnikov at his side, finger on the trigger. Perforated by six bullets, he'd died hard. The other, a young one, sprawled on shaded rows of nylon anchor line. Had the soldiers caught him napping?

A tunnel had been ground into the middle of his chest. The white coiled rope beneath him had soaked so much of his blood it seemed a red satin bed.

Yusuf breathed, "*Allah masaamax.*" God forgive us.

The pounding of guns from the port corridor continued. Yusuf gazed down on the drained boy, asking Suleiman's question of the soldiers. What kind of men are these?

He swung the Kalashnikov over his back. Dodging hawsers, masts, and anchor chains, he reached the corner of the companionway. The gun battle raged ahead. Yusuf pressed himself against the wall, Suleiman behind him. He set down the RPG.

Yusuf leaned around the corner.

Fifty meters down the port rail, three soldiers huddled in the corridor. One faced the stern, firing. Jama's men poked their

Kalashnikovs from behind cover to spray bullets wildly. The soldier in the middle swung his rifle front and rear, shooting little. The one facing backward saw Yusuf.

A flock of bullets ricocheted off the corner just as Yusuf yanked his head out of the way. Paint chips fluttered to the deck, and steel echoes yowled over the dark water.

"Cousin." Yusuf hefted the RPG. "You first."

Suleiman edged close to the corner. Yusuf backed off, bracing himself. Raising the rocket grenade to his shoulder, he fixed his eye down the flip-up sight and long tube.

"Now."

Chapter 37

A head popped around the corner. Wally peppered the steel in front of it with a quick burst, striking sparks turned green in his NVGs. The pirate ducked away.

"Targets on our six!"

Behind him, LB brought the Zastava around. Without night goggles, he could fire only at shadows. "What've you got?"

"Don't know. Someone took a look at us. Jamie."

"Sir."

"How many in front of us?"

"I count four."

Another drip of blood dribbled down Wally's left arm, collecting in the cloth at his elbow.

Four Somalis in front. Maybe two or three behind. This was what Wally had feared, getting jammed up in the corridor. He couldn't pull his eyes from the infrared sight to check his watch, but the minutes were trickling away. Somehow, they had to advance.

One more blast of crazily aimed rounds burst from the pirates ahead. The bullets ricocheted against the floor, rail, and overhang, tattooing the steel. LB stumbled backward into Wally.

"Jamie's hit!"

Wally called, "How bad?"

"In the thigh," Jamie answered, pained. "I think it's clean through. I'm good."

LB helped the young PJ back to his feet. Wally cursed under the ringing in his ears.

They were going to get chewed up in this passageway. No cover. Two wounds already, both lucky. Outgunned. An enemy more interested in standoff than in combat. LB without body armor, not even a helmet.

"Jamie, can you move?"

"Roger."

"How many flashbangs you got?"

"Two."

Wally chanced a quick look at his watch: 0137.

There wasn't a choice. The corridor was a death trap, either by bullets or in thirty-three minutes by a Predator's missile. They had to move against the pirates.

"Give them both to LB." Wally dug an elbow behind him into LB's rump. "On your mark, you throw. The two of you clear the corridor. I'll guard your six."

"Roger."

Wally spoke into the radio. "Doc."

"Juggler, go."

"Get ready."

"You okay?"

"Do it. On my mark."

"Roger."

Wally reached under his chin to unstrap his helmet and the attached NVGs. LB would need them to see through the smoke after the grenades' flash.

"LB, take these."

Before Wally could undo the strap, with a last look through the lenses, a green figure stepped into the mouth of the corridor at the bow. Wally, with a hand off the M4, could not shoot. A volley blazed from the muzzle of the pirate's AK. Wally threw himself prone on the deck, Jamie and LB following. All the rounds whizzed high; the gust had been hurried and poorly aimed.

Wally put both hands on his weapon to answer. He swung the needle-thin beam for the Somali's chest.

The pirate with the Kalashnikov leaped aside to reveal another figure behind him.

This one, a big man, balanced an RPG on his shoulder.

Before Wally could squeeze off a shot, his night goggles flared, blinding him with the exhaust of the rocket's launch.

He had only a moment to dive across LB.

Chapter 38

The rocket grenade exploded over the soldiers.

The missile struck the overhang directly above them, detonating into a fireball, rattling Yusuf's *khameez* thirty meters back. He shoved the empty tube off his shoulder to the deck, waiting for the smoke to clear.

Haze boiled over the rail, blown on the headwind. Suleiman, made bold, stood openly to fire a long burst into the mist.

Quiet flowed back from the corridor. Yusuf took his gun in hand. He stepped forward. The soldiers might be dead, or stunned enough to be overrun and finished.

A silent bullet pricked his loose blouse at the waist. The tug was like that of a child at his side. The shot drilled a channel through the smoke. Yusuf jumped aside before two more rounds zipped where he'd stood. Suleiman dropped and rolled behind the corner.

Yusuf cursed. "*Dufarr.*" Pigs. He fingered the hole in his blouse. Suleiman scrambled beside him. Yusuf growled, "How did they live through that? How do they shoot back?"

Suleiman shook his head. "Perhaps they are not pigs."

"What are they, then? Give me a better word."

"You won't accept what I have to say."

Yusuf stole a quick glance around the corner. Most of the smoke from the explosion had drifted away. Dark figures knotted in the shadow below the rail, as if the explosion had melted the soldiers together. Wisps curled off their backs. The one who'd shot at him still watched down his gun barrel.

Yusuf drew his head around the corner.

"Speak your mind."

"I asked what sort of men these were. Perhaps they're not men at all."

"Cousin, they are soldiers."

"They are *shaitann*. You saw how they kill. You see how they cannot be killed. The *jinn* that brought them to the ship, we saw it go. Why bring them here? So we can all die at their hands? I cannot believe that. Allah has another reason."

Suleiman was not wild, not afraid. He'd always been Yusuf's bedrock, wise because he was older, far-seeing, devout, braver. These fighters in the corridor were men; Yusuf would not give up that belief to turn them into *jinn* like Suleiman. But he accepted, too, that he did not know this breed of man. Were there demons inside them? It made no difference. Could just three of them kill Yusuf, Suleiman, Guleed, all the Somalis left alive on this evil ship? Without question. They'd already killed half. Could they be stopped?

Yusuf raised a hand to say he had no time to consider Allah's reasons. He was interrupted by more gunfire from Jama, who must be shocked as well to find the soldiers still alive.

"Hear me," Suleiman insisted.

"Speak. "

Suleiman hooked a thumb around the corner, into the corridor. "Men or *shaitann*, we are no match for them."

"We have the hostages."

"And we had twenty-three men to defend them. Now we have thirteen. Perhaps fewer—we cannot know standing here."

"True."

"They know we have the hostages. They came anyway. They do not care, or they do not fear us. Either way, we will all die at their hands if we do nothing more than duck and shoot back. These are powerful fighters. Think who fights for us. Jama is a coward; Guleed is a boy. We have one chance, cousin."

"And what is that?"

"Answer me, truly."

"Yes."

"If these soldiers are men, do you think we can beat them?"

Yusuf had no need to consider. "No."

"And if they are spirits, then they were brought to this ship by the hand of God. To you and me, Yusuf, to test us. I believe it in my soul. It is *kaafir* not to believe it."

"Test us for what?"

Suleiman shot a finger toward the dark bow, at more sounds of gunfire from Jama and his aimless rifles.

"Men or demons, they can be killed. But only by the faithful. That is our test. Will we trust in Allah? He has guided us all our lives to this fight, our final one together. You yourself have said so, we will quit after this." Suleiman grinned, golden. "Will we stride forward, to live or die in faith? Or will we hide on this ship until we are found, until we are shamed enough to only die?"

Another lull arose from the gunfighting around the steel corner. Suleiman continued with his hand resting on Yusuf's great shoulder, as it had rested so many times.

"On the beach. Madoowbe's blood disappeared, you recall? He was a *hooyadis*. You and I, when have we ever hidden? Never. If we are to leave our blood, let it be on Allah's hands. It will not disappear there."

Yusuf mirrored his cousin's gesture, lapping his palm behind Suleiman's long neck.

"What if you're wrong? What if they are not *shaitann*, just men?"

Suleiman pouted his lower lip over his beard. "You and I will die by the deeds of men. But if we have faith, they will talk about us for a while, at least. Eh? That's something."

Suleiman let his weapon hang by its strap. He took Yusuf into an embrace.

"*Ha cabsan*, cousin." Don't be afraid.

They released each other quickly when more bursts of gunfire beckoned them.

Yusuf led along the starboard rail. The moon had risen enough to light their way past spilled Darood blood.

Chapter 39

LB could not draw a breath.

The explosion had knocked the wind out of him. The pressure drove his eyeballs back in his head, his tongue down his throat; every joint ached from the flattening blast.

Wally lay across his back, motionless.

LB struggled to keep his wits, gasping, deaf from the ringing in his ears. He pushed against the deck, shoving himself up. Wally slid off, heavy. LB rolled over, blinking into the moonlit whorls.

He snatched a trickle of air, gagging and coughing until his airway opened enough to sit up.

His left calf stung. LB probed inside the ripped pants leg to pull out fingers tipped with crimson. He flexed his boot, testing the leg. It would hold and hurt.

Beside him, Wally had been shredded. The rear of his camos was in tatters, bare skin and razor cuts showing through a dozen slits in the legs and sleeves. The nape of his neck bled, striped and raw. The armor plates in his vest peered through the clawed webbing. Ribbons of haze rose off him.

LB flipped him over. Wally's eyelids flickered. LB slapped his cheek.

"Wake up, hoss."

Wally snorted, eyes batted open. Still woozy, LB gripped the Zastava, climbing to his knees. Jamie knelt, already alert. His head and gun pivoted to protect them front and rear. The young PJ had weathered the blast better than Wally. He, too, steamed smoke.

Someone yelled through the cotton in LB's ear. Jamie's lips were taut; Wally busied himself merging back into consciousness.

"What the fuck was that?" Doc shouted over the radio. "Juggler, LB! Respond!"

Jamie answered before LB could think to thumb the talk toggle.

"RPG."

"Shit. Sit rep."

LB jumped in. "We're okay. Wally took the worst, but he's coming around."

LB surveyed the corridor in the dim light. The blast had scored the metal overhang ten feet forward of their position, frying the paint off the metal roof, wall, and deck. If the rocket had struck directly over their heads, it would have made grease marks of all three of them.

"I'm around." Wally fought to his knees. His graveled voice revealed the pain he was in. He raised his M4 into position and turned his NVGs in the direction of the grenade. Before saying another word, Wally fired a half dozen rounds into the departing mist.

"Son of a bitch," LB whispered in admiration.

Wally shook his head to clear it. "Doc," he rasped, "what've you got?"

"We heard the explosion. The targets on the bridge must've seen it. They're riled up, waving their guns around."

"Hostages?"

"No one's been hurt. Looks like the pirates inside are waiting for someone to tell 'em what to do."

"You secure?"

"Roger. I think they're too scared to come outside. What's the plan?"

"Hold one."

"Roger."

Wally shouted over his shoulder louder than he needed. "Jamie? Can you go?"

Jamie belted out, "Roger, sir."

"LB?"

"Good to go."

"All right. Before they load up another rocket, we got to move forward."

Wally peeled off his helmet and goggles. LB strapped them on. He dropped the NVGs over his eyes to look toward the stern. Forty yards ahead, two pirates jutted out their heads and Kalashnikovs. Jamie fired a few potshots to keep them out of the corridor.

LB took a pair of flashbang canisters from Jamie.

"Are they bunched up?"

Jamie nodded. "Yeah. They're taking turns shooting at us. They're ducked in that alley under the crane. Reloading, cover me." LB brought the Zastava to bear while Jamie replaced his spent magazine with a fresh one.

The passageway was too narrow to try flinging a pair of flashbangs all the way to the pirates. If LB hit a pillar or threw the wrong distance, they'd be wasted, and they had only two.

He leaned in close to Jamie. "I'll crawl as far as I can. You keep their heads down. After I get in range, you get ready to run. When they blow, you and me take 'em."

Jamie rattled his head without looking at LB.

"No. I go. I'm wearing armor."

"And I spent ten years crawling though jungles. You got a bum leg, and you're a better shot than me."

"You got a bum leg, too."

"Shut up. Cover my ass and come when I call."

LB rapped a fist on Jamie's shoulder to seal his words, and to tell the boy he was a damn fine man.

"Juggler. We're ready."

Wally hailed Doc on the radio.

Doc answered. "Go."

"We're going to move on the pirates between us and you. It's oh–one forty. Listen to me. If we're not standing next to you by oh–one fifty-five, you assault the bridge. Be sure to call the PRCC the second you secure it."

"Roger."

"We'll take out as many targets as we can. You may have to clean up after us."

"Wally, Jesus."

"Press the mission."

"Roger."

LB lifted the NVGs to get a clear look at Wally. The wan light and Wally's dozen wounds drained his color. His bare head was tousled, unlike him. The M4 seemed weighty in his hands. Wally's eyes carried the fight.

LB grinned. "You're such an asshole."

"At least that's not my call sign."

"Fair point. See you in a few."

"Roger."

LB clicked the NVGs into place. He put his belly to the cool deck, the Zastava across his back. In each hand he gripped a canister. He wriggled forward. Moonlight washed the empty corridor.

He scrabbled ten feet, calf aching. One pirate held out the branch of a hand and a Kalashnikov without exposing his head, to squeeze off another loud, blazing burst. Bullets whizzed over LB, bouncing off the metal wall and ceiling, green tracers in the goggles. Jamie returned fire, striking emerald sparks inches from the Somali's wrist. The pirate reeled the gun back in.

LB hailed on the radio, "All good?"

Jamie answered, "Other leg. Damn it."

LB made up his mind. They couldn't stand another RPG blast, or more wild bullets. The next volley from an AK could finish one or all of them any second.

He'd gotten a good look at the location and distance of the pirates. He squirmed as fast as he could ten more yards. The slice in his calf stabbed at him.

"Jamie."

"Go."

"Can you do it?"

"I dunno. I'm pretty cut up."

"All right. Stay back. I got this. Juggler, watch our six."

"Will do."

LB lifted the NVGs to get better depth perception. He had to toss them straight down the middle of the narrow corridor.

If the flashbangs were on target, the four pirates would be blinded and stunned. If not, LB was about to rush into four Kalashnikovs by himself. He wasn't sure he could do this alone. He was certain only that he had to.

He'd done dangerous things before. He would've liked a moment to pause and rank this one. Somewhere near the top.

One lesson LB had learned from every cliffhanger moment in his life, this one, too: don't hesitate.

He curled a finger inside the primary pin on the first canister. "On my mark."

The VHF screeched.

"Break, break! Hold!"

Who was this on the team freq? LB's hearing, still stuffed by the RPG, stopped him from recognizing the voice that urged, "LB, where are you?"

"Twenty yards from the pirates, toward the bow. Who is this?"

"Robey. Stay low, all of you. Close your eyes. Now."

Robey! What was he doing here? He was in the RAMZ. With no time for questions, LB crammed his face into the crook of his arm.

Ahead, the tinny sound of rolling metal squealed down the corridor floor. The blast shivered the deck under LB, followed instantly by another.

Lifting his eyes out of his elbow, he dropped the NVGs into place to see through the swelling, roiling cloud. Two sleek green figures ran into the smoke, low and fast. They rounded the steel corner to the crane where the pirates had holed up. Three, four, five blinks of light pulsed inside the fog, matched by gunfire reports. One thin image, a pirate, staggered into the corridor. With another flicker on the mist, one more pop, he collapsed.

LB took his finger from his own grenade. He struggled to his feet, the Zastava ready in his hands.

Smoke boiled in the passageway. Through the NVGs, a bareheaded and muscular soldier stepped around the corner, lowered the muzzle of his rifle to the torso of the downed pirate, and pegged two rounds into him, like Wally.

Robey turned his way.

"Hey, LB. You fucking see me now?"

LB dragged his bad leg behind him to go give the young CRO in a wetsuit a bear hug. He shouted into the shifting haze, "Where the hell did you come from?"

Robey held his position inside the smoke, swinging his M4 back and forth.

"Been monitoring your comm from the RAMZ. Me and Sandoval climbed into the pirate skiffs and up the rope ladders. Saw a few dead targets."

From behind, Wally called out, "You secure?"

Robey answered, "Secure, sir."

Sandoval, a lean Latino, jogged out of the haze, past LB with a hand slap. He went straight to Jamie to pull the boy's arm across his shoulders and help him limp forward. Torn and wobbly, Wally backpedaled, still guarding their six.

LB lifted the night goggles to check his watch: 0143. They had time to reach the bridge, and, with Robey and Sandoval on board, extra firepower to take it.

Oily haze clung in the passage. The quarter moonlight barely pierced its folds; the headwind was slow to push it away. Robey waited inside, defending the port rail until the wounded LB, Jamie, and Wally caught up.

Twenty yards from Robey, LB stopped. A shade, like black lightning, flashed through the fog.

Chapter 40

Yusuf crept through a cloud, the steel deck beneath his sandals the only solid thing. Suleiman stayed close at his rear, Kalashnikov up. Yusuf slung his own rifle across his back to reach under his *khameez* for the knife.

A body appeared at Yusuf's feet. In the coiling mist he knelt and knew it to be Jama only because the man's loose tunic had again slipped off his shoulder, showing one bullet hole through the heart. Yusuf's next quiet strides revealed two more dead pirates, shot in the chest, too, and spreading black.

Along the port rail ahead, voices shouted in English. They sounded not like spirits but Americans.

Behind Yusuf, Suleiman muttered, *"Allahu Akbar."* He raised his rifle to fire blindly at the voices. Yusuf pressed the barrel down, shaking his head.

"Your *shaitann*," he whispered close to his cousin's ear, "can see through the fog. Stay here."

Quietly, Yusuf kicked out of his sandals. He rose to his bare toes and crouched, leading with the talon of the knife. His first steps gained him speed, silent on the pads of his feet as he charged through the cloud, low in the thickest part of the draining mist.

A shadow stood at the port rail. Yusuf ran at it, rising in the last moment to deliver the hardest blow. He struck first with his shoulder, slamming the soldier against the rail, trapping his hands there and his weapon. Yusuf drove the blade into the soldier's back, up to the onyx handle. The soldier wore only a rubber wetsuit. Staying away from the muzzle of the man's gun, Yusuf gripped the wetsuit at the collar to slam his face against the wall, the knife still in him like a windup key. Yusuf yanked out the blade, buried it again into the upper back to strike at a lung or the heart. He pulled back his knife.

Another shout entered the mist from the direction of the bow. Yusuf whirled, gripping the slumping body between him and the onrushing voice. A short gray silhouette ran down the port rail, shouting, jangling under a raised gun.

With full fury, not faith, Yusuf lifted the soldier over the rail. He did not just release but flung the body out over the water. The American fell, dying too fast even to scream as he plummeted. Let the running soldier see the first death on this ship in payment for Darood blood.

Yusuf slipped away into the blowing mist.

Chapter 41

Before he could shout a warning or lower the NVGs, the stain in the smoke struck Robey with incredible speed. LB bolted into the haze.

He ran full tilt with no clear shot, no infrared sight on the Zastava. LB got within twenty yards, close enough to see the hazy outline of the young CRO being bashed against the wall. LB screamed. The big Somali turned his way, holding the limp Robey as a shield between them. LB could not shoot.

With seeming ease, the pirate heaved Robey over the rail. The young lieutenant didn't yelp, only flopped in the air, unconscious or dead. Robey plunged out of sight. LB ran, firing the Zastava from the waist as the pirate darted away into the smoke. LB loosed another burst, the rounds hitting steel. LB bolted through the cloud to the other side, into the clear. He found no trace of the pirate.

Sandoval, with NVGs down, ran out of the mist. Together with LB they swept their rifles into the darkness, at the blowing fog.

Sandoval asked, "What the hell was that?"

"A big fucking pirate threw LT off the ship."

Through the confusion, the pain in his calf, his worry and sudden sorrow over Robey, LB recalled that he'd seen that large Somali before, by flashlight with Drozdov, looking at the railgun.

Iris had been right—LB should have shot the son of a bitch in the back.

"Can you spot Robey?"

Sandoval turned his night goggles overboard and behind the steaming ship.

"Yeah, yeah. He's still floating."

"Take the point. Get us back to the bridge."

"Roger that."

LB toggled his team radio. "Fitz, Fitz. LB. You copy?"

"LB, Fitz. Go."

"Robey's overboard, on port. He's unconscious. His wetsuit's keeping him on the surface. Find him."

From the bridge, Quincy broke in. "What, again?"

LB dismissed this. Fitz in the RAMZ replied that he was trailing the *Valnea* by two hundred yards. He'd try to get a fix on the young CRO in the wake.

"On it, LB." Fitz hailed Robey but got no answer. Fitz wouldn't quit until he found him.

LB waited in the corridor for Wally and Jamie to catch up. Wally wasn't lagging behind to help Jamie walk; he looked as if he needed a supporting hand himself, hobbling along the rail through the dissipating smoke.

When Wally came past, LB fell in behind him. The man bled out of the gash in his biceps and at least a dozen shrapnel cuts from the back of his neck to his ankles. LB took stock of the carnage they passed. One Somali lay crumpled in the corridor, cleanly killed through the heart by Robey. Three more corpses jammed the narrow alley leading to the forward crane.

He asked Wally, "How many is that?"

Wally toted up: fourteen dead targets around the deck. Two more were still alive down here somewhere, the big one and another. LB had seen just how dangerous those two intended to make themselves. Another five remained inside the bridge with the hostages.

LB checked his watch: 0145.

"Twenty-five minutes left."

Wally hailed Doc. "On our way."

Doc answered. "The pirates are freaked. They saw the flash-bangs. Still haven't come out on the wings."

"We'll be there in five minutes."

"What happened to Robey?"

LB chewed his lip; his own limp grew more pronounced as they made their way along the corridor. Since he'd seen it happen, he answered, knowing the whole team was listening.

"One of the pirates threw him overboard. I think he's dead."

No responses came over the frequency. All the cursing was done in whispers, off the radio.

Wally added, "Stay focused." Finger off the PTT, he turned to LB. "Tell me something."

"Yeah."

"You know what's on this ship?"

"I do. But it wasn't my fault."

"I don't care. Tell me."

"What about the order not to be curious?"

"That went overboard with Robey. I've lost a man, and now I want to know why. I want to know what you know."

LB opened his mouth to answer but paused. He ought to tell the entire team. All their lives, already in danger, were even more at risk because of the cargo on this ship. One of their own had just paid the price for the secrets under their feet. The clock was ticking down on a drone locked and loaded to blow them all out of the water if they didn't retake this ship on time.

Five miles off, the US warship kept pace. They couldn't call the frigate for backup. *Valnea* was massively top secret. There needed to be as few witnesses as possible to everything that happened on board.

They had their orders: this mission wasn't a hostage rescue. The Somalis could never be allowed to keep this ship. And the pirates had made it clear they weren't leaving unless it was feet first.

This was the PJs' job to finish. Do or, really, die.

The team had a right to know everything.

LB set his thumb over the PTT on his team radio. Wally nodded, okay. He pressed his own talk button.

"Listen up, team. LB's going to give us a fast brief. Eyes on your job while he talks. Go, LB."

Wally dropped behind Jamie to keep an eye on their six while LB spoke on the team freq.

"All right. You guys remember Iran-Contra, back in the eighties. The US and Israel gave Iran a bunch of missiles under the table so they'd release some hostages. Well, it's happening again; we got the twenty-first-century version. This ship is carrying state-of-the-art battlefield radar and weaponry to Iran, a swap for their nuclear weapons program. This shipment is so fucking illegal, it's off the chart. Israel, Russia, and the US are behind it. The Somalis cannot, repeat, cannot, be allowed to keep this ship. You lucky bastards were the only unit sitting alert close enough to do the job. That's the nutshell."

Doc said only, "What a world."

Quiet moments passed. Sandoval led LB and Jamie forward along the port rail; Wally backpedaled with his M4 facing backward. The missing member was Robey. His return broke the silence.

The team freq clicked. "Juggler. Fitz."

Wally answered. "Fitz, go."

"I found Robey."

"How bad?"

"He's dead. Someone cut him up pretty good."

The kid never had a chance—he was overwhelmed in the first second. Robey was likely dead when he hit the water.

They continued to move toward the bridge, all of them with watchful eyes on the moon-shadowed corners of the freighter.

Inside the bridge, the pirates paced in front of Drozdov and his hostage crew. The clock to the Predator continued to tick down: twenty-three minutes left. None of this stopped because of Robey's death. The opposite happened; things sped up. LB hadn't expected the PJs would take this ship and get away without paying for it.

Wally responded to Fitz. "Roger that. Stay close. I'll let you know if we need you."

"Roger. Good luck, guys."

Like that, Robey was put aside. This was combat, and though the dead asked for a role, they had none.

Chapter 42

Suleiman galloped in front, holding Yusuf's abandoned sandals. They left the cloud behind, gunfire rattling and fading at their backs.

They rounded a corner into the starboard rail corridor. The guns on the far side of the ship stopped snapping. Yusuf and Suleiman swept the muzzles of their Kalashnikovs left and right to be certain they were not being trailed. The moon had ridden high enough to show the corridor empty, but that meant little. The Americans could appear out of darkness and smoke anywhere on the ship. Yes, Yusuf thought, like demons. But the one he'd killed had died like any other man.

He wiped the knife on his *khameez*, a bloody man. He slid it into the sheath in his waistband.

A hundred meters toward the stern, at the top of the superstructure, the broad windshield of the bridge stayed dark. The freighter surged toward Qandala as if nothing were wrong.

"We've got to get to Guleed," Yusuf said. "As long as we hold the controls, we can make it. The sun will be up in a few hours."

Suleiman did not face him. He focused on the last wisps of smoke behind them, as though the puffs were more ghosts. Yusuf spoke to his cousin's narrow back.

"We need to get to the bridge."

"I agree."

"Let's go."

"You must go, cousin." Suleiman turned. "My brother."

"We go together."

Suleiman's gold teeth sparkled. "We have traveled beside each other a long time. We go separate ways now."

Yusuf set a palm to Suleiman's thin chest. "It doesn't have to be like that. You said we would fight together. Please, no more signs."

"This is not a sign. It is a choice." Suleiman covered Yusuf's hand with his. "There is no *jihad* in piracy. There never was. I'm done with it. I won't fight for this ship anymore."

"You said to have faith. We'll get through this. We'll get home."

Suleiman laughed. "I have absolute faith, cousin. If I am to live or die, I submit myself to Allah for a better cause than ransom."

"Those are men." Yusuf held out a stained and tacky hand. "Just men."

"They may be men and still be sent by Allah."

Suleiman scanned the stars. His words seemed intended as much for them as for Yusuf.

"I do not believe we will both survive this night."

"How can you be sure?"

"I did not say I was sure. I said I believe."

Yusuf bunched Suleiman's tunic into his fist. "This is madness."

"No. I have not gone mad. I am still a fighter, like you. And if Allah decides I must die by his hand, it will need to be a strong hand."

"What about Qandala?"

"Qandala, the ransom, Robow—those are for you, cousin. Not for me."

"What will you do?"

Suleiman squeezed Yusuf's bloodied wrist.

"I will attack. I will slow them, perhaps kill a few more, enough to give you a better chance. You go to the bridge. Save Guleed and yourself, get this ship home. If I am alive at sunup, I will pay for your wedding. But if I am to die tonight, it will be to save my two kinsmen."

Suleiman wrapped Yusuf in both arms. The Kalashnikovs bulged between them.

Yusuf whispered, "Our paths have always been side by side."

Suleiman's head shook gently. "This is not a new path for us. It's the one we've always been on. Now mine stays here. Yours leads to the bridge. Run, Yusuf. Allah rewards those who run to their destiny."

Suleiman kissed both Yusuf's cheeks, then released him. Suleiman was the elder, but Yusuf remained clan chief. Suleiman turned away but did not walk off. He faced the bow and rising moon. This let Yusuf depart first, as was proper. At his back, Yusuf heard his cousin climb a ladder, up to the cargo deck.

———

Yusuf sprinted sternward, brandishing his Kalashnikov in case he surprised an enemy in the corridor. The narrow passage stayed empty, the wake's hiss the only sound. Yusuf swung his shoulders to dodge the pillars, jumped across the bodies of clansmen.

The soldiers had gone quiet. Jama and the last three pirates on deck had died in explosions and smoke. No one was left to oppose them but Suleiman.

Yusuf ran as his cousin said. With every stride he felt the severing of their fates.

Bolting down the dark passage, he fingered the trigger of his rifle. Should he have allowed Suleiman to talk him into letting him stay behind? Yusuf was tempted to turn around and go kill the rest of the soldiers alongside his cousin. He'd throw their carcasses off this ship and shout to him, "See this! Allah has chosen for you to live!"

Yusuf reached the superstructure. He stopped to catch his wind. He pointed the Kalashnikov in every direction until all the shadows proved themselves motionless.

The six stairwells to the bridge loomed very high. Yusuf, alone and breathing hard, was tempted not to go up them. He might stand his ground and deal with whatever came out of the dark for him, like Suleiman.

He could not stay here. He was not Suleiman, did not share his destiny. Guleed, Drozdov, the hostages, the American soldiers, Qandala—all those fates waited on Yusuf to move.

He spit over the rail. He picked one star to breathe in.

Yusuf entered the superstructure to take the elevator.

Chapter 43

LB did not have his NVGs down, so he did not see the pirate who shot Sandoval.

The bark of a Kalashnikov knocked Sandoval backward. More automatic rounds clanged against the steel around them. Wally dove for the deck. LB stayed on his feet to whirl and answer with a burst over their heads, but Jamie on his two bad wheels couldn't get down fast enough. LB couldn't pull the trigger, so took a knee. Sandoval tried to sit up, one-handing his M4, but Wally pulled him back down.

LB knelt to clamp a hand over the fresh hole in Sandoval's left shoulder, then pulled his goggles down, surveying the corridor. The gunfire had been only a burst. The long alley showed green and clear.

Sandoval gritted his teeth under the pressure of LB's palm over the wound.

LB asked, "What happened?"

"Son of a bitch dropped down out of nowhere." Pained, Sandoval hissed, "*Hijo de puta.*"

Jamie was on the deck now, his face as wrenched as Sandoval's. Wally climbed to his feet, goggles down, swinging his weapon front and back to guard both directions.

LB pulled his hand away for a quick look at Sandoval's wound. The bullet had entered at the top of the chest; it might have nicked the collar bone. No exit wound—the round had stayed inside Sandoval. He needed a bandage and pain meds from their rucks stashed outside the bridge. And evac. They all did.

LB checked his watch: 0149. Twenty-one minutes.

"There's time." He told Jamie to give Wally his NVGs. The young PJ detached the goggles from his helmet and tossed them over. "Sandy, sit up now." LB helped Sandoval grunt his way to a sitting position. He arranged Jamie and Sandoval back-to-back, M4s up, facing fore and aft.

Wally finished clipping the night goggles to his helmet. He said, "We got about three minutes."

"It won't take that long." LB lowered his goggles.

He led the way up the ladder. On the white expanse, LB crouched to protect Wally's approach, scanning the breadth of the cargo deck. No glow rose above the southern horizon; Somalia was mostly an unlit land. Moon and stars were enough to paint the rows of gates and crisscrossing cables with an emerald clarity. Nothing of the steel field moved. The thing that did move was human.

The cargo deck presented the same obstacles to this pirate that it did to LB, designed to strap down containers, not for a stroll. The pirate struggled to make progress. He was headed toward the bow to lay another ambush, this time from behind the wounded PJs in the corridor. To do this, he had to climb, drop, run, and climb again.

LB and Wally crept sideways to the center of the deck, keeping low. The distance to the scrambling pirate was no more than fifty meters. Wally braced his carbine against a pillar. In LB's goggles, Wally's thin green laser landed on the pirate's moving back. It wasn't a broad back; this was not the Somali who killed Robey. There was no sign of that one anywhere up here. Just this one, thin pirate alone.

Wally waited seconds for a clear shot, then took it. The gun's suppression tube coughed; no thunder for this death. The Somali heaved forward, slammed against the steel gate he was halfway up, then slid to the deck out of sight.

Wally lowered the M4, confident in the shot. He strode forward. LB stopped him.

"You go get Sandoval and Jamie headed to the bridge. I'll do it. Then I'll catch up to you."

Wally raised his NVGs. "Tell me something."

LB took one more look at the cluttered distance between them and the downed pirate. He lifted his own goggles. "Tell you what?"

"When we were in South America. Those missions I jump-mastered for you my last year at the academy. They weren't just recon."

"No. They were black ops."

"I've never seen you kill anybody the way you knifed that pirate on the bow."

"There a problem?"

"You've done that before."

"You were a kid back then."

"I stopped being a kid pretty quick. You helped with that."

"Look, I know why you need to talk. I do. But not right now, okay?" LB said again, "I got this one."

Wally nodded. "Okay. Later."

LB dropped the NVGs over his eyes. Wally headed for the ladder down to the port corridor.

———•———

LB stood above the pirate, who lay with hands spread as if in welcome. The Kalashnikov was underneath him. Shot in the back, the Somali had rolled over to die faceup.

Wally's bullet had exited through the sternum, dead center in the torso. The pirate's eyes followed LB's last step over him.

LB lowered the Zastava's muzzle against the pirate's heart.

Blood dribbled from the corner of the Somali's mouth. The man's voice was thickened, his life draining into his throat. He spoke through spattered gold teeth.

"What...what is your name?"

"LB."

The pirate hacked weakly, swallowed once. "That is an odd name for a demon."

LB fingered the trigger. "You should never have come on this ship, pal."

The Somali nodded against the steel deck. "At the end, even enemies agree."

"You say so."

The big Zastava roared into the pirate's heart.

⸺

LB caught up with Wally, Jamie, and Sandoval at the base of the port external stairs. LB's calf pulsed. Blood warmed one boot.

Sandoval looked rough. His left arm dangled uselessly, but he held his M4 out and ready with his right. Jamie could hardly put one foot in front of the other.

LB said to Wally, "Neither of these guys can make it on the steps. Send them up in the elevator. It stops one floor below the bridge. They can backstop the inside stairwell."

Wally answered with a wan smile. LB had made no mention of the pirate on the cargo deck. That told Wally the job was done.

"All right. Jamie, Sandy, do it. We'll get you wrapped up soon as we secure the bridge."

"Don't worry about us, Captain." The two PJs propped each other up enough to hobble toward the superstructure. "Send 'em our way."

Wally took the lead up the staircases, LB close on his heels. LB couldn't count the number of rips in the back of Wally's uniform and vest. For their wounds, neither could muster much stealth, all four of their boots scuffing the steel steps.

As they reached the fourth landing, Doc called on the radio. "I hear you coming."

LB answered, "Right below you. Portside stairs."

Wally read the time: "Oh-one fifty-two."

"We'll make it."

They mounted the last steps, crouching onto the wing. Doc squatted below the pilothouse door, NVGs down to keep track of the pirates inside. Big Quincy knelt, ready with his M4. Doc gave LB a thumbs-up. After a quick look at the two of them, Quincy scrambled for his med ruck, stacked in a corner alongside a dead pirate. Wally's calling card marked the body, two black punctures in the chest.

In seconds, Quincy bound LB's right calf in gauze, then started on Wally's left biceps. The big PJ's eyes widened over Wally's shredded back. "What the fuck did you do?"

The pain in LB's leg lulled to a throb under the gauze wrap. He gestured to his own eyes, then to the bridge, asking Doc to take one last look inside the windows. Doc inched his goggles above the bottom of the dark pane, peered in, then just as slowly slid down the door. He reported over the radio.

"Six targets inside. Another one must've snuck in from the back door. He's a big one. They're all on their feet. Two on this side, three on the other, and the one jumpy little guy's still pacing between them. The hostages are crowded under the windshield. All guns are on them. How you want to play it, Captain?"

Wally worked his bandaged arm. "Like before. On my mark, Doc and Mouse open both doors. Quincy and Dow toss flashbangs. When they blow, Quincy, Doc, LB, and me assault the bridge. Mouse and Dow backstop the starboard wing. Sandoval, Jamie, copy?"

"Juggler, go."

"You both in position on the floor below?"

"Roger."

"You cover the back door. After the bridge is secure, we'll alert *Nicholas* and get that drone to stand down. Then we'll mop up. Assault team, listen up. This is vital. Mind the hostages. But taking the bridge is our priority. Move fast, shoot to kill. Confirm."

Quincy rounded an okay sign. Doc shook his head and spoke on the freq for the team to hear.

"I got to say something."

"Go."

"It's not the same as before. The pirates know something's up now. The second we toss in canisters, what if someone in there panics and pulls a trigger? It might turn into a slaughter before we can stop it."

LB checked his watch: 0154, sixteen minutes left. He readied the Zastava.

Doc finished. "I just wanted to say it, that this could go bad fast. We're all thinking it."

"Thanks, Doc. Everybody. On my mark."

LB thumbed his talk button. "Captain."

Wally gazed at LB through his NVGs. He lowered his head. The radio caught Wally's exasperated sigh before he said, "What?"

LB lifted his hands off the Serb gun. "I got another idea."

Chapter 44

When the elevator opened at F deck, Yusuf leaped out. He swept the hall with the Kalashnikov, taking nothing for granted on this ship. Satisfied, he climbed the last flight of stairs to the bridge. He pushed the door open carefully, calling out in English.

"Guleed, it's Yusuf."

The young Darood was the first to spin his gun to Yusuf's voice. His eyes were white and wild when Yusuf approached through the dark.

"What were those blasts?" Guleed urged. "What's going on? Where's Suleiman?"

"Soldiers." Drozdov spoke from the middle of his sailors beneath the windshield. All the Russians and Filipinos sat upright around him. Drozdov got to his feet. Guleed threatened him with the rifle.

"I said no talking, old man. Sit down."

"That is not you speaking, boy, is your gun. Step aside. Let the men talk."

Guleed's breathing accelerated, some action rising in him. Yusuf settled him with a strong hand to the shoulder, walking him away from the other guards.

"I will talk to the captain. Stay ready." Yusuf lowered his voice. "He's right. There are soldiers on board. We're the only ones left."

"What do you mean, the only ones?"

"There's been fighting. We still control the hostages and the ship. We will make it if you keep your head. Yes?"

Guleed's shoulder collapsed under Yusuf's grip. "All dead?"

Suleiman is not dead, Yusuf wanted to say, but could not with certainty. "Don't tell the others. Guard the hostages." He motioned Drozdov away from the windshield.

The twin radar screens outlined the Somali coast thirty miles ahead. The ship's speed and course kept steady. Yusuf waited for Drozdov in the dim glow from the dashboard. Guleed resumed his pacing. The other pirates jutted their guns at the hostages, unsure of what was happening, certain only that these captured sailors were their protection from it.

"All dead, indeed?" Drozdov asked.

"Fifteen of my men. Everywhere around the deck."

"Surrender. You will live."

Yusuf looked away from the pocked Russian to the bow, the far-off beacon on its mast.

"Minutes ago, my cousin told me we must fight."

"And where is he now? One of the dead?"

"Careful, Captain."

"*Da.*" Drozdov patted his arm. "Careful, Yusuf Raage."

The Russian turned without being dismissed. He sat among his crew. The sailors on both sides whispered urgent questions. Drozdov waved them off.

Yusuf moved to the captain's chair. He stood behind it, eyeing the dials and radar images of the dash. He was not master of the *Valnea.* He was a captive as much as Drozdov. Worse. He'd led fifteen clansmen who'd trusted him to their deaths. Before the sun rose there could be more.

In the heart of these thoughts, a soft whistle of wind tugged Yusuf's attention to the port door. The Kalashnikov rattled into his hands. Guleed halted his frantic pacing.

The guard outside on the wing did not enter the bridge. The door opened only inches, then stopped.

Something dark skidded across the floor. Yusuf could not make it out clearly and in surprise could not jump away or shout a warning.

The thing struck his sandaled foot. Yusuf braced for an explosion. He tried to capture a last thought. He pictured his home, the view of the sea.

The rush of air quit, the port door shut. At Yusuf's feet the small box did not explode. Yusuf's unclenching was almost painful.

Yusuf added the guard on the port wing to the tally of dead.

He bent for the box. Guleed screamed to leave it alone. The other gunners around Guleed shoved their weapons into the hostages' midst, yelling too. Yusuf out-bellowed them to be silent. They settled enough to be quietly tense, guns stirring among the hostages. Guleed's pacing increased, back and forth across Drozdov and the cringing crew.

Yusuf lifted the walkie-talkie. He pressed the button to speak. "Yes."

"How good is your English?"

"Better than your Somali. Who is this?"

Outside the port door window, a flashlight struck. The beam played upward across a face made shadowy and otherworldly against the night.

"First Sergeant Gus DiNardo. United States Air Force. You?"

"Yusuf Raage."

The garish head bobbed, the civil greeting of an enemy.

"We need to talk, Yusuf."

With a sweeping hand, Yusuf motioned to the twenty-five hostages and five other armed men this sergeant surely knew about even if he could not see the gesture.

"Why?"

One by one, like lanterns, more faces materialized out of the black. Three soldiers emerged beside the sergeant, two others lit on the starboard wing.

So another guard lay dead.

"That's why. And I got two more on the floor below you."

Yusuf lowered the radio, then raised it.

"Where is my cousin?"

"Gold teeth?"

"Yes."

"He's dead."

Yusuf fought against himself to hold his place inside the bridge, to not rush this soldier and drive his knife deep enough to feel the man's heart stop on the blade.

The American said, "We need to talk fast."

Yusuf returned the radio to his lips. "Of course, Sergeant. Come inside."

Chapter 45

Wally spoke straight into LB's face, without broadcasting to the team or the pirate.

"No."

Wally gave the next order over the radio. "Team, lights out."

The hovering heads on both wings extinguished. Dow and Quincy lowered their NVGs over their eyes. Quincy crept to the window to help Dow keep an eye inside the bridge, weapons ready.

LB checked the time. Twelve minutes left.

Wally, again off the team freq, said, "You got two minutes."

LB lifted the M4 strap over his head. Before he could lay the gun on the deck, Wally thrust his bandaged arm to stop him.

"I said no."

"I got to go in there. I can talk them out."

"Do it from here. Use the radio, like we said."

"For Christ's sake, he wants me inside. I can do it; I know I can."

"Listen to me. We're not hostage negotiators. We've got a mission. You have two minutes to talk them out of the bridge. Then we go in and get them. If you lack the stomach for that, stay out here. Start talking now, or I give the go."

LB slipped his rifle back across his shoulders. Wally joined Quincy and Doc kneeling at the port window.

LB peered through his NVGs for one more look inside the dark bridge. Five frantic pirates and five guns menaced the huddled hostages. Big Yusuf Raage stood in the center of the bridge behind the captain's chair, holding the spare walkie-talkie Doc had slid inside.

Doc was right. A single wrong move, and this would turn into a bloodbath.

LB lifted the goggles. He flicked on his flashlight again, training it under his chin, upward over his face as before, to talk to the pirate in plain view. He thumbed the PTT.

"Yusuf."

"Yes."

"I can't come inside."

"I understand. It would not have been good for you."

"I've got two minutes to convince you that you're all going to die."

"I don't believe you, Sergeant. You would not sacrifice the hostages."

"We would. I know you've seen what's on this ship. Down in the cargo hold, I was there. I saw you and Drozdov."

"Very good. That is a lot of machines."

"About five billion dollars' worth, all of it state-of-the-art."

"All going to Iran. Yes, I know this."

"Then you know it's an illegal shipment. Four different countries, mine included, do not want you to keep this boat. Hostages or not."

"Those are harsh orders, Sergeant."

"For everybody. So come out. Let's call it a night."

"What if I fight you?"

"Listen to me. Even if you win, you lose. In ten minutes, the United States government's going to blow this ship to the bottom if we don't have control of it. There's a drone over our heads right now with weapons locked."

"Again, I don't believe you."

"Look behind me, Yusuf. You see the American warship?"

"Yes."

"It's turned around."

"Yes. It has."

"They've got orders, too. No witnesses. I'm not lying. We're all dead, the hostages, you, me, if we don't settle this fast. If we have to come in for you, I swear, you and your men will not survive. You've seen what we can do."

"Yes."

"So end it. Give your men and the hostages their lives back. You and me, too. I'll be honest, I don't want to come in there to get you."

Off the radio, Wally said, "Time."

"Yusuf, what's your answer?"

Inside the bridge, the pirate lowered the radio. Wally stepped beside LB. He drew his hand under his chin—out of time.

LB shut off the flashlight.

Wally circled a finger in the air for Quincy and Dow. Ready.

Dow snuck his arm up to the portal handle. Quincy readied a flashbang.

LB dropped his NVGs in place. In the starboard window, Mouse and Dow watched from their dark wing. LB took a knee, Wally knelt beside him. Wally held up a fist, as per the plan, marking thirty seconds.

The team freq hissed.

"Sergeant?"

"Yeah, Yusuf."

"Can you see me in the dark?"

"We all can."

"Then watch."

Chapter 46

——.——

Yusuf approached the seated hostages. A few shied from him, shinnying away. In the center, Drozdov held firm.

Yusuf knelt before Drozdov. "Captain. I need one of your men. You pick. Or I will."

Drozdov's gray sockets and sunken cheeks might have branded him a ghost to Suleiman.

"No," the captain said. "This is not the way."

Yusuf stood to look across the seamen. The Filipinos in dungarees and T-shirts lowered their eyes from him, wanting nothing to do with sacrifice. The Russian officers in slacks and buttoned shirts crowded about Drozdov as if closeness to his courage might save them from Yusuf's choosing. The two guards in their black sweaters sat separate, distancing themselves from these sailors and their concerns.

Yusuf considered the fat first mate, Grisha. This one looked like he would blubber. Already Yusuf knew him to be a traitor. He needed a more sympathetic figure.

The Filipinos were small and too many.

A lanky officer shifted to his knees to stand, muttering, "*Sparcai-m-ash in ciorba lu ma-ta.*"

Drozdov reached to stop him. "Razvan, no." The officer shoved his captain's hand away and straightened.

Yusuf moved close to this tall officer. "What did you say to me, Russian?"

"I will shit in your mother's soup." He spat. "And I am Romanian, pirate."

Before Yusuf could take this one by the arm, Drozdov struggled to his feet to confront his tall crewman.

"Sit, Chief. That is order."

The Romanian curled his lips and winced, holding back another spit. He took his seat.

Drozdov walked away from Yusuf, again without instructions. He rounded the long dashboard to stand in the glow of his dials and screens, lit by his ship.

Dramatically, Drozdov spread his hands. Yusuf pushed talk on the radio and held it up to Drozdov so the Americans could hear him.

"Three years I have been dying slow death from pirates. Drinking, stupid, angry. Day after day. So let's go, Yusuf Raage. Kill me all at once instead of these little bits. *Po hooy.* I don't fucking care."

Yusuf raised the Kalashnikov to his shoulder. At the same time he brought the radio close to his lips.

"You are listening?"

"Yes."

"Take your men off the wings. Now. Or I will shoot the captain. I will kill another every minute until you leave or you kill me."

"Yusuf, I'm not bluffing. I can't."

"Take a moment, Sergeant. Be sure."

"I haven't got a moment. Neither do you. Put the gun down."

On both dark ends of the bridge, the doors unsealed. The wind whistled again.

At the end of the Kalashnikov, Drozdov dropped his arms.

Yusuf had run through the blood of his clansmen, sworn to walk through Robow's in revenge. In the next seconds, there would be more blood at his feet, the hostages', Guleed's, his own, perhaps the Americans'. Air gushed into the bridge from the doors cracking open; the soldiers would be next to rush in.

They would spill all to take this ship and their machines back. Suleiman had not slowed them. Yusuf could not stop them.

The American had said it. If Yusuf did not surrender, he was a dead man. If he did give up, if he betrayed his clan, his vows, Qandala, his kin, he would surely be a living dead man.

There was only one choice. Spill one man's blood. It may stop more. It had worked before.

The radio said, "One last time. Put all your guns down. Come out."

Guleed shook his head in fast, frightened trembles. "They'll kill us."

The port door opened wide enough for a big soldier, eyes hidden behind goggles, to fill the frame. The soldier did not enter but pointed his weapon at Guleed's back.

Yusuf screamed at the soldier, "No!"

His Kalashnikov flamed inside the dark bridge.

Drozdov shuddered, every round of the long blast tearing him until he buckled at the foot of the captain's chair.

Chapter 47

LB yanked Quincy out of the doorway and down. Doc slammed the door just before a burst from an AK shattered the windowpane. Bullets blistered over their heads, banging the rail. Glass shards showered the ducking PJs.

"Now!" Wally's radio voice cut across the gunfire. "Throw!"

From his back, Quincy pulled the pin to toss a flashbang through the busted window. LB shut his eyes behind the goggles and clapped hands over his ears.

The first detonation thumped deep in the steel. A second followed instantly.

Quincy scrambled off the deck, quick as a tiger. LB opened his eyes, gathering himself to move fast. Doc pulled the door wide open. Coils of smoke spilled out. Wally bulled into the cloud first, his M4 immediately sparking. Quincy moved in his wake, angling toward the windshield and hostages. LB jumped to his feet to rush into the bridge.

His goggles pierced the mist, every detail left hazy but identifiable. Emerald beams slashed back and forth, searching. The last traces of the grenades' roars rang in the metal surfaces. Near the windshield, a Somali staggered, stunned and blind. From ten feet away Quincy pinned his chest with the IR beam, put a fast pop on the dot, then plugged him again as he fell. Another Somali lurched near the hostages, hunched and holding his head. Before

LB could target this one, the pirate pulled his trigger to loose a wild arc of bullets, intending to die firing into the hostages. All of the sailors pressed chests to the floor, flattened by the grenades and gunfire. The pirate had no bearings in the smoke, deaf to the hostages shrieking at his feet. His first volley dented the wall behind them and blasted out a windshield pane, spattering glass on the crew. LB whipped his IR beam to the pirate's chest and fired. The Somali wobbled from two speed rounds to the breast but did not go down. Fading, the pirate lowered the gun's muzzle as his last act and raked the gun blazing into the hostages. From the chart table, Doc finished him with two more rounds to the rib cage. The Kalashnikov fell silent with the pirate. With more Somalis alive on the bridge, LB tore his attention from the wailing, injured hostages.

Bathed in the lights of the dashboard, another stumbling pirate went down to Wally's M4. Folding to his knees, the pirate let off a quick burst. Across the room Quincy whirled, stung. LB put two more rounds in the dropping pirate from close range. This last Somali collapsed in a heap beside the first pirate killed when Wally charged the room.

The bridge echoed like a spent bell. The PJs stabbed their targeting beams into every corner of the room. A dark ooze spread into the Somalis' blouses, drizzling onto the deck. The hostages moaned or shouted urgently through the chemical haze, unable to hear or see. Doc hustled to them, skidding on his kneepads to assess casualties. "Quincy," he yelled, "med rucks!" Big Quincy, shaking blood off his left hand, bolted for the port wing's shot-up door.

LB and Wally stepped over corpses, on crunching glass and slick blood, hunting out the last smoky hiding places on the bridge. Six Somalis had held the room when the assault started. Four were down.

"LB." Wally did not turn from his sweeping IR beam.

"Yeah."

"Hail that warship. Tell them we're secure. Have them contact AFRICOM. Stat."

LB hurried to the dash. Drozdov lay dead at the foot of his captain's chair. The digital clock on the dash read 0204. Six minutes left.

LB pressed talk on the ship's VHF.

"USS *Nicholas*, *Nicholas*. This is Air Force Guardian Angel team on board *Valnea*. Over."

The warship answered immediately. LB interrupted the sailor's response.

"*Valnea* is secure. Repeat, *Valnea* is secure. Request you contact AFRICOM immediately to relay this. Repeat, immediately."

Over the loudspeaker the frigate's radioman said he'd take care of it. He asked if any other assistance was needed.

From around the bridge, Wally, Quincy, and Doc yelled, "No!"

LB sped his words. "Not now. Just call AFRICOM. Urgent. Confirm when done."

"Roger. *Nicholas* out."

Mouse and Dow entered from the starboard wing, leaving the portal open. Mouse joined Doc and Quincy in tending to the hostages. Dow checked for a pulse on Drozdov, then the downed Somalis.

Wally finished searching in the departing mist. He moved beside the captain's chair, ignoring Drozdov's corpse. LB joined him. Both lifted their night goggles. The radioman on *Nicholas* called back to confirm. LB handled the contact. The one-word message from AFRICOM was "secure."

Dow called out that all four Somalis were dead.

Wally answered. "Casualty report on the hostages."

LB scanned the carnage of the bridge. Bits of impact glass and bullet casings glittered on the floor, lit by the ship's gauges and the moon through missing windows. Blood would not color in the sparse light and stayed black on the pirates and Drozdov.

Doc worked on hostages' wounds, wrapping limbs and scalps. The hefty first mate, Grisha, lay with his head in another's lap; Quincy was busy cutting away the shirt over the man's bulbous belly. Dow knelt beside one downed Filipino, then moved to another. All the hostages' senses remained clobbered. The ones who found their voices cried for help and answers. None tried to stand.

LB's skin prickled after the ten seconds of combat. He unlatched his hands from the rifle for it to hang loose at his chest, his first step in letting the world restore.

Dow came close. "All four targets are dead. Plus the captain and two crew. One of the Russians has a sucking chest wound; we've got to evac him. Quincy took one through the wrist. He's a bull. Says he'll wrap himself." Dow tapped a finger on the red coin seeping through the bandage around Wally's biceps. "We ought to take a look at that too, Captain."

Wally dismissed him with a nod. The PJ hesitated.

"What?" Wally asked.

"Weren't there six targets in here?"

"Two got out."

Dow surveyed the mess of the bridge. "Lucky." He moved to station himself in the center of the room, standing guard should the two missing pirates take another turn at them.

LB said, "We got lucky, too."

Wally pinched the bridge of his nose, showing strain. "No."

"Three hostages. Quincy got winged. Could've been worse."

"Robey makes it worse."

"Yeah."

"Where's Yusuf Raage?"

LB had lied to the *Nicholas* when he reported that the freighter was secure. It wasn't. Two pirates remained at large. And a female scientist.

Wally fingered his talk button. "Jamie? Sandoval? Respond."

The last of the smoke slipped along the ceiling, seeping out the busted windows and open doors. Wally hailed again.

His answer blared through the wall at the back of the bridge, a long, emptying rip from a Kalashnikov in the stairwell.

Chapter 48

The blast of the Kalashnikov did not drown out Guleed's frightened cry.

A dozen bullets threw the captain against his chair. The man was dead before he settled in shreds to the deck.

The rifle's reports pounded the bridge into a stunned silence. Yusuf's gun hovered. Guleed's hands stayed in the air as if the moment of Drozdov's killing needed more time to complete itself.

Yusuf whirled on the port door, taking fast aim at the large soldier standing in it. The soldier flew backward as if struck before Yusuf loosed a long blast, sweeping the barrel across the door, shattering the heavy pane and windows. The door slammed shut while Yusuf hammered it and the wall until the drum of his AK-47 clicked empty.

The dented bridge, its captors and hostages, paused while the racket and gunsmoke lingered.

The radio in Yusuf's hand barked.

"Now! Throw!"

Yusuf stood panting, exhilarated and blanked by the long burst from the gun. Guleed screamed again, jarring Yusuf back to action. He did not wait for the next gush of air or the bounce of grenades. He lunged to grab Guleed by the scruff of his blouse. The boy, thin like Suleiman, came to his toes in Yusuf's grasp.

Suleiman had died to save the two of them; nothing was left to Yusuf now but to honor that.

"Run!" he belted in his young cousin's ears. "The back stairs!"

Yusuf flung the boy ahead of him. Guleed, rigid with surprise, stumbled, not fathoming that they were escaping. In the next moment, he gained his feet to dash past the chart table for the rear door and steps. Yusuf did not turn to look at the hostages or the men he was abandoning to save Guleed, his kin. Yusuf had seen all his men dead on this ship; not the least honor lay with any of them. He, too, was without honor, just a pirate. Only Suleiman had died for something more than ransom.

At Yusuf's back, something small and metallic bounced against the floor, then another.

Guleed yanked open the door to dive through. Behind Yusuf, an immense bang erupted, so loud that it shoved him the last stride through the doorframe. The stairwell walls flashed with the light of a starburst. Yusuf feared the bite of shrapnel chasing him. Guleed recoiled, hands to his eyes. Yusuf barged onto the landing, pulling the door shut just before a second explosion.

Guleed gulped for breath, Yusuf listened through the door. The detonations faded fast, replaced with the shouts of the pirates left behind. "I can't see," they screamed. "Where are they?" Ratcheting noises, claps more than gunfire, snapped in twos and threes, silencing the bursts of Kalashnikovs. When the weapons quieted, the Americans were the only ones left shouting.

Yusuf pulled his small cousin into an embrace. He spoke in a whisper to the top of the boy's head.

"Listen to me. There are two American soldiers waiting on the floor below. When we come to the next landing, they will see us. We will have to fight past them. Can you do this?" He moved the boy to arm's length, leaving his great hands across Guleed's shoulders.

Guleed pushed Yusuf's hands down, as if bothersome, or as if he did not deserve them. He sniffled along his sleeve, trying to right his nerve.

"I'm sorry, cousin. I was afraid."

"I'll settle the score when you're old enough to marry. I will pick your first wife."

Guleed snorted, making him wipe his nose again on his *khameez*.

Yusuf laid down his empty Kalashnikov. The flight of stairs below led to the landing and doorway for F deck. In the hall there, the soldiers were surely gazing down gun barrels, an excellent and protected view of the stairwell.

"Give me your gun. I'll go first. I'll fire and keep them busy. You run behind me and go down the rest of the stairs as fast as you can. I'll be right behind you."

Guleed nodded. "Then what?"

"We'll get off this ship. The skiffs are still tied to the stern, but the warship will stop us. We'll head for the bow and throw a life raft over. We'll jump in it." Yusuf showed the radio the Americans had slid to him inside the bridge. "Deg Deg's behind us. We'll call him. The old man and that cat will come find us."

Guleed dug a tear from his eye. "That's not a story, is it?"

"Yes. It is. And we'll tell it at your wedding to your ugly wife."

Guleed shrugged his Kalashnikov into his narrow hands. His line was closer to Suleiman's, carrying their family's leanness and courage. The boy arranged himself beside Yusuf on the landing, facing the stairs.

Guleed said, "You did not surrender."

"No."

"I would have."

Yusuf stroked the back of his kinsman's smooth neck. "You are wrong."

Guleed smiled up at this. "Tell the story that way, cousin. *Allahu, jixinjix.*"

Allah, have mercy.

With his gun still in his hands, the boy bounded away, racing down the staircase. Yusuf leaped after him, vainly stretching to pull the boy back. Guleed jumped in the air, crying like an eagle, to land spread-legged in the doorway. Throat in full battle cry, Guleed leveled his Kalashnikov into the hallway. He braced the rifle at his hip, laying down a withering cover fire. The boy swung the flaming muzzle left and right; the soldiers must have been on both sides. Yusuf rounded the banister in time to hear Guleed shout above the gun, "Go, go!"

The first rounds made Guleed backpedal, but nothing more. He leaned forward into the blows as if into an ocean wave. The Americans struck the boy again, staggering him without silencing the Kalashnikov.

Yusuf took the last image of his young cousin with him into the stairwells below, Guleed screaming the name of Allah alongside their clan, Harti of the Darood.

Chapter 49

There seemed hardly a place on the ship without blood splashed on it.

LB gazed down at the bullet-riddled Somali boy. Jamie shifted back and forth, both legs hurting. The young PJ flicked an open hand at the body.

"What kind of son of a bitch sends out a kid to get shot up so he can run off?"

From where he slumped against a wall, Sandoval agreed, cursing in Spanish.

Wally took LB aside. "Take care of Sandoval and Jamie. Defend the bridge. Get one of the crew to stop the freighter. I'll radio when I'm done." He strode for the stairs leading down.

LB halted him.

"Move aside," Wally said. "I've got orders."

"And whoever gave you those orders wasn't thinking you'd have to chase him down by yourself on a dark freighter with how many wounds in you? Let me organize a search party; it's a big ship. We'll do it right. But if Raage is gone, he's gone."

"Do it right. Is that LB talking?"

LB ignored the jibe. Wally was hurt, tired, and not his cheerful self.

"And another thing. We've got to find Iris Cherlina, maybe before he does. You can't do that and hunt him down by yourself."

While Wally weighed this, LB added one more reason. "PJs don't work alone."

Wally nodded. LB rapped him lightly on the good shoulder. Quickly he stepped beside Jamie to loop the young PJ's arm across his shoulder. "Let's get you fixed up." To Sandoval, he said, "I'll send Dow and Mouse down for you."

"Roger, LB."

LB helped Jamie up the flight of steps to the pilothouse, Wally following. Inside the bridge, Quincy rushed over to lay the young PJ against a wall. Quincy set to cutting away both pants legs to dress the thigh wounds. Jamie, with two bullets through him, reached for the med ruck to grab bandages for Quincy's dripping hand. LB dispatched Dow and Mouse to fetch Sandoval up the stairs.

The bridge had shed the last of the flashbang smoke. LB and Wally crossed to the huddle of hostages. Two Filipinos wore Doc's gauze around their arms; a third held still while Mouse swathed his head. The chest-wounded Russian was already bandaged and plugged into a saline drip held up by a dazed shipmate. The pair of dead crewmen lay covered, one by a cloth from the coffee table, the other under a shirt from one of his Pinoy mates. Most of the hostages were still fuzzy from the flashbangs. Wally knelt before one Russian who looked clearheaded.

"Can you drive the ship?"

The man tapped his ear. "What?"

Wally leaned close. "Can you drive the ship?"

The officer raised the finger, understanding. "Yes."

"I want it stopped. Can you put it in neutral or something?"

"Of course."

The tall officer unfolded from the sheen of broken glass on the floor. "I am Razvan. Chief engineer."

LB said, "We can hear you. Don't shout."

"Sorry."

LB escorted the tall engineer around the dashboard. The ship's captain lay ruined there. Razvan hesitated.

"Can he be moved?"

Wally joined LB to lift the captain away. LB had watched and listened to this man's death; it had been gutsy. The lightness of the corpse, like a sack of sticks, saddened him. Such an end should reside in a man somehow, leave him weightier. This was LB's fear, the fear of every warrior—to die well but yet be insignificant. They carried the captain behind the map table, and LB dragged down several long paper charts to cover him.

He walked to where Jamie rested against a wall.

"Can you stand?"

"Sure."

"Take the port wing. Quincy, put him on his feet." LB pointed at the big PJ's bandaged wrist. "How's the hand?"

"Good to go."

"Mouse, you're on the starboard wing."

"Roger."

"Dow, stay with the bridge. Keep an eye on Sandy and the hostages. Call *Nicholas*. Have them stand off close on starboard until we bring them in for evac. Doc, Quincy, listen up. The three of us and Wally are going to secure the ship. There's one Somali left. You see him, shoot him. Plus a civilian out there somewhere, a woman. Be on the lookout for her. Questions?"

Doc asked, "What if the pirate surrenders?"

Wally answered. "If he throws his gun down, you keep him there for me. Then you walk away."

"But, Captain—"

Wally cut Doc off. "Those are your orders. I've got mine, and I'm done with having them questioned. I'll answer for them later. Not now."

Wally split them into two teams, Doc and Quincy on the port rail, him with LB along starboard. LB took the lead onto the wing, down the external stairs. He moved quickly, believing Yusuf Raage was not interested in making a stand, only in getting off the ship. As they reached deck level, the hiss of the wake had fallen away. The *Valnea* was slowing.

LB turned for the stern, using more care now. Wally kept an eye behind them. All three pirate skiffs were still attached to the rail, trailing on the freighter's fading momentum. The trio of Somali bodies lay undisturbed. Wally alerted Doc and Quincy on the radio, told them to watch for life rafts.

"What's Raage doing?" Wally asked.

LB pushed forward to find out. He lowered his NVGs to scan the dark waters for an inflated raft or floating container. The gulf lay flat and moon-dappled. The goggles provided a panorama of the heavens, every star highlighted.

LB let Wally take the point. They passed the midship crane, stepping over corpses every forty yards. The *Valnea* sat dead in the water now. With no masking headwind or wake, the bodies asserted themselves in silence and pitiful odors.

The radio buzzed. Quincy reported no movement in the port companionway.

Wally answered, "Stay cool. Push forward."

The pain in LB's leg grew more jabbing, his limp more pronounced. He and Wally passed another skinny body with Wally's bullets in it. LB was glad Wally had taken the lead, or, like the *Valnea*, he might just stop, drained of momentum.

Chapter 50

He ran from the boy's death. Guleed had died the same way as Drozdov, on many bullets.

Gone from Yusuf's grasp were both cousins, the ship, twenty-one clansmen, Qandala; these hounded him down the steel corridor. He slowed to hear if the soldiers chased him. They had control of the ship; would they just allow him to escape? No, they could not. Yusuf knew what was on this freighter and where it was going. They wouldn't let that knowledge loose in the hands of a pirate.

Yusuf made his way forward along the starboard corridor. He passed three life raft canisters but let them alone. He jumped over four corpses. None had weapons. Yusuf was left with only his knife.

He ran the full passageway to the bow, not knowing how much time he had. Where was Suleiman's body? Both cousins had died to save Yusuf. He could do nothing for brave Guleed, but he would try to take Suleiman home for proper burial and honor. If Yusuf could do this, he would not have lost all.

He carried the American radio in one hand, the onyx-handled knife in the other. The Americans would have to move more slowly than he did, afraid of ambush. The thought of ambush made Yusuf calculate what Suleiman might have done.

Where could his cousin have hidden, from where could he spring?

Or drop?

Yusuf leaped onto the closest ladder to the cargo deck.

The moon, high and peering white, lit the vast field. He gazed as far as the cluttered deck allowed, seeing no sign of Suleiman. Dropping to the corridor, Yusuf bolted to the next ladder, climbed again to the deck to find no trace, then ran forward to climb another. There, in the center of the white steel expanse, lay the dark blotch of his kinsman's body.

Yusuf ran across the open steel. Hatred stoked in his heart, anger hardened his grip on the knife. He knelt in Suleiman's blood without words or time to mourn. Those were for later, on Somali ground. The soldiers who'd done this and more, who would put a bullet through his heart too, could not be far behind. Tucking hands under his limp cousin, Yusuf bit his teeth to stop himself from shouting.

The body was light enough. He carried Suleiman quickly to set him beside the ladder well. He did not use the rungs but dropped down into the narrow passageway, choosing speed over silence.

The woman in the corridor could not avoid him.

She ran only a few steps toward the stern until he snared her by the back of the blouse. Yusuf yanked her to a stop, then whirled her to face him.

"You," he breathed, "are Iris Cherlina." Yusuf rolled the onyx-handled knife in his fingers. She inched away along the rail. "Don't run. I'm out of patience."

Iris Cherlina crossed hands over her breasts as a naked woman might do.

"I am Yusuf Raage. The one you sent for."

She shook her head, saying no to whatever he might do to her. She said, "I'm sorry."

"I should cut your throat."

Even with Yusuf's warning for her to stand still, the woman crept backward. He stepped forward, halting her retreat.

She said again, "I'm sorry. I didn't know this would happen."

"That is a lie. You knew what was on this ship. You knew soldiers would come take it back."

She raised one palm off her chest. "I swear I didn't. We made the accident a hundred miles from the coast because no armies could get here fast enough. I wanted the ship to reach shore. I'd never heard of these American rescuemen. And if I had, I wouldn't have believed they could…"

Iris Cherlina pulled up short in her confession. Yusuf lunged before she could speak more or back away. Snagging her wrist, he dragged her toward the bow, to the dead Darood sprawled nearby beneath the rail. He flashed his hand behind her head, pressing her to kneel into the shadows and stench. Yusuf pointed at the twin black holes over the corpse's heart glistening like coal.

"That they could do this? To *all* of my men?"

Yusuf squeezed her neck, lifting her to face him. He hauled her to the ladder, where he tugged Suleiman's body down to his arms. The woman did not move. Yusuf placed his dead kinsman on the deck, then held the blade close to Iris Cherlina's chin, twisting it to catch the moonlight.

"You are a scientist."

"Yes."

"Were you going to Iran with all the Israeli machines? Were you part of the deal?"

"Yes. I was."

"What is the machine in the bow?"

"An electromagnetic railgun. A weapon. It's what Iran wants most."

"Is that why you brought me here to hijack this ship? To stop it? Your fat sailor says you have a conscience."

"That's correct."

Yusuf, as he had with Grisha, pushed the point of the blade under her chin. This backed the woman against the steel wall. She rose onto her toes.

"I will ask once. You hid this weapon and the machines from the crew. You wanted it hijacked because you couldn't stand to see it all in the hands of Iran. Is that right?"

Her answer came without more tremors on the tip of the knife. Iris Cherlina dropped her pretense of fear.

"Yes."

"You wanted me to take this ship back to the Islamists, have them lay it all out for the world to see."

"Yes."

"And you would be the invisible hand behind it all. Because you are a patriot?"

Yusuf increased the pressure on the knife into her chin. She tried to nod but could not on the tip of the dagger.

"Yes."

"Perhaps."

She grunted. "There is no other answer."

He eased the blade from her flesh. She smoothed a pretty finger under her chin.

An ingenious scheme, if true. Use Sheikh Robow and al-Qaeda to bring forth pirates. Slow the ship to make certain they could board. Stop Iran from getting the hardware, embarrass the governments responsible, blame the pirates, all tracks covered.

"How much were the Iranians paying you to come work for them?"

"I've been paid two million dollars. I get another million per year."

Yusuf's sandals shuffled backward involuntarily.

"You must be quite the scientist."

"I am."

He pointed the dagger at her. A shame not to have been able to ransom her alongside the crew and cargo. She'd be worth a great deal.

"You've failed. The Americans have stopped me from taking the ship. It will go on to Beirut. Nothing has changed except all my men are dead."

"This ship is not going to Beirut. Iran will never see any of the machines, or the railgun, or me."

"How can that be?"

"It is going to sink. It can't be stopped."

"How did you—"

She had the fat sailor's master key. She could go anywhere.

"It will blow in less than five minutes. You'll be blamed for it."

It struck Yusuf then that this woman had pulled every string from the beginning. Starting weeks ago, when Robow arrived at the wedding, right to this moment. Suleiman said that Allah rewards those who run to their fate. Yusuf had been running to her.

He pointed at the dark heap near his feet.

"That is my cousin. Suleiman Abdikarim." He said this because everything on the ship belonged to Iris Cherlina, including the corpses.

She advanced at his raised blade. She brushed it aside, slipping past him in the narrow passage toward the stern.

"I owe you, Yusuf Raage. Get off this ship. Do it now. If you live, I will find you. I'll send you money. Again, I'm sorry."

She did not break into a run but walked away, confident that Yusuf had been settled. What sort of man did she take him for? A pirate, bought with the promise of money? He'd been that when he came on board the *Valnea*, yes, but that was when he had a ship to capture, men and kin beside him to do it. All that was gone now. Yusuf was not a pirate any longer on this ship. He was only Darood, the last living on board, and chieftain of his dead.

Yusuf surged at Iris Cherlina. Before she could turn, he'd wrapped her throat in the crook of his elbow. She struggled. He could squeeze until she choked, or cut her throat. But this woman had value greater than her own death.

Yusuf tightened around the woman's long neck enough to still her. He tugged the walkie-talkie from his waistband and brought it to his lips.

"Americans."

Chapter 51

LB started to answer, but Wally held up a hand.

"This is Captain Bloom. Yusuf Raage?"

"I am waiting for you on the bow."

Wally sped his gait, carbine up and ready. LB followed close behind. On the port rail, Doc and Quincy would be sprinting forward right now.

"Captain."

"Yes?"

"I have Iris Cherlina."

Off the radio, Wally cursed. LB passed him in the narrow corridor to break into a run. They flew past the bodies of pirates. Nearing the end of the passageway, LB leaped across the corpse of the thin Somali he'd shot ten minutes ago up on the cargo deck. How did he get here?

Reaching the end of the companionway, LB and Wally pulled up. From behind cover, LB scanned the bow through the NVGs. Yusuf Raage stood in the open between two hawsers, at the point of the hull. In the milky light of the moon and the tall beacon on its mast, the Somali could not see the pair of infrared beams pinning him from Doc and Quincy standing to port, weapons trained, one to his cheek, the other on his chest. Both dots glowed dangerously close to Iris Cherlina's head, framed inside Raage's elbow, a knife at her throat.

LB raised his goggles and lowered his weapon. Wally did the same. Both walked into the open, closer. Doc and Quincy stayed back to keep the pirate covered.

LB spoke first. "Iris, this is Captain Bloom."

Wally dipped his brow. "Ma'am."

Yusuf Raage answered by tossing the walkie-talkie overboard. He yanked the back of Iris's hair, stretching her white neck. He shaved the blade up her flesh. She breathed hard through her nose, blinking wildly.

LB held up a hand. "You don't want to do that."

Yusuf eased his head beside hers, as if to whisper in her ear. "Ah, Sergeant. You have no idea how badly I do."

Wally asked, "What do you want?"

Off to starboard, the warship *Nicholas* approached with the great mumble of her engines. Yusuf tucked the knife tighter under Iris's chin. She stood stiffly, quiet.

"Have your men lower their rifles. If they raise them again, I will kill her. You may do as you like after that."

With a wave of Wally's hand, Quincy and Doc lowered their M4s.

Yusuf shifted his dark eyes to LB. "Did you kill my cousin?"

Wally gestured for LB to give no answer. LB ignored him. "Yeah."

The Somali nodded before returning his attention to Wally. "I will make a trade."

"No."

Yusuf Raage slid the blade sideways under Iris's chin. She jerked at the sting. A dribble of her blood soaked into his sleeve.

"You will throw your weapons overboard. Then you and your men will get off this ship. He will stay behind. When I am satisfied, I will release the woman."

Wally said again, flatly, "No."

The Somali wagged his great head. "Captain. This woman has offended me in enough ways. I will slit her throat and take a bullet for it. So be it. She will die at my hand. Or he will. Either way, I am a dead man, I know that. The question is, who joins me?"

Wally did not hesitate. He raised his M4, looking keen to put a round between Yusuf's eyes.

"Quincy, Doc. Dismissed."

On the port side of the bow, both PJs held their ground.

The pirate did not duck Wally's raised muzzle. He dug the edge of his blade deeper into Iris's flesh. He showed his teeth when he said, "Captain, I've warned you."

Wally yelled at Doc and Quincy. "Dismissed!"

The two PJs wavered, unsure. Wally did not shout when he said to LB, "You, too."

The Somali waited. Another red drip pulsed down Iris Cherlina's throat.

LB lifted the Zastava's strap off his shoulder. With a spinning heave, he tossed it over the gunnel into the night.

Wally did not shift his stance.

"Doc, Quincy. Escort LB off the bow. Now." Wally lowered his voice. "I'll put you in the brig later."

LB called across the bow to the two PJs. "Hold."

Doc and Quincy steadied, both fixed on Yusuf Raage.

"Wally, he'll kill her."

"And I'll kill him. Now leave the bow."

"You got to be kidding."

Swiftly, Wally lowered his M4 from Yusuf Raage. In the same motion, he drew his Beretta sidearm to point it at LB's chest.

"Back off. That's an order."

"Or you'll shoot me?"

"Yes. Then I'll shoot him."

LB drew himself to his full height, still a head shorter than Wally.

Wally spoke down the short barrel of the pistol. "I'm going to count…"

"What are you, my fucking mom?"

LB stepped closer to Wally. The pistol's muzzle lifted to his eyes.

"That others may live, Wally. Others. Any order you get or give that contravenes that is not worth following. So go ahead and count. I'll get you started. One."

The Somali's gravelly voice interrupted. "Captain."

Wally did not turn to the pirate; the Beretta stayed on LB.

"What?"

"This sergeant you point your gun at. You wear the same uniform. You are clan."

"I suppose."

"The men you killed on this ship, they were my clan. Two were my family. Aim your gun only at me."

Wally glanced for a moment at the pirate. When he returned his focus to his pistol hand, LB had sidestepped away from the barrel.

Wally holstered the pistol.

He said to Yusuf, "Let her go. We'll all walk out of here alive, all right? You've got my guarantee."

Yusuf did not release his headlock on Iris. "Thank you for that gesture, Captain."

"Then let's go."

"But you know it's a lie. I will die here or in some African jail. My life is worth nothing in your hands, just as yours would be worthless in mine. At this moment, I prefer vengeance to keeping my life. I'm sure you think that barbaric. It may be. Now throw your weapons overboard. Leave the bow, then leave the ship. The sergeant stays behind."

Wally lowered his head and sucked his teeth. He hardened his stance, spreading his boots on the deck. Before he could bring the M4 up again, LB stepped close to stop him.

"Listen, listen to me." LB pushed the carbine down. He urged, just above a whisper. "You lift that rifle again, he's gonna kill her. You know he is, right in front of us. Let me stay."

"No."

Before LB could say more, Wally grabbed his tunic to drag him strides away. He dropped his voice to a hiss.

"It's your turn to listen. I have orders, direct orders, to eliminate this pirate. *This* specific pirate."

"Give me that order. I can do it."

Wally loosed a long sigh. "I can't say yes."

"You can. Just send me in. You've done it a hundred times before. It's a rescue. I'll do what I have to do, then I'll come back. I always do."

The pirate spoke. "Captain. Your answer?"

LB leaned his face beneath Wally's, looking up. "You know that little talk you wanted to have? About what I did in those jungles while you were pissing your pants waiting for me to come back? Let's have it now."

"Now's not the time."

"I think it is. They weren't just recon missions. They were black ops. There were targets. I killed people in those jungles. Drug lords, commies, revolutionaries, kidnappers, all on orders. All to prop up some local tyrant, or some political bullshit like this ship. After a while I couldn't sleep. I couldn't blink without seeing a face. So I stopped, Wally. I put it down and I became a PJ. I saved myself. The only way I can sleep at night is knowing I save people."

LB spun to Yusuf Raage. "You'll let her go, right?"

"My word."

"Wally, she doesn't deserve to die like this. She didn't sign up for it. We did."

Wally pursed his lips. "Shit."

LB said again, "I can do this."

Wally turned away, to the forward rail. He lifted his M4 off his shoulders to drop it into the black gulf. He gestured for Doc and Quincy to toss theirs. Both PJs looked to LB before following the order. He nodded, and they splashed their rifles.

Wally had not yet tossed away the Beretta. "It'll take us a while to get off the ship."

Yusuf Raage laughed. This struck LB as a deranged thing to do.

"I think not."

"Why?"

As if in answer to Wally's question, an explosion rumbled out of the freighter's stern, the detonation felt in the deck as much as heard. Doc and Quincy swung around, empty-handed, trying to find the source of the blast, looking to the sky. The freighter rolled to port.

What had just happened—had the Predator struck anyway? They'd called the drone off; they'd beat the deadline! LB shouted at Yusuf Raage, "What the hell was that?"

The pirate kept his grip on Iris but eased the knife from her throat.

"This ship is going to sink."

Chapter 52

The blast rocked the ship so hard the Americans adjusted their stances. Three of them searched the night sky while the captain leveled his pistol at Yusuf.

"How'd you know that was going to happen? Did you do this?"

Only for a moment Yusuf considered telling the Americans what he knew, what he'd drawn from Iris Cherlina on the tip of his knife. She set the explosives. She would sink the ship.

He could ruin the woman, cut her throat, and die after her. Pressed against her from behind, he felt her lungs working, her heart race.

"I want to know right now. Did you blow this ship?"

He could tell the truth. But that tale would mark Yusuf Raage as a fool. A woman's puppet, if he named Iris Cherlina.

He chose instead his own name.

"Yes." He spoke left and right at all four soldiers. "I have sunk your ship. I put all the machines you send to Iran on the bottom of the gulf. I send the bodies of my clansmen there too. Stay on this ship with me, Americans. Come to the bottom with us. Or go."

He pressed the blade again under Iris Cherlina's neck. She lifted to her toes.

"Throw away the pistol, Captain. And Sergeant, you remove your radio and headset."

As they were told, the American officer flung his gun overboard, the sergeant stripped himself of his communications gear.

"Take your men, the crew, your dead, and leave. When I'm convinced you are gone, I will release the woman. Then the sergeant and I can conclude our affairs."

No one moved. Out of the breezeless half-lit dark, a great groaning creak from the stern made the Americans shuffle their feet. Inside his arm, Iris Cherlina shivered. The deck rose under Yusuf's sandals. Even the *Valnea* was going to die.

"Go, Captain. The faster you get off this ship, the better this woman's chances are to survive."

The three Americans backpedaled. The sergeant gave them encouraging nods as they abandoned him. Departing, the captain issued orders into his radio to begin evacuating the freighter, for the warship to come closer.

The sergeant, a short and burly man, squatted onto his haunches like a toad. He spoke to the woman.

"It's gonna be okay."

Yusuf lowered the knife a bit from her throat. Iris Cherlina came down off her toes. Inside Yusuf's arm, her head leveled.

"It will not be okay," Yusuf said to the sergeant, "for you."

The soldier knit thick fingers between his spread knees. "Don't talk shit. I have to be nice to you right now. Soon as you let her go, that stops."

"Do you have a knife?"

The man hiked up his pants leg to slide a blade from a hidden sheath. He twisted the knife in the little light, in the fashion of a man who knew how to use one.

"Excellent," said Yusuf.

Chapter 53

At the foot of the stairwell, Wally ordered Doc and Quincy to stay on deck.

"*Nicholas* is going to send lifeboats. Find life jackets and put 'em on. We'll send the crew down to you. Get them into the rafts. Watch your asses till we're off this ship."

Wally turned for the staircase. He couldn't trust the elevator, not with the ship going under. No telling when the power was going to cut out.

Doc stopped him. "Wally."

"Make it quick."

"Let me grab a rifle. I can head back to the bow, stay out of sight until Raage lets her go. I can put a bullet into that fucker and get LB out of there."

Wally came down the few stairs he'd climbed to rest a hand on Doc's shoulder. He spoke mildly.

"I already thought of that. Raage kept my NVGs; he'll be watching. You and I both know he'll cut her throat if he sees anything he doesn't like."

Doc opened his mouth to argue. Wally cut him off.

"This ship is going down. I want my men off it. LB made the right call. He can do this. I know he can. So do you."

Wally turned for the staircase. With the slow tilting of the ship, the steps grew steeper as he labored up the six flights. The wounds in his back and legs almost tripped him several times. Out on the water, an acre of froth bubbled around the settling hull from a breach somewhere below the waterline.

Wally radioed Jamie on the port wing that he was coming up.

Reaching the bridge, Wally caught his breath. The lights had been turned on inside the pilothouse. The carnage and destruction made for a grim scene. The crew had dragged the two murdered hostages away from the windshield to lay beside Drozdov below the chart table. Four dead Somalis had been hauled out to the starboard wing. Trails of blood crisscrossed the floor, which sparkled with shattered glass. The crew had gotten on their feet now, still huddled, except for the fat Russian with the chest wound. While Wally watched from the doorway, Dow and a Filipino hoisted the Russian by the arms to skid him away to the chart table beside his crewmates. Another red track marred the floor.

The chief engineer, Razvan, stood at the dash, palms planted in front of a computer screen. He wheeled on Wally approaching.

"Captain. We are listing two percent by the stern. My engine room is flooding. Explain."

"She's sinking."

The engineer stabbed a finger at his screens. "Yes! This I know!"

"Call the warship. Alert them we need assistance for evacuation."

"This has been done. I must ask you."

"What?"

"Who has done this?" The Romanian's tone turned belligerent. "You? America? Did you decide to hide your secrets?"

"The pirates did it."

"Pirates? I think America. Grisha with bullet in chest, he tells us before dying. Everything! The machines, Iran, the pirates, and Iris Cherlina."

Wally grabbed the engineer by the lapel. "Come here."

Razvan stumbled behind him. Wally dragged him through the shot-up door onto the port wing.

Wally jammed the engineer into a steel corner. He sent Jamie with his two bandaged thighs to find Sandoval and get him down the stairs.

Wally took his hand off the engineer. Razvan lost his bellicosity, cowed now by the bloodied soldier pressing him.

Wally drew his words out slowly. "What did he tell you?" He laid a finger into the engineer's chest as if pushing Play.

Razvan sputtered a fast story about Iris Cherlina, the Chechen Mafia, Somali Sunnis, the accident on board the *Valnea*, and Yusuf Raage. Iran was to receive an illegal shipment of electronics from America, Israel, and Russia. Iris Cherlina had made up her mind to stop it. She'd sabotaged the ship and arranged to have it hijacked and exposed to the world.

When Razvan was done, Wally yanked again on the engineer's shirt. "Listen to me good. You tell your crew that no one says a thing about any of that, to anyone. They stop talking about it right now, even to each other. You understand?"

"Understood." Wally let him go. Razvan collected himself. "Captain."

"What?"

"Is it true?"

"I don't know. And trust me, you don't want to know. Let it go."

"Did you blow up my ship?"

"No. We didn't. The pirates did."

"This makes sense to you?"

"Shut up."

Razvan recognized the end of this discussion. "I will arrange crew to evacuate."

Wally asked, "How long until she sinks?"

"Hard to know. At rate of incline, I suppose thirty, forty minutes. The first half will take the most time. Once bow is in the air, the rest, *pff*, five minutes."

"Then get moving. Can your men carry the bodies?"

"Yes. But Captain, not the Somalis."

"Yes. The Somalis."

Razvan turned to his duties with a mutter: "*Du-te dracului.*"

A hundred yards off the *Valnea*'s port side, the warship eased into place, sweeping her searchlight down the freighter's hull. The first lifeboats arrived. Before going back into the bridge, Wally cast his eyes far forward to the bow. He could not make out LB and the pirate under the steaming light; the last cargo gates blocked his view. In his imagination, LB sat quiet, the way he always did before a mission.

The crew were strong, carting the nine corpses down the staircases. Drozdov and the pair of dead Filipinos were carried across the shoulders of unwounded sailors, then traded off as fatigue set in. The five dead Somalis were thin, bony men. Dow carried the machine-gunned boy. Grisha was the only burden too heavy to be taken away alone; three Filipinos hefted him. The crew said not a word leaving the ship, stalwart bearing their dead and their killers. Wally wanted to relieve the chief engineer carrying Drozdov, take the captain across his own shoulders. But his wounds vexed him, and his hands needed to be on a weapon until all were safely off the ship.

By the time they reached the main deck, the freighter's pitch was clearly accelerating. The floor sloped badly toward the stern, and each moment brought the bubbling water closer to the superstructure. Quincy and Doc handed out life vests from a locker to every crewman and PJ. Vests were secured on each corpse. Two at a time, the crew leaped over the side, followed down by the spotlight from *Nicholas*. Three rescue craft from the frigate hauled the sailors aboard. The warship had divers in the water to assist. Dow and Mouse stepped up to help drop the corpses to them.

The PJs waited until one last crewman remained on the ship, the body of Drozdov. They gave the captain the honor of letting him stay to the end, then released him into the night air. His corpse did not bob up quickly but stayed underwater for long seconds, perhaps caught in the drag of the great hull slipping below the surface. The spotlight found him in the froth, face-down, as if watching his ship slide away.

Fitz eased the RAMZ into place below the PJs. Wally teamed the wounded with the unhurt. Sandoval jumped with Mouse, Jamie with Doc, Quincy with Dow. Below, Fitz helped each over the side. Robey's body lay curled in the bow.

Wally was poised with the toes of his boots over the edge, the team waiting below. *Nicholas*'s spotlight hit him. He felt like he'd been through a grinder, his uniform full of holes. In the search-light, his hands appeared washed out.

Deep inside the ship, a giant fist seemed to beat once against the hull, followed by a trailing groan. The next moment, the emergency lights around Wally extinguished. Far forward, the steaming light on its tower snuffed. All the power on *Valnea* was finished.

"Good luck," Wally said to LB. He stepped into the air, to plunge in the spotlight away from the *Valnea*.

The salty gulf was an instant sting in his many wounds, then a soothing, cooling stroke. Fitz motored to him quickly, and Quincy hauled him in.

Wally arranged himself on the inflated edge. Robey had the bow to himself; the PJs kept toward the stern. Away from the freighter now, the big ship's backward slide into the deep was even more dramatic. She retreated into an acre-wide skirt of bub-bles and white roiled water.

Fitz pivoted the Zodiac in the spotlight cast down by the *Nicholas*, powering for the warship. Wally stood dripping as the inflatable swung alongside the lowered gangway platform. Before stepping out of the raft, he reached down for Jamie.

"Come on."

The young PJ leaned away from Wally's outstretched hand.

"Not till we find LB."

Sandoval and Quincy, the other wounded PJs, nodded in agreement.

Wally stepped onto the platform by himself. "Okay. Stay on the water till you recover LB. And the woman, Iris Cherlina."

Doc said, "Roger." Fitz motored away, back into the spume rising from the sinking freighter.

A contingent of armed marines met Wally at the top of the gangway. A sergeant approached to salute.

"An honor, sir."

"Sergeant."

"Captain Goldberg would like to see you on the bridge."

Wally motioned the guards onward.

The marines led him inside the superstructure. Wally climbed the stairs slowly. The guards were patient with him. Goldberg waited out on the port catwalk, watching the *Valnea*.

Goldberg offered a hand. "Captain." He shot a glance over his shoulder at the dark freighter a hundred yards off. Her bow rose above the waterline, the bulb fully visible.

"Makes no sense," Goldberg said, "sinking a ship like that. Pirates."

"None."

Goldberg surveyed Wally. "You okay, Captain?"

"I could use a day off, thanks."

The warship's spotlight swept the dark waters between the two hulls. The light found the PJs in their Zodiac, plying the foam around the disappearing freighter.

Goldberg turned on Wally. "Captain, why are your men still on the water? Is everyone off that boat?"

"Dismiss your guards, Captain."

Goldberg sent the pair of marines off the catwalk.

"All right. What's going on?"

Wally pointed midship at the big spotlight. "I need you to turn that off, sir. And I need you to back away one mile."

"Do what?"

Wally asked, "Sir, what are your orders?"

"Once your men are on board, I'm to put a total blackout on you. You'll have no contact with any of my crew. I'll post guards outside your quarters. I apologize. I reckon it's not the welcome you were looking for."

"I understand. Start the blackout now. Cut off that light. Everything that happens on that ship is classified."

As Wally finished speaking, the searchlight slid up the freighter's exposed hull. The beam scanned the blank, falling face of the cargo deck. It snagged on a lone figure running downhill along the starboard corridor. The beam followed Iris Cherlina over the rail, her quick drop into the foam. Fitz wheeled the Zodiac around to fish her out of the water.

"Hold it," Goldberg said. "Are there more survivors on board?"

"No, sir. There are not."

Goldberg hesitated, going against his instincts.

"Sir, do it now."

Goldberg snatched up an intercom phone. "Bridge, kill the spotlight."

The beam shut down. In the returned darkness, the *Valnea* receded into a skirt of pale water, gasping as she sank. From this distance, her backward slide was plain. She reared her head as the stern disappeared, dragged down by propeller, engine, and the inrushing void. Water reached the base of the superstructure, flowed up the corridors. Two life rafts had already popped to the surface, inflating automatically. The *Valnea* screeched, echoing in her filling hold.

Goldberg spoke into the intercom. "Helm, hold distance of one mile from that ship." He hung up. Wally thanked him. Goldberg raised a silencing hand.

"Don't say any more to me, Captain. Stay here as long as you need. I'll have your marine escort waiting inside."

Goldberg entered the bridge. Wally set elbows on the rail, watching the *Valnea* rise and recede. He took off his helmet to let the breeze cool his wet hair.

Iris Cherlina was safe. On the lifting bow, the battle had begun.

Chapter 54

CMA CGN Valnea
Gulf of Aden

LB squatted on his heels, facing Yusuf Raage and Iris ten yards away. The pirate kept a big arm around the woman's waist, knife under her chin. She was clever enough not to wriggle or speak. He hunkered his great frame behind her in case Wally had sent back a sniper. Every few minutes, Yusuf lifted the NVGs to scan the ship. LB watched, tapping the blade of his knife into his palm.

Minute by minute, Yusuf rose higher, riding the rearing bow. He kicked off his sandals for the better grip of bare feet. He dragged Iris closer to the port hawser so he could brace one leg against it. LB kept low to hold his position.

Behind him, the navy frigate idled. Rescue craft shuttled back and forth while the freighter's crew and his PJs abandoned ship. With a thud in the steel underfoot, the steaming light overhead fizzled out. The *Valnea's* engine room was flooded now, her power gone. The moving searchlight off the frigate became the only illumination, making the shadows on the bow shiver and stretch.

For long, silent minutes, LB and Yusuf pondered each other. Yusuf stared down from white eyes. LB read nothing in those eyes and gave the same back. He was afraid for his life, but he had been so before. He rapped the blade against his hand over and over to keep his mind away from it. Iris Cherlina needed rescue, Yusuf had been ordered killed, and LB was well trained to do both. He centered himself there.

The deck rose to a precarious tilt, the freighter straining and croaking as she stood herself on end. Far below on the water, unseen, all the rescue craft were done except one. A lone outboard cruised alongside the *Valnea*'s hull. That would be Fitz.

The deck climbed faster. Gushing sounds crept up both corridors. The horizon behind Yusuf had disappeared; all that framed him were stars.

Twenty minutes had passed since LB had last spoken. He rose from his crouch.

"Let her go."

With no word, the pirate lowered the blade from Iris Cherlina's throat. He unwound his arm from her waist to let her stumble away. LB caught her. Iris's sudden arms around his neck almost pulled him backward. He steadied himself and tried to let her loose, but Iris clung.

"Jump with me," she said, pent-up fear in her voice.

"Go on. Now." LB pushed at her ribs to make her stand free.

"Yes, Sergeant, jump." Yusuf glared down from the height the dying ship gave him. "I will jump the other way. And damn you for a coward."

Iris tugged. "Don't listen to him."

LB pushed her away. "I don't give a fuck what he says." He heard himself growl. Anger was no better than fear; he shut this down, too. "I got orders. That's it. Now get off the ship."

LB put his back to Iris Cherlina. He sensed her suspended there a moment. Then, in his periphery, the frigate's spotlight followed her along the starboard passage and over the rail. She splashed, the lone outboard motor revving to pluck her from the water. Yusuf kept looking down on LB, until the search beam went out.

In the darkness, the warship rumbled and pulled away. Quickly, LB and Yusuf were left with only the sounds of creaks and bursting bubbles in the water.

The slant had grown too steep to stand on the deck any longer. Yusuf climbed to the back of the port hawser. LB did the same on starboard. They faced each other three yards apart, knives in hand.

A pillar of released air blew high beside the hull. The freighter belched and gulped, shuddering as she drowned. The top of the stern crane and the last of the superstructure went under. Water rushed across the cargo deck and lashing bridges, covering the base of the midship crane.

Yusuf squared his big shoulders to LB, done with gazing at the black, claiming waters. He lifted his chin. Bloody and ragged, he reeked strength.

"I am Harti, of the Darood."

LB had no idea how this ritual worked.

"I'm from Vegas."

A grin split Yusuf's face that was still there when he launched himself at LB.

Thrusting out his knife, LB braced for the collision. In mid-air, the pirate slashed his own blade in a blurring arc. LB barely dodged, the pirate's blade ripping through his sleeve. Yusuf's shoulder caught LB by the hip, plowing him off the hawser. LB fell to the sloping deck, hacking as he tumbled. His knife sliced the back of the pirate's leg.

LB landed hard on his ribs. He slid down the deck toward the giant windlass, catching himself on the machine beneath the rusty anchor chain. He hung on, regaining his breath.

Overhead, Yusuf dangled by a long, powerful arm from the hawser. Blood dripped off one bare heel. The Somali let go, bounding against the angled deck to land with knees bent on the great windlass, an act of incredible balance.

LB scrabbled for a foothold. Again, the pirate considered him from above.

More moans sobbed in the submerging ship; another fountain of air burst beside the hull. The bow had ridden high enough to cover the moon.

Yusuf Raage jumped off the windlass, out of sight.

Before LB could turn, a hand gripped his ankle. He was yanked backward to skid down the slope into shadow. On his back, he thudded against the wall at the base of the cargo deck. A snarling Yusuf Raage loomed over him.

The pirate pounced. He raised his knife and dove, hammering the blade down at LB's heart. LB heaved up an arm to deflect but could not push the blow completely aside. The pirate's dagger raked his left shoulder, gashing the muscle. LB's arm burned but stayed in the fight. He grabbed Yusuf's wrist, forcing the knife against the wall. Yusuf coiled lower to snatch his arm out of LB's wounded grasp. The Somali was immensely powerful; he jerked himself loose, but not quickly enough. LB drove his own blade into Yusuf's exposed left side.

The pirate leaped back with the blade still plunged in his torso. LB tried to hold on, but the knife yanked from his hand. The Somali reared up, reeling back another step. With a guttural rumble, he drew the blade out of his ribs, then hurled it away.

LB scrambled to his feet. The dark ship had risen almost to vertical; the cargo wall beneath them had become their floor. LB's left arm throbbed, sapping blood and strength with every second.

Yusuf Raage shook his head to clear it. He squared off against LB, working his knife in small pendular movements, deciding how to attack.

The pirate strode forward. LB thrust out his bare hands to defend. Yusuf's tunic hung soggy with blood from the hole in his side. The man should have been on his last legs. He wasn't.

LB retreated, needing to buy seconds.

The Somali lowered his head, preparing another charge.

"Come, Sergeant. We don't have much time, either of us. Let's decide things."

LB lacked anything to say. He retreated another step. His boot landed in water, what he was waiting for.

Yusuf lunged. LB twisted sideways, parrying the thrust slowed by the onrushing, foaming gulf instantly around their ankles. He spun past Yusuf before he felt the sting of another cut, across his right forearm. LB worked his fingers, again testing to see how much he had left. No cords were severed in the arm, but he bled from one more gash.

In the instant Yusuf took to set himself for a last rush at LB, the chilly gulf rose to their waists. *Valnea* burbled, emptying herself as she dropped away below their feet. Yusuf surged at LB.

The pirate whipped the knife wildly and missed, hindered by the flooding waters. LB saw his one chance and sprang. He leaped at Yusuf before the pirate could swing his right arm back. He wrapped the big Somali in a bear hug, trapping Yusuf's arm and the knife between them. The water climbed to their chests. LB linked hands around Yusuf Raage and squeezed with the last of his strength.

The flood reached LB's shoulders; foam licked his chin. The pirate bellowed in anger, that he could not shake LB loose. In seconds the deck slid away beneath their feet. The two floated, locked together.

The pirate's eyes and mouth widened with fury. LB answered with a deep breath before his head sank underwater.

Yusuf Raage kicked madly to raise his own head above the surface for one sharp gasp. LB held tight, weighing the pirate down. His own arms would fail in the next few moments. His wounds pained him enough that he could not fully feel his clasp around Yusuf. If the pirate got loose, they were in close quarters, Yusuf could stab him. One more good cut would likely be the end.

The bow slid away around them. LB kicked once with Yusuf to lift both their heads above water. The pirate, surprised, gulped air greedily. LB filled his own lungs.

The port windlass sank to his left. Without easing his clinch around Yusuf, LB lashed out a leg at the receding machine. The toe of his boot caught inside a link of the thick anchor chain. LB was hauled under, dragging Yusuf Raage down with him.

The pirate fought with everything he had left. He pricked at LB's hip with the trapped knife, but could stab only nicks. LB rode the freighter deeper, eyes open and blurry in the salt gulf. The Somali thrashed, panicked and gaping. He worked his mouth for air that was not there while the growing depth swallowed the last of the thin light. LB clutched the pirate hard, keeping his ear pressed to the Somali's chest. He staved off his pains, fought for focus, and preserved his air.

Yusuf Raage writhed inside LB's grasp, his throat uttered muffled cries. With no notion of how deep the *Valnea* had towed them, LB pulled his boot out of the chain. The tip of the great bow slipped past in the dark, sucking at them as it disappeared.

Yusuf shuddered again. His head jerked in every direction, confounded and desperate. LB held tight until the pirate shook a last time, became sluggish, then went limp.

LB pushed the corpse away, weightless into the ghostly, tranquil water. The two drifted above the last groans of the freighter falling invisibly below them. Yusuf Raage, spread-eagled, receded into the dark.

LB followed bubbles fleeing the ship to show him the direction to the surface, but could only use his right arm to swim. His left shoulder was done.

His depth was unknown. LB kept his upward rhythm steady, expelling small breaths as he ascended. His lungs shrank, squeezing out every bit of oxygen to keep him conscious. He made his mission in the world as narrow as possible, to swim, stay alive, fight his own screaming body. Years of training lined up in his head to tell him he could do this. Memory added its images, a decade of jungle warfare, dozens of combat rescues, natural disasters, frightful conditions, always against odds. He'd done tough things in his life so that some would die and many others would live. Now was his time, LB, to take another stroke and kick upward, stroke and kick again, so that he could live.

To his salt-stung eyes, the water began to lighten. This meant starlight, moonlight, nearing the surface. LB released breath, bottoming out, easing for the last time the blaze in his lungs.

He swam as hard as he could. Behind this last push for the surface, he had nothing. Panic tripped inside his chest, his thoughts clouded. His mouth opened to draw an airless breath.

He pushed through the panic as if it were more water. On the other side, LB found calm.

He'd done his job, a proud thing. But he was alone, the place a PJ should never be.

LB stopped kicking. He floated, gazing up at the rippling surface he could not reach.

With his finished strength he made a last sound, a whimper. The water hushed.

In a span of time he could not name, the silence lingered, but did not last. An outboard engine roared past just above him. The dappled surface overhead did not stay smooth; a shallow hull cut a pale, fast swath through it.

His team was searching for him.

He was not alone.

LB, emptied, kicked one more time. It did not lift his head into the air. He kicked again, bringing both dead arms into a truly final, sweeping pull upward.

He broke the surface.

His mouth gaped to inhale the entire night. Salt water spilled down his throat with the air. He coughed, gasped, his limbs flailing to keep him afloat. A flashlight beam found him, splashing, barking coughs. The RAMZ pivoted and sped his way.

LB trod water until Fitz motored beside him. Every one of his wounds throbbed now that he was safe, and his pulse banged in his temples. LB was glad for the night; he didn't need to know how red the water was around him.

Mouse lent a hand to haul him into the Zodiac. LB kicked onto the side of the raft, but stopped before he swung his legs on board. Robey's corpse lay in the bow, facing away from him.

The team waited. Soaked Iris Cherlina prodded, "LB? Are you all right?"

He slumped back into the water. Fair was fair. LB had been the one rescued.

He gripped a rubber handle with his left hand. The ride to the frigate was less than a mile.

Quincy shook his head. "What the hell. Come on, man. You haven't had enough?"

LB said to Fitz, "Not too fast, okay?"

Chapter 55

On board the USS Nicholas
Gulf of Aden

Mouse and Dow, the best stitch men in the unit, closed wounds. They handled Quincy and Jamie first, and then Mouse worked on Wally's biceps and back. Dow took an hour to close LB's calf with eight stitches, his shoulder with eight, and his right forearm with five. Sandoval spent two hours in the ship's surgical suite having his bullet removed. In the early morning he was returned by marines on a stretcher, semiconscious. Iris Cherlina was nowhere to be seen; after giving LB a peck on the cheek once they were on board *Nicholas*, she was escorted away by her own set of marines.

The PJs slept into the late afternoon, when guards brought them a late lunch. Captain Goldberg had had their uniforms washed, and the marines handed these over with the food. The team marveled at the number of holes in Wally's tunic and pants. Mouse came up with a new call sign for him, Dartboard. Doc changed everyone's bandages.

LB finally had a chance to examine the team's wounds. Jamie hobbled around with holes in both thighs. Quincy and Wally wore slings, as did LB. Sandoval's chest was wrapped, and he was kept sedated. Robey had been bagged and laid in the ship's cold storage locker. Doc, Mouse, Fitz, and Dow were unscathed.

At 1700 hours, *Nicholas* docked at the naval pier in Djibouti. A half dozen marines escorted the PJs on deck. The rail was cleared of sailors when they stepped under a blue sky. Captain Goldberg greeted them alone. At the bottom of the gangplank, another bunch of marines waited on the quay with three Land Rovers.

Wally shook the captain's hand, then led the PJs off the ship. LB brought up the rear. Even laundered and rested, the team looked beat to hell, blood still on their boots. LB's pride swelled when the hard-jawed marines held the doors to the Land Rovers open for them. Limping, wincing, and wrapped, the PJs helped each other into the vehicles. Robey would come later in a hearse.

No one spoke. Wally had laid down the law—no talking about the mission, even among themselves, until the debriefing. In the front passenger seat, Wally slid on his sunglasses for the ride through town to the camp.

Squalid, crowded Djibouti slipped past. Skinny boys in T-shirts and sandals sat on broken walls and curbs where old women struggled under the burdens of baskets. Men loitered around garages and shops, girls hurried in shawls and long *direh* dresses. The streets were crowded with cars and vendors, slowing the convoy. LB didn't mind. This late-day bustle was the life of the real world, not the long, awful night behind him. He was glad to be stuck in traffic. He wanted to pat the annoyed marine driver on the shoulder, tell him things were all right. Instead, he put his arm around Jamie, beside him.

At Lemonnier, the Land Rovers passed quickly through the checkpoints and blast walls. They headed straight for the Barn. There the camp CO, Colonel McElroy, held open the chain-link fence, saluting to greet the arriving team. He closed the gate behind the vehicles and did not come in.

More armed marines were stationed outside the Barn. Wally led the PJs inside, into quarantine.

The Barn was locked down, marines at every door. The rest of the Fifty-Eighth RQS—unit, the SERE guys, chute riggers, med logistics team, intel specialist—all were missing. A cold-cut buffet had been spread on the long rigging table, nine cots with fresh linens set up on the concrete floor. Doc shuffled to his locker, put his wedding ring back on, then climbed to his tent on the high shelf. LB couldn't make it up the ladder, so he collapsed on a cot.

Fitz and Mouse played Ping-Pong until Doc shouted down for them to shut up.

Wally found a folded note sitting under his Air Force Academy ring in his locker. He lay gingerly on the cot next to LB and handed it over. Major Torres had scribbled the word "Dinner."

Camp Lemonnier
Djibouti

The PJs spent another night in isolation. In the morning, the marines escorted them to the head, stood outside the shower room, and afterward carted a hot breakfast into the Barn. Doc worked with Dow and Quincy, assembling new med rucks to replace the ones that had sunk. LB and Wally left their cots for pancakes, ate, then got back in them.

At noon, the marines let in a wiry man with a crew cut and civilian clothes. He wore a short-sleeved white shirt, no tie, khakis, and a blue blazer. The clothes fit as if issued to him. He doffed the jacket, entering the air-conditioned space, stood at a distance from the reclining PJs, and seemed to await a greeting. He had the veins in his forearms of a hard-ass and wore a fat gold ring. LB took a guess, got to his feet, and shouted, "Ten-hut!"

The PJs stood at attention; Sandoval was the slowest to rise. LB was right. The man was brass. He strode into their midst with the air of command. Doc clambered down the ladder.

"At ease, men."

Wally strode forward. "Captain Wallace Bloom, sir."

"Major General Raymond Piper, US Army." The general offered the hand with the West Point ring on it. Wally took it left-handed because of his sling. "Captain, can we take this into the briefing room?"

"Yes, sir. Let's go, everybody."

Wally led Piper to the doorway of the room. The general nodded approvingly at the bandaged, limping PJ team filing past. Wally closed the door when all were seated on the sofa and tiers. He sat beside LB at the rear, leaving the front to the army man.

"Gentlemen, I bring you the thanks of a grateful president. He's relieved like the rest of us that you made it back. That was a tough job, and you were up to it. The president sends his condolences for your injuries, especially for the loss of Lieutenant Robey, as do I. I understand he was a hell of a young officer."

"Saved my life," Jamie said in the front row.

Thinking of the averted Predator, LB offered, "Probably saved all of ours."

From the back, Quincy said, "Hoo-ya."

Piper liked that. "You bet, son." The general tugged at his own civilian shirt. "Sorry about being out of uniform. My bag didn't make it out of Ramstein. I didn't wait for it; I was in a hurry to get here."

Piper clapped hands, the niceties out of the way.

"I'm chief of staff for General Madson, CO of AFRICOM. Captain Bloom, the two of you have spoken."

Wally answered, "Yes, sir." LB poked him in the leg, impressed.

"You'll notice I came to debrief you alone. No intel officers, no note takers. You will not be dissecting the mission you just completed. You will not be searching for ways to do things better. Your mission to the *Valnea* is classified top secret. You will not from this day forward discuss the events of the last forty-eight hours with anyone. Absolutely no one. This includes each other. As far as you're concerned, whatever you saw or think you saw on that freighter, you did not. Violations of this order will be considered treason against your country and will be punishable as such. This order comes directly from General Madson. Questions?"

The PJs said in unison, "No, sir."

This wasn't out of the ordinary. A lot of the rescues the PJs handled were classified affairs, black ops that went wrong. LB had known this operation would be branded off-limits, but he wasn't looking for the order to come straight from a four-star, delivered by a two-star. The treason reminder seemed a little heavy-handed.

"Anyone need to speak to a psychiatrist? No? All right, then. Gentlemen." Piper hardened his stance to parade rest. "That is all. Good day."

The PJs stood, surprised collectively at the shortness of the debriefing and the rank of the officer who'd flown three thousand miles to say as little as Piper had. They left the room single file. Jamie, Sandoval, and Quincy would be on their way to the French hospital as soon as security around the Barn was lifted. LB, too.

On the top row, LB and Wally hung back. Both waited to see if, in fact, that was all. Piper held his ground until the rest of the PJs were gone from the room. He shut the door behind them.

The general crossed his arms. "Very clever. I assume this is First Sergeant DiNardo."

"Yes, sir."

"Well, I was going to talk to you two separately. But they told me you were a matched set."

Wally nodded. "Sir, the sergeant knows pretty much everything I do at this point."

"Down front, boys. Have a seat."

376

Wally and LB came down the tiers to the first row. Piper leaned against a table.

"Captain Bloom. First let me say how proud I am of how you handled this job. This could have been a major fuckup. It was not. The United States owes a lot of that to you."

"Thank you, sir."

"I've got news for you, Sergeant DiNardo. The scalded cadet will be getting skin grafts compliments of the United States. And Nikita will make a full recovery from his back injury. He says to tell you *oslayub*. Yes, I know what that means."

"Thank you, sir."

"Now, on to more important matters. Captain Bloom."

"Sir."

"General Madson gave you an order to terminate the pirate leader Yusuf Raage. I understand that was done by Sergeant DiNardo."

"Yes, sir."

"That was not your directive, Captain. The order was yours."

LB raised a hand, not knowing what else to do. "Sir. If I may."

"You got something to add?"

"Sir, by the time we isolated Yusuf Raage, the captain here had already killed a dozen men on that ship. There was a hostage situation. Yusuf had Iris Cherlina."

"So I heard from Dr. Cherlina. She is a fan of yours, DiNardo."

LB pressed past this. "I'd killed Yusuf's cousin. He demanded a trade, me for Iris. Wally was against it. I insisted."

Wally muttered, "To put it mildly."

Piper folded his arms. "Go on."

"I requested Captain Bloom give me the order to eliminate Yusuf Raage. It seemed the only way to save Iris, sir. That is what we do, you know."

"Keep the mild sarcasm in check, son."

"Yes, sir. The captain agreed. I stayed back. The team and Iris got off the ship. Me and Yusuf worked it out after that."

"Guns?"

LB patted his sling. "Knives."

Piper ran a hand under his chin. Stubble from the long flight hissed in his fingers.

"To rescue Dr. Cherlina, you stayed behind on a sinking ship for a knife fight with a Somali pirate."

LB shrugged. "Sir."

"That is a hell of a thing, Sergeant."

"Yes, sir."

"That was noble of you. I mean it. And a breach of duty. Did you have any idea of the number of orders you were violating to do that? General Madson's and Captain Bloom's? A goddamn knife fight."

"Yusuf Raage wasn't the sort of man to do things from a distance. He had some guts."

"Are you implying something to me, Sergeant?"

"Yes, sir."

"Tell me, DiNardo. You like your rank?"

"I don't mind it, sir."

"Good. Then maybe you won't mind this. You're busted down to master sergeant."

"No problem, sir."

"And why exactly is that?"

"Because those men in the next room don't follow me because of my rank."

"Probably true, son. Captain Bloom?"

"Yes, sir."

"I'm gonna let you keep your rank. For a long time."

"Understood, sir."

"Why am I not going to court-martial you both? Because I suppose you joined this unit for a good purpose. Those must've been hard orders to follow. But make no mistake, they were orders."

Both said, "Thank you, sir."

"Besides, there aren't enough PJs and CROs around to waste a couple of good ones. Even hardheaded ones. We'll say no more about it, so long as Yusuf Raage is, in fact, dead."

"Yes, sir."

"Now, gentlemen, you are likely wondering why I was sent all this way to deliver that little message myself. Someone from intel could've swung by Djibouti and told you fellas to stay quiet. The reason I'm here is because no one in intel knows what the hell was really on that ship. There aren't many of us who do. "

"The railgun."

"That's right, Captain. And all the rest. Tell me what you know about it."

Wally shook his head. "Only what LB's told me, sir. I never got a look at it."

Piper raised a hand to stop Wally. "What LB's told you. Sergeant, how much talking about this have you done?"

"What was determined on the scene to be the appropriate amount. Sir."

Wally cut in. "General, tactically, I decided LB should inform the team. The situation was confusing and dangerous. Our orders were contradictory to our PJ training. I felt it necessary to have the sergeant brief the team on what he'd found out about the ship and its cargo. We had decisions to make on the fly. Sir."

"What about the deal?"

"Yes, sir. And the deal."

Piper rubbed his stubbled cheek again. "Well, that cat's out of the bag, then. I assume with this knowledge, gentlemen, you'll both agree it's a lucky thing Iran didn't get a railgun and all that hardware. It's best to keep them out of enemy hands."

Wally asked, "Sir, what about Iran's nuclear weapons program? Doesn't this just put us back to square one?"

"Not at all. Iran had to come clean on a lot of what they're up to before that bargain could be struck. It was worth a few billion dollars down the drain to get that intel. The Israelis are beside themselves."

LB fidgeted. Piper swelled into his businessman's shirt made for a bigger frame.

"You got more to add, son? Let me have it."

"Permission to speak freely, sir."

"I got the sense you were already doing that."

Wally shot LB a tight-lipped look of caution. LB hooked a thumb at the closed door and said, "Maybe you want to step out for the rest of this."

Wally made no move to leave. Piper answered for him.

"I'll have the captain stay for this. Since I don't believe orders are enough to keep you in line, DiNardo, I'm making him responsible for you."

LB raised his palms at Wally: I tried to get you out of the way. "Proceed."

"Sir, you and I both know that ship wasn't sunk by pirates."

"Let's focus on what you know. Leave me out of it."

"Understood. I negotiated with Yusuf Raage before we assaulted the bridge. We had him and his last men surrounded."

"And?"

"He never mentioned he'd set charges to blow up the ship. I believe he would have in that situation, or else what would have been the point of mining the ship? After we had him cornered on the bow and Wally asked him, Raage looked pretty surprised when he admitted to it. It just didn't add up that he'd wait until all his men were dead to bring it up, then sink the boat. Didn't make sense to Razvan, the chief engineer, either. That's when he told Wally what he'd heard."

Wally pitched in. "Iris Cherlina caused the piston to blow." LB patted Wally gently on the back, pleased to have him at his side again.

Wally continued. "Razvan was dead certain the damage to the engine was sabotage. Then one of the Russian officers, before he got killed, confessed that he and Iris Cherlina timed the accident to slow the ship smack in the middle of the Gulf of Aden."

Piper leaned closer. "Are you two telling me Iris Cherlina was responsible for bringing pirates on board that ship?"

LB looked at his boots. "Sir, I've been blown up, sliced, and almost drowned. We all got blood on our hands that's going to take a while to wash off. One of us is dead." LB lifted his gaze. "So can you please cut the shit?"

Piper pointed at LB's sling. "You're the knife fighter, son. Cut it for me."

Wally gestured to LB with a flat palm. You've come this far— go ahead.

LB took Wally's hand for a shake, as if to say, Nice knowing you. "Iris Cherlina wasn't working for herself. No way."

Piper spoke slowly, making sure he got the tone of threat right. "Then who?"

"The United States."

Piper let the words dangle. He cocked his crew-cut head to eye LB without blinking. "That's a big statement."

"Yes, sir. But it's the only way all the pieces fit. You said it yourself a few minutes ago. This could've been a fuckup, but it wasn't. That says you're okay with the ship sinking. That means it was supposed to go down, and you knew it would."

Piper twisted the big gold ring. He nodded to himself, then asked Wally, "Does he pay attention like that when you talk, Captain?"

"Never."

"Well, Sergeant, I expect you won't be surprised if I tell you it's true."

"No, sir. I won't."

Piper's tone changed. He became conspiratorial, explaining himself and the rationales behind the secrets he was about to reveal. LB and Wally, because of their wounds and service, because they'd earned it, were going to be included.

"Listen, you both been on enough battlefields. You know how one weapon, the right weapon deployed at the right time, can determine the outcome. I assume you both know what a rail-gun is theoretically capable of."

"Yes, sir."

"The military that gets an EM launcher into the field first is going to have a huge advantage. Period. The damn thing's a game changer. It needs more R&D, about a decade's worth. A lot of us don't want Iran in on that game. When the deal first got struck with Iran, Russia, and Israel, we objected to it. We told the president it was a bad idea to let the Iranians get their hands on a weapons system like that. The president let us know this was a diplomatic initiative and not military. He and everybody else were relieved that Iran was standing down their damned nuclear development."

Wally said, "But it didn't end there."

"No, it didn't. Secretly the president agreed with us. We'd already put a lot of intel about the Irani nuke program in our pockets. So the president gave the Joint Chiefs the authority to make sure Iran would not get their hands on that ship, under any circumstances. Then he told us he didn't want anyone else to know about it. So, this became a purely military operation. We made an arrangement with a promising young Russian EML engineer, Dr. Cherlina."

LB said, "You bought her."

"Hell, son, she was buyable. We saw to it with the Russians that she accompanied the shipment. We got some of our Sunni friends in the region to find us a reliable Somali hijacker. After that, the plan was simple. Slow the boat. Bring on the pirates. Sink the boat. Blame the pirates. We made sure the *Nicholas* was in the area for the rescue. Nothing leads back to us, and the president has clean hands."

Wally asked, "But why send my team in? I mean, if the whole point of the operation was to make it look like pirates sank the ship, I don't understand dropping us in to stop them."

Piper offered this to LB. "Sergeant? You got this one figured out?"

LB nodded.

"Give it a shot."

"You had to make it look like the Somalis' hand was forced. You've got Russia, Israel, Iran, everybody, watching this cargo. It wouldn't be reasonable just to claim that pirates hijacked it, turned for Somalia, then blew it up for no reason three hours from shore. That's where we came in. We were the decoy."

Wally stiffened. "General, is that right?"

"Yes, it is."

Wally leaped to his feet. LB tugged at his pants leg to no avail, so stood with him. Because of the sling, Wally had only one arm to wave around.

"I led my men onto that ship, risked their lives, so you could have a cover story?"

"Correct."

"We killed two dozen Somalis. Lost four of the ship's crew. One of my men died, an officer, a kid. We took bullets and shrapnel in half my team, myself included. LB almost drowned. And you knew this would happen?"

"I've answered you, Captain. Sit down."

LB pressed Wally into the chair, then joined him. Wally continued to steam. He jerked a finger at LB. "I almost shot him for insubordination."

"Well, if you'd done it, we wouldn't be having this conversation."

LB rocked back. "Whoa."

"Just trying to lighten things up, boys. Calm down. I'm sorry about Lieutenant Robey. And your close call, Sergeant. But don't be prima donnas. Men die in this line of work. I expect you two know that as well as anybody."

"They're not supposed to die by our hands, General. I expect you to know that."

Wally took the momentum now, angered and wanting to get at the heart of the secrets.

"Why'd you set it up so we were the only unit that could respond? The ship's engine could've been damaged out in the Indian Ocean. The pirates would've taken her out there. You'd have had more time. You could've sent a search-and-destroy team. Why my unit?"

Piper tapped a finger to his temple. "Think about it. Your PJs were the perfect choice. Small, elite. Pararescue, excellent jump skills. Not killers by trade. We sent you in, told you to focus on the Somalis and not the hostages. We didn't want heroics, some big rescue and a body count. We figured you'd drop on the *Valnea*, fire a few shots, maybe take out Yusuf Raage, then Iris Cherlina would blow the charge. Hell, son, you're not killers anymore, just like you say. Should've been simple. The pirates would hightail it off the sinking ship in their skiffs, and you'd let 'em go. Why not? *Nicholas* would come over to rescue you and the crew, the freighter would disappear, and it would all go like clockwork."

Piper pretended to throw smoke in the air.

"Poof. All the hardware's on the bottom of the gulf, Iran loses out. Pirates get blamed. America looks like a hero for giving it the old college try to take the ship back and keep the deal alive. We didn't figure you'd go and wipe everybody out. Christ, if we'd wanted that, we would've sent in the SEALs. We just wanted Yusuf Raage dead to make sure at least one of the pirates got shot to make the story of the explosion plausible. Besides, it would keep him from talking. But Cherlina screwed up and injured two of the ship's crew when she blew the piston. DiNardo here went out on the distress call, then decided to stay on board. That wasn't part of the plan."

LB got a worse feeling than the one Piper was already giving him. It was starting to sound like, without his knowing or intending it, too much of what had happened on the *Valnea* depended on him.

The general continued, leveling a finger at LB to confirm it.

"Then this one here decided to get cute. He disobeyed his orders to show no curiosity about the cargo or Dr. Cherlina. He hid out belowdecks, saw all the toys, then cuddled up to the good doctor, who was hiding out there herself. By the time he went topside to do his job, the sergeant here knew way too damn much. Iris Cherlina was supposed to set the charge, then blow it as soon as the rescue team was on board and the pirates were on their way off the ship. Like I said, it should've been simple."

Piper swung the accusing finger to Wally.

"Then, Captain, your team went in to rescue one of your own, and you boys hit that freighter like a shit storm. Before Cherlina could trip the charge, you'd taken out all the pirates. All but one, anyway, and that one caught her up on deck after setting the timer. What do you want me to tell you? We underestimated everybody, to be honest. We didn't think the Somalis would hang so tough. Your boys are better fighters than we thought. And DiNardo here is actually charming when he wants to be."

LB asked, "Was there really a Predator?"

"There was. Worst-case scenario. And we still could've blamed it on the pirates."

Wally asked, "But why did Iris blow the ship after the deadline?"

Piper handed this one off to LB. "Sergeant?"

LB chuckled at how coldhearted it was. "They didn't tell her about the Predator."

Piper showed his palms. "Sorry if that seems harsh, fellas. But you did your job, Iris Cherlina finally did hers, and here we are. Good to go."

Wally exhaled. He seemed to believe every secret had been exposed. LB doubted it.

"Now what?" Wally asked.

"End game. We sell that story to the Iranians, Russians, and Israel. The ship was sunk by pirates. We'll reimburse the Israelis for the lost drones, the Russians for the railgun. The pirates are all dead. The ship's crew thinks Iris Cherlina did it on her own, and we've put the fear of the Almighty into them to keep quiet. Your team's not talking. Period."

Piper considered this the end of the debrief. He cast Wally and LB significant looks and said, "Boys. Your country thanks you. Now, good day."

LB rose to stand with Wally. Piper opened the briefing-room door. The general shook hands with Wally, who left the room.

LB closed the door behind him, locked it, and kept his good hand on the doorknob.

Piper eyed him. "Sergeant?"

Outside, Wally knocked.

"Sir, all due respect, I don't think the story's over."

"Sergeant, you want to take your hand off that door."

"I don't like unfinished business, sir. That's why I'm a good PJ. Nothing halfway about it, in or out."

"I admire that. You might consider mixing in a little judgment and discretion."

Wally rapped again.

"There's still a few pieces missing."

"And you just got to know."

"Yes, sir. I can obey orders I understand better than ones I don't. It's a flaw in my personality."

Piper took a seat in the second row. "All right. I'll make a deal with you. First, every word said in this room stays here. Not even your Captain Bloom out there. Agreed?"

"Yes, sir."

"Open that door."

LB unlocked the door. He opened it to find Wally standing there. Piper told him to stop knocking and go away. LB closed and locked it again.

"Second. I'll answer your questions. And every one you ask will cost you a stripe. Let's see how bad you want it. Okay, Master Sergeant. The floor is yours."

LB leaned back against the table, copying the posture Piper had taken addressing the team. He wondered what it would be like to have the kind of power over men that the generals and politicians had. To make them subordinate. Wally was right. The PJs had bled and killed on that boat. Violence always extracted a cost, whether in blood or in spirit. They asked little in return, what every man and woman in uniform asked: the chance to do their duty with honor and comrades at their sides, and that the people who sent them into the breach to do and suffer that violence weren't fucking them over. Piper, Madson, the president, and the rest had broken that pact. Someone had to call them on it. Or at least let them know they weren't so clever.

"Whenever you're ready, son."

"I think the United States pulled off a swindle. A beauty, in fact."

"Do you."

"Yes, sir. Like you said, there's no way our military would ever let Iran develop a railgun. Not before us, anyway."

"That's why it's now in a thousand feet of water."

"The gun, the drones, they were all just another cover, like us."

"Oh, the Iranians wanted all that Israeli radar, all right, if just to piss off the Israelis. But you're basically right. It was just a cover. Now, can you figure out for what? Ask me a question."

"Good. Where is Iris Cherlina?"

"She was put on a chopper that left the *Nicholas* one minute after she stepped on board. She is at this moment at an undisclosed location inside the United States. Tech Sergeant."

"You going to claim she drowned on the freighter?"

"No, Staff Sergeant. That was the original plan, but since your team killed all the pirates, we'll just say she was murdered by the Somalis. Very few people are left to contradict that, and every one of them is on an American payroll. Let Yusuf Raage have it all. Tell me something, son."

"I get a stripe back for every question you ask."

"That's fair. She talked to you a lot, I see. Why would she do that? She didn't need to."

"Actually, she did. She was hiding out in the cargo hold when the hijacking started. I was the best way for her to get information on the rescue, the timing. That explains why she acted scared, so she could be there when I called in to the JOC. And now I get why she wanted me to shoot Yusuf Raage in the back."

"She's clever, that one. Ruthless."

"A lot of both. And you know, even though I'm sure she was playing me from the minute I met her, she acted like she dug me a little."

"And a looker."

"True that. And something else."

"Yes?"

"I don't think she was just accompanying that shipment, like she said."

"No, she wasn't."

"You made her part of the bargain from the beginning. You wanted your hands on her. She was the prize all along."

"Yes, she was. Right from the start."

"Who is she?"

"You sure you want to know? Senior Airman?"

LB squinted, muttering, "Damn it." He shrugged at Piper. "What the hell. Yes, sir."

"Iris Cherlina was not simply a top EM engineer in Russia. She has become the leading electromagnetic launch designer in the world. She headed a Russian program that took the application of railguns in a whole new direction. It may speed the development of an EML by anywhere from three to five years. You understand that is immense, and could not be handed over to Iran."

"Or left in Russia, for that matter."

"Absolutely not."

"What did she do? And sir, that is part of the same question."

"Tell you what. I'll give you this one for free. You may as well know the whole enchilada. I figure you got the right. Besides, you did rescue her for me."

"I'm all ears, sir."

"She schooled you on how an EM launcher works, I assume. And the problems."

"Well enough."

"Okay. A few years back, our Dr. Cherlina and her team at Molniya came up with a very smart idea. Instead of shooting a shitload of juice in one large force into two parallel metal rails, why not ramp up the power in increments? Accelerate the projectile repeatedly as it travels down the rails. Distribute magnets along the length of the launcher, pulse the charge. You cut way back on the thermal energy, and that minimizes erosion and warping. You reduce the G-load from thousands to under a hundred, so now you can use GPS-guided projectiles."

"That's impressive."

"Not as impressive as this." Piper clapped hands and rubbed them together. Then he pointed the pistols of two fingers at LB's face. "At the Plesetsk Cosmodrome, Dr. Cherlina oversaw the design and construction of a one-mile-long elevated electromagnetic track. This big bastard railgun successfully accelerated a forty-ton load—that's what I said, a forty-ton payload—to a velocity of two kilometers per second. The projectile reached an altitude of one hundred kilometers, then separated and punched a one-ton satellite into earth orbit with a booster."

"Wow."

"And here's the kicker. Other than the obvious, do you know why this incredible technical feat is so important? Why would the United States care that a country with the biggest booster rockets in the world launched a forty-ton payload off a mile-long electromagnetic track? Can you figure that one out?"

"Because we couldn't track it."

"Because we could not goddamn track it. Exactly. There was no heat signature. It's *Sputnik* all over again—the Russians beat us to the punch. We're playing catch-up. Oh, we'll figure out how to spot an EM launch at some point now that we know we got to do it. That'll take a while. But this capability to put a load into orbit off a rail is not something we want the Russians or anyone else to corner the market on. Up to this point, our EML research has focused on the metallurgic and power problems of deploying one as a naval weapon. Frankly, we've paid no attention to sequential acceleration. But it looks like a damn ingenious approach, for orbital as well as weapons. That is why Dr. Iris Cherlina is now working for you and me, under an assumed name, of course, at an undisclosed location. She will get no credit for the intellectual property she will develop, she'll have restricted travel under US supervision, and she'll only be allowed to confer with a few of her old mentors face-to-face. This operation is blacker than black. But she'll have unlimited funds to work with and will be our lead scientist in pushing railgun technology to the lunatic fringe. Iris Cherlina pounced at the chance, to be honest. And you are now one of the few people in the world who knows it."

LB's arm ached in its sling. His calf tweaked him, too. The team would be attending a service for Robey tomorrow morning.

"So that's what she couldn't tell me."

"Beg pardon."

"Iris. She said she was just accompanying the cargo to Iran."

"That was a lie, Sergeant, one of several I'm sure you heard. No, she was going to re-create the whole shebang for the Iranians. In a couple of years, they'd be launching shit we couldn't spot, too. The railgun that got sunk was a next-generation prototype of her acceleration technology. The woman is a pioneer."

"I get the picture."

"Do you? Enlighten me."

"This whole operation was a scam. Everything my team and I went through on that ship was to cover your ass so you could screw the deal with Iran, fake Iris's death, then steal her for yourself."

Piper rocked back in his chair like a man who'd just enjoyed a performance.

"Dead center. That is what we did. Congratulations, my boy. What do you think of yourself?"

"I think, sir, that anything you take from me in this room, I can get back. The whole thing sucks, and I think you need to hear that perspective from one of the guys who did the bleeding."

Piper stood, done with LB.

"Nothing new here, son. Old men make wars, young men fight them. It's going to be that way in any future we make. Rely on it. Now I'm going to leave on that note. Got a long flight back."

LB unlocked the door and twisted the knob. He pulled open the door to let the general out. Piper took a step into the common room and stopped. LB halted in the doorway.

Wally kept watch from the Ping-Pong table; the rest of the PJs paid no attention. The general whispered over his shoulder: "You did good in there. Smart-alecky, but you held your own. Go ahead and keep your stripes. I lost count anyway."

Walking off, wrinkled and formidable, Piper lifted his voice to all the PJs in the Barn.

"Remember, boys. Mum's the goddamn word."

Chapter 56

——·——

Jamie limped on two legs, LB on one, and neither Wally nor Quincy in slings could carry five bottles. Doc fetched all the beers.

Eleven Degrees North simmered after a hot day. April had lost its mildness, beginning the short slide into a Horn of Africa summer. Even with the sun down two hours ago, the patio's concrete emitted warmth like a living thing under their boots, the metal chairs and table refusing to cool with the evening breeze off the gulf. LB wiped cold sweat from his beer on the back of his neck.

As usual after chow, the bar was crowded. One of the beauties of the place was that the men and women of the base did not clot by service. Sandy marine fatigues mingled with army-green camos. Pilots in flight suits, mechanics in overalls, anyone in T-shirts and shorts, all bought each other the next round, shared lighters for cigarettes. Japanese, French, Spanish, and British accents drifted past the PJs' table. LB listened to those other conversations around him because none of the men with him were talking, just drinking.

Major Torres dropped by. She sat for five minutes of polite chat, making no mention of the mission, their bandages and slings, or Jamie's crutches. Her presence at the table set the PJs on edge; Torres was the officer who'd started it all. Her smile at their wounds said everything for her; Torres knew less than any of them. All she could honor them with was blinks and that pretty smile.

Each of the PJs wanted to talk about what he'd done two days ago but couldn't, not for solace or teasing. They wanted to recollect and honor Robey, a young man they hardly knew who'd laid his life down for them and whose sacrifice could never be spoken of. The memory of his death was ordered wiped away, no monument anywhere, reported as a training accident. Wally excused himself and the PRCC from the table.

Doc was the next to go. He bought one more round, delivered the bottles to the table. He dared the powers that be, saying, "These are for Robey," then bid good night.

Quincy, Jamie, and LB finished their drinks silently. The bar's lights didn't blank out the African stars. All three leaned back in their chairs to study the pinpricks, using the Milky Way to stay at the table together a little longer without words. At last, with the bottles empty, Quincy rose to disappear into the crowd. He returned to tell Jamie he'd found them a ride back to the Barn. He stood one more bottle on the table, then the two left.

LB let the beer sit. He'd had enough, maybe more. He pushed it across the table when Wally sat.

Wally eased out of the sling to work his arm and slouch. LB gestured to the bottle.

"Go ahead."

Wally waved it off, tired. "No, thanks. It's yours."

"I gave it to you."

"I don't want it. You drink it."

LB lifted the beer. "That an order?"

"Don't go there."

"No, no. Don't want to disobey an order."

In one tip, LB guzzled half the bottle. Wally stretched his good arm for the second half, finishing it the same way. He set it down loudly, not between them but out of the way.

LB leaned on his good arm far across the table, less concerned with treason than loyalty. He checked to be sure no one else could hear him.

"Tell me you wouldn't have fucking shot me."

Wally took the same look-around for listeners. "Quit whining. You talked me out of it."

"Why'd you come back over here?"

"You were by yourself."

"Now I can't sit by myself?"

Wally flicked his wrist, the same gesture he used to reject the beer. He kept his voice low. "Next time I will. I'll just shoot you."

LB stood, not sure why. He got to his feet because when someone says something like that, a man stands. Wally was drunk, too, and didn't mean it, but when he slid his arm into the sling, he glared like he did.

Rising also, Wally bumped the table. The bottle toppled to its side and rolled to the edge. Both men could not stop it. The bottle hit the concrete but didn't break.

LB tapped his own chest, mimicking a bullet there. "Shoot me? Because of bullshit orders? We both got Jolly Green Giant feet tattooed on our asses. Period."

Wally pointed. "Sit down."

"Why?"

"Because I can carry two beers. Then we'll settle this."

Wally wove into the crowd. The night was too early to have drunk this much. LB thought to leave, let Wally return to an empty table. They wouldn't settle anything; they were going to argue and drink.

But LB refused to disappear.

He sat, not because he was told to.

GLOSSARY

AFRICOM. US Africa Command
BDU. Battle dress uniform
cows' tails. Lanyards clipped to rings in the floor of a helicopter
C4I. Command, control, communications, computers, and intelligence
CCS. Command and control stations
CSAR. Combat search and rescue
CQB. Close quarters battle
CRO. Combat rescue officer
CTF 151. Combined Task Force 151, the international counterpiracy task force
DKAV or D=KAV. Calculation for freefall and canopy drift, using several factors, including wind velocity, altitude, and direction
EML. Electromagnetic launcher
ERQS. Expeditionary Rescue Squadron
Guardian Angels. Overall system name for US Air Force pararescue resources
IRTC. Internationally Recognized Transit Corridor
JOC. Joint Operations Center
IP. Isolated personnel
IR. Infrared

LRP. Long range patrol
LT. Lieutenant
LZ. Landing zone
ODA. Operational detachment alpha (formerly Green Berets)
PJ. Pararescue jumper
PR. Personnel recovery
PRCC. Personnel Recovery Coordination Cell
PTT. Press to talk
RAMZ. Rigged Alternate Method Zodiac
SERE. Survive, evade, resist, escape
SIE. Self-initiated elimination
SF. Special Forces
SSAS. Ship Security Alarm System
target. Jargon for "target"
TDY. Temporary duty assignment
technical. Armed pickup truck
UAV. Unmanned aerial vehicle
UKMTO Dubai. United Kingdom Maritime Trade Operations
office in Dubai, UAE

Acknowledgments

For my several historical novels, I've been able to gather a great deal of the information I needed out of archives and nonfiction books, the recorded voices of the dead. But for a novel like this one, a contemporary tale, I've had to rely much more on the living.

At every step in my research, folks in and out of the military embraced both me and the notion of a novel about combat search and rescue (CSAR) on a massive cargo ship. I've spent time listening on three continents, four seas, and one ocean to men recounting their adventures, dangers, and wisdom. I've done my best to weave their vivid experiences into a story that not only is exciting but rings true. To a greater extent than any book I've written, this novel owes its character to the guidance and generosity of many advisers.

On Long Island, at Francis S. Gebreski Airport, the PJs and CROs of the USAF 103rd RQS showed me hospitality, trust, and just how cool and brave their lives are. While every man I spoke with contributed to my knowledge and admiration, the ones with whom I spent the most time were Maj. Scott Williams (the original LB), Lt. Colonel John McElroy, Lt. Colonel Shawn Fitzgerald, base Col. Tom Owens, and Captain Glyn Weir. Thanks to them, LB and Wally are alive and kicking each other.

In Djibouti, I was hosted by the pararescueman of the 58th RQS out of Nellis Air Force Base. While deployed with these men, I had better food, more fun, more excitement, and better sleeps than in any civilian days in recent memory. If I were a younger fellow, I would want to be like them. Since I cannot, some characters in my book (Quincy, Doc, Jamie) are. Thank you.

For two weeks, between Malta and Dubai, I was fortunate enough to sail on the *CMA CGM Hydra* in the company of Capt. Slavko "Dado" Malasic and his lovely wife, Valnea. Along with Chief Engineer Razvan Uta, they taught me everything I needed to know about massive cargo ships, traveling great distances on blue seas, Ping-Pong, Dracula, piloting a huge ship with a tiny wheel, and high spirits. I could not have conceived this book without them.

My agent Luke Janklow of Janklow & Nesbitt is a star in many rights. He, for being an impatient man, has shown me great restraint and faith. I've pledged not to vex him so greatly in the future, because he's been proven right often enough. Clare Dippel, his assistant, has been a guiding light for the journey of this book. Between the two of them, I am as confident in my representation as I've ever been.

At Thomas & Mercer, editor Andy Bartlett and his team of professionals have amazed me with their competence and eagerness to make this book a success. As any author will tell you, it's a deeply gratifying experience to work with folks who not only care about your book, but are talented and open-minded along the way.

As he has for all ten of my novels, my old friend Jim Redington, MD, helped with everything medical. The Public Affairs Office of the USAF at the Pentagon was a dream to work with.

Sherrie Najarian is not just a smart, classy beauty. She's also a first-class editor. Like so many others, she added many things to this novel for which I receive credit.

—*David L. Robbins*

About the Author

David L. Robbins currently teaches advanced creative writing at VCU Honors College. His exceptional talent is displayed through ten action-packed novels, including the classic *War of the Rats*, *Broken Jewel*, *The Betrayal Game*, *The Assassins Gallery*, and *Scorched Earth*. An award-winning essayist and screenwriter, Robbins founded the James River Writers, an organization dedicated to supporting professional and aspiring writers. He also co-founded the Podium Foundation, which encourages artistic expression in Richmond's high schools. Robbins extends his creative scope beyond fiction as an accomplished guitarist and student of jazz, pop, and Latin classical music. When he's not writing, he's often found sailing, shooting, weightlifting, and traveling the world. He lives in his hometown of Richmond, Virginia.